Ab

Initially a French... changed careers to ... happy demands of ... much a people pe... relationships, she finds the world of romance fiction a thrilling one and the challenge of creating her own cast of characters very addictive.

Annie West has devoted her life to an intensive study of charismatic heroes who cause the best kind of trouble in the lives of their heroines. As a side-line, she researches locations for romance, from vibrant cities to desert encampments and fairytale castles. Annie lives in eastern Australia with her hero husband, between sandy beaches and gorgeous wine country. She finds writing the perfect excuse to postpone housework. To contact her or join her newsletter, visit www.annie-west.com

Fiona Brand lives in the sunny Bay of Islands, New Zealand. Now that both of her sons are grown, she continues to love writing books and gardening. After a life-changing time in which she met Christ, she has undertaken study for a Bachelor of Theology and has become a member of The Order of St. Luke, Christ's healing ministry.

Australian Nights

Australian Nights: Heat of the Night

EMMA DARCY

ANNIE WEST

FIONA BRAND

MILLS & BOON

First Published in Great Britain 2021
by Mills & Boon, an imprint of HarperCollins*Publishers* Ltd,
1 London Bridge Street, London, SE1 9GF

www.harpercollins.co.uk

HarperCollins*Publishers*
1st Floor, Watermarque Building,
Ringsend Road, Dublin 4, Ireland

AUSTRALIAN NIGHTS: HEAT OF THE NIGHT
© 2021 Harlequin Books S.A.

The Costarella Conquest © 2011 Emma Darcy
Prince of Scandal © 2011 Annie West
A Breathless Bride © 2012 Fiona Gillibrand

ISBN: 978-0-263-29916-8

MIX
Paper from
responsible sources
FSC™ C007454

This book is produced from independently certified FSC™ paper to ensure responsible forest management.

For more information visit: www.harpercollins.co.uk/green

Printed and bound in Spain
by CPI, Barcelona

THE COSTARELLA
CONQUEST

EMMA DARCY

CHAPTER ONE

FRIDAY afternoon in the office of the man Jake Freedman had every reason to hate, and he could barely contain his impatience to leave. Soon, very soon, he would have all the evidence to indict Alex Costarella for the vulture he was, picking over the carcasses of bankrupted companies to feed his own bankroll. Then he could leave for good. In the meantime, the facade of aspiring to be Costarella's right-hand man in the liquidation business could not afford any cracks.

'It's Mother's Day on Sunday,' the big man remarked, eyeing Jake with speculative interest. 'You don't have any family, do you?'

Not since you helped to kill my stepfather.

Jake managed a rueful smile. 'Lost both my parents in my teens.'

'Yes, I remember you saying so. Difficult for you. Makes it all the more admirable that you pushed on with a career path and have made such a fine job of it.'

Every step of the way had been burning with the

ambition to take this man down. And he would. It had taken ten years to get to this point—accountancy, law, building up experience in Costarella's business, gaining his confidence. Only a few more months now...

'I'd like you to meet my daughter.'

Shock startled Jake out of his secret brooding and rattled his ruthless determination. He'd never thought about the vulture's family, or what effect his own actions might have on them. He raised his eyebrows enquiringly. Was the daughter about to come into her father's business or...was this some weird attempt at matchmaking?

'Laura is a stunner in any man's language. Smart girl and a great cook,' Costarella declared with an inviting smile. 'Come to lunch at my home on Sunday and find out for yourself.'

A sales pitch! And a set-up for a connection to be made!

Jake inwardly recoiled from an up-close-and-personal involvement with anyone related to this man. His hand moved instinctively in a negative gesture. 'I'd be intruding on your family day.'

'I want you to come, Jake.'

The expression on his face brooked no refusal. It was a strong, handsome face, framed by thick, steel-grey hair and dominated by steel-grey eyes—a face imbued with the confidence of a man who could and did take control of anything and bend it to his will.

Jake knew instantly that if he persisted in

declining the invitation, the approval rating that gave him access to the evidence he needed could be lost. 'That's very kind of you,' he rolled out with an appreciative smile. 'If you're sure I'd be welcome…'

Any doubt on that score was clearly irrelevant. What Costarella wanted, he got. 'Make it eleven-thirty,' he said without hesitation. 'You know where I live?'

'Yes. Thank you. I'll look forward to it.'

'Good! I'll see you then.' The grey eyes glittered with satisfaction. 'You won't be disappointed.'

Jake nodded, taking his dismissal as gracefully as he could, knowing he had to turn up on Sunday, knowing he had to show an interest in *the daughter*, and hating the idea with every fibre of his being.

Why Costarella wanted this, he didn't know. It seemed ridiculously patriarchal in this day and age to be lining up a suitor, as though people were pawns to be moved as he wished. Nevertheless, it was typical of the callous mentality of the man. He moved to his own beat, not giving a damn about anyone else's interests.

Jake had to go along with him, play for time, protect his own agenda. If he had to start dating Laura Costarella he would, but no way would he allow himself to become emotionally attached to her, regardless of how beautiful and smart she was.

She was the daughter of the enemy.

He wasn't about to forget that.

Ever.

Mother's Day...

Laura Costarella wished it could be what it was supposed to be—a beautiful, memorable day for her mother with her children showing their love and appreciation for all she'd done for them, and their father being happy with the family they'd created together.

It wasn't going to be like that.

Her father had invited a special guest to the family lunch and from the smug little smile accompanying this announcement, Laura strongly suspected that the guest would be used to show up the shortcomings in his son and daughter, as well as the failings of the mother who had raised them.

Jake Freedman—a hard name, and undoubtedly as hard in character as her father was, or he wouldn't have risen so fast to the top of the tree in the Costarella Accountancy Company, which raked in millions from bankrupt firms. Did he know how he was going to be used today? Did he care?

Laura shook her head over the futile speculation. What would happen would happen. She couldn't stop it. All she could do was cook her mother's favourite foods for lunch and try to deflect the barbs of her father's discontent with his family. Keep smiling, she told herself, no matter what.

She hoped her brother would follow that advice today, too, for their mother's sake. No eruption into a resentful rage. No walking out. Just smile and shrug off any critical remarks like water off a duck's back.

Surely it wasn't too much to ask for Eddie to keep his testosterone in check for one short day.

The doorbell rang as she finished preparing the vegetables for baking as she'd seen done on the cooking show that was one of her favourite television programs. They were ready to slip into the oven with the slowly roasting leg of lamb when the time was right. The pumpkin and bacon soup only had to be reheated. The cream was whipped and the lemon-lime tart was in the refrigerator waiting to be served.

She quickly washed her hands, removed her apron and pasted a smile on her face, determined to greet their visitor with all the charm she could muster.

Jake stood at the front door to Alex Costarella's Mosman mansion, steeling himself to be an appreciative and charming guest. The huge two-storey redbrick home was one of Sydney's old establishment houses, set in immaculately kept grounds, oozing solid respectability—a perfect front to hide the true nature of the man who had acquired it by ripping off other people.

He remembered how hard his stepfather had fought the bankruptcy officials to hold back the sale of their family home while his mother was still alive—just a few more months until the cancer finally took her. No caring, no mercy from the money men. And the whole rotten process had been started by Costarella, who had deliberately turned a blind eye to how a company and hundreds of jobs could have been saved, preferring the prospect of lining his own pockets while being in charge of selling off all the assets.

No caring, no mercy.

His stepfather's heart had given out only a few weeks after his mother had died. Two funerals in close succession. Jake couldn't lay both of them at Costarella's door, but he could certainly lay one. It amused him to think of himself as the wolf outside, waiting to be given open entry to another wolf's home.

Taronga Park Zoo was nearby.

But the dangerous animals were right here.

Costarella didn't know Jake was on the prowl, waiting for the right moment to attack. He was holding his daughter out as bait for a bright future with the young gun in the company, unaware that *he* was the targeted prey. As for Laura, herself…

The door opened and Jake was faced with a woman who instantly excited an interest. She *was* beautiful; long black curly hair, incredible blue eyes, a mouth with lush full lips stretched into a greeting smile of perfect white teeth. She wore a clingy top in purple and white, the neckline dipping down low enough to reveal the upper swell of breasts that were more than big enough to fill a man's hands. Tight purple jeans outlined the rest of her hourglass figure and emphasised the seductive length of her shapely legs. The sexual animal inside Jake growled with the desire to take.

It was several moments before he recovered wits enough to identify himself as the expected guest. 'I'm Jake. Jake Freedman,' he said, hoping she hadn't noticed how *taken* he was by her.

Alex Costarella's daughter was a man-trap.

Falling into it did not fit into his plan.

'Hello. I'm Laura, the daughter of the house.'

She heard herself say the words as though from a great distance, her mind totally stunned by how handsome Jake Freedman was. Though *handsome* didn't say it all, not by a long shot. She'd met a lot of good-looking men. Her brother's world was full of them, actors making their mark in television shows. But this man…what was it that had her heart racing and her stomach fluttering?

His hair was dark brown and cut so short the wave in it was barely noticeable. Somehow the lack of careful styling made his dark brown eyes more riveting. Or maybe it was the unusual shape of them, his eyelids drooping in a way that made them look triangular and incredibly sexy. A strong straight nose, a strong squarish jaw and a strongly sculptured mouth added to the male impact of his face. He would have been perfectly cast as James Bond, Laura thought, and had the nervous feeling he was just as dangerous as the legendary 007 character.

He had the physique to go with it, too. As tall as her father but more lethally lean and looking powerfully masculine in his black jeans and black-and-white sports shirt, the long sleeves casually rolled up to the elbows, revealing hard muscular forearms. Jake Freedman was so male, it was stirring everything female in her. Even though she knew he was her father's man, it was impossible not to feel interested in him.

'Pleased to meet you,' he said, offering his hand with a smile that made him even sexier.

'Likewise,' Laura replied, extending her own hand and finding it subjected to an electric sensation that was so shocking she wanted to snatch it away. 'Please come in,' she rattled out, needing movement to excuse the quick extraction from physical contact with him.

'Daughter of the house,' he repeated musingly as he stepped inside. 'Does that mean you still live here at home?'

The curious assessment in his eyes gave her the sense he was summing up possibilities between them. 'Yes. It's a big house,' she answered drily. Big enough to keep out of her father's way most of the time.

Jake Freedman had to be years older than her university friends, given his position in her father's business, and remembering that unpleasant fact she should avoid him like the plague, apart from getting through this visit today. They would have nothing—absolutely nothing—in common.

'The family is enjoying the sunshine on the back patio,' she said, leading him down the wide hallway that bisected the house. 'I'll take you out to Dad, then bring you some refreshments. What would you like to drink?'

'A glass of iced water would be fine, thank you.'

It surprised her. 'Not a Scotch on the rocks man like my father?'

'No.'

'What about a vodka martini?'

'Just water.'

Well, he wasn't James Bond, she thought, swallowing down a silly giggle.

'Do you have a job, Laura?'

'Yes, I'm a Director of First Impressions.' It was okay to let the laughter gurgle out at his puzzled expression. 'I read it in the newspaper this morning,' she explained. 'It's the title now given to a receptionist.'

'Ah!' He smiled at the pretentiousness of it.

'You know what they call a window cleaner?'

'Please enlighten me.'

'A vision clearance executive.'

He laughed, making his megawatt attractiveness zoom even higher.

'A teacher is a knowledge navigator,' Laura rattled on, trying to ignore his effect on her. 'And a librarian is an information retrieval specialist. I can't remember the rest of the list. All the titles were very wordy.'

'So putting it simply, you're a receptionist.'

'Part-time at a local medical practice. I'm still at

uni, doing landscape architecture. It's a four-year degree program and I'm currently making my way through the last year.'

'Working and studying? Your father doesn't support you?' he queried, obviously not quite in tune with a wealthy man who wouldn't finance his children's full education.

She slanted him a derisive look. 'My father doesn't support what he doesn't approve of. You should know that since you work with him.'

'But you're his daughter.'

'Who was expected to fall in with his wishes. I'm allowed to live here. That's as much support as my father will give to my career choice.'

'Perhaps you should have sought complete independence.'

It was an odd remark, coming from a man who had to have made an art form of falling in with her father's wishes. However, she wasn't about to discuss the dynamics of her family with an outsider, particularly not someone who specialised in siding with her father.

'My mother needs me.'

It was a brief reply and all he was going to get from her. She opened the back door and ushered him out to the patio, quickly announcing, 'Your Jake is here, Dad.'

'Ah!' Her father rose from his chair at the patio table, which was strewn with the Sunday newspapers. His whole face beamed a welcome at the man who was undoubtedly performing up to his expectations in every respect. 'Good to see you here, Jake. Beautiful autumn day, isn't it?'

'Couldn't be better,' he agreed, moving forward to shake her father's offered hand.

Confident, smooth, at ease with himself and the situation…and Laura definitely wasn't. She felt dreadfully at odds with the strong tug of attraction that wouldn't go away. It was wrong. It had to be wrong. The last thing she wanted was a man like her father messing with her life.

'Go and fetch your mother, Laura. She's showing Eddie the latest innovations in the garden. You can tell them both to come and meet our guest.'

'Will do,' she said, glad to leave the two men together, though knowing that the stirring of the family pot couldn't be delayed for long. Her father expected instant obedience to his call.

The garden was her mother's refuge. She was never happier than when discussing what could be done next to it with Nick Jeffries, the handyman who shared her enthusiasm for creating wonderful visual effects and did all the heavy work for her. Laura loved this garden, too, loved every aspect of landscape design, making something beautiful instead of tearing something down…as her father did.

And as Jake Freedman did.

It would be stupid to forget that. She could never, never be in tune with a mind that dealt with destruction.

'Mum, Eddie…' she called out. They were by the rockpool, where Nick had installed the new solar lights. 'Dad's guest is here.'

Her mother's smile of pleasure instantly drooped into a grimace. She darted an anxious look at her son, worried about an imminent clash of personalities.

Eddie hugged her shoulders, smiling reassurance. 'I promise I'll be good, Mum. No bad boy today.'

It won a wry little laugh.

Eddie made a great *bad boy* in the soap opera he currently starred in. The wild flop of his thick black hair, the designer stubble along his angular jawline, the dimple in his chiselled chin, the piercing blue eyes…all made him a very popular pin-up, especially on his flash motorbike. He was wearing black leathers today, though he was now carrying his jacket, discarded because of the heat of the morning. His white T-shirt was emblazoned with a Harley-Davidson. He played a bikie and he looked like one, much to her father's disgust.

The three of them started strolling back towards the patio, son and daughter flanking their mother, determined to keep a happy ball rolling for her. Why she stayed with their father was beyond their comprehension. There was no joy in the marriage. Having a very dominant husband who controlled everything seemed to have sapped her of any will for an independent life.

Laura always thought of her mother as a lady,

never anything but beautifully dressed and groomed, imbued with gracious manners, doing everything correctly and tastefully, making a special ritual of keeping fresh floral arrangements in the house, which she did herself. Even her name, Alicia, was somehow very ladylike.

She looked particularly lovely today, her newly dyed blond hair cut into a short, fluffy style, a blue silk tunic giving her eyes more colour. They had seemed so dull and washed out lately, Laura had worried there might be a health problem her mother was not admitting to. She was getting too thin, as well, a fact hidden by the loosely fitting long-sleeved tunic. The white slacks were also loose, affecting a casually elegant look. Certainly no one would notice anything amiss with her, not on the surface. Jake Freedman would probably pigeonhole her as the typical rich man's wife.

'What's he like?' her mother asked.

'James Bond,' popped straight out of Laura's mouth.

'What? Loaded and dangerous?' Eddie queried.

She grinned at him. 'Plus gorgeous and sexy.'

He rolled his eyes. 'Don't you go falling for him, Laura. That's bad territory.'

'Yes, be careful,' her mother quickly warned, her eyes anxious again. 'Your father might want you to like this man. There has to be some motive behind inviting him here today.'

'Could be that marrying the boss's daughter is

on Jake Freedman's agenda,' Eddie put in, grinning wolfishly, then snapping his teeth to make the point.

Marriage?

Never!

She'd walked out of every relationship she'd had once the guy started making demands on her, which always happened sooner or later. From what she'd witnessed at home, marriage was an endless string of demands, plus abuse thrown in if the demands weren't met. No man was ever going to own her as his wife.

She rolled her eyes back at Eddie. 'I'm not so easy to gobble up. I'll be feeding him lunch. He can whistle for anything more from me.'

'Humphrey Bogart,' her mother murmured.

'What?'

'Humphrey Bogart. He whistled for Lauren Bacall. It was in an old movie.'

'Well, I haven't seen it.'

'Did he get her in the end?' Eddie asked.

'Yes.'

'No doubt she wanted to be got,' Laura said, giving her brother a quelling look. 'Different story.'

'I'll be watching the mouth of Dad's man of the moment,' he tossed back at her, wicked teasing in his eyes. 'If he starts whistling...'

'It's more likely the man of the moment is about to be used to show you up as a footloose lightweight, Eddie, so watch your own mouth.'

'I don't know…I don't know…' their mother fretted.

'It's okay, Mum,' Eddie quickly soothed. 'Laura and I have put our walls up and nothing is going to crack them today. Just you relax now. We're both on guard.'

It was a relief to hear Eddie so sure that his protective armour was in place. Laura wished she could say the same for herself. Despite what her mind dictated, as soon as they came into view of the two men on the patio and she caught Jake Freedman's gaze on her, there was no wall at all to hold off the sexual chemistry he triggered in her.

Immediately she felt a wild tingling in her breasts, shooting her nipples into hard bullets. Her hips started swaying provocatively, driven by some primitive instinct to show off her femininity. Heat whooshed to the apex of her thighs and somehow melted the normal strength in her legs. Her toes curled. And turbulent temptation crashed through every bit of common sense that told her to keep away from this man.

She would love to have him.

Regardless of how wrong it would be.

She would love to have him.

Just for the experience!

CHAPTER TWO

JAKE found it difficult to tear his gaze away from Laura to make a quick assessment of the other two people he was about to meet. The mother was more or less what he expected of Alex Costarella's wife—a lady-of-the-manor type who undoubtedly kept his house as beautifully as she kept herself— but the son was a surprise…unkempt, longish black hair, designer stubble, clothes indicative of a bikie. Obviously Eddie didn't toe his father's line, either.

Two rebellious children and one submissive wife.

Was he supposed to tame Laura, draw her into becoming the kind of woman her father would approve of, sharing his world instead of striking out on her own, pleasing herself?

He looked at her again and felt a tightening in his groin. She was, without a doubt, the most desirable woman he'd ever come into contact with, dangerous to play with, yet the idea of drawing her *away* from her father made her all the more tempting. It was fair justice for Costarella to feel the loss of someone dear to him as well as the loss of the business that gave him the power to wreck people's lives.

He was acutely aware of Laura watching him as her father performed the introductions, weighing up how he responded to her family.

'Alicia, my wife...'

'Delighted to meet you,' Jake rolled out with a smile.

She returned it but there was a wary look in her eyes as she replied, 'Welcome to our home.'

'And my son, Eddie, who obviously didn't bother to shave this morning, not even for his mother.'

The acid criticism was brushed off with a nonchalant grin. 'Couldn't do it, Dad. We're shooting tomorrow. Got to stay in character.' He turned the grin to Jake as he offered his hand. 'I guess you're the son my father should have had, Jake. Happy days, man!'

Jake laughed and took his hand, shaking his head as he replied, 'Don't know about that but thanks for the good wishes, Eddie.'

'You're welcome.'

'Eddie is an actor,' Laura put in proudly. 'He plays the bad boy in *The Wild and the Wonderful.*'

Jake frowned apologetically. 'I'm sorry. I don't know the show.'

Her father snorted. 'It's rubbish. A TV soapie.'

'Rubbish or not, I enjoy doing it,' Eddie declared, totally unabashed. 'How about you, Jake? Do you enjoy doing what you do?'

'It's challenging. I guess acting is, too,' he said, careful to be even-handed in his reply.

'Totally absurd la-la-land,' Costarella jeered. 'Jake and I deal with the real world, Eddie.'

'Well, Dad, lots of people like to have a break from the real world and I help give it to them.' He deftly turned attention back to the guest. 'How do you relax from the pressure-cooker of work, Jake?'

Jake found himself liking Laura's brother. He stood up for himself and was clearly his own man. 'Something physical does the trick for me,' he answered.

'Yeah, got to say sex does it for me, too,' Eddie drawled, eyes twinkling with reckless mischief.

'Eddie!'

The shocked cry from his mother brought a swift apology. 'Sorry, Mum. It's all Laura's fault, saying Jake was sexy.'

'Did she now?' Costarella said with satisfaction.

'Eddie!' Laura cried in exasperation. 'I told you to watch your mouth.'

Jake turned to her, curious to see the reaction to her brother's claim. Her eyes were flashing furious sparks and her cheeks were flushed with embarrassment. As she met his gaze, her chin tilted defiantly and her own tongue let loose.

'Don't look at me as though you haven't heard that about yourself before because I bet you have. It's purely an observation, not an invitation.'

'Laura!' Another shocked protest from the mother.

She threw up her hands. 'Sorry, Mum. I'm off to bring out refreshments. Iced water coming up.'

Jake couldn't help grinning as she turned tail—a very sexy tail—and left the rest of them to patch a conversation together.

'I did try to bring my children up with good manners,' Alicia stated with a heavy sigh.

'No harm done,' her husband declared cheerfully.

'Actually, I like working out at a gym,' Jake said to remove sex from everyone's minds.

''Course you do,' Eddie chimed in. 'Can't get those muscles from sitting at a desk.'

'I do a yoga class,' Alicia offered, anxious to promote non-contentious chat as she gestured for everyone to sit down, tidying the newspapers on the table before sitting down herself.

Jake hadn't expected to find himself interested in Costarella's family. Even less had he expected to *like* any of them. In fact, the only one he'd given any thought to was Laura, whom he'd imagined to be a pampered princess, revelling in the role of Daddy's little girl.

The family dynamics were certainly intriguing and Jake was not averse to exploring them further… watching, listening, gathering information…and maybe, maybe, he might go after what he wanted with Laura Costarella, satisfying himself on several levels.

Laura cursed Eddie for being provocative, cursed herself for reacting so wildly, cursed Jake Freedman for making her feel stuff that completely rocked any sensible composure. Her escape to the kitchen should have settled her nerves but they were still jumping all over the place even after she'd loaded the traymobile with the preferred drinks and the platter of hors d'oeuvres.

There was no hiding from the man. He had to be faced again. She could only hope he wouldn't try capitalising on her remark or she'd be severely tempted to pour the jug of iced water over his head. Which just went to show how out of control she was and that just wouldn't do. Better to freeze him off with good manners. She had to keep remembering that Jake Freedman was her father's man and any close connection with him could not lead anywhere good.

Not emotionally.

No matter how good he might be in bed.

And she had to stop thinking of that, too.

Having taken several deep breaths and gritting her teeth with determination to behave as she should, Laura wheeled the traymobile out to the patio. It was a relief to find the four of them chatting amicably about relaxation techniques; meditation, Tai Chi, massage and flotation tanks. Even her father appeared to be in good humour. She noted glumly that the only empty chair left for her at the round table was between Jake Freedman and her mother so she couldn't avoid being physically close to the man.

She set the platter on the table for everyone to help

themselves, handed the ice-bucket containing a bottle of her mother's favourite white wine to Eddie and told him to open it, placed the jug of iced water and a crystal tumbler in front of Jake, served her father his Scotch on the rocks, and supplied the wineglasses before bowing to the inevitable of taking the designated chair and addressing the gaffe she'd made.

'I'm sorry for blowing my stack with you, Jake. I was annoyed with Eddie. And embarrassed.'

The riveting brown eyes sparkled with amusement, making her stomach flutter again. 'No offence taken, Laura. I dare say Eddie hears that said about himself so often, it's lost any currency with him. And I doubt he thought it had any currency with me, either.'

Letting her know he didn't have tickets on himself, not on that score anyway. Though Laura wasn't sure she believed him.

Her father snorted in rank disbelief. 'If it didn't have any currency with Eddie, he'd be out of a job. It's only because all the teeny-boppers think he's sexy that he's built up a fan base.'

'Lucky for me!' Eddie said flippantly. 'Though I do work at it, Dad.'

'Some people just have it,' her mother said, trying to divert a clash. 'I always thought Sean Connery...'

'Back to James Bond,' Eddie cut in, grinning at Laura.

She bared her teeth at him in warning.

He stood up to pour the wine, cheerfully saying,

'Mum's a great movie buff, Jake. I bet no one could beat her on that topic in a quiz show. And she's a champion Mum, too. Let's drink a toast to her.' He lifted his glass. 'Mother's Day!'

They all echoed the toast.

Having been handed the movie ball, Jake Freedman proceeded to run with it, giving her mother so much charming attention, Laura couldn't help liking him for it. He was probably working hard at being an amenable guest, showing off his talent for diplomacy to her father. Nevertheless, it was giving her mother pleasure, and her father, for once, was not souring it with any acid comments.

In fact, he looked surprisingly content with the situation.

Laura didn't really care why.

It was good that he wasn't putting her mother down as he usually did.

She slipped away to attend to the lunch preparations, feeling slightly more at ease with Jake Freedman's presence. It was making the day run more smoothly than she had hoped for. The only negative was his sexual impact on her.

She hadn't been able to stop herself from slyly checking him over; the neat curl of his ears, the length of his eyelashes, the sensuality of his lips, the charismatic flashes of his smiles, the light sprinkle of black hairs on his strong forearms, the elegant length of his fingers with their clean clipped nails, the way his muscular thighs stretched the black fabric of his jeans. And long feet! Didn't that mean his private parts would be…very manly?

Which, of course, would be in keeping with the rest of him.

It was all very difficult, knowing he was her father's man. It was also difficult to concentrate on getting everything right for the meal; vegetables to go into the oven, reheating the soup, greens ready for last-minute microwaving, mint sauce on the dining-room table. She would have to sit next to him again; probably a blessing since this table wasn't a round one and he couldn't see what was written on her face unless he turned to her.

So far, he wasn't giving her any special attention and it was probably better if it stayed that way—no dilemma between temptation and caution. He was bound to have a woman in the wings, anyway. Eddie had girls falling all over him and she couldn't imagine it would be any different for Jake Freedman— another reason for not getting involved with him. Being perceived as just one of an available crowd had no appeal.

Although being the boss's daughter, he would have to treat her with respect.

Which she'd hate.

Whatever way she looked at it, having Jake Freedman was no good. Besides, he wasn't exactly holding out the chance to have him, though he might before the day was over. As her mother said, there had to be a purpose behind this visit. If a connection with her was the desired end, she had to be ready for it, ready to say no.

The soup was hot enough to serve. Telling herself she was lucky to have the distraction of being the cook, Laura returned to the patio to invite everyone inside for lunch. Eddie escorted her mother to the dining room. Jake Freedman followed with her father, the two men obviously on congenial terms.

Another warning.

Her father must have once been charming to her mother or she wouldn't have married him. His true character could not have emerged until she was completely under his domination. If Jake Freedman was of like mind, thinking he had the right—the power— to rule others' lives as he saw fit, she wanted nothing to do with him.

Jake continued to get his bearings with the Costarella family over lunch. Eddie had dropped out of school and left home at sixteen, getting himself a job as a backroom boy in one of the television studios.

'One day you'll regret not going on with your education,' his father said balefully.

He shrugged. 'Accountancy was never going to suit me, Dad.'

'No. Head in the clouds. Just like your mother.'

The tone of disgust caused Alicia to flush. She was a more fragile person than her perfectly groomed image presented, very nervy and too anxious to please. He was recalling Laura's comment that her mother needed her when she leapt to Alicia's defence.

'Oh, I think Mum's totally grounded when it comes to her garden.'

'Garden…movies…' Costarella scoffed. 'Alicia has led both of you astray with her interests. I had high hopes for you, Laura. Top of your school in mathematics…'

'Well, I have high hopes for myself, Dad. Sorry I can't please both of us,' she said with a rueful smile.

'Gardening…' he jeered.

'Landscape architecture is a bit more than that, Dad.'

No hesitation in standing up for herself.

Costarella huffed. 'At least you can cook. I'll say that for you. Enjoying the meal, Jake?'

'Very much.' He shot an appreciative smile at Laura. 'Top chef standard. The soup was delicious and I've never tasted better lamb and baked potatoes.'

She laughed. 'Top chef recipes from a TV cooking show. All it takes is dedication to following the instructions. You could do it yourself if you had the will to. It's not a female prerogative. In fact, most of the top chefs are male. Do you cook for yourself?'

'No. Mostly I eat out.'

'Need a woman to cook for you,' Costarella slid in.

It was a totally sexist remark and he saw the recoil from it in Laura's eyes, followed by a derisive flash at him…if he thought the same.

He turned to Costarella and allowed himself one risky remark, grinning to take away any sting. 'Given that most top chefs are male, a man might be better.'

Eddie found this hilarious, cracking up with laughter.

'What's so funny?' his father demanded.

'It's just that lots of guys in the service industry are gay and I don't see Jake as gay,' he spluttered out.

Laura started giggling, too.

'I'm not,' Jake said.

'Certainly not,' Costarella declared emphatically.

'We know you're not,' Laura assured him, still tittering.

'Absolutely.' Eddie backed up. 'Laura wouldn't think you were sexy if you were gay.'

'Eddie, behave yourself,' Alicia cried.

'Impossible,' his father muttered, though his ill humour had dissipated at this affirmation that his daughter was vulnerable to the attraction he favoured.

Laura rose from the table. 'Now that you've embarrassed both of us, Eddie, I'm going to serve sweets, which I hope will be tart enough to glue up your mouth.' She smiled at her mother. 'It's lemon-lime, Mum.'

'Oh, my favourite!' Alicia glowed with pleasure. 'Thank you, dear.'

Jake watched her head off to the kitchen again. It would be risky business, taking on a connection with her, complicating what had been his undeviating purpose for too many years to mess with when he was in sight of the end. She could become a distraction. He'd been single-minded for so long, readjusting his thinking to include a relationship with Costarella's daughter was probably not a good idea, however tempting it was.

Cynically dating her for short-term benefits at work was no longer an option. He was genuinely attracted to her. Strongly attracted to her. She had his skin prickling with the desire for action between them. Costarella expected him to make a move on her. *He* wanted to make a move on her. The tricky part was controlling it.

'How come you're not sharing Mother's Day with your own Mum, Jake?' Eddie suddenly asked.

'I would be if she were still alive, Eddie,' he answered ruefully.

'Oh! Sorry!' He made an apologetic grimace. 'Hope the bereavement isn't recent.'

'No.'

'Guess I'm lucky I've still got mine.' He leaned over to plant a kiss on Alicia's cheek.

'Yes, since you've always been a mother's boy,' Costarella sniped.

There was a flicker of fear in the look Alicia darted at her husband. Jake imagined she had been a victim of abuse for so long, she felt helpless to do anything about it.

'I've been admiring the very artistic centre-piece for the table,' he said, smiling at her to take the anxiety away. 'Are they flowers from your garden, Alicia?'

'Yes.' Her face lit up with pleasure. 'I did that arrangement this morning. I'm very proud of my chrysanthemums.'

'And rightly so, Mum,' Laura chimed in, wheeling the traymobile into the dining room. 'They're blooming beautifully.'

She served the lemon-lime tart with dollops of cream to everyone, continuing her praise of her mother's talent for horticulture.

Jake watched her. She was beautiful. And smart. And so lushly sexy, temptation roared through him, defying the reservations that had been swimming through his mind.

As she resumed the seat beside him, he turned to her, his eyes seeking to engage hers with what he wanted. 'I'd like to see this garden. Will you show it to me when we've finished lunch?'

Startled, frightened, recoiling. 'Much better for Mum to show you, Jake. It's her creation.'

'He asked *you*, Laura,' Costarella immediately bored in. 'Not only should you oblige our guest, but your mother has already shown Eddie around the garden. She doesn't need to repeat herself, do you, Alicia?'

'No, no,' she agreed, her hands fluttering an appeal to her daughter. 'I'm happy for you to do it, Laura.'

Caught.

She had to do it now whether she wanted to or not.

Jake aimed at sweetening the deal for her. 'I'm interested in seeing it through your eyes. You can tell me how it fits your concept of landscape design.'

'Okay! I'll flood you with knowledge,' she said tartly.

He laughed. 'Thank you. I will enjoy that.'

Surrender under fire, Jake thought, but no surrender in her heart. It made for one hell of a challenge... their walk in the garden. The adrenaline charge inside him wanted to fight her reluctance to involve herself with him, yet that same reluctance gave him an out from Costarella's heavy-handed matchmaking...keeping the more important mission on track, without distraction.

He would make the decision later.

In the garden.

CHAPTER THREE

LAURA told herself it was just a job she had to take on and get through—escort Jake around the garden, bore him to death with her enthusiasm for built environments and deliver him back to her father, who had announced his intention to watch a football game on television in the home theatre.

Eddie helped clear the table, following her to the kitchen to have a private word with her as they stacked the dishwasher. 'You're the main target today, Laura. No doubt about it now,' he warned. 'I'd say Dad wants Jake as his son-in-law.'

'It's not going to happen,' she snapped.

'He's a clever guy. Been playing all sides today. And I've been watching you. You're not immune to him.'

'Which made it very stupid of you to tell him what I thought.'

'Obvious anyway. Believe me, a guy like that knows women think he's sexy. He would have had them vying for his attention from his teens onwards. Just don't say yes to him.'

Easy for him, sitting on the sidelines, Laura thought savagely. 'What if I want to?'

Eddie looked appalled.

'He *is* sexy,' she repeated defiantly, fed up with being put on the spot.

He grimaced. 'Then make damned sure you keep it at sex and don't end up hooked on him. The way Mum is should be warning enough for you.'

'I will never be like Mum.'

He shook his head. 'I wish she would leave him.'

'She can't see anything else. Better play a game of Scrabble with her while I'm doing my duty with Jake. She likes that.'

'Will do. That's a lot more fun than duty.'

Laura heaved a deep sigh, trying to relax the tension tearing at her nerves. 'I don't want to want him, Eddie.'

He gave her a look of serious consideration. 'Go for it if you must. You'll always wonder otherwise. Sooner or later he'll turn you off and I think you're strong enough to walk away.'

'Yes, I am,' she said with certainty.

'But you'd be better off not going there.'

'I know.' She made a rueful grimace. 'Maybe he'll turn me off out in the garden.'

'Unlikely.'

'Well I won't be falling at his feet, that's for sure. And you let Mum win at Scrabble, but don't be obvious about it.'

'No problem.' He grinned his devil-may-care grin. 'Let's go and fight the good fight.'

She grinned back at him. 'The *gay* bit was good.'

He laughed and hugged her shoulders as they returned to the dining room, where he immediately put their plan into action. 'Better get out the Scrabble, Mum. Since you beat me last time, I want a return match, and heaven help me if I'm swamped with all vowels again.'

'I'll leave you to your game,' her father said good-humouredly, rising from his chair, smiling at Jake Freedman. 'I'm sure you'll enjoy my daughter's company.'

'I will,' he agreed, rising to his feet, as well, ready to take on the garden seduction scenario.

Resentment suddenly raged through Laura. Jake Freedman was playing her father's game, but she didn't have to. He wasn't *her* guest. It was after three o'clock. Lunch had gone off reasonably well. The trickiest part of being together for Mother's Day was over. Her father was sparing them his presence. His wrath wouldn't fall on all of them if she didn't remain polite to the man. She could put Jake Freedman on the spot, instead of being the target herself.

She smiled at him. 'Let's go.'

He accompanied her outside, making easy conversation to start with.

'*Was* it your mother's pleasure in her garden that led you to your choice of career, Laura?'

He seemed genuinely curious and she didn't mind

answering him. 'Partly. Nick probably had more influence, the creativity he uses to generate Mum's pleasure.'

'Who's Nick?'

'The gardener and handyman Dad employs to maintain everything, but he actually does more than maintain.'

'Like what?'

'He thinks about what will delight Mum and does it. Like the solar lights he's just put around the rock-pool. I'll show you. It's over this way.'

He strolled beside her, apparently content to bide his time, ensure she was relaxed with him. Which was totally impossible, but at least he didn't know it and wouldn't know it until he made a move on her.

'A waterfall, too,' he remarked as they came to the pool.

'Yes. It makes a soothing sound. Most people enjoy sitting near falling water...fountains in a park. Also reflections in water. The lights placed around the pool shimmer in it when it's dark.'

'Does your mother come out here at night?'

'Sometimes. Though she can also see this part of the garden from her bedroom window. What's really special is how Nick lit up the figurines of the Chinese water-carriers coming down the rocks at the side of the waterfall. There's another light at the back of the pot-plant below them. It bathes them in a ghostly glow. Quite a wonderful effect.'

'Landscape architecture,' he said, slanting her a

rueful smile. 'I've never thought about it but I can see why it should be appreciated.'

'I guess in the career you've chosen, you don't take the time to smell the roses,' she shot at him.

'True. I haven't,' he conceded readily enough, as though it didn't matter to him.

It niggled Laura into asking, 'Is it worth it?'

There was a subtle shift of expression on his face, a hardening of his jaw, a determined glint in his eyes. 'Yes, it is. To me,' he answered in a tone that didn't allow for a different point of view.

Laura couldn't leave it alone. 'You like working for my father?'

'Your father is part of a system that interests me.'

It was a clever sidestep, depersonalising her question.

'The system,' she repeated, wanting to nail down his motivation. 'I can't imagine any pleasure in dealing with bankruptcy.'

'No, it can be very traumatic,' he said quietly. 'I would like to make it less so.' The dark brown eyes drilled into hers. 'Not even the most beautiful parks in the world resonate with people in that situation, Laura. All they see is their lives crumbling, their jobs gone, their plans for the future shattered. It can lead to divorce, suicide, violence, depression so dark there is no light.'

She shivered at the intensity of feeling coming from him, a depth of caring she hadn't expected in this man. It didn't sit with coldly calculated ambition.

Not only that, but he'd also somehow turned the tables on her, making his job much more seriously special than hers.

'I know that people going through trauma do find some solace in a pleasant environment,' she argued with conviction. Her mother, for one.

'I didn't mean to undervalue it.' He gestured an appeal. 'I'm not your father, Laura. Perhaps we can both work on having open minds about each other.'

'Why did you come here today?' she asked point-blank.

'Your father wanted me to meet you and I was curious enough to accept the invitation,' he answered, his eyes gently mocking the hard challenge in hers.

She planted her hands on her hips, sick of how he was churning her around and wanting open confrontation. 'So what do you think of me?'

His mouth moved into a very sensual smile. 'I think you're *very* sexy.'

A tidal wave of heat rushed through Laura. She snatched at his own words to her and threw them back at him. 'That doesn't have much currency with me.'

He laughed and stepped forward, sliding an arm around her waist and scooping her into body contact with him, his eyes glittering with reckless intent. 'I've been wanting to do this from the moment we met, so I'll do it, and you can slap me down afterwards.'

There was time—a few seconds—for her to slam

her hands against his shoulders and push away. His mouth didn't crash down on hers. It seemed to her he lowered his head in slow motion, moving his free hand to tilt her face upwards. She did nothing, waiting for the collision of the kiss, wanting it, wanting to know if it would be better than any other kiss a man had given her.

A weird exhilaration was buzzing through her at being held in his embrace, as though he was the right man for her, the perfect man—a sensation she'd never felt until now. Whether it was his intense maleness, his strength, his aggressive confidence, his sexy physique...Laura couldn't pin it down, but curiosity held her totally captive.

His lips brushed over hers with surprising gentleness, tantalising her, exciting her with a sensuality she had not expected. She *did* move her hands to his shoulders, but not to push away, to touch, to feel, to slide around his neck and hold his head to hers. She liked the shape of it, liked the clean, bristly thickness of his short hair—no gel.

He started tasting her, little flicks of his tongue slipping seductively between her lips, and she responded with her own provocative probing, wanting to taste him, a pulsing primitive streak urging her to goad him into less control. It was as though he was testing how good she was for him, whether she would be worth pursuing beyond today, and everything female in her wanted to blow him out of his mind.

A wild exultation zinged through her when he plunged into a far more passionate kiss. No more holding her face. Both arms were around her, pressing her into intimate contact with him and she revelled in the hard evidence of her desirability. He was very definitely aroused, and so was she, as fiercely passionate as he was in the meshing of their mouths, seeking and driving for more and more excitement.

He clutched her bottom, grinding her even closer, and she was so hot for him she didn't care how intimate they were. Her heart was pounding, her thighs were quivering, and the only thought she had was *yes, yes, yes*. It was powering through her. More than desire. Need that craved instant satisfaction. Urgently.

It was he who pulled back, breaking the kiss, lifting his head, sucking in air like a runner at the end of a marathon. She gulped in oxygen, too, the dizziness in her head demanding it. Her breasts were still crushed against his chest and she could feel his heart thumping in unison with hers. Then his cheek was rubbing against her hair and his voice vibrated in her ear.

'I want you, Laura, but it can't be here.'

Here...in the garden...in open view of anyone who wandered outside. Madness. She couldn't take him inside, either. Everyone would know. She recoiled from giving her father the satisfaction of thinking his plan was working. It would worry her mother. Eddie, too. It couldn't be done. The time and place wasn't right. But the man was. Which was very confusing because he shouldn't be.

'I need to sit down,' she said, acutely aware of how shaken she was. 'There's a garden bench…'

'I see it.'

He shifted, tucking her tightly against him, walking her to the bench. Laura had to concentrate on putting one foot in front of the other. He saw her seated then sat beside her, leaning forward, elbows on knees, still recovering himself from the rage of desire that had swept through both of them.

Laura breathed in the scent of the nearby lavender bush. It was supposed to be calming. It did help to clear her head to some extent. Jake Freedman might be his own man but he *was* closely connected to her father. However *right* he might feel to her, she couldn't overlook that situation.

'If you think this means I'm a pushover for the taking, it doesn't,' she blurted out. 'The chemistry between us is just chemistry and I won't be losing sight of that, so don't imagine it gives you any power over me.'

He nodded a few times, then shot her a wry smile. 'Well, you've certainly slapped me down.'

Not for the kiss. For the possible motive hidden behind it because the kiss had got to her, more powerfully than she cared to admit. She tore her gaze away from his tantalising little smile and stared at the waterfall, wishing it could soothe the deep disturbance this man had caused.

'Not so much a slap, Jake,' she said more calmly. 'Just letting you know how I feel about it. My father is obviously pushing me at you. Maybe he wants you as his son-in-law. No way will I be used as a step up your career ladder.'

No comment from him.

His silence went on for so long it began to shred her nerves. 'Sorry if I've dashed your hopes,' she said bitingly.

'Not at all.' He sat up, hooking his arms on the backrest of the bench in a totally relaxed manner, smiling at her as though he was perfectly at peace with her decision. 'I'm not looking for a wife at this point in my life and you're not looking to fill that position. With that understood, do you want any part of me, Laura?'

Which put her right back on the spot.

His eyes glittered with the knowledge that she did, but wanting and taking were two different things. As Eddie said, she'd be better off not going there. Jake could be lying, secretly thinking he could seduce her into becoming his wife. Not that he'd be able to, but if she entered into any kind of relationship with him, he could report to her father that everything was sweet between them, and she'd hate that.

Yet looking at him, remembering how it had felt with him, the thought of not experiencing more of him actually hurt. Which was probably another danger signal. He *did* have power over her.

'I want you,' he said quietly, seeing her struggle

with his question. 'Not because you're your father's daughter. I think the chemistry between us makes that totally irrelevant. I want you because I can't remember wanting any other woman quite as much.'

It echoed her response to him. Jake Freedman was definitely the ultimate ten out of ten. But he could be saying those words because they were what any woman would like to hear. He was such a sexy man, he might affect every woman this way and she was no exception at all to him. *Clever, playing all sides,* Eddie had said.

She eyed him sceptically. 'Is that the honest truth, Jake?'

'Much to my own dismay, yes,' he said with a rueful grimace.

It was an odd thing to say and she looked at him in puzzlement. 'Why to your dismay?'

The riveting brown eyes bored into hers with heart-stopping intensity. 'Because I don't want to want you, Laura. Any more than you want to want me. And with that said, why don't we both take time to think about it?'

He rose from the garden bench, apparently preparing to leave her. Laura was so startled by the action, she simply stared up at him.

'Do you have a mobile phone?' he asked.

'Yes.'

'Give me your number. I'll call you at the end of the week if I'm still thinking of you and you can then say yes or no.'

It was so abrupt, hard, cut and dried, and the turbulent feelings it set off inside her made it difficult to think. Time…yes…time to decide if she couldn't bear not to know more of him…or time to have his impact recede to something less significant.

He took a slim mobile phone out of his shirt pocket and she rattled out her number for him to enter it in his private file.

'Thank you,' he said, pocketing the phone again and flashing an ironic smile at her. 'I've seen enough of the garden. You might like to join Eddie and your mother playing Scrabble. I'll say goodbye to them and then to your father on my way out.'

Relief poured through her. No more stress today. Decision-making could wait. She returned his smile as she rose from the bench. 'I didn't have you pegged as a garden man.'

'I shall take up smelling roses.'

'You need a garden for that. The hothouse ones don't have much scent.'

He raised one eyebrow in a lightly mocking challenge. 'Perhaps we can give each other new experiences.'

She shrugged, deliberately noncommittal. 'Perhaps we can.'

No more was said.

He accompanied her back to the dining room and with every step she sensed him withdrawing from her, wrapping himself in self-containment. It was a weird, cold feeling—in sharp contrast to the wild heat of their physical connection. He was leaving her alone and that troubled her far more than it should.

Eddie and her mother said all the polite responses to his polite appreciation of the day spent with them. Her mother took him in tow to the lounge room so he could say goodbye to her father and she was left behind in the dining room with Eddie, whose eyes were full of questions.

'So?' he asked, as soon as their visitor was out of earshot.

'So, nothing,' she answered. 'I showed him the garden.'

She couldn't bring herself to open up a discussion on what had happened between her and Jake Freedman. Somehow it was too personal, too private.

Besides, it would probably come to nothing.

And it was probably better that way.

Probably.

CHAPTER FOUR

THE end of the week, he'd said.

It was the first thought Laura had when she woke up on Friday morning.

If he was still thinking of her, she mentally added, half-hoping that he wasn't so she wouldn't be faced with the decision of whether or not to see him again.

It had been impossible to get him out of her head. She couldn't look at a guy without comparing him to Jake Freedman. None of them measured up to him. Not even close. Her uni studies had suffered with him slipping into her mind when she should have been concentrating. As for being a Director of First Impressions at her receptionist job, no impressions at all had got through to her. Directing the doctors' patients had all been a matter of rote this week. It was like her whole life was revolving around waiting for his call.

Which was really, really bad.

What had happened to her strong sense of independence? It should be rising above this obsessive thinking about a man, putting him in a place of relative unimportance. She didn't like not being in full control of her life. It was as though a virus had invaded her system and she couldn't get rid of it. But as all viruses did, it would run its course and leave her, she told herself.

Especially if Jake didn't call.

However, if he did…

Laura heaved a fretful sigh and rolled out of bed, unable to make up her mind on what she should do. Would she always wonder about him if she didn't try him out?

It was an unanswerable question. Nevertheless, it plagued her all day, distracting her from the lectures at uni. By late afternoon she had decided it was best if Jake didn't call so a choice wasn't even available. She felt so woolly-headed, it was a relief to board the ferry from Circular Quay to Mosman and stand on the outside deck, needing a blast of sea breeze to whip away the fog in her mind.

The ferry was halfway across the harbour when her mobile phone rang. Her heart instantly started hammering. It might not be him, she told herself, plucking the phone out of the side pocket of her bag. He would not have finished work yet. It wasn't quite five o'clock. Her father rarely arrived home before seven.

Gingerly she raised the phone to her ear and said, 'Hello.'

'It's Jake, Laura.'

His voice conjured up his image so sharply, her breath stuck in her throat.

'Would you like to go out to dinner with me tomorrow night?'

Dinner! Her head whirled. To go or not to go…

'I thought we could try Neil Perry's Spice Temple. A new experience for both of us if you haven't been there.'

Neil Perry…one of Sydney's master chefs! His restaurants were famous for their wonderful food. The Rockpool. The Rockpool Bar and Grill. The Spice Temple. She would love, love, love to eat there, but…

'I can't afford it.'

'My treat. You gave me a great meal last Sunday.'

True. He owed her. 'Okay. I'd like that very much,' she said recklessly. A Neil Perry dinner was worth one evening with the man, regardless of what inner turmoil he caused. And maybe that would stop on further acquaintance. 'I'll meet you there,' she quickly added, not wanting her father to know she was seeing Jake Freedman again. 'What time?'

'Will seven o'clock suit?'

'Yes.'

'You know the address?'

'I'll look it up.'

'It's a basement restaurant. Go straight downstairs. I'll wait for you inside.'

'I won't be late. Thanks for the invitation.'

She ended the call, quite pleased with herself for handling it with a fair amount of control. This meeting could be contained at the restaurant…if she wanted it to be. Eddie would let her stay over at his apartment in Paddington on Saturday night so being taken home by Jake could be avoided, too.

Excitement buzzed through her…wicked, wanton excitement.

A sexy man, a sexy meal…impossible not to look forward to experiencing both.

Jake steeled himself for the Friday afternoon wrap-up meeting in Alex Costarella's office, suspecting there was only one issue of real interest on the agenda. He was right. After a half-hour chat about the week's work, Costarella leaned back in his executive chair, a smug little man-to-man smile on his face as he asked, 'Will you be seeing Laura this weekend?'

'Yes. We're having dinner together tomorrow night,' he answered, hating this matchmaking farce, but knowing that going along with it was to his advantage, keeping his position in the company ripple-free until he was ready to strike.

'Good! Good!'

Jake smiled back, playing the game to the hilt. 'Thank you for introducing me to her.'

'Pleasure. Laura needs a man to take her in hand and I hope you're the man to do it, Jake.'

The only way he was going to take her in hand was in bed, if she agreed to it. 'She's certainly very attractive.'

It was a noncommittal statement but Costarella found it encouraging enough to let the matter pass. 'Enjoy your weekend,' he said, and Jake was free to leave.

He'd thought a lot about Laura Costarella since last Sunday. She was hostile to her father, hostile to his wishes, and he'd anticipated her saying no to the dinner invitation. Since he very much wanted her to say yes, he'd deliberately used the Neil Perry drawcard, knowing that her interest in cooking had to make her something of a foodie.

Temptation...

The stronger it was, the harder it was to resist.

She wanted him, too. No doubt about that. If she was up for a wild fling with him, Jake would be only too happy to oblige. He'd been itching to oblige all week. Satisfying the lust she'd triggered in him was fast becoming a must-do, though he did feel ambivalent about taking on Costarella's daughter. He hadn't counted on liking her and he certainly didn't want to begin caring about her.

Spicy company, spicy food, spicy sex.

That had to be the limit of his involvement with the daughter of his enemy because a line would be driven between them when he brought charges against her father, ensuring that the corrupt insolvency practitioner could never again bury another struggling business to secure his obscene liquidator's fee.

Lust always burned out after a while, he assured himself.

In the meantime, the fire had been lit for tomorrow night and he looked forward to some very spicy heat.

Laura stood in front of the billowing turquoise hologram that gave an exotic curtain illusion to the doorway leading to the Spice Temple. It should have added pleasure to her dressing up for this dinner date. She was wearing her sexiest dress—a short turquoise silk bubble skirt attached to a tightly fitting black silk bodice—and the gorgeous black-and-turquoise high heels her mother had bought her for Christmas. Nothing, however, could dispel the anger festering in her mind and churning through her stomach.

Jake Freedman deserved to be stood up. Only the lure of Neil Perry's food had brought her here and she *was* owed a dinner. As for her outfit, she hoped it made Jake Freedman want her all the more because he could eat his heart out for sex tonight. No way was he going to get as much as a piece of her.

'Have a nice night with Jake!'

Her teeth gnashed over those words—accompanied by her father's beaming smile of approval. He'd been told about this date. Maybe the two men had plotted it together. Whatever… Tonight was no longer a private and personal meeting. It reeked of other agendas in the wind and she hated the thought of playing a part in either man's scheming.

Determined on focusing on the food and giving

Jake Freedman a very cold shoulder, she stepped past the doorway and made her way downstairs. Red dominated the decor of the basement restaurant. The scent of joss-sticks wafted through it. Definitely the hot, *in* place to be, Laura thought, noting that most of the tables were already occupied, even at this relatively early hour.

Jake had a table for two. He rose from his chair as he saw her being led to it, his gaze swiftly raking over the high points of her femininity, before shooting her a look of sizzling appreciation. Laura sizzled, too, not only with the acute, physical awareness he sparked off, but also with resentment at the sheer animal magnetism that clutched at her heart and turned her insides to jelly.

His clothes were completely nondescript—white shirt, grey slacks. They were irrelevant to the stunning impact of the man, as though it was his natural right to hold centre stage anywhere, in any company without any effort whatsoever. He waited for her with easy confidence and Laura wished she could knock him down and sweep him out of her life as though his existence was of no account.

Somehow she had to make it of no account.

'You look spectacular,' he said in greeting, grinning wickedly as he added, 'Great shoes!'

'They're good man-stomping shoes,' she replied, doing her best to appear cool and collected.

One black eyebrow quirked upwards. 'About to do some stomping?'

She returned a glowering look. 'I'll eat first.'

'Good idea! Work up some energy.'

He was amused.

Laura seethed over his amusement as she sat down. They were handed menus by a waitress who offered to help them make choices if they wanted anything explained.

'Not yet,' Laura said firmly. 'I want to salivate over every dish before I start choosing.'

'We'll call you when we're ready,' Jake put in, smiling his charming smile, which, of course, would bring the dazzled waitress running the moment he caught her attention.

Laura fixed her attention on the menu. She read the Spice Temple philosophy first. It described what the restaurant aimed for—unique and special dishes, seasoned by an unmistakable Chinese flavour and driven by a long-fostered passion for Asian cuisine, all designed to delight the senses with their contrasting tastes and textures. She hoped they would dominate her senses and block Jake Freedman out.

'Why do you want to stomp on me?'

She set the menu down and glared at the curiosity in his eyes. 'How many brownie points did you get for telling my father we were meeting for dinner tonight?'

'Ah!' He made a rueful grimace. 'I didn't offer the information, Laura. He asked me directly if I was seeing you again. Did you want me to lie about it?'

She was unappeased. 'I bet you knew he would

ask. That's why you called me when you did. Before you left work yesterday.'

He cocked his head on one side, the dark brown eyes challenging her stance on this issue. 'I thought you were determined on not having your father rule your life.'

'He doesn't.'

'He's influencing your attitude towards me right now.'

'Because you told him.'

He shook his head. 'You should make decisions for yourself, Laura, regardless of what anyone else knows or says. You made yours yesterday. Why let him change what you want? You've brought him here with you instead of moving to your own beat.'

She frowned, realising she had let her father ruin all her pleasure in anticipating this date. Although how could she be excited over being used?

'What about you? Are you here for me or for him?' she asked, watching for any shiftiness in his eyes.

He grinned a wickedly sexy grin. 'When I was watching you walk to this table, I can assure you I was not thinking of your father.'

Heat bloomed in her cheeks at the provocative statement. She lifted her chin, defying the desire he wanted her to share. 'I decided to flaunt what you weren't going to get.'

'Decisions, decisions,' he mocked, gesturing an appeal. 'Can we leave your father out of them for the rest of this evening? Just enjoy all there is to enjoy just between ourselves?'

He was very appealing.

The man had everything—looks, intelligence, the sexiest eyes in the world, and he was undermining her prejudice at a rate of knots. Nevertheless, she couldn't quite set aside an ulterior motive for this date with her. On the other hand, why shouldn't she take pleasure in being with him, move her father to the sidelines, denying him any power to influence the play between her and Jake? After all, she was the one with the power to decide how far she would get involved with this man.

She gave him a hard look of warning. 'As long as it's kept between ourselves, I'm happy to take a more positive attitude towards you.'

'And I'm happy to be your secret lover,' he replied, his eyes dancing with unholy teasing.

Her heart performed a somersault. 'I didn't say anything about becoming lovers.'

'Just assuring you that private moments will be kept private.' He opened up his menu. 'Let's salivate over what's on offer together. Did you see that the hottest dishes are printed in red?'

He was the hottest dish.

Laura dragged her mind off visualising him as her lover and reopened her menu. 'I prefer spicy to hot, hot,' she said, looking at the list of entrées.

'Okay. We cross out the red print ones.'

'You don't have to. Choose whatever you like.'

'There's so much to like, it will be better if we can share, don't you think? Have a taste of each other's choices? Broaden the experience?'

Sharing the taste… Laura's stomach curled. It sounded intimate. It was intimate. And suddenly she didn't care about other agendas. She wanted this experience with him.

'Great idea!' she said, and allowed herself to smile.

His eyes twinkled with pleasure, completely dissipating the anger she had carried to this meeting.

'You're incredibly beautiful when you smile,' he remarked. 'I hope I can make you smile all evening for the sheer pleasure of looking at you.'

She laughed. 'No chance! I'm going to be busy eating.'

'I'll try for in between bites.'

'I'll be drooling over the food.'

He laughed. 'Speaking of which, what entrées would you like to try?'

A smile was still on her face as she read the yummy list. The happy excitement about tonight with Jake had come bouncing back. He was right about making decisions for herself. She should trust her own instincts and go with what instinctively felt right.

CHAPTER FIVE

THE waitress advised them to choose only one main course with a side dish of vegetables to share since they were ordering two separate entrées. The helpings were large and they would surely want to leave room for dessert.

'Definitely,' Laura agreed. 'I have to try the sesame ice cream with candied popcorn and chocolate.'

'And I want the Dessert Cocktail,' Jake said with relish. 'Sounds wonderful—caramelized pear, London gin, lillet blanc and crème de cacao shaken and served with the chocolate, sesame and cashew bark.'

It sounded very James Bond to Laura who couldn't help grinning over the thought. Jake might not be 007 but he was certainly tall, dark, handsome and dangerous, especially to any peace of mind. Somehow peace of mind wasn't rating highly at the moment. A thrilling buzz was running through her veins and she was now determined on milking maximum enjoyment out of the night, throwing caution and the Machiavellian shadow of her father to the winds.

'That's a big smile,' Jake commented, his eyes simmering sexily.

'Loving the idea of having a piece of your dessert,' she tossed back, knowing she wanted a piece of him, too.

'Food, glorious food!' he quoted from the musical *Oliver*, half singing the words and making her laugh.

'We have to decide on which one of our main courses to go for now,' she reminded him.

'We'll go with your choice—the stir-fried pork, bacon, smoked tofu, garlic shoots, garlic chives and chilli oil—and I'll pick the vegetable dish.'

'Which will be?'

'Stir-fried wild bamboo pith, snow peas and quail eggs with ginger and garlic.'

'We'll probably end up with garlic breath.'

'We can try washing it away with wine.'

He ordered an expensive bottle of sauvignon blanc.

The waitress departed, having assured them of prompt service.

Laura heaved a satisfied sigh as she sat back and relaxed, happy to enjoy the ambience of the restaurant and the company of the man she was with.

'How was your week?' she asked.

He gave her a very sensual smile. 'All the better for ending here with you. How was yours?'

'Annoying.'

He raised a quizzical eyebrow.

She made a rueful grimace. 'I couldn't get you out of my head.'

He laughed. 'I'm glad the problem wasn't entirely mine. The question is whether to feed the fever or starve it?'

'I'm all for feeding tonight.'

'So am I.'

His eyes said he wanted to eat her all up and Laura couldn't deny she wanted to taste him again, too, but she wasn't ready to commit herself to becoming lovers on such short acquaintance.

'I meant here at the restaurant, Jake. I don't really know you, do I?' She eyed him seriously. 'My father obviously likes you very much, which isn't a great recommendation. I think from your visit last Sunday, you can draw a fairly clear picture of my life, but I don't have one of yours, apart from your mentioning that your mother has passed away. What about the rest of your family?

He shrugged. 'Both my parents died when I was eighteen. I was their only child. I've been on my own ever since. My life is not complicated by having to manage relationships, Laura. As I saw you doing last Sunday.'

'You move to your own beat,' she said wryly.

'Yes.'

'No live-in girlfriends along the way to here and now?'

He shook his head. 'I haven't met anyone I wanted to be with every day.'

She nodded, extremely wary of the live-in situation herself. 'It's a big ask, day in, day out. I can't see myself even wanting to try it.'

He smiled, eyes twinkling with understanding. 'You wish to be a free spirit.'

'I've seen my mother compromise too much,' she shot at him.

'Not all men are like your father, Laura,' he said seriously. 'My parents' marriage was very happy. I grew up in a loving home. I wish I still had it.'

She felt a stab of envy, though his loss triggered sympathy, as well. 'You were lucky to have what you did, Jake, but I guess missing that home life leaves you feeling very lonely.'

His eyelids dropped to half-mast, narrowing the flash of dangerous glitter. Some powerful emotion was coursing through him, belied by the offhand tone he used in his reply. 'It's been ten years, Laura. I've learnt to live with being alone.'

She didn't think so. She sensed anger in him at the loss, a deep abiding anger, so intense there was an edge of savagery to it. The image of a lone wolf endlessly prowling for some measure of satisfaction leapt into her mind.

Had he been looking for it in the career he had chosen? The bankruptcy business was centred on loss and he'd spoken almost passionately about the trauma of it and wanting to help when she'd taken him out to the garden last week. It had surprised her at the time. The conviction started to grow in her that he was not like her father. Not at all like him.

Which made the pleasure she could share with him much more acceptable.

'The self-sufficient man,' she said, smiling.

'Who doesn't want to be alone tonight.'

His smile was definitely wolfish, exciting her with the wild thought of howling at the moon together, mating on top of a mountain under the stars. Ridiculous since they were in the middle of a city, but the female animal inside her was strongly aroused, wanting to explore intimate possibilities with Jake Freedman.

The waitress returned with the bottle of wine and filled their glasses for them. Jake lifted his in a toast. 'To learning a lot more about each other.'

Laura nodded agreement. 'I'll drink to that.'

She clicked her glass to his and they both sipped the wine.

'I heard you tell Eddie that you worked out at a gym. Do you go often?'

'Usually after work. It's a good way of winding down.'

And every woman in the place would be eyeing him off, Laura thought, wondering if he also used the gym for casual pick-ups. She couldn't imagine him not having a very active sex life. Which, she strongly suspected, he kept completely separate from his work life.

'You said last Sunday you didn't want to want me,

Jake,' she reminded him. 'Is that because it's difficult to avoid it touching on your career with me being my father's daughter?'

He made an ironic grimace. 'I think it's a complication we'd both prefer not to have.' He leaned forward, his dark riveting eyes shooting a blaze of purpose at her. 'Let's shut the door on it. Just do what we want to do together, regardless of other issues. Are you brave enough to go down that road with me, Laura? Strong enough to make the choice for yourself?'

The challenge propelled her pulse into overdrive. Brave? Strong? She wanted to belief that of herself, but was it really true? She'd always shied clear of intimate entanglements, afraid of how they might affect her. The couple of sexual experiments she'd allowed herself had been more out of curiosity—a desire for knowledge—than a wish for a closer, more possessive attachment.

Jake Freedman tapped something far more primal in her and that was scary because it was uncontrollable. She wanted to explore it, to feel whatever he could make her feel, but she couldn't quite override the sense of danger with him. Already he had taken up far too much possession of her mind. Would that go away with passion spent or would she end up losing the mental independence she needed for self-survival?

She could not—would not—end up like her mother.

'I like to come and go as I please, Jake,' she said firmly. 'I don't think I'd mind joining you along the road now and then, but...'

Her mouth dried up as a dazzling grin spread across his wickedly handsome face.

'Fine...perfect...we can draw a map and meet when the time is right for both of us.'

She laughed with nervous excitement. He was so obliging, so tempting, so incredibly sexy, and surely there was nothing too scary about having an intermittent adventure with him.

The waitress arrived with their entrées. Laura had chosen the fried salt-and-pepper silken tofu with spicy coriander salad and Jake had decided on the Northern-style lamb and fennel dumplings. Both dishes looked and smelled deliciously enticing.

'We divide them in half. Right?' she said eagerly.

'Sharing is the deal,' he agreed, obviously enjoying her keen anticipation. 'Go ahead. Divvy up.'

Jake watched her halve the portions on each plate, liking her meticulous care, liking everything about her, especially the determination to run her own life as she saw fit. It freed him of any guilt over pursuing what he wanted with her. She was not looking for a happy-ever-love with him. She didn't believe in it.

Given what he'd seen of her parents' marriage, he understood where she was coming from and why she would shy clear of serious attachments. Alex Costarella had wrought damage on his own family, as well as on many others'. He'd robbed Jake of his parents, but unlike them, Laura was alive and kicking. She would survive. An intermittent relationship with him should not create a problem for either of them.

'We should start with the dumplings and finish with the salad,' she said authoritatively.

'Yes, ma'am.'

It startled her into a laugh. 'I didn't mean to be bossy.'

He grinned. 'I don't mind taking advice from a serious foodie. In fact, I would like you to extend my education on gourmet delights.'

She blushed. 'You're teasing me. I think I'll just shut up and eat.'

'Enjoy.'

She ate with obvious relish. It was a pleasure watching her appreciating each different taste. 'Please feel free to comment,' he urged. 'I wasn't really teasing you, Laura. I want you to share your thoughts on these dishes with me.'

'Tell me what *you* think,' she countered.

He did and she happily responded.

The whole meal was a pleasure, not only for the wonderful variety of tastes, but also Laura's delight in them. She made it a great sensory experience and not only on the palate. The licking of her lips, the heavenly rolling of her eyes, the rise and fall of her lush breasts when she sighed with satisfaction, the warm smiles that fuelled a burning lust to have all of her…Jake itched to sweep her off to bed and take his fill of Laura Costarella.

He couldn't recall ever having enjoyed an evening with a woman so much. It was impossible to tolerate the thought of it ending here. He had to persuade her to want what he wanted. And not just tonight. He knew one night wouldn't satisfy him. Not now.

They finished up with nougatine and rum truffle candy bars to nibble as they sipped the last of the German Riesling he'd ordered to accompany their dessert.

'This has been fantastic, Jake. Thank you so much for giving me the experience.' Her beautiful blue eyes twinkled. 'Definitely a more than fair exchange for my Sunday lunch.'

'Apart from Neil Perry, what other top Sydney chefs would you like to try out?' he asked, determined on tempting her into his company again.

She reeled off a number of names, then shook her head. 'I can't afford to go to their restaurants but one day I hope to. In the meantime, I drool over their cook books.'

'I can afford them, Laura, but I don't want to go alone. Nor do I know as much about food as you do. I'm happy to pay for you to be my educator, my companion, to share your knowledge and pleasure with me. Will you do that?'

She hesitated, frowning over his proposition.

'An adventure into fine dining,' he pressed.

'With you footing the bill,' she said, wincing over the inevitable cost.

'Why not? It's my idea.' Not to mention the desire running hot behind it.

'It's like…you're buying me, Jake.'

He shook his head. 'Buying your interest, your knowledge. Expanding my own. Say yes, Laura. It will be fun together. As tonight has been.'

Which was undeniable.

'You're right,' she said on a sigh of surrender. 'It's no fun alone. I'm sorry I can't pay my way but I simply don't earn enough with only a part-time job.'

He waved a dismissive hand. 'Don't worry about it. I'll consider it an investment in broadening my life.' He flashed her a mischievous grin. 'You could bring a garden rose for me to smell at our next restaurant. You're right about the hothouse ones sold by street vendors. They have no scent.'

She laughed, a lovely ripple of sound that was headier than the wine. 'You actually went out and tried them?'

'I did.'

'Well, there's hope for you yet.'

'Hope for what?'

'For being more aware of nature's beautiful gifts.'

'I'm very aware of one sitting directly opposite me.' He reached across the table and took one of her hands in his, lightly rubbing his thumb over its palm as his eyes bored into hers, every forceful atom of his mind willing her to concede to the strong sexual attraction between them. 'Spend the night with me, Laura. I've booked a room in the Intercontinental Hotel. It's only a short walk from here. Let's satisfy what was left unsatisfied last Sunday.'

It was blunt.

It was honest.

It promised nothing more than it said.

It had to be this way or no way.

Despite all he liked about her, she was still Alex Costarella's daughter and that fact would separate them when the time for retribution came. Jake had been moving towards that destination for ten years. Whatever he had with Laura could only be a brief sidetrack.

CHAPTER SIX

A WILD MÊLÉE of emotions pumped through Laura's heart. The response of her body to Jake's proposition was instantaneous; her stomach contracting in sheer yearning for the satisfaction he promised, her thighs pressing together to contain the rush of excitement at their apex, her breasts tingling with the need to be touched, held, given the same sensual caressing he was using on her hand.

The simple answer was yes.

She wanted to go with him, wanted to feel how it would be, wanted to know, but the surge of desire was so compelling it frightened her. This wasn't just curiosity. Nor was it an experiment over which she had control.

And there were other considerations.

She was supposed to be spending the night at Eddie's apartment. Her brother would worry if she didn't turn up there so he would have to be told, though she need not actually speak to him. A text message would suffice. Eddie would undoubtedly

repeat what he'd said before—*make damned sure you
keep it at sex and don't get hooked on him.*

Good advice. Except Laura had the fluttery feeling that she was hooked. Deeply and irrevocably
hooked. Although if Jake ever demanded too much
of her, surely she had enough backbone to walk away.
He was offering her great dinners and very probably
great sex. It shouldn't be a problem for her to take
both and enjoy both.

His thumb pressed into her palm. 'What reservations do you have, Laura?' he asked quietly, the dark
brilliant eyes scouring hers for answers, challenging
whatever barriers were in her mind.

Pride wouldn't allow her to admit she was scared
of his power over her. It suddenly seemed terribly
important to appear brave and strong, not only to
him but also to herself. She forced a smile. 'None. I
was just thinking I don't want to be left wondering,
so let's do it.'

He relaxed into a laugh—a deep rumble of pleasure that thrummed along her shaky nerves, promising all would be well between them. His eyes
sparkled delight in her as he said, 'You are one amazing woman.'

She raised her eyebrows in arch surprise. 'Why?'

He grinned. 'Before I met you I was expecting
a pampered princess or a calculating miss, used to
getting to her own way. It was a surprise to find you
were neither. But you are quite strikingly beautiful,

Laura, and beautiful women tend to use that power
to see how far a man will go for them.'

'I don't like power games,' she said sharply, hating any form of manipulation.

'No. You're wonderfully direct with what you
think.' He lifted his glass in a toast to her. 'May you
always be so.'

She cocked her head on one side consideringly.
'Were you buttering me up with the foodie thing?'

He shook his head. 'I want more than a one-night
stand with you. I'm quite certain I'll enjoy our adventure into fine dining.'

'So will I.'

'Then we're agreed on our points of contact.'

She laughed, happily giddy with the sense that this
wasn't so much a dangerous trap she might fall into
but a course of action that could give her tremendous
pleasure. Her whole body zinged with excitement at
the points of contact soon to be made.

'Will you excuse me for a few minutes?' she said,
rising from her chair. 'I need to go to the ladies' and
call my brother.'

'Why your brother?' he asked, frowning over the
possibility of third-party interference.

'I arranged to stay overnight at his apartment. I
don't want Eddie worrying about me.'

'Ah! Of course! You didn't want your father to
know. He won't know any more from me, Laura,'
he quickly assured her.

She paused a moment, eyeing him with deadly

seriousness. 'If you don't keep to that, Jake, I won't see you again.'

'Understood.'

A secret affair, Laura thought, liking the idea of it as she made her way to the ladies' room. Somehow it was less threatening than a relationship she would be expected to talk about. Eddie would have to know but she could trust him to keep it private if she asked him to. They had a solid sister/brother pact about running their own lives—away from their father.

However, she had no sooner sent the necessary text than her mobile phone rang in response. With a rueful sigh, she reopened it, knowing Eddie was going to express concern.

'You said you weren't going to fall at his feet,' he snapped in disapproval.

'I'm standing upright and walking to where I want to go. Just like you do, Eddie,' she reminded him.

'You're younger than I am, Laura. Not as street-hard. I tell you, that guy knows how to play all the angles. You should be standing back a bit, more on guard.'

She knew it was Jake's connection to her father making her brother overprotective but she had dealt with that issue. Until it raised its head again—if it did—she was determined on ignoring it and pleasing herself. 'I want this, Eddie. Let it be. Okay?'

In the short silence that followed she had a mental image of him grinding his teeth over her decision, not liking it one bit but forced to respect it. 'Okay,' he said grudgingly. 'Will I see you tomorrow?'

'If you're at the apartment when I come to pick up the things I've left there.'

'I'll be in. Hope this isn't one hell of a mistake, Laura.'

'I hope so, too. 'Bye for now.'

She stared at her reflection in the mirror as she refreshed her lipstick. Her eyes were very bright. Feverishly bright? Earlier this week she had likened Jake to a virus that had invaded her system, knocking her out of kilter. The invasion was much stronger tonight, both physically and mentally, and she didn't want to fight it. Surrendering to all the clamouring feelings inside her had to be right. By tomorrow she would know for certain if it was a mistake. That was better than wondering.

Jake rose from his chair as she approached their table again. 'Ready to go?' he asked as she reached it.

'Yes. Have you paid…?'

He nodded. 'And tipped. The service was excellent.'

'Absolutely. We didn't have to wait too long for anything.'

He smiled, the sexy simmer back in his eyes as he hooked her arm around his, drawing her into close physical contact with him and intimately murmuring, 'I'm glad you don't like waiting.'

Her ear tingled from the warm waft of his breath.

Her heart leapt into a wild hammering as the thought jagged through her mind that she was being too easy for him—not waiting, plunging headlong into bed with him. Probably all women were *easy* for him and she would be no different to any of the others. But did that really matter? Wasn't she going after what *she* wanted? She didn't have to be different. She just had to be true to herself.

She sucked in a deep breath to calm herself as they moved towards the exit. 'I daresay you don't have to wait for much, Jake,' she said drily.

'You're wrong.' He slid her an ironic look. 'Some things I've been waiting years for.'

'Like what?'

She caught a savage glitter in his eyes before he turned his head away and shrugged. 'Just personal goals, Laura. I guess you're impatient to make a start on your career, but you have to wait until you get your degree under your belt.'

'It will be good to finally strike out on my own,' she agreed, wondering what his personal goals were and why they sparked such a flow of strong feeling in him. A dangerous man, she thought again, dangerous and driven, but driven by what?

'I'm sure you'll find your work-life very rewarding, caring about the environment as you do,' he remarked, sliding straight back into an admiring expression, shutting the door on what he obviously wanted to keep private.

Laura decided not to try probing. Later in the

night when his guard was down and he was more re-laxed, he might reveal more about himself. It could wait. Or maybe his goals were connected to her fa-ther. In which case, she didn't want to know. Not to-night. Tonight was about exploring something else entirely and she didn't want anything to spoil it.

As they emerged onto the street she hugged his arm, secretly revelling in its strongly muscled mas-culinity. Her imagination conjured up images of him naked—the perfect male in every respect. Every woman should be allowed to have one, she told her-self, and this was simply seizing the opportunity. This connection to Jake Freedman didn't have to get complicated. In fact, she shouldn't let it become complicated. It was much safer to keep it simple.

'The hotel is about three blocks away,' he said, his mouth moving very sensually into a teasing lit-tle smile. 'Can you manage to walk that far in those gloriously erotic shoes or shall I flag down a taxi?'

She laughed, giddy with the thought of his mouth moving erotically all over her. 'I can walk, as long as it's a stroll and not a forced march.'

'I wouldn't force anything with you, Laura. This is all about choice,' he said seriously.

It was nice to have that assurance, to know she wasn't at physical risk with him. Strangely enough, it hadn't even occurred to her that she might be. It was the emotional risk she'd been concerned about. No man had ever affected her as Jake did.

'Why choose a hotel?' she asked as they walked towards it. 'We could have gone to your place.'

'My place is barely habitable. It's an old run-down terrace house that I'm in the process of renovating. There's stuff everywhere. I hope I can make it look great when it's finished, but that's not tonight or any night soon. I only have time to work on it at weekends.'

'You're doing the renovating yourself?'

'Not all of it. Only the carpentry. My father taught me all the skills of the trade and I'm enjoying doing the work myself.'

'Your father was a carpenter?'

'No, he was an engineer but he loved working with wood. It was a hobby he shared with me in my growing-up years.'

The tone of deep affection told her he'd shared a very special bond with his father while Eddie had only ever known criticism and disapproval from their father and she had learnt to avoid the kind of contact that inevitably led to acrimony. Such different lives…

Possibly working with wood kept the family bond alive for Jake, though he'd also said last Sunday he liked to relax by doing something physical. Going to the gym was not his only outlet, and she liked the idea of him being involved with something creative. Renovating a house was similar to building an environment to a pre-designed plan.

Jake worked for her father but he definitely wasn't like him.

She would tell Eddie so tomorrow.

In the meantime, she couldn't resist lifting her free hand to slide her fingers across Jake's. 'Your skin isn't rough,' she remarked.

He was amused by her checking. 'I wear gloves for heavy work. You must do, too.' He caught her hand and held it, caressing it as he had before, smiling into her eyes. 'Definitely no calluses.'

Laura had difficulty catching her breath he was so utterly gorgeous and her mind was spinning with the wonder of how excited he made her feel. Only belatedly did it click into the line of conversation and produce a reply, the words coming out huskily. 'My mother's training. A lady should always protect her skin from damage.'

He stopped walking, halting both of them as he released her hand to lift his to her cheek, stroking it with exquisite softness. 'No damage,' he murmured.

His thumb slid under her chin, tilting it up. He unhooked his arm from hers and wrapped it around her waist. His head bent and Laura watched his mouth coming closer and closer, her heart hammering in wild anticipation for the kiss she had been remembering all week.

It didn't matter that they were standing on a public sidewalk in the centre of the city with people passing by. Everything beyond this moment with Jake faded into insignificance. The desire, the need to feel what he'd made her feel before, was pulsing through her.

His lips grazed over hers, igniting a host of electric tingles. His tongue flicked over them, soothing, seductively seeking entry, which she eagerly gave, wanting the deeper sensations, the erotic tasting, the rise of feverish passion that would blow away any lingering doubt about choosing to have this night with him.

Eagerly she surrendered her mouth to the intimate connection with his and almost instantly her inner excitement escalated, wiping all thought from her mind, making her super-aware of physical contact with him, the delicious pressure of touching points; breasts, stomach, thighs, a wild vibrancy pouring through her, making her ache with the intensity of feelings that had never been so overwhelmingly aroused.

This kiss was not just a kiss. It was total invasion, possession, wildfire sweeping beyond any control, burning her up with the need to have all of this man. Laura lost all sense of self. She was completely consumed by her response to him, and the response was too immediate, too powerful, too real for her to reason it away.

She wanted him.

More fiercely than she'd ever wanted anything.

It was a dizzying shock when he tore his mouth from hers and pressed her head onto his shoulder, making the separation decisive. Her heart was pumping so hard, the drumming of it filled her ears. Only vaguely did she hear him suck in breath. His chest expanded with it. He rubbed her back, probably an instinctive calming action. Her quivering nerve ends were grateful for it.

'Shouldn't have done that but I've been wanting to all evening,' he muttered. 'Are you okay to walk on, Laura?'

Hotel…alone together in private…bed…uninterrupted intimacy… 'Yes,' she breathed on a sigh that relieved some of the tense ache in her chest. 'As long as you hold on to me.'

A deep sexy laugh rumbled from his throat. 'Letting you go will be the problem, not holding on to you.'

His words struck a vulnerable chord in her that Laura instantly shied away from examining. 'Let's not think about problems,' she said quickly, lifting her head to shoot him a look of needful appeal. 'I only want to think about what we can have together.'

'So do I,' he answered, tenderly cupping her cheek as though she was something very precious, his dark eyes shining with pleasure in her. 'It's not far to the hotel now.'

'Okay. Give me your arm.'

He tucked her close to him. The shakiness in Laura's legs gradually lessened as they walked the rest of the way to the Intercontinental. Neither of them spoke. They moved in a haze of mutual desire, impatient for the fulfilment of it, everything else irrelevant.

The hotel had been built around the old treasury building, making spectacular use of its special features. Laura had shared an afternoon tea with her mother there after a shopping day in the city. The main gathering place was The Cortile, a marvellous two-storeyed area covered by a huge glass dome, with colonnaded walkways surrounding it. Tonight, as Laura and Jake headed around it to the reception area, elegantly dressed people were indulging in a late supper, enjoying the ambience and the music being played on a grand piano.

It was a classy hotel and Laura couldn't help feeling pleased that Jake had chosen it. Somehow it made tonight with him more special. He collected their door-key from the receptionist and as they moved to the bank of elevators, he murmured, 'I took a Bayview room. It overlooks the Botanical Gardens. I thought you'd enjoy the view over breakfast.'

Laura's heart swelled with happiness. He'd been thinking of her, planning to give her pleasure. This wasn't just about sex with him. They were going to share more. Much more. She had made the right decision. A journey with Jake Freedman was well worth having. She no longer cared about how far it might go or where it might end. He was the man she wanted to be with.

CHAPTER SEVEN

JAKE quickly slid the door-key into the slot just inside the room and the lights came on. Everything looked fine—classy, welcoming, and most important of all, providing a private oasis, not touching on Laura's home environment nor his, completely separate to the lives they normally lived.

It had to be this way.

Bad enough that he was in the grip of uncontrollable desire for Alex Costarella's daughter. Boundaries to this affair had to be set and kept. He couldn't allow it to take over too much of his life. But right here and now he could satisfy his hunger for her, and to his immense relief she was up for it, no further delay to what they both wanted.

She walked ahead of him, moving towards the window seat with the view on the far side of the room. He watched the provocative sway of her hips, felt the tightening in his groin, started unbuttoning his shirt, impatient for action. She set her handbag on the desk as she passed it. Jake tossed his shirt on the chair in front of it, took off his shoes, his gaze fastening on her turquoise high heels with their seductive ankle straps. She had great legs and the thought of having them wound around him brought his erection to full tilt.

'Lots of city lights but it's too dark to see the botanical gardens,' she remarked.

'Won't be dark in the morning,' he muttered, unzipping his trousers.

She glanced back over her shoulder. 'I think I like this view better,' she said with sparkling interest, her eyes feasting on his bare chest and shoulders. 'I've been wondering how you'd look naked.'

He laughed, exhilarated by the honesty of her lust for him. He whipped off the rest of his clothes, dumping them on the chair with his shirt. 'Hope you're not disappointed,' he said, grinning with confidence, knowing his physique invariably drew attention from women at the gym.

'Not one bit,' she answered emphatically, examining all his *bits*, which raised the already high level of Jake's excitement.

She lifted an arm and hooked the long tumbling fall of her black curls away from her neck, her other hand reaching for the top of the zipper at the back of her dress, obviously intent on removing her own clothes.

'Let me,' Jake said hastily, finding the bared nape of her neck incredibly erotic and wanting the pleasure of slowly uncovering the rest of her, visually feasting on her lush femininity.

A few quick strides and he was taking over the task, opening up the snugly fitting bodice, exposing the satin-smooth, elegant slope of her back, which, delightfully, was uninterrupted by a bra. The line of her spine created an intriguing little valley that compelled his finger to stroke the lovely length of it. His touch raised a convulsive shiver of pleasure and he smiled, knowing her body was as taut with excitement as his own, every nerve alive with sensitivity.

Eager to see more of her, he unzipped the top of the skirt and peeled it from her hips, letting it fall to the floor. The sight of a sexy black G-string encircling her small waist and bisecting a totally luscious bottom sucked the air from his lungs and blistered his mind with urgent desire. He barely stopped himself from moving forward and fitting himself to the tantalising cleft.

Better to remove the last scrap of clothing first. He hooked his thumbs under the waistband and glided it over the soft mounds, down the long, lissom thighs and the taut curves of her calves, every millimetre raising the raging heat in his blood. The flimsy fabric caught on the straps of the erotic shoes. Couldn't leave them on. The stiletto heels could do him a damage in the throes of passion and Jake was already envisaging a huge amount of fantastic activity in bed.

'Sit down, Laura. Makes it easier to take your shoes off.'

He was still crouched, ready to free her feet when she swivelled around and sat on the window seat.

The eye-level view of her beautiful full breasts was a mind-blowing distraction. She leaned back so they tilted up at him, large rosy aureoles with peaked nipples shooting temptation. He stared, captivated for several moments before gaining his wits to lift his gaze to see if she was deliberately teasing him.

Her thickly lashed blue eyes looked darker than before, simmering with an inviting sultriness. She wanted him enthralled by her fabulous femininity, wanted to drive him wild for her. Whether it was a deliberate exertion of her woman-power or not, it reminded Jake of who she was and how careful he had to be not to become ensnared by this woman.

He fixed his attention on the shoes, forced his fingers to undo the ankle straps. In a few moments he could take all he wanted of her, revel in having it, and he would, all night long, but come the morning he had to be sane enough to walk away from her and keep her at a mental distance until the next time they were together.

Shoes off.

They were both completely naked now.

He stood up, and the act of towering over her triggered his sense of man-power. He was in charge of this encounter. He'd brought her to this cave and he would control everything that happened between them. With a surge of adrenalin-pumped confidence he leaned over, gripped her waist and lifted her off the window-seat, whirling her straight over to the bed, laying her down, positioning himself beside her with one leg flung over hers, holding her captive so he could touch the rest of her at will.

'Kiss me again,' she commanded, her voice huskily inviting, her eyes glittering with the need for passion to blow them both away.

'I will,' he promised, but not her mouth, not yet.

The rose-red nipples were pointed up at him, hard evidence of her arousal and he wanted her more aroused than he was. He closed his mouth around them, drawing on the distended flesh, sucking, his tongue swirling, lashing. She wrapped her hands around his head, fingers thrusting through his hair, dragging on his scalp, her body arching, aching for a more consuming possession.

Not yet... Not yet...

He swept a trail of hot kisses down over her stomach to the arrow of dark springy curls leading to the most intimate cleft between her thighs. He could smell the wonderfully heady scent of her desire for him as he dipped his mouth into the soft folds of her sex, intent on driving this centre of excitement to fever pitch. He exulted in tasting her hot wetness, exulted even more as she writhed to the rhythm of his stroking, crying out at the frantic tension building up inside her, jack knifing up to grab his shoulders and tug his body over hers.

He was ready to oblige now, knowing her entire being was screaming for him and he was still in control, though bursting to unleash his own knife-edge desire. As he lifted himself up, her legs locked around him, her hips already rocking, and there was no more waiting. He surged into the slick passage to the edge of her womb and dropped his head to ravish her mouth, wanting total invasion, absolute domination of this intimate togetherness.

Yet she met the attack of his kiss with an assault of her own, a fusion of heat that turned aggression into a melting pot of exploding sensations and he lost every vestige of control. Her legs goaded him into a series of fast thrusts, clamping around him at the point of deepest penetration as she moaned at the intense satisfaction of it, then rolling her hips around the hard heated fullness of him as he withdrew to plunge again, driven to hear and feel her pleasure in him over and over, wildly intoxicated by the sense of being drawn from peak to peak, each one raising the stakes to a higher level of fierce feeling.

It was like riding a storm, hurtling towards the eye of it at breakneck velocity, their lives hanging on holding on to each other until they reached beyond the violent shattering that threatened every escalating moment and landed in a place where they could peacefully return to themselves again. Jake didn't care how long that took...minutes, hours.

It was a fantastic journey—her response to him, what he felt himself, a host of primal elements whipping them towards a final crescendo. The breakthrough was a totally cataclysmic moment, both of them crying out as the storm released them into a free fall of exquisite delight and they floated down on a sweet cloud of ecstasy, still clamped together as they shifted into a more relaxed embrace, prolonging what they had shared as long as they could.

Even just cuddling her close to him was sweet, smelling the scent of her hair, winding strands of it around his fingers, rubbing his cheek over its silkiness, feeling the rhythm of her breathing in the rise and fall of her breasts against his chest, the sensual stroking of one of her legs between his, knowing she was still revelling in feeling him.

Eventually thoughts drifted through Jake's mind, carrying a need to make sense of why this sexual experience with Laura had been so incredibly intense. Never before had he been completely locked into having a woman like this, driven to take, driven beyond what he'd previously known. His liaisons with other women had been more casual pleasures, enjoyable, relaxing—what he'd considered normal. Why did the animal chemistry go deeper with Laura Costarella?

She was definitely the most beautiful woman he'd ever taken to bed. Had that heightened his excitement? Somehow he couldn't quite believe that would affect him so much. His mind kept niggling at her family connection to Alex Costarella. Was it because of *who* she was, linking her to the passion for retribution, which had consumed most of his life for the past ten years? Or did the fact that she should have remained forbidden to him cause the difference?

Impossible to pin it down. All he absolutely knew

was he couldn't allow this affair to escalate into a serious relationship. If he kept to that, surely he could simply enjoy what she gave him—her companionship over the dinners he would arrange, and the intense physical pleasure they would share in bed together afterwards.

Settling on this determination, Jake shut down on the questions, intent on making the most of this night together. 'Feeling good?' he asked, wondering what she was thinking, if she was happily satisfied with her decision to set aside her reservations about him.

'Mmmh…very good.'

There was a smile in her voice.

He didn't need to know any more. He smiled his own contentment with the situation.

She began an idle stroking of his body—slow, erotic caresses, which instantly stimulated him into touching more of her, lingering over every voluptuous curve, loving the wonderfully sensual feel of her womanliness. Touching moved into kissing as they explored each other in intimate detail, arousing the need to merge again, to feel all that could be felt between them.

It was marvellous, less frenzied this time but still incredibly exciting with the mutual abandonment of all inhibitions. It left Jake feeling flooded with pleasure, and the gradually ebbing waves of it lulled him into a deep untroubled sleep.

* * *

Laura woke to morning light. They'd forgotten to draw the curtains last night, too consumed with each other to think of anything beyond the sensational intimacy they'd shared. She rolled over to look at the man who had taken her to heights of pleasure she had never even imagined, let alone known.

He was still asleep. Despite the brilliant dark eyes being shut, his face was still strongly handsome and his body... She sighed over how perfectly manly it was, just the right amount of muscularity and everything ideally proportioned. Absolutely gorgeous. Sex appeal in spades. What a fantastic night she'd had with him! No regrets, that was for sure! Whatever happened next between them, this was one experience she would never forget.

Careful not to wake him, she slid off the bed and padded quietly to the bathroom, wanting to freshen up and look good when he did open his eyes. She grabbed her handbag off the desk in passing, glad that it contained a small hairbrush and lipstick. With no change of clothes to wear, it was a relief to find bathrobes provided for guests. She could lounge around in one of them until it was near time to leave the hotel.

Having showered and groomed herself as best she could, Laura returned to the bedroom to find Jake still asleep. Quite happy for a little time on her own, she settled on the window-seat, her back against the side wall, feet up on the cushion, arms hugging her knees, instinctively wanting to hug in all the lovely feelings generated by last night with Jake.

It wasn't just the sex, although that had been unbelievably awesome. Even now her heart swelled with the sheer joy of learning how marvellous it could be with the right man. Nothing could have felt more *right* to her, which made her wonder if it was wrong to stand back from a serious relationship with Jake. So far she liked everything he had shown of himself, and definitely wanted to know a lot more. Maybe they could have something great together.

The view of the botanical gardens caught her eye. A stroll through them would be a pleasant way of continuing the day—time to chat about their interests and look for more common ground between them. She would like to see the house he was renovating, too, the kind of home he was making for himself. The environment people chose to live in could speak volumes about them. Sharing the private life of Jake Freedman was an exciting prospect and Laura was hugging that to herself, too, when his voice broke into her hopeful reverie.

'Happy with the view this morning?'

She laughed, bubbling over with high spirits and looking at him with sparkling pleasure. 'It's lovely! The sun is shining and it's going to be a beautiful day.'

He grinned at her as he rolled out of bed, saying cheerfully, 'So let's make a start on it. Call room service and order breakfast for both of us while I freshen up in the bathroom.'

'What would you like?'

'You choose. I have great faith in your food judgement.'

He left her grinning, enjoying the back view of him as he headed off to the bathroom. Only when this vision was cut off did she swing her legs off the window-seat and set about ordering their breakfast, choosing what she wanted herself and hoping Jake would be pleased with everything.

He came out of the bathroom, wearing the other bathrobe and checking his watch. 'It's eight o'clock now. How long before room service arrives?'

'About another twenty minutes.'

The dark eyes twinkled sexily. 'Only time for a good-morning kiss then. And no disrobing.'

'We have the rest of the day,' she suggested happily as he drew her into his embrace.

He frowned. 'No. No we don't. There's work I have to get done on the house before the plumber comes tomorrow.'

'Can I help you?' she asked impulsively, wanting to be with him.

He shook his head. 'You would be a major distraction, Laura. I'll work more efficiently on my own.'

He grazed his lips over hers—a distraction that didn't quite soothe the stab of disappointment over the rejection of her offer. She told herself his reasoning was fair enough and opened her mouth for a whole-hearted kiss. He'd given her a wonderful night and there would be more in the future. No need to be greedy, asking for today, as well.

It was a soft, very sensual kiss, and he withdrew from it before it escalated into wild passion, brushing her hair tenderly from her face, smiling into her eyes. 'Thank you for last night. We'll do it again soon,' he promised her.

'Thank *you*. I'll look forward to it,' she said, inwardly craving much more from him but doing her best to accept the situation gracefully.

'I'll book a taxi to take you from the hotel to Eddie's apartment after we've had breakfast.' He stepped back from her and moved towards the telephone on the desk, asking, 'Where does he live, Laura?'

'Paddington.'

'That's handy.' He grinned at her as he picked up the receiver. 'We can share the taxi. I'll see you to his place first before going on home.'

'Where do you live?'

'Next suburb. Woollahra.'

Virtually in walking distance from Eddie's apartment, she thought, watching him make the call. She wanted to ask what street, but held her tongue, knowing she would be tempted to go there and suddenly frightened of how deeply she was being drawn by this man.

Jake didn't want a full-on relationship. He'd told her so at dinner last night. And she had been

super-cautious about going down that road, too.
Obviously nothing had changed for him. It shouldn't
have changed for her, either. She had to keep her head
straight about this, not get twisted up by emotions
that could mess with the decisions she'd made about
her life.

A journey with meeting places.

Best to keep to that.

But somehow she couldn't really take pleasure
in the breakfast they shared. It didn't sit right in her
stomach. And she hated the taxi trip to Paddington,
knowing Jake was travelling on without her. It took
an act of will to smile her goodbye at him. And then,
of course, she had to face Eddie and say everything
had been fine.

Which was the truth.

Though not quite.

It had been fantastic, brilliant, totally engaging.

Too engaging.

And that was dangerous.

CHAPTER EIGHT

To Eddie's inevitable query about her night with Jake Freedman, she breezily answered, 'Great food, great sex, and marriage is not on the menu for either of us so don't worry about my becoming a victim of secret agendas. That's definitely out!'

Later in the day, she settled her mother's concern with, 'It won't become a serious relationship, Mum. It was just a dinner date, which I might or might not repeat.' With a mischievous smile, she added, 'Depends on how good the restaurant is if he asks me out again.'

It made her mother laugh. 'Oh, you and food!'

And she cut off her father's probe into the personal connection by regaling him with details of every spicy dish she'd tasted, virtually dismissing Jake's company as pleasant enough but relatively unimportant.

However, it was easier to establish in other people's minds that an involvement with Jake was not a big issue than it was to convince herself. Life simply wasn't the same as before she met him. He dominated her thoughts, especially at night when she was alone in bed, her body restless with memories of their intense intimacy. It was impossible to block him out for long and she grew angry and frustrated with herself for not being able to set him at a sensible distance, especially as day followed day without any contact from him.

He hadn't given her *his* mobile telephone number.

He obviously had a silent land number at his Woollahra home because his name wasn't listed in the telephone directory.

No way could she call him at work because her father might get to hear about it.

Control of any connection between them was all on *his* side and she had no control whatsoever over yearning to be reconnected. Which was turning her into a stupid, love-sick cow and she hated being like that, hated it so much when he did finally call her on Friday afternoon, the zoom of pleasure at hearing his voice was speared through by resentment at his power to affect her so deeply. She only grudgingly managed a polite 'Hi!' to his greeting.

He didn't seem to notice any coldness in her response, rolling straight into the business of the call without any personal enquiries about her or her well-being. 'I've been trying all week to book us a table at one of your top restaurants for tomorrow night. Can't be done. They're all booked up and there hasn't been any cancellations. However, I have managed to get us a table at Peter Gilmore's Quay restaurant for next Saturday night. Is that okay with you?'

Peter Gilmore's Quay—listed as one of the top fifty restaurants in the world! It was a totally irresistible invitation. A rush of excited enthusiasm flooded over all other feelings.

'Fantastic!' tripped off her tongue. 'I saw his amazing Snow Egg dessert on a television show. It started with a layer of guava purée mixed with whipped cream. On top of that was guava-flavoured crushed ice. Then a meringue shaped like an egg and an inside that was creamy custard apple. It was topped off with a thin layer of toffee melted over it. Absolutely to die for!'

His laughter flowed through her like a fountain of joy. She couldn't help smiling, couldn't help feeling happy.

'Shall we meet there at seven o'clock? Same as last time?' he asked.

'Yes.'

'Great! See you then, Laura.'

Click!

That was it from him.

The happiness deflated into a rueful sigh. It was what they had agreed upon—meetings for an adventure into fine dining. Jake probably thought of any sexual follow-up as icing on the cake. And she should, too. She couldn't fault him for not suggesting they do something else together this weekend.

The problem of wanting more was entirely hers and she had to deal with it, get over it.

On the whole, Laura thought she managed that fairly well over the following week. Probably knowing they had a definite date to meet made it easier to concentrate on other things. She promised herself that at this meeting she would not expect an extension of their time together beyond the night, nor hope for it. After all, it was better for her to maintain her independence and not become slavishly besotted with the man.

Despite all her sensible reasoning, she could not control the fizz of excitement as she prepared for the big evening out. In an attempt to lessen its importance to her and show Jake she was taking this journey as casually as he was, she chose a far less dressy outfit—her best jeans, which were acceptable almost anywhere, and a peasant-style top with some wild costume jewellery she'd bought at the markets. Beaded sandals completed the look she wanted— fun, not seriously formal or serious anything else.

Eddie had been warned she would be staying overnight at his apartment again. Before leaving home she deliberately picked a yellow rose, not a red one, from her mother's garden. It was a Pal Joey rose and it had a fabulous scent. Jake might not remember asking her to bring one to their next dinner together but it definitely showed she was keeping to her side of their deal.

The ferry ride across the harbour from Mosman

to Circular Quay brought her close to the site of the restaurant. There was an excited lilt in her step as she walked around to the overseas passenger terminal where all the big cruise ships docked. Jake would be waiting for her inside Quay on the upper level and tonight would undoubtedly be brilliant all over again.

For Jake it had taken rigid discipline to wait through the fortnight before indulging himself with Laura again. It would only be a week next time, and the next, and the next, provided, of course, she wanted to go on with it. Why shouldn't he have as much of her as he could within reasonable limits? As long as he kept the end in mind, his involvement with her would not get in the way of what he had to do. It was no good wishing she wasn't Alex Costarella's daughter. Nothing could change that.

She walked into the restaurant looking like a wonderfully vivid gypsy with her black curly hair all fluffed out around her shoulders, lots of colourful beads around her neck and a peasant blouse that clung to the lush fullness of her breasts. Tight jeans accentuated the rest of her sexy curves and the instant kicks to his heart and groin told Jake she was having too big an impact on him.

He shouldn't have started this.

Shouldn't be going on with it.

But she smiled at him as he stood up from their table to greet her and a rush of pleasure had him smiling back. Just before she reached him, her hand dived into the bag she carried and brought out a full-blown yellow rose.

'For you to smell,' she said, her blue eyes sparkling a flirtatious challenge.

It surprised him, delighted him, and the pleasure she brought him intensified as he took the rose and lifted it to his nose. 'Mmmh...I shall always connect this glorious scent with you.'

She laughed. 'And I shall always connect glorious food with you. I can't wait to salivate through Peter Gilmore's menu.'

He laughed and quickly held out her chair with an invitational wave. 'At your service.'

Once they were both seated, a waiter arrived, handing them menus, and Jake asked him to bring a glass of water for the rose to keep it fresh.

As soon as they were left alone together, Laura leaned forward with another heart-kicking smile. 'I'm glad you like it.'

He grinned. 'I have plans for this rose.'

'What plans?'

'For later tonight.' Like rubbing it all over her skin and breathing in the scent as he kissed her wherever he wanted. 'I've booked us a room at the Park Hyatt at Campbell Cove....'

'Another hotel,' she broke in with a frown.

'My place is still a mess,' he explained with an apologetic grimace. 'Can't take you there, Laura.'

He never would. He *had* to keep her separate from his real life.

'But I know that hotel is terribly expensive, Jake. And on top of this dinner tonight, which will undoubtedly cost the earth...'

'The cost is not a problem to me,' he assured her.

Still she frowned. 'Does my father pay you so well?'

He shrugged. 'Well enough, but I don't count on him for my income.' *Because that was always going to end and quite soon now.* He would probably become unemployable in the bankruptcy business after he'd blown the whistle on how corrupt some of it was and he'd prepared for that outcome. 'I have a side interest that has proved very profitable.'

It piqued her curiosity. 'What is it?'

There was no harm in telling her. He doubted she would tell her father and it didn't really matter if Costarella knew, not this close to his resignation from the company. 'I buy run-down houses, renovate them in my spare time, then sell them on.'

'Ah!' She looked pleased. 'The property ladder. That's another show I sometimes watch on TV. It's always fascinating to see how each property is improved before reselling. How many houses have you done?'

'I'm currently on my fifth.'

'I'd love to see it sometime. See what you're doing to it,' she said with eager interest.

He had to clamp down hard on the strong impulse

to share it with her, to hear her views on the renovations he was doing, enjoy her interest. She was so
attractive in so many ways. But anything beyond
sexual intimacy had to be discouraged or he risked
becoming far too hooked on Laura Costarella. Bad
enough that he couldn't go to bed without wanting
her in it.

'Maybe when it's further along,' he said ruefully.
'It's virtually a shell right now. Nothing to see but
mess.'

She grimaced in disappointment. 'Okay. I guess
you'd prefer to feel some pride in showing off your
work. I take it you've made a good profit from each
house you've done.'

'Good enough not to worry about paying for a
great night out with you, Laura, so don't you worry
about it, either. I can well afford special treats like
this and having you share them doubles the pleasure.'

She visibly relaxed, smiling her heart-kicking
smile at him again as she picked up her menu. 'In
that case, I'm very happy to share your pleasure. I
shall have no inhibitions about ordering whatever I
want to try.'

No inhibitions in bed, either, Jake thought happily, relieved that she wasn't pressing the house issue.
Their time together had to be time out from his real
life. He couldn't consider anything else with her however much he would like to.

Laura let herself wallow in the pleasure of being with
Jake. He was so attractive in every respect—looks,

wit, charm. There was nothing about him she didn't like. However, he was big on control, and she shouldn't forget that. Although there was a plus side to that, too. It had obviously taken a great deal of inner strength to set the trauma of losing his parents aside and drive himself towards establishing a professional career, and his enterprise in climbing the property ladder, as well, was truly admirable.

Something Eddie had said popped into her mind—*sooner or later he'll turn you off*—but she honestly couldn't see that happening, definitely not tonight. In fact, she was so turned on, it was impossible to find any wrongness in him.

He was the best company over dinner, relishing and enjoying the amazingly wonderful food as much as she did. The conversation between them was fun. The sexy twinkle in his eyes kept her excitement bubbling. She loved every bit of him, which should have set warning signals off in her head, but it was so giddy with delight, no sense of caution was even registered.

Again it was an easy walk to the hotel. Her body was humming with delicious anticipation. Her feet wanted to dance all the way. Jake had brought the rose she'd given him at the restaurant, twiddling it in his fingers as they walked, smiling down at it, and she smiled at it, too, imagining he intended taking it home with him as a romantic reminder of her.

She knew this wasn't supposed to be a romantic relationship. It was probably crazy wanting it to turn into one, yet all her female instincts were insisting this man was the right man for her. He wasn't *demanding* anything of her. It was simply great being together.

The hotel was brilliantly sited right below the harbour bridge. A set of glass doors on the far side of their room showcased a fabulous view of the opera house. Laura couldn't help loving the luxury of it, couldn't help loving the man who was giving it to her. As soon as the door was closed behind them, she turned to hug him tightly and kiss him with every fibre of her being, unable to wait another second to feel all he could make her feel.

Almost instantly they were on fire for each other, quick hungry kisses turning into fierce, needful passion. The barrier of clothes was unbearable. She broke away to get rid of hers and laughed as she saw Jake clamping the stem of the rose between his teeth to free his hands for the same purpose.

'Just as well I picked off the thorns,' she tossed at him.

'Mmmh…' was all he could answer.

Naked and still laughing with wild exhilaration, she raced him to the bed, landing and rolling until her caught her, trapping her into stillness with one strong leg flung over hers. She looked up into wickedly glittering eyes, her chest heaving for breath, her heart hammering with excitement.

'You can't kiss me with that rose between

your teeth,' she teased, her lower body wriggling provocatively against his.

He plucked the rose free and started caressing her face with it. 'I've been fantasising about doing this all evening. Lie still, Laura. Close your eyes. Feel the petals gliding over your skin. Breathe in the scent of them.'

It took enormous control to follow his instructions but it was worth the effort, focussing on the amazing sensuality of what he was doing, the soft graze of the rose, tantalisingly gentle, followed by a trail of kisses that had all her nerve ends buzzing. It made her feel like a pagan goddess being worshipped, anointed with perfume and brought to tingling life by a ceremony of slowly escalating physical ministrations.

She had never been so acutely aware of her body, hadn't realised she had erotic zones below her hipbones, behind her knees, on the soles of her feet. To be touched like this everywhere, to be kissed as though every inch of her was adored…it was an incredible experience, mesmerising, heavenly.

Finally he came to her most intimate parts, caressing her to an exquisite tension, making it impossible for her to lie still any longer. Her body arched in need for release and she cried out his name, desperately wanting him to take her to the end now.

He moved swiftly to oblige and it was wondrous all over again, the ebb and flow of extreme sensations gathering momentum to a fantastic climax, then the delicious aftermath of sweet contentment, the scent of the yellow rose still lingering on her skin, adding its heady pleasure to their intimate togetherness.

Laura had never felt so blissfully happy. To have a lover like Jake…she was incredibly lucky to have met him. She could even find it in her heart to be grateful to her father for bringing him into her life. This journey was definitely worth taking and she hoped it would go on for a long, long time.

As they were leaving the hotel the next morning Jake asked, 'Will you be free to join me next Saturday night? I've booked a table at Universal, Christine Manfield's restaurant.'

Free for you anytime, she thought, her heart skipping with pleasure at not having to wait more than a week to be with him again. Glorious food was no longer the seductive temptation it had been, though she would absolutely enjoy it, having Jake as her dining partner.

'That would be lovely,' she said, trying not to sound too eager for his company, which was now the main drawcard. This relationship did have to be controlled. Jake was not falling all over himself to be with her every free moment he had and it was better for her if she could hold him at a distance, too, in between their meeting points,

'Same time?' he asked.

'Suits me.'

'Good!'

He gave her his brilliant, sexy smile and Laura

managed a smile back though her insides clenched, wanting, needing much more of him. She had to bite down on her tongue to stop herself pleading, *Why can't we be together today? I won't get in the way of your working on the house renovations. I'll help. We can chat, laugh, enjoy being with each other.*

The words kept pounding through her mind as they settled in the taxi that would take her to Eddie's apartment before driving on to Jake's place, but she couldn't let herself voice them. It would put Jake in a position of power over her, knowing she wanted him more than he wanted her.

Had her mother fallen into that trap with her father, showing how needy she was? If so, he'd certainly taken advantage of her vulnerability. She wasn't sure if Jake would be like that or not, but her gut feeling told her not to show any weakness that could be exploited.

It was best to keep to what they had agreed upon. If anything changed further along the line, the change had to come from him, not from her and certainly not today.

CHAPTER NINE

TETSUYA'S, a Japanese-French fusion eatery many times listed amongst the top fifty restaurants in the world, was Jake's choice for his last night with Laura. It had the longest waiting time to secure a table—two months—and he'd actually held back his own agenda, just to have this very special dinner together before he took her father down.

He checked his watch as he waited for her to arrive, conscious of not wanting her to be late, not wanting to have a minute of this final encounter wasted. It wasn't quite seven o'clock. The hell of it was he would miss the pleasure of her company, miss the fantastic sex they had shared even more, but knew it was stupid to try spinning out their time with each other any further.

It had been good. Great. But she was her father's daughter and once the axe fell on Costarella he would come out fighting for blood in return and the first casualty would be any personal association with his accuser. Laura would be turned out of the Mosman mansion if she didn't toe that line. Even if she chose not to and fled to her brother's apartment… No, she wouldn't do that. She would stay by her mother to deflect as much of her father's venom as she could.

Tonight was it—the end.

No point in looking for any way around it.

Besides, once he'd achieved the objective he'd set for himself he wanted to move on, find the kind of relationship he'd seen between his mother and stepfather, have a family of his own, hopefully sharing good times with his wife and children. Regardless of how powerfully drawn he was to Laura Costarella, he couldn't fit her into that picture.

As hot she was in bed, she kept a cool head out of it, content to go about her own life without trying to get him involved in it. This was confirmation to Jake that marriage had no appeal to her—understandable given *her* family background. Part-time lovers was as far as any man would get with Laura. It made the end of their affair easier in so far as he knew it carried no deep importance to her. He'd given her pleasure. He hoped the memory of it would not get too tainted by the angst his actions would inevitably cause in the Costarella household.

All this past week he'd been tossing up whether to tell her, warn her what was about to happen, explain why. Somehow that smacked too much of justifying himself and he didn't need to do that, not when he was meting out justice, which would eventually be evident to everyone. Besides, he'd told Laura right from the beginning he didn't want to want to her.

Understanding would come soon enough. Better for them both to enjoy this one last night.

Laura was smiling, aglow with excited anticipation as she entered Tetsuya's. She was ten minutes late, due to the public transport connections needed to get to Kent Street in the inner city—where the restaurant was located—but she was finally here for another night with Jake. And there he was, rising from the table where he'd been seated.

Her heart skipped a beat. Every time he had this impact. And his smile of pleasure on seeing her… it was like a fountain of joy bursting through her. She loved this man, loved being with him, fiercely wished they could be sharing much more than one night a week.

Though she told herself it was sensible not to get too involved, not when she still had to earn her university degree. It was halfway through the year now. In a few more months… Was Jake waiting for her to be fully qualified before inviting her into more of his life? There was quite an age gap between them. Maybe he was conscious of that, too. Whatever his reasons for keeping their relationship so strictly limited, Laura felt sure they would wear out eventually. They were too good together—great together—for this journey to ever end.

She couldn't resist planting a greeting kiss on his cheek before sitting down. 'Sorry I'm a bit late. The bus trip was slow. Lots of people getting on and off.'

'No problem,' he assured her, his deep rich voice curling around her heart, warming it with pleasure. 'You're here. And I've been perusing the menu. This promises to be a fantastic dining experience.'

'Oh, wow! I've been *so* looking forward to it.'

He laughed at her excitement as they both took their seats. Laura loved his laugh, the sexy male rumble of it, the way it lit up his handsome face, the dancing twinkles in his eyes.

'I want us to do the gustatory menu—all eight courses of it. Are you up for it?' he asked.

Laura goggled at him. 'Eight courses!'

'They won't be big. Just a marvelous range of tastes.'

'Let me see.' She held out her hand for the menu and he passed it over. The list of dishes Jake wanted proved irresistible. 'I'm up for it,' she said decisively.

It would obviously cost Jake another small fortune, but also obviously he didn't care so Laura refused to feel guilty about the expense. It was his choice. He grinned at her, knowing she was happy to succumb to temptation.

She sighed. 'You're spoiling me rotten with all this, Jake.'

An oddly rueful expression twisted his grin. 'You've given me more than money can buy, Laura. I should probably thank you for being you.'

Why did that sound…almost as if he was saying goodbye to her? Laura frowned over the uncomfortable niggle. Surely he was just trying to balance out what they had together, make it feel okay to her. 'It's no big deal being me,' she said critically.

He shook his head, his eyes gently mocking her. 'I can't imagine enjoying our dinners so much with anyone else.'

She relaxed into a relieved smile. 'Then I should thank you for being you because I can't imagine it, either.'

'Good to be in accord on that point.'

She laughed. 'I think we're in accord on many points.'

'True. Shall we order now?'

He signalled their readiness to a waiter while Laura happily assured herself that everything was fine between them.

Again it was another brilliant evening with Jake. The dinner was sensational. It was great fun enjoying and discussing the various tastes, comparing it to what they'd eaten in other restaurants. Laura visited the ladies' room just before they were about to leave and on her way back to their table, she was struck by another little stab of uncertainty.

Jake was not looking for her return. He sat in pensive mode, a dark, bleak expression wiping out all the sparkles he'd shot her way during dinner. It didn't take much intuition to realise something was wrong—something in the private life he didn't share with her. Wasn't it time that he did? They'd been seeing each other on a very intimate basis for almost three months now. Surely he knew her well enough to trust her with what was in his mind.

He brightened as she reached the table, pulling himself back from the place he'd travelled to without her, but Laura's fighting spirit had been pricked into taking a stand. 'What were you thinking of just now, Jake?'

He shook his head, a wry little smile curling his mouth as he rose from his chair. 'A piece of the past. Nothing to do with you, Laura. I've called a taxi for us. It's waiting outside.'

He tucked her arm around his as she frowned over his evasive reply. 'I want to know,' she said, shooting him a searching look.

He grimaced at her obstinacy, but did answer her. 'I was thinking of my parents. How much they enjoyed sharing meals together.'

'Oh!' Laura's heart instantly lifted. The memory had obviously saddened Jake but she felt it did have something to do with her—a connection to what *they* were doing, which he enjoyed with her! It made her feel their relationship was more meaningful to him than he was willing to admit at this point.

'I've booked us into the Park Hotel tonight,' he told her as they made their exit from the restaurant.

Another hotel. She knew it overlooked Hyde Park in the city centre, which gave them only a short trip to Paddington and Woollahra in the morning. It always disappointed her that he didn't ask her home with him but she'd decided never to push it. Besides, she was still cherishing that link to his parents, whom he'd loved very much.

They didn't chat in the taxi. Laura was keenly anticipating the sexual connection with Jake and she imagined his mind was occupied with it, too. It seemed to her he held her hand more tightly than usual, his long fingers strongly interlaced with hers, their pads rubbing her palm. She silently craved more skin-to-skin contact, barely controlling her impatience to dive into bed with him.

Certainly their desire for each other hadn't waned at all. As soon as the door of the hotel room was closed behind them they were locked in a fierce embrace, kissing like there was no tomorrow, shedding clothes as fast as they could on their way to the bed, totally consumed with a wild passion that demanded to be slaked before easing into a more sensual lovemaking.

Even that seemed to carry more intensity than usual, more need for continually intimate contact, and Laura revelled in it, believing it meant Jake felt more for her now, on a personal rather than just a sexual level. It was a long time before they fell asleep and in the morning she woke to the sense of having her body being softly caressed by a loving hand. She rolled over to fling her arm around Jake, who proceeded to arouse her more acutely. They'd never had sex *the morning after* but they did this time, and Laura took it as another heart-hugging sign that their relationship was beginning to change to a closer one.

They ate a very hearty breakfast.

Showered, dressed and ready to leave, they were at the door of their hotel room when Jake turned and kissed her again, a long, passionate kiss that left Laura tingling with excitement on their elevator ride down to the foyer. Her mind swam with the hope he was going to ask her home with him instead of their going separate ways today.

A taxi was waiting outside the hotel entrance. Jake opened the passenger door for her and she got in, sliding along the back seat to make room for him. Instead of following her he leaned in to tell the driver Eddie's address and hand him a twenty dollar note.

Startled, Laura blurted, 'Aren't you coming with me?'

His dark eyes met hers, flat dark, almost black, devoid of any brilliance. 'No. I have somewhere else to go, Laura,' he stated decisively. He reached out and touched her cheek. 'It's been good. Thank you.'

Then the brief caress was withdrawn, as swiftly as Jake withdrew himself, shutting the passenger door and signalling the driver to take her away. Which he did, given no reason not to.

Laura was too stunned to protest the move. She sat in total shock, her hopes, her dreams, her expectations crashing around her. That was a goodbye! Not a *see you next time*. Jake hadn't mentioned a next time. Her hand lifted and clapped her cheek, holding on to what a creeping tide of panic was telling her had been his farewell touch.

Her mind railed over why it should be so. Surely there was no reason to give up what had been good. He would call her during the week. This couldn't be the end. Yet the more she thought about it, the more she felt he had been saying goodbye to her all last night. And this morning. Last dinner, last sex, last kiss, last touch!

But maybe she had it wrong. Maybe, maybe...

The taxi pulled up outside Eddie's apartment. Laura pulled herself out of her mental torment enough to thank the driver and step out onto the pavement. A glance at her watch showed almost eleven o'clock. She hoped Eddie was having a Sunday brunch with his friends somewhere because she wasn't up to chatting normally with him, not when her mind kept running on this awful emotional treadmill.

No such luck!

He was seated at his dining table in the living room, a cup of coffee to hand as he perused the newspapers. The moment she let herself into the apartment he looked up to shoot an opening line at her. 'Hi! Had another great night with Dad's golden boy?'

'Yes. A great night.' Even to her own ears it was a hollow echo of Eddie's words. It was impossible to work any happy enthusiasm into her voice.

He looked at her quizzically. 'Tetsuya's up to your expectations?'

'Yes. Absolutely.' That was better, more emphatic.

'Are you sick or something?'

'No.'

He sat back in his chair and gave her his wise look. 'Then why do you look like death warmed up, Laura?'

She sighed, accepting the fact there was very little she could hide from Eddie. He had a very shrewd talent for boring straight through any camouflage she put up. 'I think Jake said goodbye to me this morning and I'm not ready to say goodbye to him,' she said, shrugging in an attempt to minimise her dilemma.

Eddie grimaced and rose from his chair, waving her to the table. 'Come and sit down. I'll get you a cup of coffee. It might perk you up a bit.'

She slumped into a chair, feeling weirdly drained of energy.

'Why do you *think* he said goodbye?' Eddie asked as he poured coffee from the percolator.

Laura relived the scene in her mind. 'He put me into the taxi at the hotel, touched my cheek and said, "It's been good. Thank you." Usually he shares the taxi with me and tells me where we'll meet next week, but this morning he shut the door on me and waved me off.'

'It's *been* good,' Eddie repeated, musing over the past tense. He shook his head as he brought her the shot of caffeine and resumed his seat across the table from her. 'If he'd said *was* good...'

'No, it was *been* good. I'm not mistaken about that, Eddie.'

He grimaced. 'Got to say it sounds like a cut-off line to me. Do you have any idea why?'

'No. None. Which is why I'm so…in a mess about it.'

'No little niggles about how he was responding to you? Like maybe getting bored with the routine you'd established?'

'I'm not stupid, Eddie. I'd know if he was bored,' she cried, though right now she didn't feel certain about anything.

'Okay. He wasn't bored but he was saying good-bye regardless of the pleasures you both shared. That only leaves one motive, Laura,' Eddie said ruefully.

'What?'

'You've served your purpose.'

She shook her head in helpless confusion. 'I don't understand. What purpose?'

'You can bet it's something to do with dear old Dad.'

'But we've kept our whole relationship away from him,' she protested.

'You have, but how can you possibly know that Jake has?'

'He promised me…'

'Laura, Laura…' Eddie looked pained. 'I warned you from the start that this is a guy who plays all the angles. He's not our father's right-hand man for nothing. He's obviously worked at winning Dad's trust. He's worked at winning yours. But let me remind you, James Bond plays his own game and I think you've just been treated to one of them—*love 'em and leave 'em.'*

James Bond... She'd stopped connecting Jake to the legendary 007 character. He was the man she wanted, the man she loved, the man she'd dreamed of having for the rest of her life. Had she been an absolute fool, getting so caught up with him? Hadn't Jake felt anything for her beyond the desire to take her to bed? How could the strong feelings he'd stirred in her be completely one-sided?

The intensity of his love-making last night and this morning had made her believe he felt a lot for her. Eddie had to be wrong. She couldn't think of any purpose Jake could have in loving her and leaving her. He might very well have somewhere else he had to be this morning—somewhere he wished he didn't have to go because of wanting to be with her—and that past tense he'd used could have been simply a slip of the tongue. Maybe she'd worked herself into a stew for nothing and he would call her during the week.

Eddie shook his head at her. 'You don't want to believe it, do you?'

'I guess time will tell, Eddie,' she said flatly. 'Let's leave it at that. Okay?'

'Okay.' He gave her a sympathetic look. 'In the meantime, chalk up the positives. You've had the experience of dining in some of the finest restaurants, staying in very classy hotels, plus a fair chunk of great sex. Not a bad three months, Laura.'

She managed a wry smile. 'No, not bad at all.'
But I want more.
Much more of Jake Freedman.
And I desperately hope I get more.

CHAPTER TEN

THE rest of Sunday went by without a call from Jake.

No contact from him on Monday, either.

It would probably come on Friday, Laura told herself, doing her best to concentrate on her uni lectures and not get too disturbed by the lack of the communication she needed. Regardless of the situation with Jake, she still had to move on with her life, get the qualifications necessary for her chosen career. Yet all her sensible reasoning couldn't stop the sick yearning that gripped her stomach when her thoughts drifted to him. And telling herself he would call soon didn't help.

It surprised her to see her father's car parked in the driveway when she arrived home on Tuesday afternoon. He never left work early and it wasn't even five o'clock. A scary thought hit her. Had something bad happened to her mother? An accident? Illness? She couldn't imagine anything but an emergency bringing her father home at this hour.

She ran to the front door, her heart pumping with

fear as she unlocked it and rushed into the hallway. 'Mum? Dad?' she called anxiously.

'Get in here, Laura!' her father's voice thundered from the lounge room. 'I've been waiting for you!'

She stood stock-still, her heart thumping even harder. He was in a rage. No distress in that tone. It was total fury. The only concern she need have for her mother was being subjected to his venom again.

The double doors from the hallway into the lounge room were open. Laura stiffened her spine, squared her shoulders and forced her feet forward, knowing that her mother would be spared the full-on brunt of savage remarks when he turned them onto her. It didn't matter how much she hated these vicious scenes. Better for her to be here than not here.

On entering the war zone, she found her mother cowering in the corner of one of the sofas, white-faced and hugging herself tightly as though desperately trying to hold herself together. Her father was standing behind the bar, splashing Scotch into a glass of ice. *His* face was red and the bottle of Scotch was half-empty.

'Are you still seeing Jake Freedman?' he shot at her.

No point in trying any evasion when her father was in this mood. He'd dig and dig and dig.

'I don't know,' she answered honestly.

'What do you mean "you don't know"?' he jeered, his eyes raking her with contempt. 'Don't pretend to be stupid, Laura.'

She shrugged. 'I was with him on Saturday night but he made no plans for us to meet again.'

Her father snorted. 'Had a last hurrah, screwing my daughter.'

'Alex, it's not Laura's fault,' her mother spoke up, showing more courage than she usually did. 'You introduced him to her.'

It enraged him into yelling, 'The bloody mole played his cards perfectly! Anyone would have been sucked in by him!'

'Then don't blame Laura,' her mother pleaded weakly, wilting under the blast.

What had Jake done? Laura's mind was in a whirl as she crossed the room to where her mother was scrunched into as small a space as possible and sat on the sofa's wide armrest next to her. 'What's going on, Dad?' she asked, needing to get to the crux of the problem.

He bared his teeth in a vicious snarl. 'That bastard has taken all my business to the Companies' Auditors and Liquidators Disciplinary Board and had me suspended from any further practice in the industry, pending further investigation.'

'Suspended?' This was why he was home, but... 'Investigation of what?'

His hand sliced the air in savage dismissal. 'You've never been interested in my work, Laura, so it's none of your concern.'

'I want to know what Jake is accusing you of.'

He shook a furious finger at her. 'All you have to

know is he was hell-bent on taking me down every minute he was supposedly working *for* me. Rolling you was icing on the cake for him.'

'But why? You're making it sound like a personal vendetta.'

'It *is* a personal vendetta.' His eyes bitterly raked her up and down. 'How personal can you get with his hands all over you, exulting in taking every damned liberty he could.'

'Alex!' her mother cried in pained protest.

She was ignored.

'And you let him, didn't you? My daughter!' her father thundered.

Laura refused to answer.

He sneered at her silence. 'He would have revelled in every intimacy you gave up to him.'

'This isn't about me, Dad,' she said as calmly as she could. 'I'm obviously a side issue. Why does Jake have a personal vendetta against you?'

'Because of JQE!' The words were spat out.

'That doesn't mean anything to me,' Laura persisted.

He glared at her contemptuously as though her ignorance was another poisonous barb to his pride.

Her chin lifted defiantly. 'I think I have the right to know what I've been a victim of.'

'JQE was his stepfather's company,' he finally informed her in a bitterly mocking tone. 'He believes I could have saved it and chose not to. The man died of a heart attack soon after I secured the liquidator's fee.'

*Step*father! 'Was his surname different to Jake's?'

'Of course it was! If I'd had any idea they were related, he would never have been employed by me.'

'How long has he been working in your company?'

'Six years! Six damnable years of worming his way through my files, wanting to nail me to the wall!'

A man with a mission…James Bond…Dark and dangerous…

Her instincts had been right at their first meeting, but she hadn't heeded them, hadn't wanted to.

'Could you have saved his stepfather's company, Dad?' she asked, wanting to know if the mission was for justice or some twisted form of vengeance. Jake had loved his stepfather, possibly the only father he had known.

'The man was an idiot, getting in over his head,' her father snarled. 'Even with help he was in no state to rescue anything. His wife was dying of cancer. Trying to hang on was stupid.'

A judgement call. Had it been right or a deliberate choice for her father to make a profit out of it, charging huge fees to carry out the liquidation process?

What was the truth?

Laura knew she wouldn't get it from her father. He would serve his own ends. Always had.

As for Jake, he must have been totally torn up

with grief when the seeds of his mission had been sown—his mother dying of cancer, his stepfather driven into bankruptcy and dying of a heart attack. It must have been a terribly traumatic time, having to bury both parents in the midst of everything being sold up around him. She had sensed the darkness in him, seen signs of it, heard it in his voice that first day in the garden when he'd described the terrible downside of bankruptcy, but hadn't known how deep it went, hadn't known that she was connected to it by being her father's daughter.

The bottle of Scotch took another hit. A furious finger stabbed at her again. 'Don't you dare take his side in this bloody whistle-blowing or you are out of this house, Laura! He used you. Used you to show me up as even more of a fool for trusting him with my daughter.'

Had that been Jake's intention behind tempting her into an affair? An iron fist squeezed her heart. He'd controlled every aspect of their meetings, kept their involvement limited to Saturday nights. Had he been secretly revelling in having her whenever he called? Because of who she was?

'What there was between us is over,' she said flatly.

'It had better be, my girl!' Threat seethed through every word. 'If he contacts you…'

'He won't.' Laura was certain of it. He *had* been saying goodbye on Sunday morning.

'Don't bet on it! It would be an extra feather in his cap if he sucked you in again.'

'He won't,' she repeated, sick to her soul. She'd loved him, truly deeply loved him, and the thought of having been used to drive a dagger further into her father was devastating.

'You be damned sure of it, Laura, because if I ever find out otherwise, you'll pay for it!'

'I'm sure.'

'You're looking sick around the gills. He got to you all right.'

The savage mutter was followed by another hefty swig of Scotch.

'I'm not feeling well,' her mother said shakily. 'Will you help me up to my bedroom, Laura?'

''Course I will.' She quickly moved off the arm-rest to give support.

'Running away as usual,' her father said scath-ingly. 'We'll be living with this hanging over our heads for months, Alicia. No escaping it.'

'It's just the shock, Dad,' Laura threw back at him. 'Mum needs some recovery time.'

'Recovery! I'll never recover from this! Never! That bastard has me hamstrung!'

Not for nothing, Laura thought as she helped her mother from the room. Jake must have presented a considerable body of hard evidence against her fa-ther for him to be suspended from practice. And had still been gathering it while he was seeing her on the side.

She needed recovery time, too.

Her mother felt terribly frail. Laura put her to bed and tucked the doona around her. 'It's not your fault, either, Mum,' she said gently.

The pale blue eyes were teary and fearful. She grasped Laura's hand. 'I don't think I can bear it if your father is home every day.'

'You don't have to. Eddie would take you in. You have only to ask.'

She shook her head fretfully. 'It wouldn't be fair on him. You don't understand, Laura. Your father wouldn't tolerate my leaving him. He'd...do something.'

Laura hated the fear but she knew there was no reasoning against it. She and Eddie had tried many times. 'Well, I don't think Dad will be at home all the time. He'll be out networking with people, fighting this situation with everything in his power.'

'Yes. Yes, he will. Thank you, Laura. I'm sorry... sorry that Jake...'

'Let's not talk about him. You just rest, Mum.'

She kissed the slightly damp forehead and left the room before her own tears welled up and spilled over—tears of hurt and shock and grief that pride had insisted she hold back in front of her father. And her mother.

In the safe haven of her bedroom she wept until she was totally drained of tears. Her mind was wiped blank for a long time as she lay in limp misery, but gradually it began to turn over everything that had happened between her and Jake in the light of what she now knew and it kept coming back to the one line that felt critically important—the line he'd spoken after their first kiss in the garden.

I don't want to want you.

But he had.

He most definitely had wanted her, and quite possibly not because of who she was but *in spite of* who she was.

Which made a huge difference to her father's interpretation of Jake's conduct where she was concerned.

It meant she was not part of his vengeance plot.

She was an innocent connection to the man whom he saw as the prime cause of the darkest time of his life. The words he'd used describing bankruptcy came back to her—lives crumbling, futures shattered, depression so dark there is no light. The emotional intensity that had surprised her in that forceful little speech had obviously erupted from personal experience.

Looking back, she began to make much more sense of how Jake had run their affair, always keeping the end in sight, ensuring their involvement was limited, not escalating into something too serious. He'd known it was ill-fated from the start, but he'd found her as irresistible as she'd found him and he'd taken the small window of opportunity for them to enjoy each other before circumstances made it impossible.

It's been good. Thank you.

He hadn't been *using* her.

They'd both chosen to give themselves the pleasure of mutual desire and it had been good. The more Laura reasoned it out, the more she believed the journey they'd taken together was completely separate from the road Jake had been travelling to put her father out of business.

She remembered the intensity of his love-making on Saturday night, the long passionate kiss before they left the hotel room, the flat darkness—no... light—of his eyes as he touched her cheek in the taxi.

Maybe he hadn't wanted to say goodbye.

Maybe he loved her as deeply as she loved him.

Maybe he just couldn't see a future for them, given what he was about to do.

That might be true...or it might not.

It depended on how much he felt for her.

She had to see him, talk to him, find out the truth.

CHAPTER ELEVEN

LAURA wished she could have borrowed Eddie's car to tour the streets of Woollahra, looking for the houses that were being renovated, noting them down for further investigation. It would have been the most time efficient way of searching for Jake's current home, but she knew her brother would not have been sympathetic to her quest. Better not to ask. Better to go on foot, however long it took.

When she'd broken the news to Eddie, he'd leapt to the same interpretation of Jake's interest in her as her father, being quite smug about having been right that Laura should never have *gone there*, right about Jake having a mission, too. The latter was impossible to deny, but Laura could not set aside the need to *go there* again.

At least Eddie had taken their mother out today, giving her a break from the wretched tensions at home. It left Laura enough free time to cover a fair bit of ground in her search, though it was now Sunday—no tradesmen's trucks around to mark possibilities. After three hours of walking one street after another, and feeling somewhat dispirited at her lack of success, she decided to take a break for lunch and give her feet a rest.

Heading up another street that led to a public park where she could sit and eat her home-made sand-wiches, Laura could hardly believe her eyes when she actually spotted Jake. He was on the upstairs balcony of a terrace house, painting the iron-lace railings—the same shade of green as the front door and the window frames. It was a rich forest green that looked really good against the old red bricks of the house.

He looked good, too, a fact her heart was register-ing by thumping painfully. She stood still, staring up at him, wracked by a terrible uncertainty now that the moment of truth was at hand. Was she being an utter fool, coming to him like this? So what if she was, she fiercely argued to herself. A sharp dose of humiliation wouldn't kill her. And she wasn't about to die wondering, either.

His head lifted, his gaze suddenly swinging to her as though some invisible force had drawn it. 'Laura!' He spoke her name in a tone of angst, jerking up from his crouched position on the balcony, frown-ing down at her. 'What are you doing here?'

'I need to talk to you,' she blurted out.

He shook his head. 'It won't do you any good.' His gaze shot to a van parked on the other side of the street. 'That's been here since Wednesday. I'd say your father has me under surveillance and he won't like getting a report of your coming to me. Just keep walking and maybe nothing will come of it.'

Her father's threat jangled through her mind— *you'll pay for it.*

Right now Laura didn't care. Jake had just proved his caring for her. That was more important than anything else. Or was he just trying to get her out of his life again as fast as possible?

'I have to know,' she said with immovable determination. 'I won't go until you lay out the truth to me.'

A pained grimace twisted his mouth as his hand waved in a sharp, dismissive gesture. 'You already know it had to come to an end. Remember it for what it was and move on.'

'What was it, Jake?'

'You know that, too,' he shot back at her.

'No, I don't. You kept me in the dark about what meant most to you. I don't know if it gave you a thrill to have me while plotting to bring my father down, if I was some kind of sweet icing on the cake for you. I want to know that before I move on.'

Jake stared at the woman he should never have touched, his mind torn by the deep hurt emanating from her. She was still the most beautiful, most desirable woman he'd ever known, quite possibly would ever know, and he hated having to part from her. It had to be done, but did it have to be done with her mind poisoned against what they'd shared?

He wanted her to have a good memory of him, not a bitter one. Yet how was he to soothe the hurt and protect her from her father's wrath at the same time? The surveillance man was surely watching, taking note of this encounter. The longer it went on, the worse it would be for Laura at home.

'There's a public park at the end of this street,' he said, pointing the direction as though she had asked for it.

'I know!' she cried in exasperation. 'Can't you just answer me?'

He shot a warning look at the van. 'I'll meet you there when I've finished this painting. Go, Laura. Go now.'

He turned his attention to the work in hand, bending down to the tin of paint again, hoping the intense urgency in his voice would spur her into moving away from him. After a few moments' hesitation that tied his gut into knots, she did walk on, hopefully proving there was nothing in this meeting worth reporting.

He maintained a steady pace with the brushwork, exhibiting no haste to finish the job. It gave him time to think, time to reason out he should keep his answers to Laura short, avoid the tempting impulse to take her in his arms and prove his passion for her had been real, was still real. The ache in his groin had to be ignored. This meeting had to be limited to setting her straight, then letting her go. Anything else could not be sustained in the climate of her father's venomous animosity.

The narrow alley that ran along the back of this row of terraces allowed him to leave his house unobserved. He would return the same way. A last meeting. No more.

He does care for me. He does.

It was like a chant of joy in Laura's mind, making every step towards the park a light one for her tired feet. Jake would have no reason at all to give himself the trouble of meeting with her if she meant nothing to him. If she'd been part of his vendetta against her father, he would have shamed her in the street. He had certainly not been amused by her coming to him nor titillated by his power to draw her. He'd been pained by her presence, reminding him of what they'd shared, what he'd been trying to shut out as finished.

Except it wasn't.

Not for her and not for him.

The connection was too strong to obliterate.

Laura was sure of it.

She found a park bench under a tree and sat down to wait, not bothering to unpack the sandwiches in her handbag. Her heart was too full of other needs for eating to be a priority anymore. Jake would come to her soon—Jake, whom she loved…whom she would always love. Did he feel the same way about her?

Was it only the situation with her father that had driven him to break it off with her?

She had no idea how long she waited. Her mind was obsessed with finding some way to continue their relationship—safe places to meet, secret places, whatever it took for their journey not to end. When she spotted him approaching her at a fast stride she leapt to her feet, barely quelling the urge to run to him and fling her arms around his neck. Talking had to come first, she told herself, though if he wrapped her in his embrace…

He didn't. There was no smile on his face, no joy at seeing her, no sexy twinkle in his eyes. When he reached her he took hold of her hands, squeezing them as though to prevent any other touching. 'I never meant you to be hurt, Laura,' he said gruffly. 'I thought we could simply satisfy ourselves with the pleasures we could give each other. None of that had anything to do with your father. It was all about you, the woman I wanted to be with, not whose daughter you are.'

His thumbs were dragging across the skin on the back of her hands, wanting his words to sink in, go deep, expel the nastiness of the motivation that her father had given him. The earnest sincerity in his voice, the blaze of need to convince her in his eyes… Laura believed he spoke the truth. She *wanted* to believe.

'You should have told me what you were about to

do, Jake,' she blurted out. 'It wouldn't have been so bad if you'd told me.'

His mouth twisted into a rueful grimace. 'I didn't want to spoil our last night together, bringing your father into it, bringing my family background into it. And telling you wasn't going to change anything.'

'It would have prepared me.'

'Yes. I see that now. I'm sorry. I thought you'd understand. What we had was time out of time, Laura.' He squeezed her hands hard. 'You must let it go and move on.'

'I don't want to, Jake. It was too good to let go. You must feel that, too,' she pleaded.

He jerked his head in a sharp negative. 'There's no way. Your father will see to that and bucking him would make things much worse for both you and your mother. You told me she needs you. And you still have to get your uni degree for the career you want. Any association with me will cost you too much.'

If he was under surveillance… Yes, it would be too risky. The tensions at home were volatile enough already. Yet letting this connection she felt with Jake go… Everything inside her railed against giving it up.

'What about when this is all over, Jake. Could we pick up again then?'

He shook his head but there was a pained expression on his face as he answered, 'The process of indicting your father for corruption may go on for years, Laura.'

'Is he guilty?'

'Without a doubt.'

'Will he go to jail?'

'He'll be ousted from the industry. It's unlikely that any further action will be taken.'

No relief for her mother. No escape unless…

'Once I get my degree and hopefully a well-paid position, I'll be independent. And perhaps I can persuade my mother to come and live with me. We'll be free and clear of my father.'

'Perhaps…' he repeated, but there was no belief in his eyes.

Her hope for at least some distant future with him was being crushed. It begged for a chance to survive. 'Do you really want this to be goodbye, Jake?'

'No. But I can't honestly see any good way forward,' he said flatly.

'You have my mobile phone number. You could call me from time to time, check on how things are going,' she suggested, trying to keep a note of desperation out of her voice.

He wrenched his gaze from the plea in hers and stared down at their linked hands. Again his thumbs worked over her skin. After a long nerve-tearing silence, he muttered, 'You should close the door on me, Laura. You'll meet someone else with no history to make your life difficult.'

'I won't meet anyone else like you,' she said

fiercely, every instinct fighting for a love she might never feel with any other man.

He expelled a long breath with the whisper, 'Nor I, you.' Then he visibly gathered himself, head lifting, meeting her gaze squarely again. 'I won't call you from time to time. I won't keep any hold on you. When I'm done with your father—however long that takes—I'll catch up with you to see where you are in your life and how we feel about each other then.'

She knew there was no fighting the hard decision in his eyes, in his voice. 'Promise me you'll do that, Jake. Whatever happens between now and then, promise me we'll meet again.'

'I promise.' He leaned forward to press a soft warm kiss on her forehead. 'Stay strong, Laura,' he murmured.

Before she could say or do anything, he'd backed off, released her hands and was walking away. She stared at his retreating figure, feeling the distance growing between them with each step he took, hating it yet resigned to the inevitability of this parting.

He'd promised her they'd meet again.

It might be years away but she didn't believe any length of time would make a difference to how she felt with him.

And she did have things to achieve—her qualifications, building a career and hopefully persuading her mother that there was another life to be led, free of abuse and oppression.

It would not be time wasted.

She would be better equipped to continue a journey with Jake Freedman when they met again—older, stronger, more his equal in everything. She could wait for that.

CHAPTER TWELVE

STAY STRONG...

Laura repeated those words to herself many times as she tried to minimise her father's savagery over the next few weeks, protecting her mother from it as best she could. She had half expected a vicious blow-up about her visit to Jake's house, but that didn't eventuate. Either there hadn't been a surveillance man at all, or he hadn't reported the incident, not seeing anything significant in it.

Strangely enough her mind was more at peace with Jake's promise. She didn't fret over his absence from her life. It was easier to concentrate on her landscape projects than when she was seeing him each week. Knowing what he was doing, knowing why, helped a lot, as did good memories when she went to bed at night. Besides, there was hope for a future with him, which she kept to herself, not confiding it to her mother or Eddie, both of whom would probably see it as an unhealthy obsession with the man.

She spent as much time with her mother as her uni studies and part-time receptionist work would allow. Nick Jeffries seemed to be finding a lot of maintenance jobs that had to be done, coming to the house two or three times a week. Laura wondered if he knowingly provided a buffer between her parents, giving her mother an excuse to be outside with him, supervising the work. He was a cheerful man, good to have around, in sharp contrast to her father, who was never anything but nasty now.

One evening she was in the kitchen with her mother, helping to prepare dinner, when he arrived home bellowing, 'Laura!' from the hallway, the tone alone warning he was bent on taking a piece out of her.

Her heart jumped. What had she done wrong? Nothing she could think of. 'I'm in the kitchen, Dad!' she called out, refusing to go running to him or show any fear of his mean temper.

Stay strong...

She kept cutting up the carrots, only looking up when he announced his entry by snidely commenting, 'Good sharp knife! You might want to stick it into someone, Laura.'

Like him? He had a smug smile on his face, in no doubt whatsoever that she wouldn't attack him physically. He was the one who had the power to hurt and that knowledge glittered in his eyes. He stood there, gloating over whatever he had in mind to do. Laura waited, saying nothing, aware that her mother had also stopped working and was tensely waiting for whatever was coming next.

'I've had Jake Freedman under surveillance,' he announced.

The visit to Jake's house! But that was so long ago. It didn't make sense that her father would keep such a tasty titbit until now.

He waved a large envelope at her. 'Hard evidence of what a slime he is.' He strolled forward, opening the envelope and removing what looked like large photographs, and laid them down on the island bench in front of her.

'Thought you'd like to see Jake Freedman's steady screw, Laura,' he said mockingly, pointing to a curvy blonde in a skimpy, skin-tight aerobic outfit, her arms locked around Jake's neck, her body pressed up against his, as was her face for a kiss.

It was like a kick in the gut, seeing him with another woman.

'Meets her at the gym three times a week.'

Every word was like a drop of acid eating into her heart.

The pointing finger moved to the next photograph. 'Goes back to her place for extra exercise.'

There was the blonde again, the pony-tail for the gym released so that her shiny hair fell around her face and shoulders in soft waves. It was a very pretty face. She was opening the door of a house, smiling back invitingly at Jake, who was paused at the foot of the steps leading up to the front porch.

'Woman works at a club on Saturday nights,' her father went on. 'Very handy. Left him free to have his delectable little encounters with you. Shows what a two-faced bastard he is in every respect.'

She didn't speak, couldn't speak. Sickening waves of shock were rolling through her. It was a huge relief that her father didn't wait for some comment from her.

'Need a drink to drown the scumbag out,' he muttered and headed off to make his usual inroads into a bottle of whisky, leaving the damning photographs behind to blast any faith she might have in Jake's love for her.

Laura stared at them. It was only a month since her meeting in the park with him—a meeting he hadn't wanted, a meeting to ensure she wouldn't pester him again, coming to his house where she had never been invited. She had accepted his reasoning, believed in his promise, and here he was with another woman, enjoying her company, having sex with her.

Two-faced…

Of course he had to be good at that—brilliant—to fool her father.

Fooling her, too, had probably been a fun exercise in comparison.

A dark, dangerous man… She should have trusted that instinct, should have said no to him, should never have allowed him to play his game with her because it had been *his* game all along, *his* arrangements, *his* rules. She had read into them what she wanted to believe and he had let her with his rotten promise.

Tears welled up and blurred her vision. She shut her eyes, didn't see her mother move to wrap her in a comforting hug, only felt the arms turning her around, a hand curling around her head and pressing it onto a shoulder. She wasn't strong in that moment, couldn't find any strength at all. She gave in to a storm of weeping until it was spent, then weakly stayed in her mother's embrace, soaking up the real love coming to her from the rubbing of her back and the stroking of her hair.

'I'm sorry you've been so hurt by this,' her mother murmured. 'Sorry you were caught up in your father's business, in past deeds you had nothing to do with. So wrong...'

'I loved him, Mum. I thought he loved me. He promised me we'd meet again when this was all over,' she spilled out, needing to unburden the pain of the soul-sickening deception.

'Perhaps that was a kinder way of letting you down than telling you the truth. You're a wonderful person, Laura. Even he had to see that, care for you a little.'

'Oh, Mum! It's such a mess!' She lifted her head and managed a wobbly smile. 'I'm a mess. Thanks for being here for me.'

Her mother returned an ironic little smile as she lifted her hand to smear the wetness from Laura's cheeks. 'As you are for me. But please don't think you always have to be, my dear. I want you to have a life of your own, away from here. Like Eddie.'

'Well, we'll talk about that when I'm through uni. Now let's do this dinner. I don't want Dad to know I've been upset.'

Pride lent her strength again. She snatched up the photographs. 'I'll just take these up to my room as reminders of my stupidity, clean myself up and be right back down to help. And don't worry about me, Mum. I'll be okay now.'

She dumped the photographs on her bed, bitterly thinking how *easy* she had been for Jake, how vulnerable she had been to his strong sex appeal, how willing to go along with *his* journey, letting him call all the shots. He'd probably had this other woman all along. Even if the pretty blonde was only a more recent acquisition for his sex life, the very fact of her spelled out that he felt no deep attachment to Alex Costarella's daughter.

Washing her face, she wished she could wash Jake Freedman right out of her head.

Stay strong...

Oh, yes, she would. She had to. Nobody was going to wreck her life; not her father, not Jake, not any man. This steadfast determination carried her through dinner, sharpening her wits enough to dilute her father's barbs with good-humoured replies. It also formed her resolution when she returned to her bedroom and was faced with the photographs again.

She scooped them up and shoved them straight back into the envelope her father had left with them.

It was a blank envelope and she wrote Jake's address on it, grimly pleased that the search for his house had not been completely wasted time. She wanted him to know that she knew about his other woman and he would not be sucking up any more of her time.

To underline that fact, she wrote an accompanying note—

> *As for any future meeting between us, you can whistle for me, Jake. I'm moving on. Laura.*

No angst in those words. She liked the *whistle* bit. It carried a flippant tone, as well as implying he was just another jerk to be ignored.

Having slipped the note into the envelope, she sealed it and put it in her briefcase to be posted tomorrow. Over and done with. Her life was her own again.

Jake sorted his mail, frowning over the business-size envelope with the handwritten address. It wasn't standard practice to handwrite anything that wasn't personal these days. Curious about its content, he slit it open and drew out the photographs and the damning little note from Laura.

A lead weight settled on his heart.

He'd been sucked in by the dancer at the gym. She'd been Costarella's tool. That was bleeding obvious now. He hadn't suspected a set-up when she'd grabbed at him as he was leaving the gym, expressing what seemed like genuine fear of being stalked and pleading with him to walk her home—just a few blocks to where she knew she'd be safe. It wasn't much to ask, wasn't much to do—a random act of kindness that was coming back to spike him with a vengeance.

Then the embrace of gushing gratitude a week later, an over-the-top carry-on that he'd backed away from, not wanting it, not liking it, certainly not encouraging any further involvement with the woman. But that didn't show in the photograph. It didn't serve Costarella's purpose to give Laura shots of his reaction.

He carried the mail into his house, despondently dumping it on the kitchen bench on his way to the small backyard, which provided a sunny haven from the rest of the world. He slumped into one of the deck chairs he'd set out there, still holding Laura's note that brought their journey to a dead end.

He stared at the words—*I'm moving on.*

It was what he had meant her to do, advised her to do, and most probably it was the best course to chop him completely out of her life. Costarella was not about to tolerate any future connection between them. Even if he explained this photographic set-up to Laura and she believed him, Costarella would look for other ways and means to drive wedges into their relationship. It gave him a focus for getting back at Jake for bringing him down and he'd relish that malicious power.

Definitely best that what he'd had with Laura ended here and now.

No future.

He folded the note and tucked it into his shirt pocket.

He'd known all along that this was how it would have to be, but it was still damned difficult to accept. Achieving what he'd set out to do to Alex Costarella felt strangely empty. Like his life after his mother and stepfather had died. But he'd picked himself up then and moved forward. He could do it again.

There should have been warmth in the sunshine.

He couldn't feel it.

The emptiness inside him was very cold.

CHAPTER THIRTEEN

FOR the rest of the year Laura applied herself so thoroughly to her uni course, she not only attained her degree, but also graduated with honours in every subject. This gave her an extra edge over other students entering the workforce for the first time. She was snapped up by a firm of architects, wanting a landscape specialist to enhance their designs. It was a wonderful buoyant feeling to know all her hard work had paid off and she was actually going to begin her chosen career.

The phone call notifying her of her successful interview came in the first week of December and her new employers wanted her in their office the following Monday. After revelling in the news for a few moments, she rushed out to the back garden to tell her mother, who was trailing after Nick Jeffries as he checked the sprinkler system.

'Mum! I got it! The job I interviewed for!' she called out, causing both of them to turn and give her their attention. She grinned exultantly at them as she added, 'And they want me to start next week!'

Her mother's face lit with pleasure. 'That's fantastic, Laura!'

'Fantastic!' Nick repeated, grinning delight at her. 'Congratulations!'

'And before Christmas, too,' her mother said with an air of relief, turning her face up to Nick's and touching his arm in an oddly familiar manner. 'Can we do it?'

He nodded. 'The sooner, the better.'

'Do what?' Laura asked, bemused by what seemed like an intimate flow of understanding between them.

Nick tucked her mother's arm around his and they faced Laura together as he told her their news. 'Your mother is leaving your father and moving in with me. We've just been waiting for you to have some freedom of choice, Laura, and now you're set.'

She was totally thunderstruck. Her mother and Nick? She had never imagined, never suspected there was anything beyond a casual affection between them, born out of sharing the pleasure of a lovely garden. She knew Nick was a widower, had been for years, but he'd always been very respectful to her mother, caring about what she wanted but never taking liberties that might not be welcome. When had their relationship moved to a different level?

'I can see you're shocked,' her mother said on a deflated sigh.

Her air of disappointment jolted Laura into a quick

protest. 'No! No! Just surprised! And pleased,' she quickly added, beaming a smile at both of them.

'It's not good for Alicia here,' Nick said, appealing for her understanding.

That was the understatement of the year!

'I'm sure Mum will be a lot happier with you than with Dad,' Laura said with feeling. 'Both Eddie and I have always liked you, Nick. And appreciated how much you've lightened Mum's life. I think it's brilliant that you're stepping in and taking her away, but I've got to warn you, Dad's bound to be horribly mean about it. He's not a good loser.'

Which was another huge understatement.

Nick patted her mother's hand reassuringly. 'Alicia doesn't need to take anything from him. I can provide for her.'

'There's very little I want to take from this life, Laura. Nick can fit it into his van,' her mother said, looking brighter now that her decision had been so readily accepted by her daughter. 'But you'll have to move on the same day. Either come with us or go to Eddie's until you can afford a place of your own. I can't leave you here, not with your father finding out I've walked out on him.'

'No, that would not be a good scene,' Laura heartily agreed.

The biggest understatement of all!

'I'll go to Eddie's, let you two start your lives together on your own,' she decided. 'It won't be for long. As soon as I get my first pay cheque, I'll look around for an apartment close to my work.'

'We must tell Eddie now,' her mother said anxiously, looking to Nick for his support again.

'Yes, he has to be brought into the plan,' Nick agreed.

'No problem. I'll call him, let him know,' Laura suggested. 'And don't worry, Mum. Eddie will be all for it.'

She shook her head. 'I must tell him, dear. It's only right.'

'Okay. Just trying to save you trouble, Mum.'

'I know. It's what you've been doing for years,' she said sadly. 'But no more, Laura.'

'That's my job from now on,' Nick said with a cheerful grin. 'All you have to do, Laura, is choose what you want to take with you, pack it up and be ready when Alicia nominates the day.'

'A day when I'm sure your father will be out. I'm not going to face him with this. I'll leave him a letter. Let him rage to an empty house.'

'Best course,' Nick said decisively. 'I wouldn't put it past him to stoop to physical violence and I won't have Alicia subjected to any risk of that.'

'Definitely the best course,' Laura agreed. 'What about Friday, Mum? I'm sure Dad said that was when he was meeting with his barrister to plan the counter-attack to the accusations against him.'

Give him some dirt on your lover-boy, Laura, he'd

jeered. *Jake Freedman won't come out of this clean, I can promise you that.*

None of my business, Laura had firmly recited to herself, determined not to encourage her father into elaborating on *the dirt,* refusing to go anywhere that involved Jake. Despite all the intervening months, she hadn't been able to bury the hurt of her disillusionment with him and it was quite impossible to become interested in any other man.

'Yes, Friday!' her mother cried excitedly.

The day of freedom.

She turned to the man who had opened another door for her. 'No way will Alex miss that meeting, Nick. As soon as he's left the house I'll call you.'

'And I'll be here,' he assured her.

It was really heart-touching seeing the caring for her mother written on Nick's face, seeing her open trust in him. Laura had to clear a lump in her throat before she could speak.

'Now we've got that settled, I'm off to my room to start selecting what I want to take with me. You two can start planning a happy future together.'

She kissed them both on their cheeks and skipped away feeling even more light-hearted at the prospect of her mother's escape to a new life. No more oppressive abuse, no more fear, no more misery. Nick Jeffries was not an impressively handsome, wealthy man, but the kindness running through his veins was obviously more attractive to her mother than anything else.

And maybe that was what she should look for in a man.

Forget Jake Freedman's strong sex appeal.

Forget everything she had loved about him.

There had been no real kindness in him.

A kind man would never have used her as Jake had.

Next week she would be starting a new phase of her life, leaving everything and everyone connected to her father behind, and that would surely make forgetting Jake easier. She would be busy working her way into her career, forging a path of her own without having to worry about her mother's well-being, and looking forward to a really happy, tension-free Christmas for once!

Joy to the world!

Smiling over the words that had sung through her mind, Laura raced upstairs to her room to start organising the big move. Having perused the contents of her wardrobe, she decided large plastic garbage bags were needed for easy transportation. A lot of old stuff need not be taken. She stared down at the turquoise shoes Jake had called erotic on her first date with him at Neil Perry's Spice Temple. Gorgeous shoes. A gift from her mother. But could she ever wear them again without remembering him, remembering how it had been in the hotel after he'd taken them off?

A knock on her door interrupted the miserable train of thought.

'It's just me,' her mother called.

'Come in,' Laura quickly invited, wanting some private time with her mother, mostly to feel totally assured that going with Nick Jeffries was the right move for her, not an act of desperation or some kind of sacrifice to her children's peace of mind.

'Nick has stacked some boxes in the laundry for us to use,' she said, her blue eyes sparkling with happy anticipation.

'Mum, you are sure about this?' Laura asked earnestly. 'You're not just taking some...some easy way out?'

'No, dear. I'm very sure.' She walked over to the bed and sat on the end of it, looking at Laura with a soft, dreamy expression on her face. 'I lost myself with your father. I want to find the person I could have been and Nick will let me do that. I know I'm different with him and I like the difference. He touches my heart and makes me feel good, Laura, good in a way I've never felt before.'

She'd felt good with Jake until... But this wasn't the time to be thinking of him. She had to *stop* thinking of him. 'That's great, Mum,' she said warmly, giving her an ironic smile. 'I guess I'm still a bit surprised. When did you two open up to each other?'

'It was just after my birthday...'

Tenth of October

'Your father had been particularly nasty to me and I was sitting out on the garden bench near the pool, weeping over my miserable existence, wishing I were dead. Nick had come to work and he found me there.

There was no hiding my wretched state and he was so kind, so comforting. We talked and talked....'

She sighed, shook her head as though it was too difficult—or too private—to explain, but the reminiscent smile on her face spoke of unexpected pleasure found and treasured. 'Anyhow, the more we talked, the more I realised *I* wanted to be with him, and *he* wanted me to be with him, too. We both believe we can make a beautiful little world together. You can't imagine, Laura. Everything feels so different with Nick. So very different...'

Yes, she could imagine. No problem at all in imagining how it was or how it could be. She pulled her mother up from the bed for a hug. 'I'm so glad for you, Mum. Make sure you tell Eddie all that so he won't worry about you.'

'I will, dear. And you must both come to Nick's house for Christmas. We'll have a lovely celebration of it this year.'

'Mmmh...' Laura grinned. 'We'll be able to have fun together.'

'Yes, fun!' Her mother seized the concept with delight and sailed out of the room, no doubt eager to share it with Nick.

Over the next few days Laura and her mother secretly packed what they wanted to take, storing the boxes in Laura's room, where her father never ventured. Eddie was cock-a-hoop about the plan and in total agreement that it be carried out without their father's knowledge, not risking any explosive confrontation.

Friday morning came. Alex Costarella duly left for his meeting. Nick arrived in his van within minutes of the all-clear call. He and Laura packed the boxes and bags into it while her mother removed her personal papers—birth and marriage certificates from her father's safe—and made a last-minute check that nothing important had been missed.

There were absolutely no regrets on driving away from the Mosman mansion. It was like having a huge weight lifted off their hearts. The sense of freedom was so heady they couldn't help laughing at everything said between them. Laura called Eddie on her mobile phone to inform him of their successful escape and he was out on the street waiting for them when they arrived at his apartment block.

They all moved her belongings into his second bedroom and once that task was complete, she and Eddie accompanied their mother and Nick back to the van to say goodbye and wish them well. Oddly enough her mother looked strained as she nervously fingered a large envelope she'd left on the passenger seat, finally thrusting it at Laura.

'I don't know if it's right or wrong to give you this,' she said anxiously. 'It was in your father's safe and I looked into it while I was searching for my papers. It holds more photos of Jake Freedman—ones he didn't show you, Laura. I think he lied about those he did. Lied to drive a wedge between you and Jake, wanting to hurt. He always wanted to hurt when he didn't get his own way. Maybe seeing these will lessen the hurt a bit. I hope so, dear.'

It felt like a knife was twisting in her heart as she took the envelope, but she managed a smile, quickly saying, 'Don't worry, Mum. What's done is done and it's all in the past anyway. Go with Nick now. Be happy.'

They drove off and she stood so long staring blankly after the van, Eddie picked up the vibes of her distress and hugged her shoulders. 'It might be in the past but it's not done with, is it, Laura?' he said sympathetically. 'I know you haven't got over the guy. So let's go inside and look at what Dad's Machiavellian streak came up with to destroy what you had together.'

They were before-and-after photographs—before and after the damning shots that had driven her to reject any future with the man she had loved. Jake hadn't followed the pretty blonde into the house. She'd gone inside alone. Even the shots of them walking down the street together had no hint of any intimacy between them—just a man accompanying a woman.

As for the kiss at the gym, it was clear that the woman had thrown herself at Jake. There were snaps of his face showing surprise, annoyance, impatience, rejection, none of which had been visible in the photo her father had shown her.

'It was a set-up,' Eddie muttered, tapping a clear

shot of the blonde. 'I've seen this woman around the traps. She's a fairly high-class working girl. This would have been an easy gig for her and no doubt Dad paid her well for it.'

A set-up...and she'd fallen for it; hook, line and sinker.

'I didn't give Jake a chance to explain,' she said miserably. 'I posted him the incriminating photos with a message that wrote him out of my life.'

'Don't fret it, Laura. I'm sure Jake was smart enough to realise Dad wasn't going to tolerate a connection between the two of you. He probably thought he was saving you grief by letting it go.'

Yes, he would think that. But he wouldn't contact her when the business with her father was all over. Not now.

'I didn't believe in him enough. I didn't *stay strong*,' she cried, gutted by her failure of faith in his caring for her.

Eddie frowned. 'You think there was genuine feeling for you on his side?'

'Yes! It was just the situation making everything too hard. He promised me we'd meet again but I've messed it up, Eddie, taking Dad's word instead of his. I've completely messed it up!'

'Not necessarily. You must have his home address if you posted the photos to him,' he said thoughtfully. 'You're free of Dad now, Laura, and so is Mum. Why not pay Jake a visit, find out where you stand with him? Better to know than not know.'

'Yes!' She jumped up from her seat at Eddie's table where they had laid out the photographs, gripped by a determination to set everything right, if she could. 'I'll go. It's a chance to nothing, isn't it?'

He nodded. 'If you have to go there, go there.'

She did.

A wild hope zinged through her heart every step of the way, right until the front door of Jake's house was opened and she was faced with a young woman holding a baby on her hip.

'Hello. Are you one of our new neighbours?' the woman asked with bright-eyed interest.

'No, I…I was looking for Jake Freedman,' Laura blurted out.

'Oh, I'm sorry. He's gone, I'm afraid, and I don't have a forwarding address. We bought the house from him two months ago and moved in last week. I have no idea where you can find him.'

'It's okay. Thank you. Have a nice life here.'

A nice life in the house Jake had worked on and sold…and he had now moved on.

And Laura had no idea where to, either.

But it wasn't the absolute end, she told herself on the long trudge back to Paddington. The case against her father was set down to be heard in March next year—three more months away. Jake was the prime witness against him. He had to attend the court hearing, give evidence—fulfil the mission that had driven them apart.

A court of law was a public place.
She could go there.
She would go there.

CHAPTER FOURTEEN

LAURA dressed carefully for the first day of the hearing, choosing to wear the professional black suit she donned for business meetings. She wanted Jake to see her as a fully adult woman, established in her career and capable of standing on her own. However, the suit was figure-hugging, accentuating her feminine curves, and she left her hair loose, wanting him to see her as sexy, too, reminding him of the pleasures they had shared.

She had all week to make contact with him, having arranged for the time off work, but her heart was set on sooner rather than later. Arriving early at the court house, she tensely searched the waiting rooms and corridors, hoping to cross paths with Jake. Having no luck at even catching a glimpse of him, she entered the inquiry room, settling on one of the back seats, sure that she would see him here sometime today.

Her father was seated beside his barrister. He saw her, giving her a bulletlike stare before turning away.

She didn't care what he thought of her presence. Only what Jake thought mattered.

The hearing started. Jake had not entered the room. Laura set aside her frustration and listened to the accusations her father had to answer. This was what Jake had been secretly working on—more important to him than their relationship.

Sixteen companies were named—JQE amongst them. Struggling companies that could have been saved by arranging bridging loans but which her father had chosen to bury, gouging millions out of selling off their assets by charging outrageous fees for his services as liquidator.

The judge described it as 'Churning and burning.'

The day dragged on with no sight of Jake, not in the morning session, not in the lunch-break, not in the afternoon session.

Her father was the only witness called. He admitted to earning between four and six million dollars a year from failing companies but belligerently insisted it was by carrying out due process and he was innocent of any wrongdoing. His air of contempt for the court did not endear him to the judge. Laura hated listening to him. She kept darting glances around the room, hoping to see Jake, willing him to appear.

Why wasn't he here?

Surely this was the culmination of his mission for justice.

Shouldn't he be listening to what her father said so he could rebut it?

Jake was sitting in the consultation room, waiting for the prosecuting barrister to report on the afternoon session, feeling buoyantly confident that Alex Costarella would finally be nailed for the fraudulent bastard he was. The glass panels of the door gave him a view of the area directly outside the enquiry room. A rush of people into it signalled that the session was over.

Jake recognised the reporters who had tried to interview him. The case was drawing quite a bit of interest from the business sector of the media. Which was good. Too much skulduggery was hidden from the public. The more people were aware of what went on, the more they could guard against it, or at least question what was happening.

Laura!

Jake bolted to his feet, shocked at seeing her amongst the departing spectators, his mind instantly torn by uncertainty over what she was doing here and the wild urge to stride out and sweep her into a fiercely possessive embrace. It had been so long—almost a year—but just the sight of her had his body buzzing with the need to have her again.

She looked stunning, the black suit barely confining her voluptuous curves, her glorious hair bouncing around her shoulders. His fingers itched to rake through its silky mass. His groin was tingling hotly from a swift rush of blood. He'd never wanted a woman so much. If he reached out to her now, would she happily respond, or…?

More likely she would spurn him, he realised, the surge of excitement draining slowly away. Given that she had believed whatever story her father had spun around the photographs she'd sent him, no doubt believing she'd been used as a malicious thrill on the side, as well, the probability was she was here to support her father against him.

Love…hate—they could colour anyone's judgement.

He watched her join the group of people waiting for the elevator, watched her until steel doors closed behind her, and ached inside for what had been lost. He'd let the past rule his decisions, the long-burning need for justice. It was a crusade for good over evil, yet he knew he would feel no joy in the victory. Satisfaction, perhaps, but no joy.

He had to take the witness stand tomorrow. If Laura attended the hearing again… A violent determination rampaged through him. He would make her believe every word he said, every revelation of the kind of man her father was. It might not win him anything from her on a personal level, but at least she wouldn't be able to sustain any support for her rotten father, who had ruined any chance they might have had for a future together.

The second day...

Laura had no sooner settled on a back-row seat in the inquiry room than her father was on his feet, pushing back the chair he had occupied at his barrister's table so violently it tumbled over. He ignored it, glaring furiously at her as he strode down the aisle, obviously intent on confrontation.

She sat tight, steeling herself to ride out his wrath. Since she and her mother had left the Mosman mansion before Christmas, none of the family had had any personal contact with him. No doubt he contemptuously considered them rats that had deserted the sinking ship, but he had no power over them anymore. He couldn't actually *do* anything to her, not here in public, but if looks could kill, she'd certainly be dead.

'What the hell are you doing here?' he demanded, the thunderous tone of voice promising punishment for her sins against him.

'Listening,' she answered curtly, refusing to be cowed.

Burning hatred in his eyes. 'Are you on with Jake Freedman again?'

'No.'

His lips curled in a sneer. 'Chasing after him.'

She met his vicious mockery with absolute self-determination. 'You lied to me about him, Dad. I've come to hear the truth.'

'Truth!' he scoffed. 'You benefited from his

stepfather's fall. That's the truth. And Freedman isn't about to forget it, not when he's been brooding over it for years.'

The judge's entrance demanded her father's return to his barrister's side. Laura was shaken by the encounter. She'd been all keyed up, hoping that a meeting with Jake might lead to a resumption of their relationship. Fixated on the photographs, she hadn't given any thought to other factors. When all was said and done, she was still her father's daughter, and Jake may well have killed any feeling he'd had for her and moved on, especially after she'd used false evidence to blow him away.

A chance to nothing, she'd said to Eddie, and the truth was she was probably fooling herself about having any chance at all. She sat in a slump of silent despair, not hearing anything until Jake's name was called.

Tension instantly stiffened her spine and pressed her legs tightly together. Her eyes automatically drank in everything about him as he entered the room and was led to the witness box. He wore a sober grey suit and the air of a man all primed to carry out deadly business. James Bond—sleek, sophisticated, sexy, making her heart kick at how handsome he was, making her stomach flutter at how devastating this day could be to her. Even the sound of his voice as he was sworn in evoked memories of intimate moments, making her ache for more.

He shot his gaze around the room before sitting

down. For one electric moment it stopped on her. There was no smile, not the slightest change of expression on his face at seeing her. She didn't smile at him, either. The feelings inside her were too intense. She fiercely willed him to know she was here for him. The moment passed all too quickly, his gaze flicking to the prosecuting barrister as he settled on his chair.

He didn't look at her again.

Not once.

Laura listened to his testimony, hearing a biting edge in every word. It became perfectly clear that her father's intent as a liquidator was exploitation, without any regard to the interests of any company or its creditors. Billable hours extended to clerical staff, even to the tea and coffee lady—each at three hundred dollars an hour. At one meeting with creditors, the coffee served to them came to eighty dollars a cup.

'Nice cup,' the judge remarked acidly.

'Not exactly sweet when the creditors never get their entitlements,' Jake said just as acidly.

The flow of evidence went on and on, backed up by facts and figures that could not be denied. They painted a picture of shocking corruption. Laura felt ashamed of her connection to the man who hadn't cared how many people he hurt in amassing more and more money for himself. She'd known he had a cruel nature. She hadn't known his contempt for others extended so far.

It was sickening.

She understood now how much this mission had meant to Jake, especially given what had happened with his parents. Apart from the personal element, it was right to take her father down, saving others from suffering similar situations. He was doing good, more good than she had ever done in her life, showing up the faults of a system that was a feeding ground for liquidators without any conscience.

It took a big person to stand up and blow the whistle on it, regardless of any cost to himself. She admired Jake's drive to get it done. But her father was right about one thing. She was his daughter and her life had been cushioned in the luxury of his greedy profiteering. It wasn't her fault but she was definitely tainted by it in Jake's mind.

I don't want to want you.

And there was no sign of him wanting her now. He wouldn't even look at her, though she had been willing him to all day. He probably hated the sight of her—a memory of weakness on his part, not to be revisited.

Stay strong.

His whole demeanour, his voice, his laying out of undeniable facts, had been relentlessly strong today. He was not going to reconnect with her. Laura slipped out of the inquiry room as soon as the afternoon session ended, carrying the misery of lost hope with her. There was no point in coming back tomorrow. Jake had obviously shut the door on her and she must now do it on him.

She forced her legs to walk straight to the elevator, forced her finger to jab the *down* button. Other people clustered around her, waiting for the elevator to arrive. Minutes crawled by. There was a buzz of voices commenting on the hearing. Laura heard her father called *one hell of a shark*. No sympathy for him. Nor should there be.

Her own heart suddenly rebelled against leaving Jake believing that she had been here to support her father. The elevator doors opened. The surge forward carried her into the compartment but she wriggled out again, telling herself there was one last stand she had to make—a matter of self-respect if nothing else.

Jake emerged from the inquiry room with his barrister, the two men conferring with each other as they walked out. Laura didn't care if she would be interrupting something important. What she had to say would only take a couple of moments and it was important to her. Her hands clenched in determination. Her chin instinctively lifted. Every nerve in her body was wire-tight as she closed the short distance between them.

As though sensing her approach, Jake's head jerked towards her. His gaze locked on hers, hard and uninviting, twin dark bolts boring into her head. The barrister murmured something to him. Jake's hand sliced a sharp dismissive gesture, his attention not wavering from Laura. She stopped a metre short of him, close enough to be heard, her mind totally focussed on delivering a few last words.

'I found out that my father lied about the photographs. I'm sorry that I let him influence my belief in you, Jake. I wish you well.'

That was it.

She turned and walked back to the elevator where another group of people had gathered, waiting for its return. She could go now, having righted the wrong she had done Jake. And she did wish him well. He was a good man.

She didn't hate him!

The steel guard Jake had put around his feelings for Laura Costarella cracked wide open at this stunning realisation. He was in instant tumult over her apology, wanting to know more, but she had already turned away and was heading for the elevator, not waiting for any response from him. What did that mean? She didn't want one? Didn't expect one?

How long had she known about her father's lie? If it was before this hearing, she wouldn't have attended it to support him. Was it simply curiosity that had drawn her here, a need to know everything that had limited their relationship and made it so impossible to sustain? But surely she wouldn't have bothered unless…she still had feelings for him.

I wish you well….

It was a goodbye line.

He didn't want it to be. He wanted…

The elevator doors opened. Laura was following the group of people into it. She was going and everything within him violently rebelled against letting her go.

Without any conscious thought at all he lifted two fingers to his lips and whistled the most piercing whistle he'd ever produced in his life.

CHAPTER FIFTEEN

THE whistle startled everyone who heard it. Conversations were momentarily cut off. Feet stopped moving. Heads turned. Laura's heart felt as though it had been kicked. Her mind instantly recalled the kiss-off line she'd written to Jake.

As for any future meeting between us, you can whistle for me.

Had he done it?

Please…let it be him wanting a meeting with her.

A meeting with a future in mind.

The other people resumed their movement into the elevator. Laura didn't. She had to turn around, had to see. If it was Jake who had whistled, he'd be looking at her, perhaps holding out a hand in an appeal for her to stay where she was, wait a minute.

A chance to nothing, she told herself, her heart hammering as she acted on her need to know, throwing a quick glance over her shoulder. Jake had left his barrister's side and was striding towards her, determined purpose burning in the eyes that locked onto hers, holding her still until he could reach her.

The elevator doors closed. Laura was the only person left behind. But Jake was coming to her. They hadn't talked to each other for almost a year. She had no idea what was on his mind, yet the leap of hope in hers was so strong, it was impossible to put a guard of caution around it. He could probably see it in her eyes, the wanting, the needing. Pride couldn't hide it. She had none where he was concerned.

He stopped about a metre away from her, tension emanating from him, making her nerves even tighter.

'It's been a long time,' he said.

'Yes,' she agreed, the word coming out huskily. Her throat was choked up with a mountain of tumultuous emotions.

'There's a good coffee shop on the corner of the next block. Can I buy you a cappuccino?'

She swallowed hard to get rid of the lump. He was offering time together, wanting time together. A meeting. 'I'd like that very much,' she answered, her voice still furred with feelings that were totally uncontrollable.

'Good!' he said and stepped around her to press the elevator button, summoning it to this floor again.

Third time lucky, Laura thought giddily.

Jake flashed her a smile. 'I wish you well, too, Laura. I always have.'

She nodded, yearning for far more than well-wishing from him.

'Are you still living with your father?' he asked.

'No. I have a full-time job now. Landscape

designer for a firm of architects. I can afford my own apartment.'

'What about your mother?'

'She moved out the same time I did. She's okay. Much happier.'

'Sharing your apartment?'

'No. Nick Jeffries, our former handyman/gardener, carried her off to his home. He's a widower and they're very much in love.'

'Wow!' Jake grinned, surprised and seemingly delighted by this turn of events. 'I guess you don't have to worry about her anymore.'

'No, I don't. Having nothing to fear from Nick, she's already blooming into a far more positive person.'

'That's good. Great!'

He really did look pleased—pleased because he didn't want anyone to be her father's victim, or pleased because she was completely free and clear of any continuing connection with her father? Was he checking to see if he could reasonably resume a relationship with her with no negative fallout from it? Did he want to? She was still her father's daughter. Nothing could change that.

The elevator arrived and Jake waved an invitation to precede him into it. They were the only people occupying the small compartment on this ride. Jake stood silently beside her on the way down. Laura was too conscious of his close presence to think of anything to say. She had been intensely intimate with this man and the memories of it were flooding through her mind—the passionate kisses, the exquisite sensitivity of his touch. She had to press her thighs tightly together to contain the hot, searing need to have him again.

As they walked out to the street she was fiercely wishing he would take hold of her hand but he didn't attempt even that simple physical link with her. The evening rush hour hadn't quite started. The sidewalk wasn't crowded. There was no reason for Jake to take her arm to keep them together and he didn't. They reached the coffee shop without touching at all and Jake led her to a booth, waiting for her to slide in on one bench seat before seating himself across the table from her.

'Like old times,' she remarked, managing an ironic smile to cover the sick feeling that this might be the last time she shared a table with Jake.

He returned the smile. 'A lot of water has passed under the bridge since then. Are you happy with the career you've chosen?'

She nodded. 'It's very challenging but I'm loving it. What about you, Jake? Have you moved on to renovating another house?'

'Yes. I sold the last one.'

'I know.'

He looked quizzically at her and she flushed, realising she had given away the fact that she had tried to visit him. Too late to take back those revealing words. She heaved a sigh to relieve the tightness in her chest and plunged into telling the truth. What point was there in holding back?

'On the day we left Mosman—it was just before last Christmas—Mum found a bunch of other photographs of you in Dad's safe. They made me realise he'd set you up, then spun a false story to make me believe...' She hesitated, inwardly recoiling from repeating the horribly demeaning picture her father had drawn.

'That I was a liar and a cheat,' Jake finished for her with a wry grimace. 'I didn't blame you for believing him, Laura. It was my fault. I should never have touched you. It put you in a rotten position when I made my move against him.'

His use of the past tense hurt. If he regretted their relationship, what hope was there for a future one? But she was halfway through her explanation and she wanted to finish it.

'Anyhow, it made me feel really bad about how I'd completely written you off, so I went to your house at Woollahra, wanting to apologise, except you were gone and other people had moved in. I had no means of contact with you unless I came to the hearing, and I'm glad I did. Listening to everything being laid out made me understand why you had to take my father down. You were right to do it. And I do wish you well, Jake.'

There!

Definitely water under the bridge now!

And she'd managed it with reasonable dignity.

A waiter arrived to take their order and Jake asked for two cappuccinos, quickly inquiring if she wanted something to eat as well—a toasted sandwich? Laura shook her head. Her stomach was in knots. After the waiter had left them, Jake regarded her seriously for several moments, making the knots even tighter.

'It's not over, Laura,' he said quietly. 'There will be ugly things said about me in the days to come.'

The dirt her father had up his sleeve.

'Will they be true?' she asked.

'Not on any professional level. He can't deny the evidence against him. It's too iron-tight. So I'm confident that nothing will change the eventual outcome. He's gone from the industry, regardless of what he uses in an attempt to discredit me.'

'Do you know what he'll try to use?'

He made a wry grimace. 'You were my only weakness, Laura. I'm anticipating an attack on my character revolving around my involvement with you.'

She frowned. 'But that had nothing to do with how he ran his business.'

'I think he'll try to link it up.'

A fierce rebellion swept through Laura. Her father had been too successful in hurting others, deliberately doing it and taking malicious pleasure in it. She wanted him to fail for once, and be shown up as the liar he was—some justice for the months of misery he'd given her.

She leaned forward, earnestly pressing for Jake

to agree with her. 'I've taken this week off work. I could testify on your behalf. I know you didn't do me any wrong, Jake.'

His face tightened in instant rejection. 'This isn't your war, Laura. It was wrong of me to put you in the line of fire and I won't do it again. I'll ride it through.'

'It *is* my war,' she cried vehemently. 'I've taken the bullets and I want to return them. I'm not ashamed of my involvement with you. It makes a much stronger stand if we ride this through together. Publicly together. Surely you can see that any capital my father might think he could make out of our connection becomes utter nonsense if we're still connected.'

He didn't offer any quick rebuttal this time. The riveting dark eyes scoured hers with blazing intensity. Laura had the sinking feeling he was unsure of her staying power. She hadn't remained strong against her father's manipulation in the past.

'There's no other man in your life, Laura?' he asked quietly.

The question startled her—not what she had been expecting. It offered hope that Jake was considering her suggestion. 'No. I'm free and clear,' she stated firmly.

It suddenly occurred to her that he might not be. He hadn't touched her. Just because the memory of him had made her disinterested in other men didn't mean he'd felt a similar detachment. She'd certainly opened the door for him to move on when she'd shut it on her life.

'I'm sorry. I didn't think,' she blurted out, flushing self-consciously over her single-mindedness, her hands fluttering an apologetic dismissal of her impulsive ideas. 'If you're in another relationship, of course this won't work.'

'I'm not,' he said swiftly, reaching across the table to take one of her hands in his, long strong fingers stroking, soothing her agitation. 'There's nothing I'd like more than to be connected to you again, Laura. I just want to be sure it's right for you.'

A wild joy burst through her heart. She stared at him, scarcely able to believe she did have another chance with him. Warmth from his touch ran up her arm and spread through her entire body, a blissful warmth, promising her the loving she craved. She wanted this man so much, yet it hadn't really been right for her before, not with him limiting their relationship to great dinners and great sex. The temptation to take whatever she could of him played through her mind, but she knew that would never be enough.

'Will you show me the house you're now working on?'

It was a critical question, challenging how much he wanted to be connected to her.

His face relaxed into a smile, his eyes twinkling sexy delight. 'Would after we drink our coffee be too soon?'

She laughed in sheer ecstatic relief. 'No, not too soon. Where is it?'

'Petersham. It's about ten minutes in the train from Town Hall, then a short walk from the station. An easy commute to the city centre.'

'Is it another terrace house?'

'No. A two-bedroom cottage with a yard, both of which have been neglected for years.' He grinned. 'Maybe you can give me some ideas on what to do with the yard.'

It was so wonderful that he was willing to share this project with her, she grinned straight back. 'I'd love to design a cottage garden. Something delightfully old-fashioned. All I've done so far at work is very modern landscape.'

'Then you'll have to go shopping for plants with me,' he said decisively. 'Guide me into buying the best.'

More sharing. Laura's cup of happiness was suddenly bubbling to the brim. 'No problem,' she assured him, revelling in allowing herself to love this man all over again.

The waiter returned with their cappuccinos. Jake released her hand and they sat apart again, but another journey had begun—one that shimmered with the promise of far more than the first they'd taken together. Laura couldn't remember a coffee ever tasting so good.

Jake could scarcely believe this incredibly fortunate turn of events. Laura hadn't moved on. Not from him. And the time apart had not been wasted. She had achieved complete independence from her father and quite clearly would never allow herself to be subjected to his influence again. It was now totally irrelevant that she was Alex Costarella's daughter. She was simply herself—the beautiful, strong, giving woman he had come to love. And since her mother no longer needed her in any protective sense, the way ahead for them was free of any insurmountable complications.

He could throw caution to the winds, share whatever he wanted with Laura without any sense of guilt over how hurt she might be from associating with him. The whole truth was out in the open now. There was no reason to hold back on anything. Where the future might take them as a couple was entirely in their own hands. The most important thing was he could have her again. Nothing else really mattered.

Froth from the cappuccino coated her upper lip. He wanted to lick it off. Her tongue slid out and swept it away. Her beautiful blue eyes twinkled at him teasingly as though she knew what he'd been thinking.

'I haven't wanted any woman since you, Laura,' he said softly. That was the truth, too, and he needed her to know it. The damning photographs could have left doubts in her mind about how deeply he'd felt connected to her. This was a new start and he couldn't bear anything marring it.

She smiled, happiness lighting up her lovely face.

'It's been the same for me, too, Jake, though I did have a lot of bad thoughts about you.'

'The woman in the photographs…she said she was being stalked and pleaded with me to walk her home from the gym. It was an act of kindness, Laura, nothing more.'

The smile broadened. 'I like kindness in a man. Nick is very kind to Mum. She never had that from Dad.'

Neither did you. Only demands and abuse if they weren't met.

Jake understood where Laura was coming from, why marriage was not an attractive proposition to her, but maybe he could change her view of it, given enough time together. She was certainly seeing the difference for her mother.

He wanted a family in his future. The loss of it had driven him all these years and now that the goal he had set himself had been reached, he could plan a different scenario for his life, hopefully with Laura. It was like a miracle that it was possible at all.

She put down her cup and gave him a look of eager anticipation. 'Are we done here? Ready to go?'

Desire roared through him like an express train. He couldn't get her out of the coffee shop fast enough. They started the walk towards Town Hall hand in hand, a joyous bounce in their step. It was rush hour, people crowding past them either way. They came to a building with a recessed entrance and Jake instantly pulled Laura out of the mêlée on the sidewalk and into his embrace against a sheltered side wall.

'I've been wanting to do this ever since I saw you yesterday,' he murmured, his eyes blazing with naked need.

'Yesterday?' she echoed quizzically.

'I thought you'd come for your father. If I'd known you'd come for me…'

He couldn't wait. Like in the garden the first day they'd met, like on their first date on the way to the hotel…he had to kiss her and she wrapped her arms around his neck and kissed him right back, their passion for each other as wildly exhilarating as ever, more so with the freedom from all restrictions.

But they couldn't give it full expression in this public place.

They had to move on.

And they did.

Together.

* * * * *

PRINCE OF SCANDAL

ANNIE WEST

For Karen, Reeze and Daisy,
who celebrate with me
and who understand all the rest.
Thank you!

CHAPTER ONE

RAUL stared unseeingly out of the chopper as it followed the coast south from Sydney. He shouldn't be here when the situation at home was so delicately poised. But he had no choice.

What an unholy mess!

His hands bunched into fists and he shifted his long legs restlessly.

The fate of his nation and the well-being of his subjects were at risk. His coronation, his right to inherit the kingdom he'd been born to and devoted his life to, hung in the balance. Even now he could scarcely believe it.

Desperately the lawyers had sought one legal avenue after another but the laws of inheritance couldn't be overturned, not till he became king. And to become king…

The alternative was to walk away and leave his country prey to the rivalries that had grown dangerous under the last king, Raul's father. Civil war had almost ripped the country apart two generations ago. Raul had to keep his people safe from that, no matter what the personal cost.

His people, his need to work for them, had been what kept him going through the bleak wasteland of disillusionment when his world had turned sour years before. When paparazzi had muckraked and insinuated and his dreams had shattered around him, the people of Maritz had stood by him.

He would stand by them now when they most needed him.

Besides, the crown was *his*. Not only by birthright. By dint of every long day, every hour he'd devoted to mastering the myriad royal responsibilities.

He would not renounce his heritage. His destiny.

Tension stiffened every sinew and anger simmered in his blood. Despite a lifetime's dedication to the nation, despite his experience, training and formidable capacity, it had all come down to the decision of a stranger.

It scored his pride that his future, his country's future, depended on this visit.

Raul opened the investigator's report, skimming familiar details.

Luisa Katarin Alexandra Hardwicke. Twenty-four. Single. Self-employed.

He assured himself this would be straightforward. She'd be thrilled and eager. Yet he wished the file contained a photo of this woman who would play such a pivotal role in his life.

He closed the report with a snap.

It didn't matter what she looked like. He wasn't weak like his father. Raul had learned the hard way that beauty could lie. Emotions played a man for a fool. Raul ruled his life, like his kingdom, with his head.

Luisa Hardwicke was the key to safeguarding his kingdom. She could be ugly as sin and it would make no difference.

Damn! The cow shifted, almost knocking Luisa over. Wearily she struggled to regain her footing in the bog at the edge of the creek.

It had been a long, troubling morning with early milking, generator problems and an unexpected call from the bank manager. He'd mentioned a property inspection that sounded ominously like a first step to foreclosure.

She shuddered. They'd fought so long to keep the small farming co-operative going through drought, illness and flood. Surely the bank couldn't shut them down now. Not when they had a chance to turn things around.

Overhead came the rhythmic thunder of a helicopter. The cow shifted uneasily.

'Sightseers?' Sam shouted. 'Or have you been hiding some well-heeled friends?'

'I wish!' The only ones she knew with that much money were the banks. Luisa's stomach coiled in a familiar twist of anxiety. Time was fast running out for the co-op.

Inevitably her mind turned to that other world she'd known so briefly. Where money was no object. Where wealth was taken for granted.

If she'd chosen she could be there now, a rich woman with not a financial worry in the world. If she'd put wealth before love and integrity, and sold her soul in that devil's bargain.

Just the thought of it made her ill.

She'd rather be here in the mud, facing bankruptcy with the people she loved than be as wealthy as Croesus, if it meant giving up her soul.

'Ready, Sam?' Luisa forced herself to focus. She put her shoulder to the cow. 'Now! Slow and steady.'

Finally, between them, they got the animal unstuck and moving in the right direction.

'Great,' Luisa panted. 'Just a little more and—' Her words were obliterated as a whirring helicopter appeared over the rise.

The cow shied, knocking Luisa. She swayed, arms flailing. Then her momentum propelled her forwards into the boggy mess. Wet mud plastered her from face to feet.

'Luisa!' Are you OK?' Her uncle, bless him, sounded more concerned than amused.

She lifted her head and saw the cow, udder swaying, heave onto firm ground and plod away without a backward glance. Gingerly Luisa found purchase in the sodden ground and crawled to her knees, then her feet.

'Perfect.' She wiped slime from her cheeks. 'Mud's supposed to be good for the complexion, isn't it?' She met Sam's rheumy gaze and smiled.

She flicked a dollop of mud away. 'Maybe we should bottle this stuff and try selling it as a skin tonic.'

'Don't laugh, girl. It might come to that.'

Ten minutes later, her overalls, even her face stiff with drying mud, Luisa left Sam and trudged up to her house. Her mind was on this morning's phone call. Their finances looked frighteningly bleak.

She rolled stiff shoulders. At least a shower was only minutes away. A wash, a quick cup of tea and...

She slowed as she topped the hill and saw a helicopter on the grass behind the house. Gleaming metal and glass glinted in the sun. It was high-tech and expensive—a complete contrast to the weathered boards of the house and the ancient leaning shed that barely sheltered the tractor and her rusty old sedan.

Fear settled, a cold hard weight in her stomach. Could this be the inspection the banker had mentioned? So soon?

It took a few moments before logic asserted itself. The bank wouldn't waste money on a helicopter.

A figure appeared from behind the chopper and Luisa stumbled to a halt.

The sun silhouetted a man who was long, lean and elegant. The epitome of urbane masculinity.

She could make out dark hair, a suit that probably cost more than her car and tractor put together, plus a formidable pair of shoulders.

Then he turned and walked a few paces, speaking to someone behind the helicopter. His rangy body moved with an easy grace that bespoke lithe power. A power that belied his suave tailored magnificence.

Luisa's pulse flickered out of rhythm. *Definitely not a banker.* Not with that athletic body.

He was in profile now. High forehead, long aristocratic nose, chiselled mouth and firm chin. Luisa read determination in that solid jaw, and in his decisive gestures. Determination and something completely, defiantly masculine.

Heat snaked through her. Awareness.

Luisa sucked in a startled breath. She'd never before experienced such an instant spark of attraction. Had wondered if she ever would. She couldn't suppress a niggle of disturbing reaction.

Despite his elegant clothes this man looked…dangerous.

Luisa huffed out a choked laugh. Dangerous? He'd probably faint if he got mud on his mirror-polished shoes.

Behind the house, worn jeans, frayed shirts and thick socks flapped on the clothes line. Her mouth twitched. Mr stepped-from-a-glossy-magazine couldn't be more out of place. She forced herself to approach.

Who on earth was he?

He must have sensed movement for he turned.

'Can I help you?' Her voice was husky. She assured herself that had nothing to do with the impact of his dark, enigmatic stare.

'Hello.' His lips tilted in a smile.

She faltered. He was gorgeous. If you were impressed by impossibly handsome in a tough, masculine sort of way. Or gleaming, hooded eyes that intrigued, giving nothing away. Or the tiniest hint of a sexy cleft in his chin.

She swallowed carefully and plastered on a smile.

'Are you lost?' Luisa stopped a few paces away. She had to tilt her chin up to look him in the eye.

'No, not lost.' His crisp deep voice curled with just a hint of an accent. 'I've come to see Ms Hardwicke. I have the right place?'

Luisa frowned, perplexed.

It was a rhetorical question. From his assured tone to his easy stance, as if he owned the farm and she was the interloper, this man radiated confidence. With a nonchalant wave of his hand he stopped the approach of a burly figure rounding the corner of the house. Already his gaze turned back to the homestead, as if expecting someone else.

'You've got the right place.'

She looked from the figure at the rear of the house whose

wary stance screamed *bodyguard*, to the chopper where the pilot did an equipment check. Another man in a suit stood talking on a phone. Yet all three were focused on her. Alert.

Who were these people? Why were they here?

A shaft of disquiet pierced her. For the first time ever her home seemed dangerously isolated.

'You have business here?' Her tone sharpened.

Instinct, and the stranger's air of command, as if used to minions scurrying to obey, told her this man was in a league far beyond the local bank manager.

An uneasy sensation, like ice water trickling down her spine, made her stiffen.

'Yes, I need to see Ms Hardwicke.' His eyes flicked to her again then away. 'Do you know where I can find her?'

Something in that single look at her face, not once dropping to her filthy clothes, made her burningly self-conscious. Not just of the mud, but the fact that even clean and in her best outfit she'd feel totally outclassed.

Luisa straightened. 'You've found her.'

This time he really looked. The intensity of that stare warmed her till she flushed all over. His eyes widened beneath thick dark lashes and she saw they were green. The deep, hard green of emeralds. Luisa read shock in his expression. And, she could have sworn, dismay.

Seconds later he'd masked his emotions and his expression was unreadable. Only a slight bunching of sleek black eyebrows hinted he wasn't happy.

'Ms *Luisa* Hardwicke?'

He pronounced her name the way her mother had, with a soft s and a lilt that turned the mundane into something pretty.

Premonition clamped a chill hand at the back of her neck. The accent *had* to be a coincidence. That other world was beyond her reach now.

Luisa wiped the worst of the dirt off her hand and stepped forward, arm outstretched. It was time to take charge of this situation. 'And you are?'

He hesitated for a moment, then her fingers were engulfed in his. He bowed, almost as if to kiss her hand. The gesture was charming and outlandish. It sent a squiggle of reaction through her, making her breath falter. Especially as his warm, powerful hand still held hers.

Heat scalded her face and she was actually grateful for the smearing of dirt that concealed it.

He straightened and she had to arch her neck to meet his glittering scrutiny. From this angle he seemed all imposing, austere lines that spoke of unyielding strength.

Luisa blinked and drew a shaky breath, trying to ignore the butterflies swirling in her stomach and think sensibly.

'I am Raul of Maritz.' He said it simply but with such assurance she could almost imagine a blare of trumpet fanfare in the background. 'Prince Raul.'

Raul watched her stiffen and felt the ripple of shock jolt through her. She yanked her hand free and took a step back, arms crossing protectively over her chest.

His mind clicked up a gear as interest sparked. *Not* the welcome he usually received. Fawning excitement was more common.

'Why are you here?' This time the throaty edge to her words wasn't gruff. It made her sound vulnerable and feminine.

Feminine! He hadn't realised she was a woman!

From her husky voice to her muddy boots, square overalls and battered hat that shadowed her grimy face, she had as much feminine appeal as a cabbage. She still hadn't removed the hat. And that walk! Stiff as an automaton.

He froze, imagining her in Maritzian society where protocol and exquisite manners were prized. This was worse than he'd feared. And there was no way out.

Not if he was to claim his throne and safeguard his country.

He clenched his teeth, silently berating the archaic legalities that bound him in this catch-22.

When he was king there'd be some changes.

'I asked what you're doing on my land.' No mistaking the animosity in her tone. More and more intriguing.

'My apologies.' Automatically he smiled, smoothing over his lapse. It was no excuse that the shock of seeing her distracted him. 'We have important matters to discuss.'

He waited for her answering smile. For a relaxation of her rigid stance. There was none.

'We have nothing to discuss.' Beneath the mud her neat chin angled up.

She was giving *him* the brush-off? It was absurd!

'Nevertheless, it's true.'

He waited for her to invite him in. She stood unmoving, staring up balefully. Impatience stirred.

And more, a wave of distaste at the fate that decreed he had to take this woman under his wing. Turn this unpromising material into—

'I'd like you to leave.'

Raul stiffened in indignation. At the same time curiosity intensified. He wished he could see her without that mask of mud.

'I've travelled from my homeland in Europe to speak with you.'

'That's impossible, I tell you. I have no—'

'Far from being impossible, I made the trip for that sole purpose.' Raul drew himself up and took a pace closer, letting his superior height send a silent message. When he spoke again it was in a tone that brooked no opposition. 'I'm not leaving until we've concluded our business.'

Luisa's stomach twisted in knots and her nerves stretched to breaking point as she hurried through the house back to the veranda where she'd left her visitor.

The crown prince of Maritz, her mother's homeland, here at her house! *This couldn't be good.*

She'd tried to send him away, turn her back rather than face anyone from that place. The memories were too poisonous.

But he'd been frighteningly immovable. A single look at that steely jaw told her she wouldn't succeed.

Besides, she needed to know why he was here.

Now, armoured as best she could manage by scouring hot water and clean clothes, she tried to stifle rising panic.

What did he want?

He filled up her veranda with his larger than life presence, making her feel small and insignificant. His spare features reminded her of pictures of the old king in his youth—impossibly handsome with his high cut cheekbones and proud bearing. From his top notch tailoring to his air of command, this man was *someone*.

Yet royalty didn't just pop in to visit.

Disquiet shivered through her. A shadow of the stormy past.

He turned to her. Instantly she felt at a disadvantage. With those chiselled aristocratic features and that uncompromising air of maleness he was…stunning. Despite her wariness, heat ricocheted through her abdomen.

His eyes narrowed. Luisa's heartbeat pattered out of kilter and her mouth dried. With a jolt of shock she realised it was the man himself, as much as his identity that disturbed her.

Luisa laced her fingers rather than straighten her loose shirt, her only clean one after weeks of rain. She wished she could meet him on equal terms, dressed to the nines. But her budget didn't run to new clothes. Or a new hairdryer.

She smoothed damp locks from her face and pushed back her shoulders, ignoring the way her stomach somersaulted. She refused to be intimidated in her own home.

'I was admiring your view,' he said. 'It's lovely countryside.'

Luisa cast her eyes over the familiar rolling hills. She appreciated the natural beauty, but it had been a long time since she'd found time to enjoy it.

'If you'd seen it two months ago after years of drought you wouldn't have been so impressed.' She drew a deep breath, fighting down the sick certainty that this man was trouble. Her skin crawled with nervous tension but she refused to let him see. 'Won't you come in?'

She moved to open the door but with a long stride he beat her to it, gesturing for her to precede him.

Luisa wasn't used to having doors opened for her. That was why she flushed.

She inhaled a subtle, exotic scent that went straight to her head. Luisa bit her lip as tingles shot to her toes. None of the men she knew looked, sounded or smelled as good as Raul of Maritz.

'Please, take a seat.' She gestured jerkily to the scrubbed kitchen table. Luisa hadn't had a chance to move the buckets and tarpaulins from the lounge room, where they'd staved off the leaks from the last downpour.

Besides, she'd long ago learnt that aristocratic birth was no measure of worth. He could sit where her friends and business partners met.

'Of course.' He pulled out a chair and sank into it with as much aplomb as if it were a plushly padded throne. His presence filled the room.

She lifted the kettle, her movements jerky as she stifled hostility. She needed to hear him out. 'Would you like coffee or tea?'

'No, thank you.' His face was unreadable.

Luisa's pulse sped as she met his unblinking regard. Reluctantly she slid into a chair opposite him, forcing herself into stillness.

'So, Your Highness. What can I do for you?'

For a moment longer he regarded her, then he leaned forward a fraction. 'It's not what you can do for me.' His voice was deep, mellow and hypnotic, holding a promise to which she instinctively responded despite her wariness. 'This is about what I can do for you.'

Beware of strangers promising gifts. The little voice inside sent a tremor of disquiet skidding through her.

Years before she'd received promises of wonderful gifts. The future had seemed a magical, glittering land. Yet it had all been a hollow sham. She'd learned distrust the hard way—not once but twice.

'Really?' Her face felt stiff and she found it hard to swallow.

He nodded. 'First I need to confirm you're the only child of Thomas Bevan Hardwicke and Margarite Luisa Carlotta Hardwicke.'

Luisa froze, alarm stirring. He sounded like a lawyer about to break bad news. The voice of warning in her head grew more strident. Surely her ties with Maritz had been completely severed years ago.

'That's right, though I can't see—'

'It pays to be sure. Tell me—' he leaned back in his seat but his eyes never wavered from hers '—how much do you know about my country? About its government and states?'

Luisa fought to remain calm as painful memories surged. This meeting had a nightmare quality. She wanted to scream at him to get to the point before her stretched nerves gave way. But that glittering gaze was implacable. He'd do this his way. She'd known men like him before. She gritted her teeth.

'Enough.' *More than she wanted.* 'It's an alpine kingdom. A democracy with a parliament and a king.'

He nodded. 'My father the king died recently. I will be crowned in a few months.'

'I'm sorry for your loss,' Luisa murmured, struggling to make sense of this. *Why was he here, interrogating her?* The question beat at her brain.

'Thank you.' He paused. 'And Ardissia?'

Luisa's fingers clenched as she fought impatience. She shot him a challenging look. He was like a charming bulldozer, with that polite smile barely cloaking his determination to get his own way.

'It's a province of Maritz, with its own hereditary prince who owes loyalty to the King of Maritz.' Her mouth twisted. 'My mother came from there, *as I'm sure you know.*'

She shivered, cold sweeping up from her toes and wrapping around her heart as bitter memories claimed her.

'Now, my turn for a question.' She planted her palms on the table and leaned forward, fixing him with a stare. 'Why are you here?'

Luisa waited, her heart thudding hectically, watching him survey her beneath lowered brows. He shifted in his seat. Suddenly she wondered if he were uncomfortable too.

'I came to find you.' His expression made her heartbeat speed to a pounding gallop.

'Why?'

'The Prince of Ardissia is dead. I'm here to tell you you're his heiress, Princess Luisa of Ardissia.'

CHAPTER TWO

RAUL watched her pale beneath her tan. Her eyes rounded and she swayed in her seat. Was she going to faint?

Great. A highly strung female!

He thrust aside the fact that anyone would be overcome. That his anger at this diabolical situation made him unreasonable.

She wasn't the only one whose life had been turned on its head! For years Raul had steered his own course, making every decision. Being fettered like this was outrageous.

But the alternative—to turn his back on his people and the life to which he'd devoted himself—was unthinkable.

'Are you all right?'

'Of course.' Her tone was sharp but her eyes were dazed.

They were surprisingly fine eyes, seen without that shadowing hat. Blue-grey a moment ago, now they sparkled brilliant azure. Like a clear summer sky in the Maritzian Alps. The sort of eyes a man could lose himself in.

She blinked and shifted her gaze and Raul was astonished to feel a pang of disappointment.

He watched her gnaw her lip. When she looked up and flushed to find him watching, he noticed the ripe contours of her mouth. With the grime washed away, her features were pleasant, regular and fairly attractive.

If you liked the artless, scrubbed bare style.

Raul preferred his women sophisticated and well groomed.

What sort of woman didn't take the time to style her hair?

Pale and damply combed off her face, it even looked lopsided. Anyone less fitted for this—

'I can't be his heir!' She sounded almost accusing.

His brows rose. As if he'd waste precious time here on a whim!

'Believe me, it's true.'

She blinked and he had the sense there was more going on behind her azure eyes than simple surprise.

'How is it possible?' She sounded as if she spoke to herself.

'Here.' Raul opened the briefcase Lukas had brought. 'Here's your grandfather's will and your family tree.'

He'd planned for his secretary, Lukas, to take her through this. But he'd changed his mind the moment he saw Luisa Hardwicke and how unprepared she was for this role. Better do this himself. The fewer who dealt with her at this early stage the better.

Raul suppressed a grimace. What had begun as a delicate mission now had unlimited potential for disaster. Imagine the headlines if the press saw her as she was! He wouldn't allow the Maritzian crown to be the focus of rabid media gossip again. Especially at this difficult time.

He strode round the table and spread the papers before her.

She shifted in her seat as if his presence contaminated her. Raul stiffened. Women were usually eager to get close.

'Here's your mother.' He modulated his tone reassuringly. 'Above her, your grandfather, the last prince.'

She lifted her head from examining the family tree. Again the impact of that bright gaze hit him. He'd swear he felt it like a rumbling echo inside his chest.

'Why isn't my uncle inheriting? Or my cousin, Marissa?'

'You're the last of your family.'

Her brow puckered. 'She must have been so young. That's awful.'

'Yes.' The accident was a tragic waste of life. And it altered the succession.

She shook her head. 'But I'm not part of the family! My mother was disinherited when she fell in love with an Australian and refused to marry the man her father chose.'

She knew about that? Did that explain her animosity?

'Your grandfather blustered but he never disinherited her. We only discovered that recently when his will was read.' The Prince of Ardissia had been an irascible tartar but he had too much pride in his bloodline to cut off a direct descendant. 'You're definitely eligible to inherit.'

How much easier life would be if she weren't!

If there were no Ardissian princess he wouldn't be in this appalling situation.

'I tell you it's impossible!' She leaned forward, her brow pleating as she scanned the papers.

The scent of lavender wafted to him. Raul inhaled, intrigued. He was used to the perfectly balanced notes of the most expensive perfumes. Yet this simple fragrance was strangely appealing.

'It *can't* be right.' She spoke again. 'He disinherited me too. We were told so!'

Startled, he looked down to find her eyes blazing up at him. Her chin was angled in the air and for the first time there was colour in her cheeks.

She looked…pretty. In an unsophisticated way.

And she knew more than he'd expected. Fascinating.

'Despite what you were told, you're his heiress. You inherit his fortune and responsibilities.' He summoned an encouraging smile. 'I've come to take you home.'

'Home?' Luisa shot to her feet, the chair screeching across the floor. 'This is my home! I belong here.' She gestured to the cosy kitchen she'd known all her life.

She fought a sense of unreality. This had to be an appalling mistake.

From the moment he'd mentioned Ardissia and Maritz bitter recollection had cramped her belly and clouded her brain. It had taken a superhuman effort to hear him out.

'Not any more.' Across the scrubbed table he smiled.

He really was unbelievably good-looking.

Until you looked into those cool eyes. Had he thought her too unaware to notice his smile didn't reach his eyes?

'You've got a new life ahead of you. Your world will change for ever.' His smile altered, became somehow more intimate, and to her surprise Luisa felt a trickle of unfamiliar warmth spread through her body.

How had that happened?

'You'll have wealth, position, prestige—the best of everything. You'll live a life of luxury, as a princess.'

A princess.

The words reverberated in Luisa's skull. Nausea rose.

At sixteen she'd heard those same words. It had been like a dream come true. What girl wouldn't be excited to discover a royal bloodline and a doting grandfather promising a life of excitement and privilege?

Luisa's heart clutched as she remembered her mother, pale but bravely smiling, seated at this table, telling her she had to make up her own mind about her future. Saying that, though she'd turned her back on that life, it was Luisa's choice if she wanted to discover her birthright.

And, like the innocent she was, Luisa had gone. Lured by the fairy tale fantasy of a picture book kingdom.

Reality had been brutally different. By the time she'd rejected what her grandfather offered and made her own way home, she'd been only too grateful he hadn't publicly presented her as his kin. That he'd kept her a cloistered guest during her 'probation' period. Only her closest family knew she'd ever been tempted by the old man's false promises of a joyful family reunion.

She'd been naïve but no more.

Now she knew too much about the ugly reality of that aristocratic society, where birth and connections mattered more than love and common decency. If her grandfather's actions hadn't been enough, she only had to recall the man she'd thought she'd loved. How he'd schemed to seduce her when he realised her secret identity. All because of his ambition.

Luisa's stomach heaved and she reached out blindly for the table, shaking her head to clear the nightmarish recollections.

'I don't want to be a princess.'

Silence. Slowly she turned. Prince Raul's hooded eyes were wide, impatience obliterated by shock.

'You can't be serious,' he said finally, his voice thickening with that appealing accent.

'Believe me, I was never more so.'

Revulsion filled Luisa as she remembered her grandfather. He'd invited her to join him so he could groom her into the sort of princess he wanted. To do his bidding without question. To be the sort his daughter had failed to be.

At first Luisa had been blind to the fact he merely wanted a pawn to manipulate, not a granddaughter to love.

He'd shown his true colours when news arrived of her mother's terminal illness. He'd refused Luisa's tearful, desperate pleas to return. Instead he'd issued an ultimatum—that she break off all contact with her parents or give up her new life. As for Luisa's begging that he fund further medical treatment, he'd snarled at her for wasting time on the woman who'd turned her back on his world.

That heartless betrayal, so blatant, so overwhelming, still sickened Luisa to the core.

That was who she was heir to! A cruel, ruthless tyrant. No wonder she'd vowed not to have anything to do with her bigoted, blue-blooded family.

She recalled her grandfather bellowing his displeasure at her ingratitude. At her inability to be what he wanted, play the part.

A hand on her arm tugged her from her thoughts. She looked up into a searing gaze. Black eyebrows tilted in a V and Raul's nostrils flared as if scenting fear.

This close he was arresting. Her stomach plunged in free-fall as she stared back. Tingling sensation spread from his touch.

Luisa swallowed and his eyes followed the movement.

The intensity of his regard scared her. The beat of her blood was like thunder in her ears. She felt unprotected beneath a gaze that had lost its distance and now seemed to flare with unexpected heat.

'What is it? What are you thinking?' Gone was the smooth tone. His words were staccato sharp.

Luisa drew a shaky breath, disoriented by the arcing heat that snapped and shimmered in the air between them. By the hazy sense of familiarity she felt with this handsome stranger.

'I'm thinking you should let me go.'

Immediately he stepped back, his hand dropping. 'Forgive me. For a moment you looked faint.'

She nodded. She'd felt queasy. That explained her unsteadiness. It had nothing to do with his touch.

The electricity sparking between them was imaginary.

He thrust a hand through his immaculately combed hair as if, for an instant, he too felt that disturbing sensation. But then his dark locks fell back into perfect position and he was again cool, clear-eyed and commanding.

Swiftly Luisa turned to grab a glass. She gulped down cold water, hoping to restore a semblance of normality. She felt as if she'd been wrung inside out.

Finally she willed her scrambled thoughts into order. It didn't help that she sensed Prince Raul's gaze skewer her like an insect on a pin.

Setting her jaw, she turned.

He leaned against the dresser, arms folded and one ankle casually resting on the other. He looked unattainably sexy and a little scary. His brow was furrowed as if something perplexed him, but that only emphasised the strength of his features.

'When you've had time to absorb the news, you'll see going to Maritz is the sensible thing.'

'Thank you, but I've already absorbed the news.' Did he

have any idea how patronising he sounded? Annoyance sizzled in her blood.

He didn't move but his big body was no longer relaxed. His folded arms with their bunched muscles drew her eyes. Suddenly he looked predatory rather than suavely elegant.

Her skin prickled.

'The money doesn't tempt you?' His mouth compressed. Obviously he thought money outweighed everything else.

Just like her grandfather and his cronies.

Luisa opened her mouth, then snapped it shut as her dazed brain cells finally revved into action.

Money!

In her shock that hadn't even registered. She thought of the looming debts, repairs they'd postponed, Sam's outdated milking machine and her own rattletrap car. The list was endless.

'How much money?' She wanted nothing of the high society position. But the cash…

The prince unfolded his arms and named a sum that made her head spin. She braced herself against the table.

'When do I get it?' Her voice was scratchy with shock.

Did she imagine a flash of satisfaction in those dark green eyes?

'You're princess whether you use the title or not. Nothing can alter that.' He paused. 'But there are conditions on inheriting your wealth. You must settle in Maritz and take up your royal obligations.'

Luisa's shoulders slumped. What he suggested was impossible. She'd rejected that world for her own sanity. Accepting would be a betrayal of herself and all she held dear.

'I can't.'

'Of course you can. I'll make the arrangements.'

'Don't you listen?' Luisa gripped the table so hard her bones ached. 'I'm not going!' Life in that cold, cruel society would kill her. 'This is my home. My roots are here.'

He shook his head, straightening to stand tall and imposing. The room shrank and despite her anger she felt his formidable magnetism tug at her.

'You have roots in Maritz too. What have you got here but hard work and poverty? In my country you'll have a privileged life, mixing in the most elite circles.'

How he sounded like her snobbish grandfather.

'I prefer the circles I mix in.' Fire skirled in her belly at his condescension. 'The people I love are here.'

He scowled. 'A man?' He took a step closer and, involuntarily, Luisa retreated a pace before the fierce light in his eyes.

'No, my friends. And my father's brother and his wife.' Sam and Mary, almost a generation older than Luisa's parents, had been like doting grandparents through her sunny childhood and the darkest days. She wouldn't leave them, ageing and in debt, for a glamorous, empty life far away.

The sharp-eyed man before her didn't look impressed.

Had her grandfather once looked like Prince Raul? Proud, determined, good-looking and boy, didn't he know it!

Standing there, radiating impatience, Raul embodied everything she'd learned to despise.

Determination surged anew.

'Thank you for coming to tell me in person.' She drew herself up, level with his proud chin, and folded his papers with quick, precise movements. 'But you'll have to find someone else to inherit.' She breathed deep. 'I'll see you out.'

Raul's mouth tightened as the chopper lifted.

Thrilled! Luisa Hardwicke had been anything but. Just as well he'd told her only about her inheritance, not the more challenging aspects of her new role. She'd been so skittish it was wiser to break that news later.

He'd never met a more stubborn woman. She'd all but thrown him out!

Indignation danced in his veins and tightened his fists.

Something motivated her that he didn't know about. He needed to discover what it was. More, he had to discover the trigger that would make her change her mind.

For an instant back there he'd been tempted simply to

kidnap her. The blood of generations of warriors and robber barons as well as monarchs flowed in his veins. It would have been easy to scoop her up in his arms and sequester her till she saw reason. *So satisfying.*

An image of Luisa Hardwicke filled his mind. She stared defiantly up with flashing cerulean eyes.

Raul recalled her shirt lifting when she reached for a glass, revealing her lusciously curved bottom in snug jeans. The feminine shape outlined by her shirt when she moved. A shape at odds with his original impression.

Fire streaked through Raul's belly.

Perhaps there would be compensations after all.

Luisa Hardwicke had a wholesome prettiness that appealed far more than it ought. He'd made it his business these last eight years to surround himself only with glamorous, sophisticated women who understood his needs.

He grimaced, facing a truth he rarely acknowledged. That if he'd once had a weakness it had been for the sort of forthright honesty and fresh openness she projected.

The sort he'd once believed in.

Sordid reality had cured him of any such frailty. Yet being with her was like hearing an echo of his past, remembering fragments of dreams he'd once held. Dreams now shattered beyond repair by deceit and betrayal.

And, despite his indignation, he responded to her pride, her pluck.

It was an inconvenience that complicated his plans. Yet perversely he admired the challenge she represented. What a change from the compliant, eager women he knew! In other circumstances he'd applaud her stance.

Besides, he saw now, a spineless nonentity would never have been suitable for what was to come. Or so surprisingly appealing.

Raul tugged his mind back to business. He needed a lever to ensure she saw sense. Failure wasn't an option when his nation depended on him.

'Lukas, you said the farming co-op is in debt?'

'Yes sir, heavily so. I'm amazed it's still running.'

Raul looked back at the tiny speck that was her home. A sliver of regret pierced him. He'd wanted to avoid coercion but she left him no choice.

'Buy the debts. Immediately. I want it settled today.'

The roar of a helicopter brought Luisa's head up.

It couldn't be. After rejecting her inheritance yesterday there was no reason for her path and Prince Raul's to cross again. Yet she was drawn inexorably to the window. It couldn't be but it was. Prince Raul—here!

To Luisa's annoyance, her heart pattered faster as she watched his long, powerful frame vault from the chopper.

Twenty-four hours had given her time to assure herself he wasn't nearly as imposing as she remembered.

She'd been wrong.

Luisa had searched him on the web yesterday, learning his reputation for hard work and wealth. The reports also referred to discreet liaisons with gorgeous women.

Yet no photos did justice to his impact in the flesh. Her breath caught as he loped up the steps. Good thing she was immune.

'Luisa.' He stood before her, wide shoulders filling the open doorway, his voice smooth like dark chocolate with a hint of spice as he lingered on her name.

A tremor rippled through her as she responded to the exotic sound of her name on his tongue. It maddened her that she should react so. She pulled herself together, fiercely quelling a riot of unfamiliar emotions.

'Your Highness.' She gripped the door hard. 'Why are you here? We finished our business yesterday.' Surely he had VIPs to see, deals to forge, women to seduce.

He bent over her hand in another courtly almost-kiss that knotted her stomach. She had to remind herself not to be impressed by surface charm. *Been there, done that.*

Yet her gaze riveted on his austerely handsome face as he straightened. The flash of green fire in his eyes sent tendrils of heat curling through her. His fingers squeezed and her pulse accelerated.

'Call me Raul.'

It went against the grain but to refuse would be churlish.

'Raul.' It was crazy but she could almost taste his name in her mouth, like a rich, full-bodied wine.

'Aren't you going to invite me in?' One dark eyebrow rose lazily as if her obstinacy amused him. She bit down on a rude response. He must have good reason to return. The sooner she heard it the sooner he'd go.

'Please, come in.' She led the way to the lounge room, ignoring the jitter of nerves in her stomach.

Instead of making himself comfortable, he took up a position in front of the window. A commanding position, she noticed uneasily as premonition skittered across her nape.

She didn't like the glint in his eye or his wide-legged stance, as if claiming her territory for his own. She stood facing him, refusing to be dominated.

'You haven't changed your mind?'

She lifted her chin a fraction. 'Not if the cash comes with strings attached.'

Desperate as she was for money, she couldn't agree.

She'd spent yesterday afternoon consulting her solicitor. There *must* be a way to access some of the money she was in line to inherit without giving up her life here. She didn't trust Raul, a man with his own agenda, to be straight with her on that.

It was too soon to know, but the possibility she could negotiate enough funds to give the co-op the boost it needed had given her a better night's sleep than she'd had in ages. It buoyed her now, strengthening her confidence.

'Can I persuade you to reconsider?' His mouth turned up in the barest hint of a smile, yet even that should have come with a health warning.

Her breath sawed in her throat and her pulse quickened.

Luisa thought of the enquiries being made on her behalf.

She'd be a fool to give in to his preposterous suggestion. 'Absolutely not.' The very thought of accepting made her ill.

'That's unfortunate.' He paused so long her nerves stretched taut. 'Very unfortunate.' He looked grim.

Finally he reached into his jacket pocket. 'In that case, these are for you.'

Bewildered, Luisa accepted the papers. 'You want me to sign away my inheritance?' She'd sign nothing without legal advice.

He shook his head. 'Take your time. They're self-explanatory.'

Confused, she skimmed the papers. Unlike yesterday's, these weren't rich parchment. They looked more like the loan documents that were the bane of her life.

Luisa forced herself to concentrate. Hard to do with his stare on her. When finally she began to understand, the world spun around her.

'You've bought the co-op's debts.' Disbelieving, she shuffled the papers, eyes goggling. 'All of them!'

And in one day. Each paper had yesterday's date.

Was it even possible?

Bewildered, she looked up. The gravity of his expression convinced her more than the typed words.

Luisa sank abruptly onto the arm of a chair, her knees too wobbly to take her weight, her breath choppy.

What strings had he pulled to manage that in a single day? Luisa couldn't conceive of such power. Yet, staring up at the man before her, she realised he wielded authority as easily as she managed a milking machine.

The realisation dried her mouth.

'Why?' Her voice was a hoarse rasp.

He paced closer, looming between her and the light from the window. 'On the day you sign the documents accepting your inheritance, I'll make a gift of them. You can rip them into confetti.'

Relief poured through her veins so suddenly she shook.

He was so obstinate! He still didn't accept her rejection. No doubt he thought it embarrassing that the heir to a royal title was neck-deep in debt.

It was a generous gesture. One she'd compensate him for if she found a way to access the funds.

'But I'm not going. I'm staying here.'

'You won't.'

Had anyone ever denied him what he wanted?

Impatient energy radiated off him. And that chin—she'd never seen a more determined face.

Luisa stood. She needed to assert herself and end this nonsense. It was time he accepted she knew her mind. 'I've got no plans to leave.'

He held her gaze as the seconds stretched out. His expression didn't change but a frisson of anxiety skipped up her back, like a spider dancing on her vertebrae.

'Knowing how committed you are to the well-being of your family and friends, I'm sure you'll change your mind.' His voice held steel beneath the deep velvet inflection. 'Unless you want them to lose everything.'

He spoke so matter-of-factly it took a moment to register the threat.

Luisa's face froze and a gasp caught inside as her throat closed convulsively.

Blackmail?

She opened her mouth but no sound emerged. Paper cascaded to the floor from her trembling hands.

'You…can't be serious!'

Slowly he shook his head. 'Never more so, Luisa.'

'Don't call me that!' The way he said her name, with the same lilting accent her mother had used, was like a travesty of a familiar endearment.

'Princess Luisa, then.'

She took a furious step forward, her hands clenching in frustration. 'This has to be a joke.' But no humour showed on his stern features. 'You can't foreclose! You'd destroy the livelihood of a dozen families.' And her father's dream. What she had worked for most of her life.

After she'd returned home to nurse her mother, Luisa had never found time to go back and finish school. Instead she'd stayed on to help her father, who'd never fully recovered from the loss of his wife.

'The decision is yours. You can save them, if they mean as much as you claim.'

He meant it! The grim determination in his granite-set jaw was nothing to the resolution in his glittering eyes.

'But…*why?*' Luisa shook her head, trying to find sense in a world turned topsy-turvy. 'You can find another heir, someone who'd be thrilled to live the life you're offering.' Someone happy to give up her soul for the riches he promised. 'I'm not princess material!'

The gleam in his eyes suggested he agreed.

'There *is* no one else, Luisa. You are the princess.'

'You can't dictate my future!' Luisa planted her hands on her hips, letting defiance mask her sudden fear. 'Why are you getting so personally involved?'

When her grandfather had made contact it had been through emissaries. He hadn't come to her. Yet Raul as crown prince was far more important than her grandfather.

He took her hand before she could snatch it away. Heat engulfed her, radiating from his touch and searing her skin even as his intentions chilled her marrow.

'I have a stake in your future,' he murmured.

Automatically she jerked up her chin. 'Really?' The word emerged defiantly.

'A very personal stake.' His grip firmed, all except for his thumb, which stroked gently across her palm, sending little judders of awareness through her. 'Not only are you the Ardissian heiress, you're destined to be Queen of Maritz.' He paused, eyes locking with hers.

'That's why I'm here. To take you back as my bride.'

CHAPTER THREE

LUISA watched his firm lips shape the word 'bride'. Her head reeled.

There was no laughter in his eyes. No wildness hinting at insanity. Just a steady certainty that locked the protest in her mouth.

Her lungs cramped from lack of oxygen as her breath escaped in a whoosh. She lurched forward, dragging in air. He grasped her hand tight and reached for her shoulder as if to support her.

Violently she wrenched away, breaking his grip and retreating to stand, panting, beside the window.

'Don't touch me!'

His eyes narrowed to slits of green fire and she sensed that behind his calm exterior lurked a man of volatile passions.

'Explain. Now!' she said when she'd caught her breath.

'Perhaps you'd better sit.'

So he could tower over her? No, thank you! 'I prefer to stand.' Even if her legs felt like unset jelly.

'As you wish.' Why did it sound like he granted her a special favour in her own house?

He had royal condescension down to an art form.

'You were going to explain why you need to marry.' For the life of her, Luisa couldn't say 'marry me'.

His look told her he didn't miss the omission.

'To ascend the throne I must be married.' At her stare he

continued. 'It's an old law, aimed to ensure an unbroken royal lineage.'

A tremor scudded through her at the idea of 'ensuring the royal lineage'. *With him.*

It didn't matter how handsome he was. She'd learnt looks could hide a black heart. It was the inner man that counted. From what she'd seen, Raul was as proud, opinionated and selfish as her detested grandfather.

The way he looked when she challenged him—jaw tight and eyes flashing malachite sparks, was warning enough.

Luisa's heartbeat pounded so hard she had trouble hearing his next words.

'It's tradition that the crown prince take a bride from one of Maritz's principalities. When we were in our teens a contract was drawn up for my marriage to your cousin, Marissa, Princess of Ardissia. But Marissa died soon after.'

'I'm sorry,' Luisa said gruffly. She searched his features for regret but couldn't read anything. Didn't he feel *something* for his fiancée who'd died?

She pursed her lips. Obviously the heartless arranged marriage was still alive and thriving in Maritz!

'After that I was in no hurry to tie myself in marriage. But when my father died recently it was time to find another bride.'

'So you could inherit.' Luisa shivered, remembering that world where marriages were dynastic contracts, devoid of love. She crossed her arms protectively. How could he be so sanguine about it?

'My plans were curtailed when your grandfather's will was read and we discovered you would inherit. Before then, given what he'd said about disowning your mother, your branch of the family didn't feature in our considerations.'

He made them sound like tiresome complications in his grand design! Indignation rose anew.

'What has the will got to do with your marriage?'

'The contract is binding, Luisa.' He loomed far too close. Her lungs constricted, making her breathing choppy.

'But how?' Luisa paced away, urgently needing space. 'If Marissa is—'

'Everyone, including the genealogists and lawyers, believed your grandfather's line would die with him. The news he had a granddaughter who hadn't been disinherited was a bombshell.' He didn't look as if the news had pleased him. 'You should be thankful we were able to find you before the media got the story. You'd have had press camped here around the clock.'

'You're overdramatising.' Luisa's hands curled tight as she forced down growing panic. 'I've got nothing to do with your wedding.'

One dark eyebrow winged upwards. 'The antiquated style of the contract means I'm bound to marry the Princess of Ardissia.' He paused, his mouth a slash of pure displeasure. *'Whoever she is.'*

'You're out of your mind!' Luisa retreated a frantic step, her stomach a churning mess. This truly *was* a nightmare. 'I never signed any contract!'

'It doesn't matter. The document is legal.' His lips twisted. 'The best minds in the country can't find a way out of it.'

She shook her head, her hair falling across her face as she backed up against the window. 'No way! No matter what your contract says, you can't take me back there as—'

'My bride?' The words dropped into echoing silence. Luisa heard them repeat over and over in her numbed brain, like a never-ending ripple spreading in a still, icy pool.

'Believe me; I'll do what's necessary to claim my throne.' His chin lifted regally, making clear what he hadn't put in words: that he didn't wish to marry someone so far beneath him. Someone so unappealing.

Why was he so desperate? Did power mean so much?

Luisa choked on rising anger. Twenty-four years old and she'd received two marriage offers—both from ambitious men who saw her as nothing but a means to acquire power! Why couldn't she meet a caring, honest man who'd love her for herself? She felt soiled and cheap.

'You expect me to give up my life and marry you, a total

stranger, so you can become king?' What century had he dropped out of? 'You're talking antiquated nonsense.'

His look grazed like shards of ice on bare skin. 'It may be antiquated but I must marry.'

She jutted her chin. 'Marry someone else!'

Something dangerous and dark flashed in his eyes. But when he spoke his words were measured. She sensed he hung onto his control by a thread.

'If I could I would. If you hadn't existed or if you'd already married, the contract would be void and I could choose another bride.'

As if choosing a wife took a minimum of time and effort!

Though in his case it might. With his looks, sexual magnetism and wealth there'd be lots of women eager to overlook the fact they tied themselves to a power hungry egotist!

His deep voice sent a tremor rippling through her over-wrought body. 'There's no more time to find a way out. I need to be married within the constitutional time limit or I can't inherit.'

'Why should I care?' Luisa rubbed her hands up chilled arms, trying to restore warmth. 'I don't even know you.'

And what she did know she didn't like.

He shrugged and unwillingly Luisa saw how the fluid movement drew attention to those powerful shoulders. The sort of shoulders that belonged on a surf lifesaver or an outback farmer, not a privileged aristocrat.

'I'm the best person for the kingship. Some would say the only suitable one. I've trained a lifetime for it.'

'Others could learn.'

He shook his head. 'Not now. Not in time. There was unrest in the last years of my father's reign. That's growing. A strong king is what the country needs.'

The sizzle in his eyes stopped her breath.

'That leaves only one option.'

She was his only option!

'I don't care!' Cool glass pressed against her back as he

took a pace towards her and she stepped back. 'Let them crown someone else. I'm not a sacrificial lamb for the slaughter.'

His lips curled in a knowing smile that should have repelled her. Yet her heart hammered as she watched his eyes light with a gleam that warmed her from tip to toe.

'You think marriage to me would be a hardship?' His voice dropped to a low pitch that feathered like a sultry breeze across her suddenly flushed skin. 'That I don't know how to please a woman?'

Luisa swallowed hard, using her hands to anchor herself to the windowsill behind her rather than be drawn towards the glittering green gaze that seemed now to promise unspoken delights.

He was far more dangerous than she'd realised.

'Be assured, Luisa, that you will find pleasure in our union. You have my word on it.'

A beat of power, of heat, pulsed between them and she knew how an animal felt, mesmerised by a predator.

'The answer is still no,' she whispered hoarsely, shocked at the need to force down a betraying weakness that made her respond to his sensual promise. Why did her dormant hormones suddenly jangle into life around *him*?

For a long moment they stood, adversaries in a silent battle of wills.

'Then, sadly, you leave me no choice.' The fire in his eyes was doused as if it had never been. A flicker of what might have been regret shadowed his gaze then disappeared. 'Just remember that decision, and the outcome, are entirely yours.'

Already he turned away. Only her hand on his elbow stopped him.

'What do you mean?' Fear was a sour tang in her mouth.

He didn't turn. 'I have business to finalise before I leave. Some farms to dispose of.'

Panic surged. Luisa's fingers tightened like a claw on the fine wool of his suit. She stepped round to look up into his stern face.

'You can't foreclose! They haven't done anything to you.'

His stare pinioned her. He shook off her hand.

'In a choice between your relatives and my country there is no contest.' He inclined his head. 'Goodbye, Luisa.'

'I'm sure Mademoiselle will be happy with this new style. A little shorter, a little more chic. Yes?'

Luisa dragged herself from her troubled reverie and met the eyes of the young Frenchwoman in the mirror. Clearly the stylist was excited at being summoned to the Prince's exclusive Parisian residence. Unlike the nail technician who'd barely resisted snorting her displeasure when Luisa had refused false nails, knowing she'd never manage them. Or the haughty couturier who'd taken her measurements with barely concealed contempt for Luisa's clothes.

The hair stylist hadn't been daunted at the prospect of working on someone as ordinary as Luisa.

Perhaps she liked a challenge.

'I'm sure it will be lovely.' Another time Luisa would have been thrilled, having her hair done by someone with such flair and enthusiasm. But not today, just hours after Raul's private jet had touched down in Paris.

It had all happened too fast. Even her goodbyes to Sam and a tearful Mary, crying over the happy news that Luisa was taking up her long lost inheritance.

How she wished she were with them now. Back in the world she knew, where she belonged.

Luisa gritted her teeth, remembering how Raul had taken the initiative from her even in her farewells.

When she'd gone to break the news it was to find he'd been there first. Her family and friends were already agog with the story of Luisa finally taking her 'rightful place' as a princess. And with news their debts were to be cancelled.

Yet Luisa had at least asserted herself in demanding Raul install a capable farm manager in her place to get the co-op on its feet. She refused to leave her friends short-handed.

In the face of their pleasure, Luisa had felt almost selfish, longing to stay, when so much good came out of her departure. Yet she'd left part of herself behind.

Her family and friends would have been distraught, knowing why she left. They wouldn't have touched the Prince's money if they knew the truth. But she couldn't do that to them. She couldn't ruin them for her pride.

Or her deep-seated fear of what awaited her in Maritz.

She shivered when she thought of entering Raul's world. Being with a man who should repel her, yet who—

'These layers will complement the jaw line, see? And make this lovely hair easier to manage.'

Luisa nodded vaguely.

'And, you will forgive me saying, cut even on both sides suits you better, yes?'

Luisa looked up, catching a sparkle in the other woman's eye. Heat seeped under her skin as she remembered her previous lopsided cut. She tilted her chin.

'My friend wants to become a hairdresser. She practised on me.'

'Her instincts were good, but the execution…' The other woman made one last judicious snip, then stepped away. 'Voila! What do you think?'

For the first time Luisa really focused. She kept staring as the stylist used a mirror to reveal her new look from all sides.

It wasn't a new look. It was a new woman!

Her overgrown hair was now a gleaming silky fall that danced and slid around her neck as she turned, yet always fell sleekly back into place. It was shorter, barely reaching her shoulders, but shaped now to the contours of her face. Dull dark blonde had been transformed into a burnished yet natural light gold.

'What did you do?'

Luisa didn't recognise the woman in the mirror. A woman whose eyes looked larger, her face almost sculpted and quite… arresting. She turned her head, watching the slanting sunlight catch the seemingly artless fall of hair.

The Frenchwoman shrugged. 'A couple of highlights to accentuate your natural golden tones and a good cut. You approve?'

Luisa nodded, unable to find words to describe what she felt. She remembered those last months nursing her mother, poring with her over fashion and beauty magazines borrowed from the local library. Her mother, with her unerring eye for style, would point out the cut that would be perfect for Luisa. And Luisa would play along, pretending that when she'd finally made her choice she'd visit a salon and have her hair styled just so. As if she had time or money to spare for anything other than her mother's care and the constant demands of the farm.

'It's just long enough to put up for formal occasions.'

Luisa's stomach bottomed at the thought of the formal occasions she'd face when they reached Maritz.

This couldn't be real. It couldn't be happening. *How could she have agreed?*

Suddenly she needed to escape. Needed to draw fresh air into her lungs, far from the confines of this gilt-edged mansion with its period furniture and discreet servants.

It hit her that, from the moment Raul had delivered his ultimatum, she'd not been alone. His security men had been on duty that final night she'd slept at home. Probably making sure she didn't do a midnight flit! After that there'd been stewards, butlers, chauffeurs.

And Raul himself, invading her personal space even when he stood as far from her as possible.

The stylist had barely slid the protective cape off Luisa's shoulders when she was on her feet, full of thanks for the marvellous cut and turning towards the door.

Her thoughts froze as the Frenchwoman looked at something over Luisa's shoulder then sank into a curtsey.

'Ah, Luisa, Mademoiselle. You've finished?' The deep voice curled across her senses like smoke on the air. She reminded herself it was distaste that made her shiver.

'Yes. We've finished.' Stiffening her spine, she turned.

Clear afternoon light spilled across the parquet floor and highlighted Raul where he stood just inside the doorway. Once again his splendour hit her full force. Not just the elegance of hand-stitched shoes and a beautifully crafted suit that clung to his broad shoulders. The impact of his strong personality was stamped on his austere features.

Even knowing his ruthlessness, it was hard not to gawk in appreciation. Luisa saw the stylist surreptitiously primping.

Annoyance sizzled. It wasn't just her. He had this effect on other women.

'I like your new look.' Raul's sudden smile was like warm honey. The flare of appreciation in his eyes even looked genuine. She told herself she didn't care.

'Thank you.' Her tone was stiff.

Yet Luisa's pulse raced. She put it down to dislike. How dared he come here with his gracious smile and his fluent French, charming her companion as if he were a kind benefactor!

Finally, after a long exchange of compliments, the stylist headed to the door. Luisa followed.

She should have known it wouldn't be so easy. A firm hand grasped her elbow as she walked past Raul.

'Where are you going?'

'Out.' She looked pointedly at his restraining hand.

'That's impossible. You have another appointment.'

The simmering fury she'd battled for days spiked.

'Really? How strange. I don't recall making any appointment.' She raised her head, meeting his regard head-on. Letting her anger show.

Ever since she'd consented to go with him it had been the same. Exquisite politeness from him and deference from his staff. Yet every decision had been made for her.

At first she'd been in a state of shock, too stunned to do more than be swept along by the force of Raul's will. But her indignation had grown with each hour. Especially when she'd been told, not asked about appointments with the beautician, the pedicurist, the manicurist, the hair stylist, the couturier…

As if she were an animated doll, not a woman with a brain of her own.

His hand dropped.

'You're upset.'

'You noticed!' She drew a slow breath, fighting for control. She was rigid with outrage and self-disgust.

Luisa had spent enough time battling bullies. From her despotic grandfather to big banks eager for immediate returns. To this man who'd taken over her life.

She should have been able to stand up to him!

She'd never felt so helpless.

That scared her more than anything. And provoked her fighting spirit. She'd had enough!

'You're tired after the long journey.' Did his voice soften? Surely not.

She hadn't slept a wink, even in the luxurious bed assigned to her on the long haul flight to Europe. Yet fatigue was the least of her worries.

'I'm tired of you managing my life. Just because I gave in to blackmail doesn't mean I've relinquished the ability to think. I'm not a doormat.'

'No one would presume—'

'*You* presume all the time!' Luisa jabbed a finger into his broad chest then backed up a step, resolving to keep her distance. She didn't like the tiny pinprick of heat tickling her skin where she'd touched him. It was there too whenever he took her arm, helping her from a plane or car.

'You haven't once *asked*!' She spread her hands. 'Your staff simply tell me what you've decided.'

His hooded eyes gave nothing away, but the sharp angle of his jaw told her she'd hit home. Good! The idea of getting under this man's skin appealed. It was about time he found out what it felt like not to get his own way.

'Royalty works on a strict timetable.'

'And dairy farms don't?' She planted her hands on her hips. 'After you've spent your life getting up before dawn for early milking, *then* talk to me about managing my time!'

'It's hardly the same thing.'

'No, it's not.' She kept her voice calm with an effort. 'My life might not have been exciting but it was about honest hard work. A real job, doing something useful. Not—' she gestured to the exquisitely decorated salon and the man who stood so haughtily before her '—not empty gloss and privilege.'

A dull flush of colour streaked across Raul's razor-sharp cheekbones. Deep grooves bracketed the firm line of his mouth and his long fingers flexed and curled. Energy radiated from him, a latent power so tangible she had to force herself to stand her ground.

'You'll find royal life isn't a sinecure.' His words were glacial shards, grazing her overheated cheeks. 'Running a country is a demanding full-time job.'

Luisa refused to be cowed. Nothing excused his treatment of her. That had to change. Now.

'Under extreme duress I agreed to go to your country and accept my inheritance. That doesn't give you carte blanche to run my life.'

'Where were you going?' His question surprised her.

She glanced at the full length windows with their view of a wide, elegant boulevard and a distant park.

'I've never been to Paris.' She'd never travelled. Except to her grandfather's home and to Sydney when her mum visited specialists. Neither had been pleasant experiences. 'I want to explore.'

'You haven't time. Your new clothes are here and you need to be fitted. It's important you look like a princess when you step off the plane in Maritz.'

'In case I don't photograph well for the press?' She almost laughed at the idea of being media-worthy, but the way his face shuttered instantly at her mention of the press distracted her.

'It's for your sake as well, Luisa. Imagine arriving in the full blare of public interest, dressed as you are.'

Was that a hint of sympathy in his expression, or did she imagine it?

'There's nothing wrong with my clothes! They're...'

Cheap and comfortable and a little shabby. It wasn't that she didn't want beautiful clothes. It was the idea of pretending to be someone she wasn't, as if the real Luisa wasn't worth knowing. Yet a tiny voice inside admitted she didn't want to face a nation's press as she was.

She didn't want to face the press at all!

'Clothes are like armour.' His voice held a note of understanding that surprised her. 'You'll feel more comfortable in clothes that make you look good.'

Did he speak from personal experience? Seeing the proud tilt of his head, Luisa guessed Raul could walk naked before a crowd and not lose one ounce of his regal attitude.

Her breath hitched on the idea of Raul naked. With those long, powerful thighs and that rangy powerful torso...

With an effort she dragged her mind back on track.

'I don't need permission to go out.' She kept her voice low and even but her chin crept up. 'I don't answer to you and I *do* intend to see some of the city.'

She wouldn't let him dictate to her any more.

'Then what if I take you out myself, tonight?' Luisa blinked in astonishment. 'I have appointments for the rest of the day but after dinner, if you like, I'll show you some of the sights of Paris.' He paused for a long moment, his mouth easing into what could almost pass for a smile. 'Would that suit?'

Blankly Luisa stared. A compromise? That must have cost him!

Instantly suspicion grew that he was up to something. Yet the idea of escaping this gorgeous, claustrophobic house was irresistible.

'Agreed.'

Six hours later Luisa stood against the railing of a river cruiser, straining forward as each new sight came into view. From the Ile de la Cité with Notre Dame's flying buttresses illuminated like spread wings against the darkness, to the Pont Neuf and the glittering Eiffel Tower. Paris slid around them, gorgeous and outrageously seductive. Yet still the tension twisted through her.

She and Raul were the only passengers.

Another reminder of what his wealth could buy.

Like her clothes. Stylish black wool trousers and a chic winter-weight cream tunic. Boots and a long coat of leather so soft she had to force herself not to keep smoothing her hands over it. A designer silk scarf in indigo and burnt orange that brought colour to her cheeks.

Except her cheeks burned anyway, remembering the designer's whispered asides to his assistant about Luisa's shape, size, posture and walk. Her posture was good, apparently, but her walk! A stride, like a man's. And she had no notion how to carry off a dress. None!

Yet, despite being an apparently insurmountable challenge, she'd been transformed.

Not that Raul had noticed. He'd escorted her to the car with barely a word. Luisa's bruised pride had been lacerated that he hadn't commented on her appearance. Clearly it was a matter of the utmost indifference to him.

And this the man who'd spoken of marriage!

She drew a slow breath. Once in Maritz she'd consult local lawyers. There must be a way out of the wedding contract. Fear scudded through her at the idea of marrying—

'You're enjoying yourself?' In the darkness she saw movement as Raul stood beside her. A trickle of heat warmed her belly and she swallowed hard. She hated the way her traitorous body responded yet she couldn't douse her excitement. Even in her teens, bowled over by what she thought was love, she hadn't felt this way.

'The city is beautiful. Thank you for the cruise.'

'So you admit there are benefits to our arrangement?'

His satisfied smile set her teeth on edge. He took credit for the beauty of the city, forgetting the blackmail that had forced her hand! It was a relief to let her frustration and indignation surge to the surface.

'They don't outweigh the negatives.'

He made an abrupt movement with one hand, a rare sign of impatience that surprised her. Usually he was so calm. 'You refuse to be pleased, no matter what you are offered.'

'I don't recall any *offer*. That implies choice.'

'You would rather be with your precious cows instead of here?' His wide gesture encompassed the magical vista. 'I give you the chance to be *queen*.'

'By *marrying* you!' She backed a step. 'I'll go with you to Maritz, but as for marriage...' Luisa shook her head.

The sharp glimmer of his stare triggered her innermost anxieties, releasing a tumble of words. 'You can't give me anything I truly desire!'

Years before a man had tried to take her, not out of passion, but calculating ambition. It had left her feeling unclean. That was when she'd decided she'd never settle for anything less than love.

'I want to marry a man who makes my heart race and my blood sing—'

Strong hands closed on her upper arms and she gaped up at the starkly sculpted face suddenly so close. A passing light played over him. Far from being coolly remote, heat ignited in Raul's eyes. His expression sent adrenalin surging.

His head lowered and his warm breath feathered her face. 'Like this, you mean?'

CHAPTER FOUR

RAUL's mouth claimed Luisa's, pressing, demanding, till on a gasp her lips parted and he took possession.

Too late he realised his mistake.

The spark of indignation and guilt that had urged him to silence her grievances flared higher. Hotter. Brighter. He tasted her and heat shimmered, molten in his blood. He delved into her sweet, lush mouth and discovered something unexpected.

Something unique.

He slanted his mouth, demanding better access. Needing more. A ripple of stunned pleasure reverberated through him. He'd suspected almost from the start that there was something unique about Luisa. But this…!

His tongue slicked across hers, laved and slid and explored and there it was again.

An excitement, an anticipation he hadn't felt since he was a green boy.

Still it persisted. The feeling this was *different*.

He tugged her satisfyingly close between his wide-planted legs. His other hand slid up into the thick silken mass of bright hair that had caught his eye as he'd walked into the salon this afternoon. He'd wanted to touch it ever since.

It felt even better than it looked, soft as seduction.

The fire dropped to his belly, kindling like a coiling Catherine wheel that jetted sparks in all directions.

Tension screwed unbearably tight as her hand fluttered at his throat, a barely there touch that weakened his knees. When she slid both arms over his shoulders to clasp his neck a great shudder rocked him.

How could a kiss ravage his senses?

Trying to staunch the feeling that he spun out of control, Raul moved his lips to the corner of her mouth but she turned her head. Instead of an almost chaste caress, he found himself transfixed as her lips opened beneath his. Her body pressed close and her tongue slipped into his mouth in a move that he'd have called tentative if it hadn't sent every blood cell in his body rushing south.

Her kiss was slow and deliberate. Unbelievably provocative as she treated him to a devastating sensual exploration that almost blew the top off his head. Shivers of delight coursed through him.

Once or twice she hesitated as if unsure how to proceed. But the feel of her tongue mating with his in slow, lush pleasure soon obliterated such crazy notions.

Raul slid a hand under her long coat, over the tight curve of her bottom. His splayed fingers dragged her close, where that flicker of heat was now a blazing furnace. He tilted his pelvis and felt her welcoming feminine softness. Lust shot through him.

He swallowed her gasp, returning her kiss with growing fervour. Every nerve was sharp and aware, as if it had been an age since he'd held a woman.

Luisa tasted like sunshine, felt warm and soft and luscious like a summer peach.

Heat spiked in his groin and a hard weight surged there. The audacious notion rose that here, now, they should let passion take its inevitable course. He'd never felt such an unravelling of control.

Dimly he registered astonishment as desire blasted him. He met her kisses hungrily, her soft little whimper of pleasure driving him on even as he tried to slow down.

Luisa, with her sweet sensuality and her delicious hesitation, piqued an appetite jaded by over-eager women.

Brightness spilled over them, a wash of cold sanity.

Raul blinked in the light from an overhead bridge. He raised his head but his hands were still on her, their lower bodies welded together, even as they passed a group of sightseers peering down at the Seine.

Even now hunger gripped him.

Hell!

What was he doing, giving free rein to passion in public? It was unheard of! Raul kept his sex life scrupulously private after the nightmare scandal eight years ago. He'd worked tirelessly since to shore up his people's belief in and respect for the monarchy.

Yet he couldn't drag his eyes from Luisa, couldn't force himself to step away.

Her lips were parted. Her dark eyelashes fanned, concealing her eyes. She looked wantonly inviting and the heat in his groin intensified. His hold tightened.

Could this be the same woman he'd once thought unfeminine? She was beautiful.

Yet more was at work here than a no-expenses-spared makeover. Even if the result surpassed his expectations.

He met lovely women all the time. But none made him feel like this.

The women in his life were easy company, a pleasure to look at. They satisfied his need for sex. He treated them well and they were eager to please. Simple. Uncomplicated.

Yet with Luisa he didn't merely respond to a pretty woman. Her fire, her determination, her strength made her unique. He *felt* as well as desired.

She stirred against him and a bolt of erotic energy speared him.

No! He imagined things. This desire was so intense because he'd allowed her to provoke anger.

He avoided dwelling on the fact that in itself was unusual. He'd learnt years before to channel all his energies into his work. Emotion had led him to the brink of disaster. The eventual fallout of that error had destroyed his family and threatened the state. Now he knew better. He controlled his world. Never again would he be a hostage to sentiment.

Luisa's eyes flickered open and a jewel-bright stare skewered him. His heart thudded out of kilter as his rationalisations crumbled.

Abruptly he released her and stepped away.

What had she done?

Heat blasted Luisa and she swayed, legs wobbling, as unfamiliar sensations cascaded through her.

She couldn't—surely she couldn't have kissed the man who'd *blackmailed* her into doing his bidding?

Surely she hadn't…*enjoyed* it?

Cool air chilled her face and crept in the open front of her jacket. Yet she burned up, her cheeks fiery. Heat seared through her stomach and down to the terrible hollow throb between her legs.

Inwardly she cringed. So much for defiance. And for self-respect. What had happened to the reserve that had kept her impervious to the masculine sex for so long? The wariness borne of disillusionment and hurt?

Raul had hauled her into his embrace, kissed her and her brain had shorted. She'd gone from indignation to helpless need, craving each demanding caress.

How could she have responded to a man she surely hated?

And to have revealed her inexperience to him! No way could her shaming enthusiasm have made up for her lack of expertise. He knew now just how naïve she was. How he must be smirking. The country bumpkin, easy to twist around his little finger. Show her a taste of what she'd never had and she'd be eating out of his hand.

Sickening echoes of the past filled her brain. Hadn't she learned? How could she be susceptible again? Self-disgust was bitter on her tongue.

Reluctantly she opened her eyes.

Instantly he moved away, his brows drawing down in a ferocious scowl as if he couldn't believe he'd touched her.

Pain speared her. No doubt she didn't measure up to his exacting royal standards. Déjà vu swamped her, recalling the scathing revelations of her long-ago suitor.

'I don't want you touching me.' Her voice was raw, husky with distress.

Raul loomed taller, his frown morphing in an instant to a look of cool composure.

'That wasn't the impression you gave a moment ago.' He tugged at his shirt, straightened his jacket, and Luisa felt about an inch tall, realising she'd pulled his clothing askew.

'I didn't invite you to maul me.' Conveniently she ignored the way she'd given herself up to his kiss. Even now she held onto the railing to stay upright. He turned her bones to water.

In the dimming light as the boat slid away from the bridge, it looked like colour rose in his cheeks. But that had to be her imagination. His expression grew haughty and his eyes glittered.

'My apologies. You can be sure I don't make a habit of *forcing my attentions* where they're not wanted.'

Raul drew himself up like a guard on parade. Then with a flourish of one elegant hand he bowed formally. 'I'll leave you to your contemplation of the view.'

He turned and strode to the wheelhouse. He looked utterly calm, as if their passion had been a figment of her imagination. As if he'd felt nothing.

Surely not! He'd been as hungry for her as she'd been for him.

Or had he? She bit her lip, all too aware she had next to no experience to draw upon and that her judgement of men was flawed. Years ago she'd been dumbfounded when her ardent suitor finally revealed his true self when thwarted. His disdainful dismissal of her attractiveness and lack of sophistication was still vivid.

The possibility that Raul too had feigned desire made her want to sink through the deck.

Why should he do it?

The answer came too readily. To reduce her to starry-eyed compliance.

Luisa sagged against the railing.

It had worked. When he kissed her all her doubts and anger fled. She was putty in his hands. His kisses had been white-hot lightning, blowing her mind and leaving her body humming with a desperate craving.

She stared at his tall form as he disappeared into the darkness. Vivid as her recall was of that near seduction years ago, Luisa couldn't remember kisses as devastating as this. Was her memory faulty? Or had years focused on work and family, shying from any tentative male interest, made her more susceptible?

The trembling in her knees grew to a quaking that shook her whole body.

Her impossible position had just become impossibly complicated.

Raul thrust aside a surge of regret as Luisa emerged from her suite. It was unfortunate he'd had to force her hand. Her vulnerability and her desperate pride struck a chord with him. And her passion—

No! Last night was over. A passing weakness.

He was in control now. Impossible that his feelings were engaged by the woman at the top of the staircase. He didn't do feelings. Not any more. One disastrous mistake had cured him.

Though in her chic honey-gold trouser suit and black silk shirt, Luisa was eye-catching. The suit skimmed ripe curves he'd held just hours ago. His fingers flexed at the memories, still vivid after a night of no rest.

She cast a flickering half glance in his direction and chewed on her glossy lower lip.

A ripple of something urgent disturbed his inner calm.

Stoically he ignored it, focusing an appraising eye on how she descended the grand staircase. She gripped the banister tight, clearly unsure of herself in high heels.

As he'd suspected. She'd need help when they arrived in Maritz in a few hours. He didn't want her falling down the steps from the plane and breaking her neck.

His gaze lingered on the long line of her throat. She had a natural elegance her farm clothes had camouflaged. His hands tingled as he recalled the feel of her soft skin, the temptation of her lips, the way her eyes flashed when she challenged him.

Her gaze snared his and his pulse slowed to a weighted thud.

Raul frowned. It was one thing to feel desire with a warm woman pressed intimately against him in the night. Quite another to experience it here, with his butler waiting to usher them on their way to the airport.

Worse, this felt more complex than lust. In a couple of short days she'd somehow got into his head.

Instantly he rejected the idea. It was simple desire he experienced.

'Luisa. I hope you slept well.'

He walked forward as she reached the bottom step. She stumbled and his hand shot out to steady her, but she jerked her arm away, hurrying past him, heels clicking on inlaid marble.

Raul drew a sharp breath. After a lifetime fending off eager women he discovered he didn't like this alternative.

He recalled how she'd clung so needily last night and assured himself her response was contrived. Women were devious. Was it any wonder he kept relationships simple?

What sort of relationship would he have with his wife?

'Yes, thank you. I slept well enough.'

Liar! Despite the make-up accentuating the smoky blue of her eyes, Raul saw signs of fatigue.

'And you?' To his surprise challenge sizzled in her gaze, as if she knew he'd spent most of the night wakeful, reliving those few moments when she'd melted into him like a born seductress.

Even now he wasn't sure about her. There'd been more than a hint of the innocent about her last night.

But then feigned innocence could be such an effective weapon. As he knew to his cost. A spike of chill air stabbed the back of his neck.

'I always sleep well in Paris.' He offered his arm again, this time holding her gaze till she complied.

He covered her hand with his, securing it possessively. The sooner she grew accustomed to him the better. 'And now, if you're ready, our plane is waiting.'

He felt the shiver race through her. Saw her eyes widen in what looked like anxiety.

There was nothing to fear. Most women would sell their soul to be in her place, offered wealth, prestige and marriage to a man the press insisted on labelling one of the world's most eligible bachelors. But already he began to see Luisa wasn't most women.

He heard himself saying, 'I'll look after you, Luisa. There's no need to be anxious.'

It was on the way to the airport that Raul discovered the cost of his unguarded actions last night. The discreet buzz of his mobile phone and a short conversation with Lukas, already waiting for them at the airport, had him excusing himself and opening his laptop.

Not that Luisa noticed. She was busy pressing her nose to the glass as they drove through Paris.

He focused on his computer, scrolling through page after page of newspaper reports. The sort of reports he habitually ignored: 'PRINCE'S SECRET LOVER.' 'RAUL'S PARISIAN INTERLUDE.' 'SIZZLING SEDUCTION ON THE SEINE.'

There wasn't much to the articles apart from speculation as to his new lover's identity. Yet acid curdled his stomach and clammy heat rose as he flicked from one photo of last night's kiss to another.

He frowned, perplexed by his reaction.

It wasn't the first time the paparazzi had snapped photos of him with a woman. He was a favourite subject. Typically the press was more interested in his mistresses than his modernisation plans or regional disarmament talks. Usually he shrugged off their reports.

But this time…

Understanding dawned on a wave of nausea.

This time the photographer had unwittingly caught him in a moment of rare vulnerability. The press couldn't know, but Raul had been careening out of control, swept away by dangerously unfamiliar forces. Prey to a compulsion he hadn't experienced in years.

Eight years in fact.

Since the feeding frenzy of press speculation about a royal love triangle. The memory sickened him.

Since he'd learned to distrust female protestations of love and displays of innocence. Since he'd rebuilt his shattered world with determination, pride and a complete absence of emotion that made a man vulnerable.

His gut cramped as he remembered facing the press, made rabid by the scent of blood—*his* blood. The effort of appearing unmoved in the face of the ultimate betrayal. Of how he'd had to claw back his self-respect after making the worst mistake of his life. How day after day he'd had to appear strong. Till finally the façade had become reality and he'd learned to live without emotional ties. Except for his love of Maritz.

He shut the laptop with a snap.

The cases weren't the same. Then he'd been naïve enough to believe in romance. He'd hurt with the intensity of youthful emotions. Now, at thirty, Raul was in control of his world. What he'd felt last night had been lust, more intense than usual perhaps, but simple enough.

Besides, public interest in Luisa could be used to advantage. It wouldn't hurt to hint that there was more to his approaching nuptials than fulfilment of a legal contract. People liked to believe in fairy tales and it would ease the way for her.

A lost princess, a romantic interlude in Paris, an early wedding. It was the sort of PR that would focus interest on the monarchy and dampen the enthusiasm for political rabble-rousing in the lead up to his coronation.

He'd planned a quiet arrival in Maritz to give Luisa time to acclimatise. Yet in the circumstances revealing her identity had definite benefits.

He'd arrange it with Lukas at the airport.

'You can unfasten your seat belt, ma'am.' The hostess smiled at Luisa on her way to open the plane door.

Foreboding lurched in the pit of Luisa's stomach.

The idea of stepping out of the aircraft and into the country that had once been her mother's, and her detested grandfather's, terrified her. Some atavistic foreknowledge warned that this next step would be irrevocable.

Again she experienced that sense of the world telescoping in around her, shrinking to a dark tunnel where her future lay immutable before her.

Desperately she sought for something positive to hang onto. The determination to get legal advice on that marriage contract as soon as she could. To find an escape clause that would allow Raul to inherit the throne he coveted without marrying her.

'Here.' A deep voice cut through her swirling thoughts. 'Let me.' Warm hands, large and capable, unclipped the seat belt and brushed it off her lap.

Sensation jittered through her stomach and across her thighs. Luisa looked up sharply to find Raul bending over her, his eyes warm with an expression she couldn't fathom.

Her heart rose in her throat, pounding fast. The memory of last night's madness filled her. The feel of his tight embrace and her need for more. Despite today's polite formality, nothing could obliterate the recollection. Even the knowledge it had been a lie. He'd felt nothing.

He stepped back and she sucked in an uneven breath.

'It's time to go.' He extended an arm.

Luisa nodded, her tongue glued to the roof of her mouth. What was happening to her? She had no desire to fall into Raul's arms again, yet she imagined warmth in his gaze. When all he cared about was her usefulness to him.

Silently she let him drape a cashmere coat over her shoulders, then stepped to the door. The sooner she reached their destination, the sooner she could sort out this mess.

A roar filled her ears and she stopped abruptly at the head of the stairs. She blinked into the bright light, wishing she'd brought sunglasses.

'It's all right,' Raul said. 'They're just glad to see us.'

He slid an arm slid round her, drawing her to him. Instinctively she pulled away but his hold was unbreakable.

'Relax,' he murmured. 'I'm just making sure you don't trip on those high heels. Come on.'

At his urging they descended, Luisa clinging to the railing and inordinately grateful for his support. Sheer bravado had led her to wear the highest heels in her new wardrobe, determined to look as sophisticated as possible. The move had backfired when she'd come face to face with Raul and discovered the extra height merely brought her closer to his knowing gaze.

Another roar made her blink and focus on the scene ahead.

Crowds massed behind the fence at the edge of the tarmac. Maritzian flags waved and excited voices called out. Luisa's Maritzian was rusty so all she could make out was Raul's name. *And hers.*

She stumbled to a stop on the narrow stairs and only Raul's firm grip saved her. Adrenalin pumped hard in her blood. From the near fall or perhaps from the impact of meeting his intent scrutiny head-on.

'What's happening?'

He shrugged and she felt the movement against her as he kept a tight hold of her waist.

'Well-wishers. Nothing to worry about.'

Luisa frowned, battling a rising sense of unreality. 'But how do they know my name?'

Something flickered in his eyes. 'Your identity isn't a secret. Is it?'

Dazedly she shook her head, beginning her descent again at his urging. 'But it makes no sense. How could—'

The sight of a placard in the throng cut off the words mid-flow. It showed her name and Raul's, linked in a massive love heart topped with a crown.

She swung round and read satisfaction in his face.

'What have you done?' Every muscle tightened as she fought the impulse to run back up the steps and hide in the royal jet.

His brows arched. 'I authorised my staff to confirm your identity if queried. Now, it's time we moved.'

Mutinously Luisa stared up at him, her hand tightening on the rail.

His eyes flashed, then his lips tilted in a one-sided smile that obliterated the grimness engraved around his lips, making him look younger. 'As you wish, madam.'

He bowed. But it wasn't a bow, she realised as his arms circled her.

Seconds later he hefted her up against his chest. The noise of the crowd crested in a swell of approval. But Luisa barely heard it over the thunderous beat of blood in her ears.

She should hate being manhandled. She did! Almost.

'What are you doing?' she demanded, trying not to focus on the feel of tough muscle and bone surrounding her.

His smile deepened and something flipped over inside Luisa's chest. He shrugged again and this time the movement rippled around her, drawing her closer.

It scared her how much she enjoyed being held by Raul.

'Carrying my bride down the stairs.'

CHAPTER FIVE

LUISA walked across the tarmac towards the crowd. It was daunting. So huge, so excited. For an insane moment she wished she were back in his arms. To her consternation she'd felt…safe there.

Her knees shook with every step. His arm around her waist was both a torment and a support.

She swallowed hard, nervous at what she faced. And furious.

'Don't faint on me now, Luisa.'

'No chance of that,' she managed through gritted teeth as instinctively she tried to respond to the broad smiles on so many faces. 'I'm not going to swoon in your arms. Even for the sake of your audience.'

'*Our* audience.'

A barrage of flashes set up around them. He raised one hand in acknowledgement and the crowd cheered harder.

The information she'd found on the web mentioned his dedication to his country but she hadn't realised how popular he was. Cynically she did a quick survey of the crowd and noticed women outnumbered men three to one. That explained some of the excitement.

It would be easy to fall for Raul if you didn't know the man behind the gorgeous exterior.

He swept her towards a gleaming limousine. No lengthy wait for passport and customs checks for him.

They'd almost reached the car when Luisa saw what had

provoked such interest. Someone held up a page from a newspaper, with a blown up photo of a couple embracing so passionately it felt voyeuristic to look at them.

It took a moment for the truth to slam into her. The man staring so intently down at the woman he held possessively was Raul. His face was harsh with stark sexual hunger. Or intense calculation.

And the woman with her kiss-swollen lips, apparently swooning in his arms, was her!

Luisa's skin crawled in horror. Bile rose in her throat and she swallowed frantically. She felt…violated at the knowledge anyone else had seen that moment. Had viewed her vulnerability. Bad enough Raul knew her appalling weakness, but to have others witness it, splash it in newsprint…

She gasped, her breath sawing painfully in cramped lungs.

'Come, Luisa.' Raul urged her forwards. 'Don't stop here in front of the cameras.'

The mention of cameras moved her on till she found herself seated, shivering, in a limo. Her brain seemed to have seized up and her teeth were chattering.

'Luisa?' Warm hands chafed her icy ones. Dazedly she heard a muttered imprecation, then her knees were swathed in warmth as Raul tucked his jacket around her legs.

'I don't need it. I'm fine.' Her voice sounded overloud in the thick silence now the privacy screen had been raised. But a chance glance out of the window to the people milling about, watching their vehicle, made her shrink back into the soft leather.

'You've had a shock. I apologise. I should have warned you.' Luisa could almost believe that was genuine regret in his deep voice.

But her brain was branded with the memory of his expression in that photo. She wasn't stupid enough to believe he'd been overcome by passion. He'd recovered too fast and too completely. He'd probably been calculating how successful his seduction had been. Assessing how compliant she'd be in future.

Fury pierced the fog of shock.

'*You* did that!' She rounded on him, too angry to feel more than a tremor of surprise at how close he sat, his thigh warm against hers. 'You set me up for that photo.' How could she have forgotten her suspicion last night when he'd suggested taking her out? She should have guessed he was up to something.

Hauteur iced his features.

'I don't do deals with the paparazzi.'

Luisa shook her head. 'Someone did! They were there, waiting for us. You can't tell me—'

'I *do* tell you, Luisa.' His voice held a note of steel that silenced her. 'I have nothing but contempt for the media outlets and the photographers who spend their time beating up such stories.' His jaw tightened and Luisa found herself sinking back into her seat.

Gullible she might be, but everything from the set of his taut shoulders to the glitter in his dark eyes convinced her he was telling the truth.

'The press are always on the watch for photo opportunities. They follow constantly, though given my security detail, usually at a distance. It's part of being royal. A fact of life.'

'I don't think much of being royal then.' Her stomach was painfully tight after the sudden welling nausea.

To her surprise, Raul's mouth lifted in a rare smile that made something inside her soften. 'I don't either. Not that part of it.'

His hand enfolded hers and for an instant she knew a bizarre urge to smile back, sharing a moment of intimacy.

Except it was a mirage. There *was* no intimacy.

'I regret the photo, Luisa. If I'd realised we were visible…' He shrugged.

To her amazement she found herself wanting to believe him. 'But even if the press had reported our—' she swallowed, her mouth dry as she remembered his kiss '—our trip on the river,

I don't see why the crowd would be excited about my arrival. Surely they don't turn out to see all your...girlfriends.'

His smile faded and his grip tightened. Clearly he didn't like explaining himself.

Tough!

Luisa dragged her hand from his, refusing to notice the loss of warmth.

'I told you. I instructed my staff to explain who you are if asked.'

'But my name wouldn't mean anything!'

Silently he surveyed her as if waiting for her to catch up. 'Your title does. Princess Luisa of Ardissia.'

Luisa froze as the implications sank in. 'I'm not princess yet. I haven't signed—'

'But you will.' His voice was a rich, creamy purr. 'That's why you came, isn't it?'

She nodded, feeling again that hated sense of being cornered. Suspicion flared.

'That's not all they said, is it?' Urgently she leaned towards him, thrusting his jacket off her legs, uncaring she was close enough to see the individual long lashes fringing his eyes, or the hint of a nick on his smoothly shaven jaw. To inhale the warm scent of his skin.

'They just happened to mention the marriage contract, didn't they?'

Raul held her gaze unblinkingly and for one crazy moment she felt an echo of last night's emotions when he'd hauled her close and introduced her to bliss.

Heat scorched her cheeks and throat.

'Didn't they?'

'It's not a secret, Luisa, though the details weren't widely known.'

She sat back, her heart pounding.

'You don't give up, do you?' It shouldn't come as a surprise. Not after he'd manoeuvred her into coming here. 'What did you hope to achieve? Pressure me into agreeing?'

It was as if he'd known she still held out hope of avoiding

marriage. Wearily she raised a hand to her forehead, smoothing the beginning of an ache there.

'I won't be forced into marriage because your precious public expects it. If I pull out the story would be all about you. How you were jilted. Not about me.'

In an instant his face whitened to the colour of scoured bone. His nostrils flared and the flesh seemed to draw back, leaving his clear cut features spare and prominent. Almost she could believe she'd scored some unseen injury.

Energy radiated from him. A sense of barely controlled power. Of danger.

This time she did retreat.

'*There will be no jilting.*' Fascinated, Luisa saw the tic of Raul's pulse at his jaw.

'I will not leave my people to the chaos that would come if I gave up the throne.' He paused. 'Remember why you agreed to come here.'

Blazing eyes meshed with hers and any hope she'd harboured that he wouldn't follow through on his threat vanished. This man would do whatever it took to get what he wanted. How had she let last night's fake tenderness blind her to that? Or his solicitude here in the car?

Luisa pulled her jacket close and turned to face the window. She couldn't face him with her emotions so raw.

They'd left the highway for the old part of the city. Cobblestones rumbled under the wheels as they crossed a wide square of pastel-coloured baroque buildings that housed expensive shops.

The car turned and before them appeared a steep incline, almost a cliff. Above that, seeming to grow from the living rock, towered the royal castle. Dark grey stone with round towers and forest green roofs just visible behind the massive battlement.

Guidebooks said the castle was a superb example of medieval construction, updated with spectacular eighteenth century salons and modern amenities. That it commanded extraordinary views to the Alps and down the wide river valley. That its treasure house was unrivalled in central Europe and its ballroom an architectural gem.

But what stuck in Luisa's mind was that in almost a millennium of use no one had ever escaped the castle's dungeons once locked up by order of the king.

Her suite of rooms was airy, light and sumptuous. Not at all like a dank prison cell. Yet Luisa barely took in the silk and gilt loveliness.

She stood before the wide windows, staring to distant snow-capped mountains. That was where Ardissia lay. The place that tied her to wealth and position and a life of empty gloss instead of emotional warmth and security. Tied her to Raul. A man whose ambition repelled, yet who made her tremble with glorious, dreadful excitement.

Luisa trailed her fingers appreciatively over the antique desk. It wasn't that she didn't like beautiful things, or the designer clothes wealth could buy. It was that she knew they weren't any substitute for happiness. For warmth and caring and love. She'd grown up with love and her one disastrous foray into romance had taught her she couldn't accept anything else.

On impulse she snatched up the phone. A dialling tone buzzed in her ear and her heart leapt at the idea of calling home. She looked at her watch, calculating the time difference. With the help of the phone book she found the international code and rang home.

'Oh, pet! It's so good to hear your voice.' Mary's excited chatter eased some of the tension drawn tight in Luisa's stomach. She sank back onto a silk upholstered chair in front of the desk.

'We've been wondering how you are and what you're doing. Are you well? How was the trip? Did that lovely Prince Raul look after you?'

Luisa bit her lip at the memory of how well Raul had looked after her. He'd played on her vulnerability and used his own compelling attraction to lay bare naïve longings she hadn't even realised she harboured.

'The trip was fine, Mary. I even had my own bed on the plane. And then we stopped in Paris—'

'Paris? Really?'

Soon Luisa was swept along by Mary's demands for details, peppered with her aunt's exclamations and observations. Eventually the talk turned to home.

'We've been missing you, love. It seems strange with that new bloke and his son in your house. But I can't deny they've made a good start. He's a decent manager, by the look of it. And he reckons the changes you and your dad began to modernise the co-op were spot on. Well, I could have told him that! And between you and me, it's such a relief knowing that debt's going to be settled. Sam is like a new man without that weighing on him. And Josie's all agog about moving into town to take up an apprenticeship, now we'll be able to afford to help her with rent. And little Julia Todd is looking so much better these days. I was worried about her being so wan. It turns out the poor thing is pregnant again and was worried about how they'd afford another child. But now she's positively radiant...'

Luisa leaned forward to put her elbow on the desk, letting her head sink onto her hand.

Mary's voice tugged at something deep inside. The part of her that longed for everything familiar and dear.

Yet with each new breathless revelation it became clear Luisa couldn't go back. Her past, the life she'd loved, were closed to her.

The last vestige of hope had been torn away today when she looked into fathomless emerald eyes and a stern, beautiful face. Raul would do whatever it took to get the crown he coveted.

Already the people she loved were moving on, anticipating the cancellation of the co-op's debts. Luisa had understood that, but not till this moment had the devastating reality of it all hit her fully.

Luisa had no choice.

She lifted her head and looked around the delicately lovely room. *A room for a princess.*

She shuddered at the enormity of what faced her.

But her parents' example was vivid in her mind. No matter what life threw at them, they'd battled on, making the most of life without complaint.

Luisa set her jaw. It was time she faced her future.

'Raul.'

He looked up from the papers he and Lukas were discussing—disturbing reports of more unrest.

Luisa stood in the doorway. A dart of heat shot through him as he took in her loveliness and remembered the taste of her lips beneath his.

There was something different about her. Gone was the distressed woman of mere hours ago. And the woman endearingly unsure of herself in high heels. This was Luisa as he'd first seen her—confident and in control, yet with no hint of the farmyard about her.

She looked…magnificent.

He shoved back his chair and stood. 'We'll continue later, Lukas.' His assistant hastily packed up the reports and bowed himself from the study, closing the door.

'Please take a seat.'

She crossed the room to halt before his desk. 'This won't take long.' She paused, her slightly stunned gaze taking in his state-of-the-art computer equipment and the large document storage area behind him. As if surprised to discover he actually worked.

Raul paced around the desk. 'What can I do for you, Luisa?' It was the first time she'd sought him out.

Clear blue eyes met his and he felt that now-familiar frisson of anticipation.

'I've come to tell you I'll do it. I'll marry you.'

Raul breathed deep as the knot of tension that had screwed his belly tight for so long loosened.

He'd manipulated her into coming here. He'd overseen a new look for her, introduced her to his people in such a way she'd be cornered by their expectations, and still he hadn't been sure he could go through with it. Force her into marriage.

Despite his determination and his desperation, doubts had preyed on him.

'What made you change your mind?'

She shrugged. 'Does it matter?'

Raul opened his mouth. Part of him believed it did. The part that wanted to know Luisa better, her thoughts and feelings. The part of him, he supposed, that had made him emotionally susceptible all those years ago. The part he'd thought he'd erased from his being.

He shook his head. What mattered was her agreement.

'I thought not.' Her eyes blazed with what might have been anger. Then, in a moment, the look was gone.

He took her hand in his. She didn't resist.

'I promise you, Luisa, I will do everything in my power to ensure you never regret this.' His skin grew tight over tense muscles as he thought of the enormity of her decision. Of all it meant for him and his people.

He lifted her hand to his lips.

'You will have my gratitude and my loyalty.' Her flesh was cool, her expression shuttered and yet he felt the trembling pulse at her wrist. He inhaled her delicate scent. Something far stronger than gratitude stirred in his belly.

'You owe me more.'

Startled, he raised his head. She slipped her hand free and clasped it in her other palm as if it pained her.

'What do you want?'

She'd almost convinced him she didn't care for wealth and glamour. Now suspicion rose. He should have known better. Hadn't Ana taught him anything? What was her price?

'I want…' She paused and gestured abruptly with one hand. 'I *don't* want to be treated as some brainless doll. As far as possible, I want to make my own decisions. Don't expect to dictate to me.'

Raul took in the defiant glimmer in her eyes, the determined jut of her chin and felt the tension leach away.

No unreasonable demands? No tantrums or tears?

Pride stirred, and respect for this remarkable woman.

Perhaps after all Luisa was as unique as she seemed.

His lips curved in a smile of genuine pleasure. 'I wouldn't expect anything less.'

Raul saw Luisa led past the royal councillors, across the vast reception room. The soon-to-be-Princess of Ardissia was quietly elegant in shades of caramel and cream. Her back was straight and her chin up as if unfazed by the presence of so many august people. Yet she was pale and there was a brittle quality to her composure that made his brow knot.

Guilt pinched. A few days ago she'd been leading a completely different life. Had he been right to move so fast to cement this arrangement?

Raul stiffened, refusing to follow that line of thought. This was for the best. For the good of the nation. The alternative would plunge the country into chaos.

The sooner this was done the better.

He strode across the room, silently berating himself for getting sidetracked by urgent negotiations. He'd meant to support her as she entered the room.

He'd nearly reached her at the ornate desk when she saw him and started. Disappointment flared. This wasn't the first time she'd reacted as if his touch contaminated.

It took a moment to realise that in flinging out an arm involuntarily Luisa had knocked over the baccarat crystal inkwell. Black liquid sprayed across the hand woven heirloom carpet and his suit.

The room inhaled a collective gasp. In a moment Luisa had ripped blotting paper from the embossed blotter on the desk and dropped to her knees, soaking up the stain.

Servants rushed to assist but she didn't notice. 'We need something to soak this up.'

Raul dragged a pristine handkerchief from his pocket and hunkered beside her. 'Will this help?'

'Not much.' Her words were crisp. 'But it's better than nothing.' The snowy cloth joined the dark pulpy mass on the carpet.

'Excuse me, ma'am. Ma'am?' One of the senior staff appeared with materials to clear the worst of the mess.

'Luisa.' Raul took her elbow, gripping tight enough to make her look up. 'The staff will deal with this.'

She opened her mouth as if to protest, then looked over his shoulder, eyes widening. As if she'd only just remembered every member of the High Court, the royal advisors and sundry VIPs here to witness the formalities.

Heat flooded her face and she looked away. Gently he drew her to her feet.

She felt surprisingly fragile beneath his touch. Not like the woman who'd seduced him witless with just a kiss, or the proud woman who'd agreed to marry him.

'I'm sorry.' She watched the staff deal with a stain that was probably immovable, worrying at her lower lip.

'It's all right,' he murmured, leading her away to the other side of the desk.

'But the carpet! It's old and valuable, surely?' Her hands clenched tight.

'No such thing. It's amazing how well they make reproductions these days.'

He heard his butler's breath hiss at the blithe lie. In Raul's father's day, damaging an heirloom like this would have resulted in severe punishment. But, seeing Luisa's distress, feeling her arm tremble beneath his hold, Raul didn't give a damn about anything but allaying her guilt.

'Come,' he said. 'Here's a seat for you.'

She sank into the chair and Raul swept the blotter aside, motioning for the accession document to be brought forward. Reaching in his jacket, he withdrew his own pen.

Maritz needed to move with the times. There was absolutely

no need to continue the tradition of signing and witnessing important documents with old-fashioned ink pens.

Lukas presented the document which, when signed, would confirm Luisa as Princess of Ardissia, inheritor of her grandfather's wealth. And Raul's wife-to-be.

It was spread wide on the desk and the witnesses stepped forward. Raul handed her the pen.

And waited.

For Luisa didn't sign. Instead, she read the English translation, slowly and methodically. Her finger marked a difficult clause and she lifted her head, turning to Lukas who hovered helpfully on her other side.

'Would you mind explaining this reference?' she murmured softly.

'Of course, ma'am.' After a quick look at Raul, Lukas bent over the parchment, explaining the clause. Then after a few moments, another.

The audience grew restless. Raul noticed one or two raised brows among some of the more old-fashioned advisers. He could imagine what they whispered. That the woman should gratefully accept what was offered, without question.

Luisa was aware of the buzz of comment. Her cheeks grew brighter and he saw her neck stiffen. Yet still she read each line.

It should have annoyed him, this delay to his plans. Even now, on the edge of achieving what was so necessary, ripples of anxiety spread through his belly. He couldn't be completely happy till this was settled.

Yet his impatience was tempered by admiration. Luisa was naturally cautious.

Like him. He'd never sign anything without careful consideration either.

Raul recalled the advice he'd recently received. That on investigation Luisa's farming co-op was found to be surprisingly well run. That the financial difficulties were due to the economic downturn, a massive drought and a series of unfortunate health problems, including the death of her father last year.

According to the accountants, the business was poised to become very successful, once money was freed up for new equipment. Luisa had done an excellent job.

Once more curiosity rose. She wasn't like other women. He'd been so intent on achieving his ends he'd initially thought of her as a convenient bride, not a real woman. Now he pondered exactly what sort of woman he would wed.

He looked at her bent head, how she bit her lush bottom lip in concentration. Fire arced through his gut.

She fascinated him, he admitted now. Her obstinacy, pragmatism and quiet pride. Her unassuming ways and her disquieting sensuality. *How long since a woman had intrigued him so? Since a kiss had made him lose his head?*

Finally, with a swift movement, Luisa picked up his pen and signed. Only Raul, close beside her, saw the way her hand shook. It pained him to see what this cost her.

Yet relief swamped him. It was almost done. Soon the crown would be his. His destiny was within his grasp. His country would be safe.

He picked up the pen, still warm from her fingers, and with a flourish added his signature as first witness. 'Thank you, Luisa,' he murmured.

At his words she tilted her head and their gazes meshed. Heat ricocheted through his belly and groin, the reverberations spreading even as she looked away, letting her lashes veil her eyes.

Now she was bound to him, this intriguing woman so lacking in sophistication yet with an innate grace and integrity he couldn't ignore.

Theirs would be a convenient marriage. A marriage of state for the well-being of the nation.

Yet, to his astonishment, Raul registered a purely personal satisfaction at the prospect.

CHAPTER SIX

'I COULDN'T have done a better job of botching that if I'd tried.' Luisa grimaced as she followed Lukas through a maze of corridors to her suite.

She'd do better in future.

Her skin crawled at the memory of censorious eyes on her: an upstart foreigner, not only gauche but clumsy.

'Nothing of the sort, ma'am. You carried it off with great composure.'

Luisa smiled gratefully. Lukas really was a nice man. Surprisingly nice for someone in the Prince's employ.

'Thanks, Lukas, but there's no need to pretend. I saw the way they looked, and their impatience that I wanted to read what I signed.'

'It's true some of the advisers are rather old school.' Lukas cleared his throat and gestured for her to precede him down another wide corridor. 'I'm sure His Highness wouldn't mind me saying that's been one of his challenges in running the country as a modern state—bringing them along in the process of reform.'

Luisa's eyes widened. It hadn't occurred to her Raul would have difficulties. With his take charge attitude and formidable determination she couldn't imagine it.

'You talk as if he's been in charge of the country a long time. I thought the King only died recently.'

A hint of a flush coloured Lukas' cheeks. 'That's correct, ma'am.' He paused and then, with the air of making a sudden decision, added, 'But His Highness was in many ways responsible for running the country long before that. The previous king…left a lot in the Prince's hands.'

Luisa's mind snagged on Lukas' words, trying to read the subtext. There was one. Something he skated around rather than spelling out. It was on the tip of her tongue to press for an explanation, till she read his discomfort.

'And is it still difficult?'

Lukas shrugged. 'The Prince has made his mark and even the more old-fashioned courtiers see the benefits. But there are some who resent change. Some who'd rather vie for personal power than cooperate in a national effort to modernise.'

Her steps slowed. Lukas' assessment echoed Raul's words. She'd half dismissed that as a smokescreen, veiling the fact he simply coveted the crown. Though lately she'd wondered. Seeing him with others, she'd caught glimpses of a reasonable man, even a caring one.

Was there more truth in Raul's words than she'd thought? He claimed he acted for the country as well as himself. Was it possible? It was tempting to hope so.

Yet nothing excused Raul's behaviour towards her.

'As for today, ma'am,' Lukas said, 'I know the Prince was very pleased with your first official appearance.'

She just bet he was! She'd signed his precious documents. Yet she hadn't missed the way he'd hovered, eager for her to sign and be done with it. If she was truthful, it wasn't just the habit of reading legal papers carefully that had made her delay. A tiny part of her had wanted him on tenterhooks, wondering if she'd go through with it.

As if she'd had a choice! Besides, she'd given her word.

Her heart plunged at the implications of what she'd just done. No turning back now.

'Lukas, I've changed my mind. Can you show me the way to the gardens? I need some fresh air.'

Forty minutes later Luisa felt less claustrophobic. Wandering through the courtyards she'd found a gardener. They'd discussed the grounds with enthusiasm and sign language since her Maritzian was sparse and Gregor, the gardener, spoke a particularly thick dialect.

They'd toured the terraces and rose garden, where Luisa recognised the names of gorgeous old roses her mother had mentioned. They'd visited an orchard in the moat, a walled garden with fountains and arbours and the kitchen garden where Luisa struggled to identify the rarer herbs.

For the first time in days she felt as if she'd stepped out of her nightmare and into the real world, with the scent of rich soil and growing things around her.

She breathed deep as she climbed the spiral staircase in the battlements. Gregor had said, if she understood right, that she'd see the parterre garden from here. She'd read about such gardens, with their intricate patterns laid out in plants and gravel paths, but the view from the ground didn't give the full effect.

She could have seen it from the castle. But she didn't want to meet any of the disapproving VIPs who'd witnessed her accession to the title of Princess of Ardissia.

Princess! Her stomach curdled, thinking about it. Or was that because of the tower? She didn't have a head for heights and the open window beside her gave a dizzying view to the city below.

Luisa pressed a damp palm to the wall and kept moving. Soon she emerged at a low opening looking towards the castle. Someone had been working here and she side-stepped a pile of tools. The opening was so low she felt safer on her knees, her hands on the stonework.

The garden was spectacular, though overgrown. She made out the remnants of the Maritzian dragon, the one flying on the flag from the topmost turret, laid out in the hedges below. Shrubs with gold foliage denoted its eyes and a straggling group of red-leaved plants might have been its fiery breath. Its tail was missing and a path cut through one claw, yet it was still magnificent.

Enchanted, Luisa leaned a little further out.

She'd inherited her mother's love of gardens, though she'd had little time to indulge the interest.

Movement caught her eye. She looked up to see a familiar figure striding through the garden. Raul. Instantly, absurdly, her pulse fluttered.

He saw her and shouted something as he raced forward.

Instinctively Luisa recoiled, feeling as if she'd been caught trespassing. She pushed back and again that dizzy sensation hit. Only this time it wasn't just in her head.

To her horror, the wall beneath her hands shifted. Instead of rising up, her movement pushed her further out, the stone sliding forward with a terrible grinding noise.

She scrabbled back but her centre of gravity was too far forward. With a loud groan, the old sill tumbled out of her grasp to fall, with dreadful resounding thuds, to the ground below.

Luisa lurched forward, spreadeagled over jagged rock, her arms dangling into space and her eyes focused disbelievingly on the sheer drop below. Masonry bruised her ribs but she couldn't get breath to try inching back. Fear of another fall, this time with her in it, froze her.

She couldn't see Raul now and the staccato beat of blood in her ears drowned every sound. Her throat closed so she couldn't even yell for help. Swirling nausea made her head swim.

Her breath came in jerky gasps as she tried to crawl backwards, only to slide further forward as another block tumbled with a reverberating crash.

Any minute now, that could be her.

'It's all right.' The deep, soothing voice barely penetrated her consciousness. 'I've got you.' On the words strong arms slid beneath her waist.

'No!' she gasped, terror freezing her muscles. 'Keep back. It's too dangerous.' Surely Raul's weight with hers on the unstable wall would send them both plummeting.

'Don't move. Just relax and let me do this.'

'Relax?' He must be kidding. Luisa squeezed her eyes shut as swirling dots appeared in her vision.

Her body was rigid as he hauled her back, his arms locked around her. She waited, breathless, for the ominous groan of rock on rock. Instead she heard Raul's indrawn breath as he took her weight against him, dragging her slowly but inexorably to safety.

There was heat behind her. Searing heat that branded her back as he held her to him. His breath feathered her nape and his hands gripped so hard she wondered if she'd have bruises. But they'd be nothing to the bruises on her ribs from the stones. Or to her injuries if she'd fallen.

A shudder racked her and she squeezed her eyes even tighter, trying to block the pictures her mind conjured.

'Shh. It's all right. You're safe. I promise.' Yet the tremors wouldn't subside. Her teeth began to chatter.

Desperately she sought for composure. 'I n-never did l-like heights.'

'Open your eyes.' He held her away and the shaking worsened. Her eyes snapped open in protest but he was already lowering her to sit on the floor.

Luisa slumped like a rag doll, her bones water. Even now the view down to the distant flagstones was emblazoned on her brain.

'Here, lean forward.' She did as she was told and heat enveloped her as Raul draped his jacket around her quaking shoulders. A subtle spicy scent surrounded her. The scent of Raul's aftershave. Or perhaps the scent of him. Luisa breathed deep, letting the fragrance fill her lungs.

She lifted her head. He stood before her, hands on hips, brow pleated and mouth a stark line.

Luisa had seen him without a jacket only once, briefly, in the limo. Always he was impeccably dressed. It shocked her that beneath that tailored elegance was a broad chest of considerable power.

Her eyes trailed over his heaving torso, noting the way his stance drew the fine cotton of his shirt taut, moulding to a body that wasn't that of an effete clothes horse but a strong, very masculine man. Luisa's heart skittered to a new rhythm as she remembered that solid muscle pressed against her on the boat in Paris. No wonder he'd felt so good!

'We need to get you inside where it's warm.' Yet he didn't move to help her rise. Did he see how weak she was?

Shakily she nodded, drawing his jacket close. 'Soon. I need to get my b-breath.' She had to pull herself together but she couldn't quite manage it.

'Here.' With a quick stride, Raul moved behind her. Next thing she knew, those capable hands were on her again. He pulled her up and across his lap as he sat leaning against the wall opposite the gap.

Luisa should protest. She didn't want to be this close to him. But she didn't have the energy to resist and had to be content holding herself as stiff as she could in his arms. As if she could ignore the heat of those solid, muscular thighs or his arms around her!

'I hope that wall's safe!'

'It's fine. Don't worry. It's only the other side that's a problem.' He hauled her closer so her shoulder was tucked into his chest. 'Didn't you see the warning sign?'

She recalled a neat sign at the base of the tower but she'd barely glanced at it.

'The door was unlocked.'

'It won't be in future.' His voice was grim. 'Not until it's safe.' He tugged her closer but she resisted. Any nearer and her head would be on his shoulder. The idea both attracted and horrified her.

'Why did you come up here? You get finer views from the other side of the castle.'

She shrugged jerkily. 'I wanted to see the parterre garden. Gregor showed it to me, but you don't get the effect from the ground.'

'Gregor?' A steely note in his voice made her turn and meet his eyes head-on. They had darkened to a shade of rich forest-green. This close she was surprised to find a glimmer of scintillating gold sprinkled there too.

'Yes.' She found she was leaning towards him and drew back abruptly. 'One of your gardeners. He showed me around.'

The frown returned to Raul's face and his mouth flattened. But, instead of marring his features, it made him look like a sulky angel.

A quiver began low in her stomach that had nothing to do with her recent scare.

'He didn't encourage you to come up here, did he?'

'Of course not.' It was only now she realised Gregor's gestures had been to warn her away from the unsafe structure.

'Thank you for saving me.' She should have thanked Raul immediately but her brain was too frazzled.

'I'm just glad I saw you when I did.' His hold firmed and his frown became a scowl, as if he'd like to blame someone.

Luisa looked at his concerned expression and tried to remember how callous he was. That he'd forced her hand.

'Just think. If you hadn't reached me, you mightn't have had a princess to marry. Then you'd never inherit.'

A large firm hand cupped her jaw and cheek. His gaze snared hers and her breath caught. The gold in his eyes seemed to flare brighter. Or was that because he was nearer?

He shook his head slowly. 'If there was no princess, the contract would no longer bind me.' His thumb slid under her chin and Luisa's eyelashes fluttered as a strange lethargic heat stole through her. 'I'd have been free to marry whomever I want.'

'Is there someone you *want* to marry?' The notion clawed Luisa back from the brink of surrendering to his caress.

'Don't worry, Luisa.' His face loomed closer. 'You're not coming between me and the love of my life.'

'So there's no one special?' It confirmed his cold-blooded approach to marriage. But right now, dazzled by his brilliant stare, lulled by his rhythmic caress and the encompassing heat of his body, Luisa couldn't scrape the energy to be outraged. She felt…distanced from pain. Who'd have thought she'd find solace in Raul's embrace? There was unexpected pleasure in the sense that, for this moment at least, they could be frank.

'No one who matters.' His warm breath caressed her face and she struggled to find the anger that had burned within her before. Surely she shouldn't enjoy being here, with him.

'You really are ruthless, aren't you?' Her tone was conversational, curious, rather than accusing.

It was as if, after the shock of her accident, she floated on another plane where all that mattered was that she was safe in Raul's strong arms.

He shifted and she found her head lolling against his shoulder, his body cradling hers. She almost sighed at how good that felt. She felt boneless, like a cat being stroked in the sun.

'If you mean that I plan to get what I want, then yes.' His lips curved in a smile that held something other than humour. His intense focus reminded her of the way he'd watched her in Paris. Heat filled her.

'Have you always managed to get your own way?' She should protest about how he held her but it felt so good and Luisa liked this new, unreal world where she and Raul weren't at daggers drawn. Where that fragile connection shimmered in the still air.

He shook his head. 'Far from it. I was anything but spoiled. My mother died in childbirth and my father was impatient with children.'

Her heart clenched. No wonder Raul was so self-sufficient. She stared up at his perfectly sculpted mouth, just made for reducing women to mindless adoration.

'But as an adult. With women, I bet you've always—'

'Luisa.' The hand at her jaw slid round to thread through her hair and hold the back of her head. His eyes gleamed with an inner fire. 'You're talking too much.'

She watched those lips descend in slow motion. As if he gave her a chance to pull free. Or to savour their impending kiss. Excitement raced through her.

By the time his mouth covered hers Luisa's breath had

stalled, her lips opening to meet his, her pulse an insistent, urgent beat.

Their kiss was slow, a leisurely giving and receiving of pleasure. Delight swamped her in a warm, sultry wave. This wasn't like the forceful, hungry passion they'd shared in Paris.

A voice in her head tried to point out that in Paris they'd shared nothing. Raul hadn't felt anything.

But Paris seemed so far away.

Here, now, this felt like something shared. Something offered and accepted. Not dominance or submission. Not demand or acquiescence, but something utterly, satisfyingly mutual.

Luisa slipped an arm around his waist, revelling in how his muscles tensed then relaxed to her touch, testament to the leashed power of the man caressing her so gently. The realisation heightened her pleasure.

His tongue curled against hers as he drew her deeper into his mouth and the little voice of sanity subsided, overwhelmed by the magic Raul wove with his kiss, his big body, his tenderness.

Desire unfurled within her like a bud opening to the sunlight. Tendrils spread low to the feminine hollow between her legs. Up to her breasts that tingled as he pulled her closer, as if to absorb her into his body.

Her other hand rose to splay across his neck, discovering the pulse thudding heavily at his jaw. Then up to tangle in the rough silk of his hair.

Raul growled at the back of his throat. The raw sound of pleasure thrilled across her skin and sent heat plunging through her.

The languor that had held her spellbound dissipated and she wriggled against him, wanting more. The tingle of sensation at her hardening nipples became a prickle of need. The lavish, slow swirling eddy of delight in her belly grew more urgent.

Then, abruptly, he pulled back. Just enough for her to see his face. Stunned, it took a moment to read the heat in his hooded gaze and realise he was breathing heavily.

He grasped her wrist and tugged it down, holding it securely away from him.

'Next time—' his nostrils flared as he drew a deep breath '—if you want a tour, ask me. I'll arrange to come with you or have someone guide you. Agreed?'

Silently Luisa nodded, her mind abuzz, her world rocked out of kilter. Could she blame shock for the fact that she wanted to fall back into the arms of the man she'd been so sure she detested?

Two weeks later, in conversation with a gallery curator, Raul found his gaze straying to Luisa. She stood before a display of botanical studies, talking to the junior curator who'd organised the exhibit.

Raul's gaze slid appreciatively up her slender legs. It was the first time he'd seen her in a dress and he couldn't keep his eyes off her. Especially when she smiled at her companion with all the warmth of her sunny homeland.

The impact was stunning. Heat flickered along his veins and pooled in his groin.

She was blossoming into a lovely woman. That had to explain why she'd been knotting his belly with thwarted desire since Paris.

And why he'd succumbed to temptation and kissed her in the tower. His pulse jumped and a spike of something like fear drove through his chest at the memory of her sprawled out over that fatal drop. The need to hold her and not release her had been unstoppable. The hunger for another sweet taste of her lips inexplicable.

It disturbed him, the force of this unexpected attraction.

She was utterly unlike his usual companions. She was unpolished, preferring flats to high heels and avoiding even the simplest of her inherited jewellery. She had a habit of talking to anyone, particularly the staff, rather than to VIPs. He sensed she'd be as happy chatting to the gardeners as attending a glitzy premiere occasion.

Yet his heart lifted when he was with her.

He told himself that was sentimental twaddle. Yet there was definitely *something* about his bride-to-be.

Raul shook his head. Didn't he prefer his women sophisticated, assured and sexy?

Why did Luisa infiltrate his thoughts at every turn? Why had he found it so hard to release her that day in the tower? Or to pursue his own busy agenda while she began her lessons in language, etiquette, history and culture?

Because he wanted her. And, almost as much as he wanted her, he wanted her company.

Raul turned to his companion. 'Could the Princess and I have time alone to view the rest of the exhibition?'

The curator agreed enthusiastically. Such interest boded well. Two minutes later Raul and Luisa were alone. Even the guard at the door discreetly melted into an adjoining space.

'Thank you.' She turned to him and he saw her eyes were overbright. His heart thumped an unfamiliar beat and his hand closed automatically over hers.

'Are you OK?' He'd thought to please her with this visit, not upset her. Show her she *did* have a connection with his homeland.

'I didn't expect to see my mum's work on show. It was a lovely surprise.'

Raul shrugged. 'She was a talented artist. It's a shame she didn't continue her botanical painting.'

Luisa looked away. 'She dabbled but she said it was a discipline that needed dedication. She couldn't give that. Not with the farm.'

He nodded. It was clear what a toll that place had taken on Luisa's family. Her mother should have more than early works on display. She would have if she'd not embraced a life of hardship. All for the supposed love of a man who could give her so little.

People were fools, falling for the fantasy of love.

So-called love was an illusion. A trap for the unwary. Hadn't he learnt that to his cost?

'It was kind of you to bring me.' She touched his sleeve and looked up from under her lashes in an unconsciously provocative way that made heat curl in his gut. 'Lukas told me you rarely have time for such things, especially now.'

'It was nothing. It's been a while since I visited and there were issues to discuss.' The last thing he needed was for her to get the idea he'd changed his schedule for her. Even if it was true.

Luisa had been stoically uncomplaining through her first weeks in Maritz. Yet the change must be difficult for her. Despite her heavy tuition schedule he'd often glanced up from a meeting to see her wandering in the gardens and he had the discomfiting notion she was lonely, despite her ever-widening acquaintance.

Guilt blanketed him. She was here because of him, his country, his needs. What did she personally get out of it?

She wasn't interested in riches or prestige. The only money she wanted was to save her friends.

His lips twisted. She didn't see *him* as a prize, even if she couldn't conceal the passion that flared when he kissed her. Luisa Hardwicke was a salutary lesson to his ego.

'I had no idea Mum's work was so well regarded.' She turned to examine a delicate drawing of a mountain wildflower and he followed, not wanting to lose the warmth of her hand on his arm.

'Tell me about her.'

Luisa swung round. 'Why?'

He shrugged, making light of his sudden need to understand Luisa's family, and her. 'She must have been strong to have stood up to your grandfather.'

Luisa grimaced. 'Maybe it's a family trait.'

'Sorry?'

She shook her head. 'I thought she was remarkable. And so did my dad.'

Raul threaded his fingers through hers, pleased when she didn't pull away. 'Tell me.'

For a long moment she regarded him. Then she seemed to make up her mind. 'She was like other mums. Hard working, making do, running a household and doing the books. Always busy.' Luisa paused. 'She made the best cinnamon Christmas biscuits and she gave the warmest hugs—guaranteed to make you feel better every time. She loved roses and had an eye for fashion, even if we couldn't afford to buy it.'

Luisa moved to the next picture and he followed. 'She hated ironing and she *detested* getting up early.'

'Not suited to be a farmer's wife then.' The change from palace to dairy must have been hard. Had the marriage been a disaster? He frowned. It didn't sound so.

Luisa laughed, a rich, lilting chuckle and Raul's senses stirred. 'That's what Dad used to say. He'd shake his head and pretend to be scared she'd go back to her glamorous world. Mum would smile that special smile she saved for him and say she couldn't possibly leave till she mastered the art of cooking sponge cakes as well as my aunt. Dad would say no one could ever make sponges like Mary, so Mum would just have to stay for ever. Then he'd kiss her.'

Raul felt the delicate tremor in her hand and watched a wistful smile flit across Luisa's features. He knew an unaccountable desire to experience what she had. The warmth, the love. A childhood of cinnamon biscuits and hugs. How different from his own upbringing!

'But how did it work?' He found himself curious. 'They were so different.'

She shrugged. 'They came from different worlds but they made their own together. Dad said she made him feel like a king. Mum always said he made her feel more like a princess than she'd ever felt living in a palace.' Luisa swung to face him. 'Life with my grandfather wasn't pleasant. He tried to force her into marrying someone she detested, just to cement a deal. There was no laughter, no fun. Not like in our home.'

Someone she detested. Did Raul fit that category for Luisa? He told himself the country must come first, yet he couldn't squash regret.

'They were in love; that was the secret.'

It didn't take a genius to know that was what Luisa had wanted for herself. Till he'd come along.

Never before had Raul's duty seemed so onerous. He was doomed to disappoint her. He didn't even believe in love. He'd never experienced it.

'But she loved it here.' Luisa turned to him, her smile a shade too bright. 'Mum wanted to bring us one day to see it.'

'I'm glad.' He paused, clasping her hand more firmly. 'In time I hope you come to love it too. It's a special place. There are no people like Maritzians.'

'You're not biased, are you?'

'Surely that's my prerogative.' He led her towards the rest of the exhibition, regaling her with a traditional local story. It surprised him how much he wanted to hear her laugh again.

Raul strode swiftly to his study. There was a crushing amount of work to do and, though the unrest in the provinces had abated a little, he couldn't afford to be complacent.

Yet the wedding tomorrow, a small affair since the nation was in mourning for his father, would pave the way for his coronation and go a long way to solving his problems.

Taking his bride to bed would go a long way towards easing the permanent ache in his groin.

Anticipation pulsed in his blood at the thought of his wedding night to come. His desire for Luisa grew daily.

The more time he spent with his bride-to-be the more she fascinated him. She was vibrant, engaging, determinedly independent and down-to-earth. Different from every other woman he knew.

Even now he never knew what to expect from her.

Lukas approached as he reached the study.

'Your Highness.' He fell into step beside Raul.

'Yes? Am I late for my meeting?'

'No, not that.' His secretary hesitated, his mouth turning down. 'You have a visitor. I wanted to warn—'

'Raul. Darling!' The husky female voice came from the

door ahead. For one shattered instant Raul felt his feet rivet to the floor as shock vibrated through him. His hands clenched into fists. Then, bracing himself, he slowly approached the blonde draped in the doorway.

'This is unexpected, Ana. What are you doing here?'

'Surely you didn't expect me to miss your wedding, darling?' She straightened and lifted her head, her lips a crimson pout. 'Your invitation didn't reach me. Luckily I heard about it on the grapevine.'

He stopped a metre away, distaste prickling his skin. Foolishly, he'd thought he'd seen the last of her, for the time being at least.

They weren't in public so there was no need for a courteous bow. And she could wait till hell froze over before he took up the invitation implicit in that pout.

Not when she was the woman who eight years ago had dragged him to hell.

CHAPTER SEVEN

'LUISA, you look so lovely!' Tamsin said. 'This pearly cream is wonderful with the golden tone of your skin.'

'You think so?' Luisa stood stiffly, uncomfortable in the full length gown of silk. The fitted bodice covered with cobweb-fine hand-made lace. The diadem of finely wrought gold and pearls.

The bridal dress showcased the finest traditional Maritzian products. Lace from one province. Hand woven silk from another. The exquisite filigree gold choker necklace that made her throat seem elegant and impossibly fragile was by craftsmen in yet another province. Beaded slippers from still another.

Only the bride hadn't been involved in the design of her wedding clothes.

Gingerly Luisa turned to the mirror, feeling a fraud under the weight of this charade.

Yet the image awaiting her took her breath away. Could that really be *her*? A woman who till recently had spent her days in jeans and gumboots?

'You look like a fairy princess.' Tamsin shook a fold of embossed silk so the flaring skirt draped perfectly.

'I don't feel like it.' Nausea churned in Luisa's stomach. It was only through sheer willpower that she'd nibbled at a fruit platter for lunch. She whose appetite was always healthy!

'Believe me.' Tamsin clasped her hand briefly and smiled. 'You'll take everyone's breath away. Especially Raul. He won't be able to take his eyes off you.'

Luisa saw the other woman's secret smile and wondered if she was thinking of her recent marriage to Prince Alaric, Raul's distant cousin. It was clear that the big man with the steely jaw and face almost as handsome as Raul's was deeply in love with his new English wife.

For a moment Luisa let herself imagine what it would be like to marry for love. Burnt so badly years ago, she'd buried herself on the farm, shunning any hint of male interest. She'd longed to experience true love but had she been too craven to open herself to the possibility?

The day Raul had saved her from falling and kissed her so tenderly she'd allowed herself to be swept along by his deep voice, his gentle hands and the unstoppable cravings that welled at his touch.

For one fragile interlude she'd longed to believe something warm and special could grow from their union.

Then there was his unexpected kindness, taking her to see her mother's work.

But the fantasy was too painful. It scraped too close to the bone for a woman who'd been chosen, not for love or respect. Not even for convenience. But because Raul had no other option!

'It's good of you to help me get ready.' She sent a shaky smile in Tamsin's direction. Though this wasn't a romantic match it was her wedding day. The day women looked to their mother for support.

Luisa had never missed her mum more.

'It will be all right.' Again Tamsin took her hand, chafing warmth into it. 'I know how daunting it is marrying into a new world. Marrying royalty. But Raul will look after you. He's like my Alaric. Strong and protective.' She sent a speculative glance at Luisa. 'And I suspect behind that well bred calm, very passionate.'

Heat roared through Luisa's cheeks, banishing the chill that had frozen her all day.

Tamsin giggled, blushing herself. 'Sorry. I didn't mean to

embarrass you. It's just sometimes I feel like pinching myself. It all seems so unreal!'

'I know what you mean.' Tamsin was an outsider too—a commoner and a foreigner who'd married her prince in a love match that had intrigued everyone. But Tamsin had fallen in love. Luisa would face her royal marriage and the weight of public expectation without love to cushion the shock. Their circumstances were so different.

'I'm glad you're here,' she added, grateful to this initially reserved but warm-hearted woman.

'So am I! And when you settle in, after your honeymoon, I hope we can spend more time together.'

Luisa nodded, not bothering to disabuse her. Raul was a workaholic. That was why the trip to the gallery had been such a lovely surprise. He wouldn't take time off for a honeymoon. Not with a wife he didn't really want.

A wife who was simply a solution to a problem.

A cold lump of lead settled in the pit of her belly as a soft knock sounded on the door.

'It's time, Your Highness.'

The music swelled and the massive doors swung open and Luisa stepped over the threshold into the castle chapel.

Multicoloured streams of light shone through ancient windows. A cloying wave of fragrance hit. Hothouse flowers and incense and a multitude of perfumes. Hundreds of faces turned to stare. She didn't know a single one.

A rising tide of panic clawed at her, urging her to turn tail and run, as fast and as far as she could. Her heart slammed against her ribs and her knees shook.

She faltered, her hand curling into Alaric's sleeve. He covered her hand with his and leaned close. 'Luisa?'

'This is a *small* wedding?' Dazed, she saw heraldic banners, including some of the Maritzian red dragon, streaming from the lofty ceiling. The crowd murmured and it sounded like a roar.

'Courage, little one. It'll soon be over.' He paced forward

and she had no option but to follow. 'Tamsin and I have a bet on who spots the most absurd hat. Weddings incite women to wear the most monstrous things on their heads, don't you think?'

His *sotto voce* patter continued all the way down the aisle, almost distracting her from the throng of hungry-eyed guests. Watching. Judging. Finding her wanting.

Suddenly she caught a smile. Tamsin, in muted gold, giving her an encouraging nod. Behind her was another woman, platinum blonde, dripping jewels yet sour-mouthed.

Then, abruptly, they were at the end of the aisle. Bands of steel squeezed the breath from her lungs as, with a sense of inescapable inevitability, she turned her head towards the dark figure she'd avoided since she entered.

Raul, tall and heart-stoppingly handsome in a uniform of scarlet and black that made him look like the model for Prince Charming.

Something in her chest rose and swelled. Was it possible that perhaps they could make this work? The other day they'd surely started building a fragile relationship.

Then she read his expression. Austere, proud, stern. Not a scintilla of pleasure. A complete absence of anything that might one day turn into love. His mouth was a stern line, his jaw chiselled rock.

She blinked quickly, hating herself because even now, faced with his indifference, she yearned for the tenderness he'd begun to show her.

How could she? She knew what she was to him. How could she be so weak as to want the impossible?

Luisa gulped. It was like swallowing shards of glass.

Just as well she hadn't allowed herself to pretend he reciprocated her inconvenient attraction.

Her hand tightened, talon-like as Alaric ushered her forward. But Raul took her hand in his, his other hand at her elbow as she swayed.

She had to quell this anxiety. She'd *agreed* to this. She looked away, to the mass of flowers by the altar: a riot of roses, orange blossom and lilies. Their scent was too pungent for her roiling stomach.

The priest spoke but Luisa didn't listen. She was thinking that at home lilies were traditional for funerals.

'Who *is* that woman?' Luisa watched the petite platinum blonde lean into Raul, her hand possessive on his arm. Her scarlet dress matched his jacket perfectly and her plunging neckline showed a stunning cleavage. She smiled up, her face hardly recognisable as the one that had scowled at Luisa in the chapel.

'She wasn't in the reception line,' Luisa added.

Raul stood on the other side of the reception room, his back to Luisa, but from here she'd almost swear the woman flirted with him. A spike of heat roared through her. Heat and anger. 'Is she an ex-girlfriend?'

Beside her Tamsin spluttered, choking on champagne.

'Are you OK?'

Tamsin waved her away. 'I inhaled some bubbles. I'm not used to champagne.'

Luisa knew the feeling. This evening she'd sipped some, standing beside Raul for a formal toast. The wine had tickled her senses and tingled all the way down her throat. But it was Raul's presence beside her, like a wall of living heat, that had made her giddy. His stern expression had eased for a moment and his lips had curved in a heady smile as he toasted her. The impact had knocked her for six and Luisa had felt as if she were floating.

As if this were a real wedding and she a bride smitten with her handsome husband! Instead of a woman blackmailed into cooperating. That still rankled.

Luisa stiffened. It scared her that Raul affected her so. That she might be jealous of the woman pawing at his jacket. It should be impossible, yet...

'You don't know her?'

Finally Tamsin looked up. A flush tinted her cheeks.

'Tamsin?' Her new friend's expression made Luisa tense.

'The woman with Raul? No one you need worry about.' The words came out in a rush. 'She lives in the US now.'

'But who *is* she?'

Tamsin took another quick sip of wine. 'That's Ana. Raul's stepmother.'

Stepmother?

'But she's too young!' She didn't act like a stepmother. The other woman was flirting outrageously. Luisa's only consolation came from the fact Raul stood as stiffly as he had through the wedding ceremony, though he inclined his head as if listening intently.

'I think she and Raul are about the same age.'

Through her shock Luisa heard Tamsin's intense discomfort. She saw Tamsin's gaze dart away as if seeking a diversion and uneasiness stirred.

Intuition told her there was something Tamsin wasn't saying. Luisa turned back, finally noticing how the guests kept their distance from the pair. No one had approached Raul since his stepmother had claimed his attention but they all watched speculatively. An undercurrent of whispers eddied around them.

The frisson of uneasiness grew to stark suspicion.

No! Luisa refused to draw conclusions about Raul's relationships. No matter what her eyes told her.

Yet she couldn't stifle a feeling of betrayal.

As if sensing her scrutiny, Raul turned sharply, his gaze skewering her. Fire seared her blood and she felt as if she'd been caught out spying on him.

But she had every right to be here. This was *her* wedding reception. *Her* day. Even if it wasn't her choice.

Hysterical laughter bubbled in her throat. Today should be the happiest day of her life!

If she didn't laugh at the absurdity surely she'd cry.

Holding Raul's eyes, she lifted her chin and downed the rest of her champagne.

'If you'll excuse me, Tamsin, I'd better introduce myself to my mother-in-law.' Luisa passed her glass to a waiter and picked up her skirts, grateful now for the formal dress that kept her posture perfect and made guests move aside as she stalked forward.

She was magnificent. She cut a swathe through the crowd as if it didn't exist, her eyes locked with his.

A pulse of heat thudded deep in his belly at the sight of her: jaw angled, eyes glittering, chest swelling against the demure V neckline. She skimmed across the polished floor, her train sweeping magnificently behind her. Tiny bursts of fire peeped from beneath her hem as her jewel-encrusted slippers caught the light. It was as if she set off sparks with each step.

Absently Raul brushed Ana's clawing hand away. He'd done what he had to—accepted her presence publicly. But he'd had enough.

He'd had enough of her eight years ago!

He barely registered her protest as he strode instead towards the woman he'd just married and pleasure surged.

All day tension had ridden him. Worries for the state. Fury at Ana's return. Discomfort at the idea of marrying. Guilt at forcing Luisa's hand. The need to bury his thoughts deep behind a cloak of royal calm. Now the tension morphed into something that had nothing to do with concerns and everything to do with his long-suppressed needs.

And with the challenge he read in his bride's expression, her posture, her firmed lips.

Her eyes flashed azure fire and heat danced in his veins. He drew a breath, the first free breath all day.

He'd done his duty in marrying. Now he wanted to forget about duty, about diplomacy and building bridges with intransigent politicians and soothing the bruised egos of his father's cronies. About his own doubts.

He wanted…Luisa.

A smile cracked his carefully schooled features.

'Luisa, you look enchanting.' Her pace propelled her forward and he took full advantage, stepping before her at the last moment and putting a hand to her waist, ostensibly to steady her. Through the lace and silk he felt warmth and lithe muscle and the deep exhalation of her breath.

He grasped her other hand in his and lifted it to his mouth. Her eyes blazed and he almost smiled at the provocation in her glare. Instead he turned her hand and pressed his lips to her wrist. He heard her breath catch and a satisfying tremor rippled through her. Slowly he moved his mouth, kissing her palm and touching his tongue to the erogenous zone at its centre.

Her eyes widened and he felt pleasure tug through his belly. She tried to draw her hand away but he held her.

'Aren't you going to introduce me to your mother?'

He read the doubt and hurt pride in her eyes and silently applauded her front.

'You mean my father's second wife. Not my mother.'

'My mistake.' She bit the words out precisely with her even white teeth. 'You two looked so close…'

Little cat.

This was what he'd missed. Much as he enjoyed having his plans go smoothly and the tantalising sense of closeness he'd experienced with Luisa now and then, he'd missed her vibrancy. From the first she'd sparked with energy and defiance. She'd obstructed him and argued and defied him. Even consenting to wed she'd been proud as an empress.

He enjoyed her sassiness when she stood up to him. He'd grown accustomed to fireworks. He enjoyed them more than he'd thought possible. Especially when it wasn't argument that fuelled the conflagration.

Even the hint of jealousy in her tone pleased him. Did her desire match his? A bolt of excitement shot through him. He recalled her passion, the way she melted in his arms. How she watched him when she thought he didn't see.

He leaned forward and whispered, 'I'm not going to introduce her. You wouldn't like her.'

She gaped at his honesty. He wanted to kiss those lush lips till she forgot how to speak. He wanted that sizzling energy channelled in more satisfying directions.

Urgent heat swirled in his loins as he visualised it.

'Why not?' Luisa looked stunned.

'Because she's not at all nice.' It surprised him how much pleasure there was in saying it out loud, even if in a murmur for Luisa's ears alone. How long he'd been constrained by the need to keep up appearances!

'But surely I need to meet her.'

'Hardly. She's leaving for LA tonight. Grabbing a lift with her newest boyfriend, a Hollywood producer.'

Raul didn't even feel the usual simmering anger. Ana couldn't be bothered to feign mourning for her dead husband. Their marriage had been a farce, his smitten father turning a blind eye to anything in his young wife's behaviour that might dent his royal pride.

Raul was tired of pretending his father's marriage was anything but a sham. His father was dead and his ego couldn't be battered any more. Ana didn't deserve more than the merest observance of courtesy. Her attempt just now to wheedle more cash from the royal coffers had been expected but her timing had surprised even Raul, who'd believed himself inured to her grasping ways.

'Come,' he said, turning Luisa with him towards the dais where the royal throne rested. She grabbed her wide skirts and followed. The scent of lavender that accompanied her movements was refreshing after Ana's cloying perfume. He breathed deep and helped his wife up the steps.

The flush colouring Luisa's cheeks was charming. His gaze descended her throat, gorgeous in its gold filigree and pearl choker, down to where her breasts rose and fell rapidly. His palms itched to touch.

Leaving the reception early would cause a stir. But he wasn't in the mood to worry about protocol. After years acceding to duty and convention, trying to compensate for the trauma of earlier royal scandal, Raul chose for the first time to flout tradition.

It felt good. The gossips could go hang.

He reached for his wife's hand, enjoying the way it fitted his own so neatly. Enjoying her presence beside him.

'Highnesses, ladies and gentlemen.' Raul addressed the assembly. When he'd finished the sound of clapping made him turn. There were Alaric and Tamsin, smiling broadly. The applause spread.

Raul raised a hand in acknowledgement, then turned to Luisa. 'It's time we left.'

Her eyes rounded but a moment later she conjured a smile and a wave for their audience. She really was superb.

A moment later Raul ushered her out through the double doors behind the throne, held open by footmen.

Then they were walking down the private corridor, her hand still in his. The doors closed behind them, muting the swell of applause.

Satisfaction filled him. He was alone with his bride.

It happened so quickly Luisa was dazed as he led her through the labyrinth of corridors.

Only two things were real. Raul's warm hand enfolding hers and the fact she was married. Even in the chapel it hadn't seemed real. But hearing Raul tell their guests to enjoy their wedding hospitality, seeing the curiosity, the goodwill, even the envy on some of the faces staring up at her, it had suddenly hit.

She'd bound herself to this man. No turning back.

Her spurt of indignation over his stepmother dwindled. Now she felt only shock.

Raul's hand tightened and sensation streaked through her.

No, she felt more than shock. A tiny bud of something curled tight inside. Something that kept her hand in his even when she knew she should withdraw it. Something that shortened her breath as Raul halted before an unfamiliar door then stood aside, waiting for her to precede him.

She stepped in then halted. She shouldn't be here in his private apartments.

The door closed, silence enveloping them. Her breathing was overloud as she sought for something to say.

'Come.' A hand at her elbow propelled her forward. 'You need food. You ate nothing at the reception.'

'How do you know?' For much of the reception they'd been on opposite sides of the room.

'I watched you.'

She started, stunned at the idea of Raul concentrating on her all the time he'd chatted with dignitaries. The notion sent a ribbon of heat through her.

'And you had just one glass of champagne.'

Her gaze melded with his. The kindling heat she saw made her look hastily away.

'Maybe a bite of something would be a good idea.' Then she'd go. She felt too aware of him beside her.

Aware of herself too, in a new, unsettling way. Of the swish of rich fabric around her legs as she moved. Of the tight clasp of the fitted bodice at her waist and breasts as she struggled to draw in oxygen. The fabric of her bra seemed suddenly abrasive, drawing her nipples to taut peaks.

She stepped away, only to stop again abruptly. Her eyes widened. 'This looks…intimate.' It sounded like an accusation.

'Does it matter?'

'Of course it matters!' Luisa bit her lip at her high pitched response. She sounded like a schoolgirl, not a mature woman.

A low table was drawn up before a massive sofa long enough for even Raul to recline full length. Velvet cushions made it look plush and inviting. A foil-topped bottle nestled in a silver cooler. Cold lobster lay sumptuously arrayed beside a bowl of fresh ice that cradled gleaming beads of caviar.

Luisa stepped back abruptly, only to find Raul behind her. She spun round, hands planted on his chest as if to ward him off. So why did her fingers curl into his jacket?

Hurriedly she retreated. 'Is this someone's idea of a joke? It's like a clichéd set for a seduction.'

'You don't like lobster?'

'Well, yes.' She'd only tried it here in the castle and had loved every mouthful.

'Or fruit?' He gestured and she spied a platter of her favourite fruits: peaches and cherries and glowing navel oranges. Beside them was a bowl of fresh berries. Beyond that a basket of bread rolls—not the fine dinner rolls that graced the royal table but the malty whole-grain bread, thick with seeds, that she'd discovered when she'd invited herself to the kitchens. Traditional peasant fare, she was told. The best bread she'd tasted.

Luisa leaned closer. Beyond that were fat curls of butter, a board of cheeses and a silver bowl of cashews. Her favourites.

A familiar jar at the end of the table caught her eye. Mary's spidery writing on the label: raspberry jam.

Luisa blinked hard, her pulse thudding. She reached out and stroked the thick glass jar of her aunt's home-made jam, the jam she'd been helping make since she was a child. A taste of home. Luisa could barely believe he'd taken the trouble to ask Mary for this.

Raul hadn't just clapped his hands and ordered a feast. This was just for her. Something special. His unexpected thoughtfulness blindsided her.

'How did you…?' Her throat closed on emotion.

'How did I know you prefer fruit to gateaux, cheeses to chocolate?'

Shaken, Luisa turned. He stood so close she saw again that sparkle of gold in his dark green gaze.

'Because I notice everything about you.' His voice was deliciously deep. 'You are my wife now. I want you to be happy.' The warmth in his tone made her tremble inside.

Not even to herself would she admit how those words eased her wounded soul.

'But not like *this*.' Her wide gesture encompassed the sofa, the crystal flutes, the whole seductive scene. 'We agreed to a marriage of convenience!'

Was she trying to convince herself or him? From the

moment she'd stepped into his chamber she'd had the delicious sense of walking on a knife-edge of excitement.

Raul said nothing. Yet his look heated her skin. His mouth was a sensual line of temptation she had to resist.

Luisa's heart drummed an urgent tattoo. Part of her wanted nothing more than to touch him. To feel his power beneath her hand. That was why she forced her hands behind her back and kept them there.

Did he read her desire? His brilliant green eyes were hot with an inner blaze and Luisa realised how close she came to being singed.

'We married for legal reasons.' Her words were slurred because her tongue was glued to the roof of her mouth. 'So you can inherit. Remember?'

'I remember.' His voice was low, resonating through her body to places she didn't know existed before. 'I remember how it felt to kiss you too. Do you recall that, Luisa? The fire between us? The need?'

She shook her head and her veil swirled between them. It snagged on the gold braiding that marched across his tunic, emphasising the breadth of his chest.

'It wasn't like that. You just…'

Her throat closed as he untangled her veil. His fingers were centimetres from her breast and she sucked her breath in, trying not to think of him touching her there.

But breathing meant movement. Her breast brushed his hand. She gasped as sensation pierced her and she trembled.

He didn't look up but she saw his lips curve.

'I'm not some passing amusement.' She gritted her teeth, trying not to breathe too heavily.

'I never thought you were. I take you much too seriously for that.' His eyes snared hers and she forgot about breathing. His hands dropped away to hold hers, warm and firm. 'You are my bride. You'll be the mother of my children. I don't take you lightly at all.'

His mouth curved up in the sort of smile mothers had

warned their daughters about for centuries. Luisa felt its impact like a judder of power right down to the soles of her feet.

Her heart raced—in indignation she assured herself. Yet indignation had nothing to do with the hunger coiling inside or the febrile heat flooding her body.

'I never agreed to share your bed.'

She tried to summon anger but discovered instead a jittery thrill of dangerous excitement.

'You don't want children?' His brows rose.

'Of course I want—' She stopped and tried to harness her skittering thoughts. 'One day.' Once she'd dreamed of a family. But with Raul? She'd thought this a paper marriage. Or had she deliberately deceived herself? Heat poured across her skin and eddied deep in her womb.

The trouble was he tempted her with the very thing she'd tried unsuccessfully to deny wanting: him. From the first she'd been unable to prevent herself responding to him at the most basic level.

He took desire for granted but for her it was momentous. Life-changing. She'd learnt distrust too young.

His smile would reduce a lesser woman to a puddle of longing. Luisa it merely turned to jelly. Her knees gave way with a suddenness that astounded her.

Why didn't it surprise her when he swept her up against his chest in one fluid, easy move?

'I never said…'

He crossed the room as if she weighed nothing, entering another chamber and kicking shut the door. This room held a wide bed that seemed to stretch for hectares. The sight of it dried her mouth.

He lowered her and Luisa shut her eyes, wishing she didn't delight in the friction of each slow, tormenting centimetre as she slid against him.

'I thought you had spirit, Luisa. Why are you afraid?' His tone sharpened. 'Did someone hurt you?'

Her eyes snapped open at his husky anger.

'No, I wasn't hurt.' Not physically at least.

Yet he was right. She was afraid: of these new overwhelming feelings. Afraid she'd lose herself if she gave in to this longing. That it was a betrayal of her moral code—giving herself to a man she didn't love.

Yet standing here, bereft now of his touch, feeling the heat of his breath on her face and his body so close, desire twisted deep. Hunger for an intimacy she'd never had. Would never have with love, not now she'd given herself in a cold, practical bargain.

He'd robbed her of that chance.

The realisation was an icy hand on her heart.

She'd never experience true love. Would never have what her parents had shared. That was what she'd always hoped for, especially after the disaster of her first romance.

The knowledge doused her fears and made her angry as never before. Scorching fury rose, stronger than regret or doubt.

Raul had taken so much from her.

'Is it so wrong to find pleasure together?' He voiced the thoughts that already ran, pure temptation, through her head. 'You disappoint me, Luisa. I thought you woman enough to admit what you feel.'

Luisa stared up into his hot gaze and wanted nothing more than to wipe away his smug self-satisfaction. For him desire was easy. No longing for love. No doubts or fears.

A tumble of images cascaded in her head. Turning on her heel and storming out. Or walking serenely, with a cool pitying expression on her face as she left him behind. None of them did justice to the roiling tide of emotion he'd unleashed.

Instead Luisa stepped in, slamming hard against his body. She took his face in her palms and kissed him full on the mouth. She leaned in to him till, with a flurry of billowing silk, they collapsed onto the bed.

CHAPTER EIGHT

IT WAS like holding a flame, or a bolt of lightning.

Luisa was all urgent energy. Her touch, her body, igniting explosions in his blood.

Sensation speared through him. White light flickered behind his eyelids as she pushed her tongue into his mouth in an angry, urgent mating. There was little finesse but her hunger incited the most possessive urges.

She grabbed his scalp as if to imprison him with her scorching passion.

Raul welcomed it, meeting her questing tongue in a desperate kiss that was more like a battle for supremacy than a caress.

He felt alive as never before, caught by a throbbing force that drove every thought from his head but one.

The need for Luisa. Now.

He growled in his throat as he lashed one arm around her waist and the other lower, clamping his hand on her bunched skirts to pull her tight against his groin as he sank back on the wide bed. He was on fire.

Splayed over him, she wriggled as if she too couldn't get close enough. He pushed his hips up and felt her legs slide satisfyingly wide to surround him.

Yes!

It was as if she'd smashed the lock on his self-control. All those primitive urges that he, as a civilised man, had learned to suppress, roared to the surface, stripped bare by this woman who kissed as if she hated him.

He knew passion, used it as a release from the difficulties of life under the spotlight. But never had it been this blistering current of untrammelled power.

Again he rocked up into her encompassing heat and she pushed down to meet him with a jerky movement that spoke of need rather than grace.

Raul scrabbled at the mass of her skirts, pulling it higher and higher around her back till finally he touched silky bare skin. His pulse throbbed in his throat and his groin simultaneously as he clamped both hands to the taut warm silk over her backside. He could almost swear flames crackled around them.

The sound of her cry, a wordless mew of encouragement against his mouth, notched the tension impossibly higher.

Holding her tight, he drew her pelvis to his in a circling movement and sparks ignited in his blood.

A moment later he had her on her back, a tumble of silk and lace and femininity. Hands around her slim waist, he tugged her higher up the bed with a strength born of urgency.

She was flushed, her eyes a narrow glitter of heaven, her lips open and inviting as she gulped in air. Her breasts strained against the tight bodice and he allowed himself a moment's diversion. He covered one breast with his hand, feeling her arch into his touch, her nipple a pebbled tease to his palm. He rotated his hand, squeezing gently and she groaned, her eyes slitting shut and her body moving restlessly.

With his other hand Raul was already busy scooping metres of silk up and away to uncover her calves, her thighs. But a man could do two things at once. He ducked his head and kissed her open-mouthed on the breast, drawing lace and silk and her hard little nipple against his tongue.

Her hands clamped his head close and her breath was a hiss of delight. Beneath him she twisted and bucked as if seeking the weight of his body on hers.

He'd never had a woman so wild for him. No games, no subtlety, just a devastating need that matched his own.

Such pure passion was liberating.

Raul let his hand skim up Luisa's thighs to her panties, pressing hard and discovering damp proof of her need. It was all the encouragement he required.

Seconds later he'd loosened his trousers and freed himself enough to slide his length against her hot apex in a move so arousing he had to pause and gather his scattered wits.

Luisa wouldn't wait. She circled her hips in hungry little movements that tore at the last vestige of his control.

Propped on one arm, Raul ripped away the delicate fabric of her panties and settled himself on her.

'Is this what you want?' His voice was thick, rough with desire and the promise of unsurpassed pleasure.

Azure fire blazed from her eyes. He read passion and something fierce and unfamiliar. But her body eased beneath him. She was enticingly soft, reassuringly strong and vibrating with erotic energy.

She panted for him yet he wanted to hear the words. Why, he had no idea.

He fitted one hand to her upthrust breast and felt her jolt beneath him.

'Tell me, Luisa.' He pushed against her, torturing himself as much as her with the luscious friction of body on body. 'What do you want?'

Her eyes widened and he felt himself sink into their brilliance. She rose, tugging his head down and her mouth took his, greedily, tongue swirling and plunging.

Raul struggled against the force of her ardour and his own pleasure. But it was too much. Too close.

With a muffled groan he gave in and reciprocated, tasting her, almost taming her mouth with his then retreating so the kiss became a mutual give and take of sensual combat.

Using his thighs, he nudged her legs wider and settled himself at her entrance. He slid one hand over blonde downy hair to find the nub of her pleasure. One stroke and she shivered. A second stroke and she shuddered.

'Raul!' His name was a tiny, breathless gasp that shattered his fragile control.

A moment later, his mouth claiming hers, he drove inside. Pressure screamed through him as tight, hot, silken walls enclosed him. Tighter than was surely possible. Raul felt her tremble around him, her raised thighs quaking against his hips.

Stunned, he made to draw back but Luisa fastened her hands in his hair and kissed him with a desperation that made his head swim. Or was that from the relief of finally being sheathed in her body?

She wrapped her legs around him and he sank deeper, lodging fully in exquisite pleasure. He braced himself as the trembling spread from her body to his, making his nape prickle and every muscle quake with tension.

It was no good. Stillness was impossible. Clamping his hands on her hips, he slid back, seeing stars behind closed eyelids as sensation rushed through him.

Another second and he thrust again, harder, longer, as he gave in to the force of a desire that had ridden him ever since that night in Paris.

'I'm sorry. I can't…' His words were swallowed by the roar of blood pounding in his ears.

Dimly he heard a cry rend the air. Luisa convulsed around him, tearing at his strength and his consciousness as he lost himself in delight.

Frantically his body pumped, driven by a force so strong only Luisa's gasps anchored him to reality. His movements crescendoed, wringing out every last vestige of white-hot pleasure, till, with lungs bursting and the world spinning away, Raul sank into oblivion.

Despite his weight on her, Luisa felt as if she were floating. Echoes of incredible pleasure shimmered through limbs taut with the aftershock of tension.

Finally she gathered the strength to move a fraction and let her legs, impossibly heavy, sink to the cushioned mattress. She felt the hint of an ache in untried muscles but even that felt satisfying. Her arms clasped Raul tight. She could barely breathe but the feel of him blanketing her was...comforting.

Stunned, she thought about opening her eyes, but the notion of reality intruding on the single most remarkable experience of her life stopped her.

Even now she couldn't put a name to the feelings that had burst out of nowhere when she'd confronted Raul at their wedding reception. Or when he'd dared her to make love with him. No...have sex with him.

She swallowed, trying to ignore the strange winded sensation in the region of her heart.

If that was having sex, what would making love be like?

How could something so glorious have come out of such turbulent emotions?

Luisa waited for shame to engulf her. For regret that she'd given herself to a man who, though her husband, didn't truly care for her, didn't love her.

Yes, there was regret. Sadness that she'd never know what it was like to be with a man she loved and who loved her.

Yet she couldn't hide from the fact that with Raul she'd felt...different, glorious, powerful. The words didn't do justice to the sensation of soaring, of life and excitement and pleasure bubbling through her veins when they'd come together. Even when they argued it was there, a hidden promise that egged her on to defy him.

What did it mean? Luisa's brow knotted as she tried to work through her feelings. But she was too dazed by the enormity of what had just happened. Thinking was too hard when simply lying here with Raul was so wonderful.

A knuckle gently grazed her brow. 'Don't frown. It's not the end of the world.'

Luisa's eyes snapped open and she found herself staring into Raul's face. He looked as perplexed as she felt. A lock of dark hair tumbled over his brow, making him seem younger,

more approachable. Her hand itched to brush it from his forehead but, despite what they'd just shared, the act seemed too
intimate.

He moved, easing his weight onto his elbow, and she flushed,
realising they were still joined intimately. She looked away but
he turned her head towards him.

'You didn't tell me.'

'Tell you what?' The lovely lax feeling of contentment vanished and her muscles tensed.

'That you hadn't done this before.' His beautiful mouth
twisted.

Had it been that obvious? While the passion lasted it hadn't
mattered to Luisa. All that counted was her need and the fact
that Raul reciprocated with equal urgency. Had he been disappointed? Her stomach dived.

'Does it matter?' She kept her gaze fixed on his mouth
rather than his knowing eyes.

His lips thinned. 'Of course it mattered. I would have made
sure it was better for you.'

Her gaze flew up, colliding with an intense green stare. It
was on the tip of her tongue to ask how it could possibly be
better, but she managed to stop herself.

At the memory of what they'd done Luisa breathed deep,
internal muscles clenching. To her shock she felt an answering
throb inside as Raul stirred. His mouth tipped into a smile that
was rueful and devastatingly glorious and Luisa's heartbeat
picked up speed.

'I could do that now,' he offered. To her amazement, Luisa
felt her body hum with answering desire. So soon!

It frightened her how easily he'd made her need him. How
readily she responded. Despite his occasional devastating tenderness, to him she was a convenience.

If she tried she'd convince herself what they'd just done
meant as little to her as it must to him.

She just had to try harder.

'I need to get up. This dress will be a mess.'

Abruptly he withdrew, his smile fading. Luisa bit her tongue rather than cry out for him not to move. Without his weight pressing on her she felt lost.

How could she miss his touch so soon?

Shakily she drew her crumpled skirts down over her nakedness while he stood and adjusted his trousers. She had to remember he was used to dealing with desire. With sex. For him it was nothing special.

'Here, let me.' He took her arm and drew her up to a sitting position.

Avoiding his eyes, Luisa looked down at her creased and rumpled silk. Her throat clogged. 'It's ruined.'

'Nonsense. It just needs a little attention. Don't worry, the palace has expert launderers.'

Shakily Luisa stroked the fabric, noticing a tear in the fine lace, feeling dampness at her bodice where Raul had suckled. What had seemed magnificent just minutes ago now seemed anything but. 'They'll know what we've done.'

'No one expects us to be celibate.' Once more he tilted her chin up. 'You shouldn't be ashamed of what we did.' He paused and she sensed he hesitated. 'Are you?'

Something passed between them, a surge of heat, a sense memory of passion. Luisa felt fire flicker in her belly. So, it wasn't over after all. It was still there, this…craving for his touch.

That was when she faced the truth. 'No, I'm not ashamed.' She wanted her husband still, again.

She shouldn't crave intimacy with the man who'd treated her so. Yet the feelings he unleashed subverted her pride.

'Good. Because I intend for it to happen often.' His hand slipped up to caress her cheek and she caught her breath at the gleaming promise in his look. 'Turn around and I'll help you out of that dress. You'll feel better after a bath.'

Luisa twisted sideways, telling herself she wasn't disappointed at his prosaic request.

It was only natural she'd enjoy sex with her virile, handsome husband. They were young and healthy. These…urges were to be expected. Yet she couldn't shake the feeling that nothing was quite that simple.

Luisa didn't understand her feelings. One minute he outraged her. The next he intrigued. He wasn't the sort of man she told herself she wanted, yet there were times when she liked him too much.

Perhaps she'd fallen for his expert seduction? He was vastly experienced and she a complete novice. Yet there'd been precious little seduction. He'd seemed as out of control as she. Luisa recalled the dazed look in his eyes and how he'd gasped an apology because he hadn't been able to hold back. As if she'd wanted him to!

Her lips curved and her thighs squeezed as satisfaction curled within her.

'Hold still while I get this veil.' The feel of his hands fumbling in her hair sent rivulets of heat through her. Finally he drew the veil aside and tossed it onto a plush chair, a stream of heirloom lace. A reminder, if she needed one, that they came from separate worlds. She couldn't imagine treating such a work of art so cavalierly.

Then she remembered how she'd thrown herself at him, heedless of the beautiful things she wore.

He brought out a side to her she didn't know.

The touch of Raul's fingers at her nape made her breath catch as the mattress dipped behind her.

'This will take a while.' The couturier had insisted on a myriad of buttons, each with its own tiny loop.

Raul sat close, his breath feathering her bare skin. She straightened, nipples tingling. In the silence she heard her breathing grow shallow.

'I wondered…'

'Yes?' She'd never heard Raul hesitant.

'Why were you so set against coming here? It wasn't just the prospect of marriage. From the first you were negative, instantly opposed to inheriting.'

'It bothers you that I didn't swoon at your feet?' Yet from the first Raul had got under her skin as no other.

'If I ever expected that, I know better now. Besides, I prefer you as you are.' Instead of annoyance, she thought she heard admiration in his voice.

Did her senses conspire to fool her?

His fingers brushed her back and her flesh drew tight. A coiling pulse began low in her belly. He devastated her defences. Luisa drew a sharp breath, seeking control.

'Won't you tell me?' His voice was a dark velvet caress.

She shut her eyes. What would it hurt?

'When I was sixteen my mother was diagnosed with a terminal illness. I looked after her.'

'I'm sorry. That must have been hard.'

She nodded, her throat tight. 'At least I was with her. But the point is, just before that some strangers came to the farm, wanting to talk to me. They were sent by my grandfather.' Even now she had to force that word out. The man didn't deserve the title.

'Not to see your mother?'

'No.' A sour taste flooded her mouth. 'His offer was for me alone. He invited me to live with him and learn to be a real princess.' She paused, clasping unsteady hands as she recalled the grandiose promises and the demands.

'At first I was excited. I was thrilled to see him, to be in his home. It was like a fairy tale. Even though he kept me busy at the palace, training me, he said, for when I'd be ready to take my proper place with him.'

'You actually came here? I didn't know.'

She nodded. 'No one did. Obviously I wasn't up to his high standards. But I was here long enough to get his measure and that of the people he mixed with. That put me off ever returning.' She laughed hollowly. 'I was naïve. It took a while to realise I was just a puppet to manipulate. No choices. No career. No control over my own destiny.'

The skimming touch of Raul's fingers was gentle, almost a caress. She knew a ridiculous desire to sink back against him.

'When news came of my mother's illness I saw him for what

he really was. He insisted I sever all links with my parents. He
hated that my mother had walked out on the life he'd planned
for her—a duty wife to some crony. He never forgave her.
When I begged for help to get her better care, he was furious.
According to him, she'd ceased to exist the moment she'd left
her home.'

Luisa shuddered as she recalled the old man's vitriol. His
cruelty.

'By marrying a commoner she'd diluted her aristocratic
bloodlines. It was only his extreme generosity that enabled
him to overlook my tainted birth and offer to take me in.'

A stream of low-voiced Maritzian cut the air. No mistaking
its furious, violent edge.

'I knew he was old-fashioned.' Raul's voice was a lethal
whisper. 'But that's just vicious.'

Luisa felt tears prickle, hearing his outrage and sympathy.
It wrapped round her like a warm blanket.

She'd never told her parents. Couldn't bear to repeat it,
though she suspected her mum had guessed some of it.

Relief filled her at finally spilling the awful truth.

'So you went back to the farm.'

'Mum needed me. And so did Dad. When she died it almost
broke him.'

'Which is when you started taking responsibility for the
co-op. I'm sorry, Luisa.'

She stiffened. 'There's nothing to be sorry for. I *wanted* to
be with them.'

'I meant I'm sorry your first contact with Maritz was so
poisonous. No wonder you hated the idea of the place.'

Her laugh was bitter. 'You can say that again. I thought the
place full of the worst sort of people.'

'Not just your grandfather?'

She hesitated, aware she'd again strayed into territory she'd
never shared.

'Luisa?' He paused. 'Do you want to tell me?' It was the
concern in his tone that did it. The gentleness.

'There was a guy a little older than me at my grandfather's

palace.' She sucked in a breath. 'No one knew I was the prince's granddaughter but when we met in the gardens it didn't seem to matter who I was. We talked and talked.' She cut herself off. How gullible she'd been!

'We met daily. And I…fell for him.' He'd kissed her and she'd believed herself in love. 'He wanted to elope but I refused.' She'd wanted her parents at her wedding.

'That upset him. He tried…' Foul memories surged, chilling her to the marrow and she was grateful for Raul's warmth. 'He tried to force me but I fought him. He left with a black eye, but not before he'd explained the reason he'd bothered with me was because of who I was. He'd found out and decided to use that to his advantage. He was ambitious, you see. Marrying a princess would be a coup.'

'Luisa—' Raul's deep voice was gruff '—I'm sorry.'

'It's not your fault.'

'But it's my country, my people.' No mistaking his regret and indignation.

A touch feathered between her shoulder blades as if he'd pressed his lips there. She was so tempted to ask him to love her again till the disturbing memories receded and all she knew was ecstasy.

Raul made her needy. He made her want things she shouldn't.

On wobbly legs she stood, clasping the loose dress close. She needed to take control. She'd already revealed enough. Despite the relief of sharing, she felt raw.

'I can manage now, if you point me to the bathroom.'

'Let me help.' From behind he tugged the dress.

Resisting would tear the fabric so she cooperated, only to find her bra had somehow got caught up with the gown. Hurriedly she crossed her arms over bare breasts.

'That's enough. I—'

He dragged the cloth down till it pooled at her feet.

Too late she remembered her panties lay in shreds somewhere. She clamped a hand between her legs, feeling moisture there, a reminder of the sex they'd shared. There wasn't even a robe or a towel to cover her nakedness.

He circled before her, tall in his exquisite finery while she wore nothing but stay-up stockings. She felt vulnerable, especially before his magnificent height.

'You're stunning.' The thickening timbre of his voice splintered her thoughts. 'Let me look at you.'

The avid glitter in his eyes, the way his nostrils flared as if to drag in oxygen, spoke of a man at the edge of control. She felt his hands tremble as he took hers. He swallowed jerkily and tendons stood out in his neck.

She'd never been naked before a man. Embarrassed heat flushed her skin. But with it came a buzz of excitement, a rising sense of power.

For Raul looked…enthralled.

Again he swallowed and she saw the rapid pulse in his throat. It mirrored her heartbeat.

He looked like a starving man before a feast, not sure where to begin. She felt again that stirring of power.

With a visible effort he dragged his gaze up. His eyes had a strange unfocused look. Slowly he shook his head. He released her and stepped back.

'You were a virgin. You'll be sore. I shouldn't…'

She didn't feel sore. Not much. She felt wonderful. Because he wanted her as she wanted him? Or because he cared enough to hold back? To put her needs first.

She hugged the knowledge close. It was a small thing but it felt significant.

When he gently scooped her in his arms Luisa curled into him. She delighted in the steady thump of his heart as he carried her to the bathroom.

Minutes later she sank back with a sigh in warm scented water. It was bliss on the gentle ache of muscles.

Under lowered lashes she watched Raul strip off his jacket, roll up the sleeves of his collarless shirt and reach for a large sponge. Anticipation zinged through her.

His swirling touch with the sponge was impossibly erotic.

She gripped the massive tub rather than reach up to brush back the dark lock tumbling over his forehead. He tended her so gently. As if she were precious.

Sweat sheened his face. It trickled down his throat and she wanted to slide her hand along his skin. But his taut frown and grim mouth deterred her.

Until she noticed the bulge in his trousers. No wonder he looked in pain. No wonder his big capable hands shook so badly he'd dropped the soap more than once.

The knowledge set every nerve ablaze.

'I'm getting out.' Luisa struggled to rise.

'Wait!' Heedless of the water, Raul hauled her out with an ease that reminded her of the power hidden under his clothes. She sank into him, spreading her hands over his saturated shirt and muscled chest.

'You need rest.' His jaw set hard as if with strain.

'That's not what I need.' She tilted her chin and met his gaze. 'I need you.'

There, she'd said it and the world hadn't collapsed around her! In fact it felt good.

'*Now.*' Her fingers curled tight in his sodden shirt. She raised herself on tiptoe and pressed her lips to his.

In a flurry of urgent movement he lifted her, strode out and laid her on the bed. Seconds later he'd ripped his shirt open and shrugged it off. Luisa's pulse rocketed as she took in his sculpted torso with its smattering of dark hair. His hands went to his trousers as he heeled off his shoes. A moment later he stood naked and imposing.

She forgot to breathe as she surveyed his perfect form, felt the power radiating from him. Then thought ended as he joined her. He was like a furnace, burning hot.

He touched her all over, palms smooth, fingers teasing. He skimmed and stroked and even tickled till she squirmed and tried to reciprocate. But he held her, his thigh clamped her still, his hands capturing her wrists.

The torture began as he used his lips, tongue and teeth on her body. Minutes turned into an aeon of pleasure.

It was as if he tried to compensate for the speed of their earlier coupling. Delight piled upon delight till Luisa was strung out, quivering with need and pleasure. It was too much, too intense.

'Please, Raul,' she gasped. 'Don't tease.'

He looked up under hooded lids and her breath snagged as he tugged with his mouth at her breast. He held her gaze as his tongue circled her nipple then lapped hard, drawing hot wires of desire through her taut body. She groaned and instantly his hand slid down, stroking at her most sensitive point.

That was all it took.

She cried out as waves of ecstasy crested and crashed within her. Still he held her gaze, even as the world swirled around her and she bucked helplessly beneath his touch. It was wonderful; it left her speechless.

But it wasn't *Raul*.

Luisa clutched at his shoulders and finally, as she sagged spent against the mattress, he settled between her thighs. The feel of his hot flesh there sent a spark of energy through her lax bones and a searing sense of familiarity. Of rightness.

This time he slid home easily. She rejoiced in each magnificent centimetre, excitement stirring anew as he propped his weight above her. His solid chest brushed her sensitive nipples. Friction built to combustible levels with each measured thrust.

But it was his eyes that transfixed her. The connection between them was different this time. She read arousal and restraint in his gaze. And more. Something unguarded and raw. Something honest.

Raul moved faster and Luisa tilted her hips to meet him. Pleasure coiled tighter, lashing them together. It reached breaking point and still their eyes locked.

The climax came. Earth-shattering, mind-blowing ecstasy that went on and on. Through it all their gazes held in silent communication.

It felt like they shared as equals.

CHAPTER NINE

REALITY hit when Luisa woke.

Last night she'd almost believed they shared more than their bodies. But waking alone in Raul's bed reminded her where his priorities lay. Their marriage was about his desire for power. Sex was a bonus they shared.

Her chest tightened as she forced herself to think of it as sex. *It had felt like making love.*

Yet he'd left it to a maid to wake his bride, discreetly pretending not to notice the rumpled bed or that Luisa was naked beneath the fine linen.

Fire scorched Luisa's skin as the girl swept up the rumpled wedding gown, folding the metres of fine hand-worked veil with the reverence it deserved.

Memories seared, of Raul flinging the veil away. Of her standing with the dress at her feet as he held her arms wide and feasted on the sight of her. Of their blazing passion, utterly heedless of her exquisite finery.

Thrumming arousal beat low in her body, just remembering. Appalled, Luisa realised the need Raul had awoken was far from sated. How much she'd changed in one night!

She nodded vaguely as the maid, eyes carefully averted, pointed out the door in the panelling connecting to Luisa's room, for when she wanted to dress.

Luisa hadn't known the apartments were connected. She hadn't even recognised the corridor when Raul had brought her here! She'd been so caught up in her response to him.

Alone at last, Luisa stared at the empty pillow beside her.

She had no right to feel disappointed. She'd known what she was doing. She'd initiated it! But through a night of intimacy, curled close in his arms, she'd forgotten.

What they'd shared had been purely physical. Her skin prickled as she recalled how eager she'd been. It had been almost a relief to let anger push her into reckless desire.

She'd given herself, *knowing* where she fitted in his world. Raul viewed her in terms of her usefulness to him. Despite his tenderness, in that he was like her grandfather.

Pain cramped her belly. Her dream of one day finding love like her parents was dead. This—the ecstasy and the loneliness—would be her lot.

Maybe that was why she'd imagined the fragile connection between them: because it was easier than facing reality.

But she couldn't hide from the world for ever.

Ignoring the breakfast tray, Luisa wrapped a sheet around herself and hurried to the connecting door, determined not to yield to weak regrets. She'd made her bed and now…

She grabbed the door frame and braced herself as sudden realisation smote her. Her knees shook so hard she feared she'd slide to the floor.

They hadn't used contraception! How could she only just have realised?

It scared her—how much Raul scrambled her thoughts. How she changed when she was with him. He raised passions she'd never known. Her every emotion, from anger to joy, seemed so much more intense because of him.

Giving herself to him surely made her more vulnerable to his potent influence. But it was too late to turn back.

All she could do was try to be sensible, remembering they shared a pragmatic, convenient relationship. She couldn't afford to fall into the trap of foolish dreams.

She'd begin with contraception. She wasn't ready to bring a baby into such a situation.

* * *

'Your Highnesses, welcome.' The mayor bowed low, his bald head gleaming in the sun.

But Raul's attention wasn't on the resplendent figure before the town hall. It was riveted on Luisa. In her pale suit and with her golden hair swept up she looked coolly elegant. Yet a darting glance at her full lips and the slenderness of her throat brought waves of memory crashing in on him.

Of Luisa beneath him last night, writhing with a desperate pleasure tinged by innocent wonder that had held him in thrall despite his urgent need for completion. Of her unrestrained passion that blasted through his sophistication and years of experience and reduced him to slavering, uncontrolled need.

As if *he* was the virgin and she the seducer!

Even the feel of her arm as he guided her over the uneven cobblestones made hunger spring to gnawing life. He had to call on all his experience to mask his feelings.

That was what worried him. The fact that she made him *feel*. Not merely mind-blowing lust. Nor simply relief and gratitude that the crown was assured.

A cocktail of emotions had stirred last night as she'd spoken of her grandfather and her would-be seducer. A fierce protectiveness utterly unlike that he felt for his country. Fury at her hurts. Sadness. Tenderness he'd never known.

And joy so profound it had shocked him to the core and driven him from bed this morning, seeking work as a distraction.

Instinctively he tried to deny the intensity of his emotions. He didn't do feelings. That was how he'd survived and rebuilt his life in the face of humiliating public speculation and private pain.

What did Luisa do to him?

Even as a youth, when he'd been smitten by what he'd foolishly deemed love, he'd functioned better than this.

The crowd cheered and it was all Raul could do to remember to wave in acknowledgement. For the first time he had difficulty remembering his duty.

The realisation terrified him.

Duty had been his life. He'd devoted himself to his country with a dedication other men gave to wives and families. It gave him purpose. Had kept him going in that bleak time when his world crashed around him.

'Prince Raul, Princess Luisa, welcome.' The mayor's eyes gleamed admiringly as he bowed to Luisa.

Raul tensed at his blatant stare. He knew an unreasoning desire to pull Luisa behind him out of sight. Or take her to the castle and lock her in his bedroom.

Now *there* was a thought!

The crisp wind brought colour to her cheeks. Last night's passion had softened her lips to a lush, inviting bow that played havoc with his self-control and sent blood surging to his groin. Any minute now and the snapping cameras would catch him in rampant arousal.

'Your Highness?'

A look at the mayor's puzzled face told Raul they were waiting for him.

Dredging up his control, Raul spoke, finding calm in the give and take of official welcome. Yet the undercurrent of awareness heightening every sense disturbed him. A night of passion should slake desire, not increase it.

The mayor turned to Luisa, holding out a huge ornamental key that signified her free entry to every locked building in the capital.

'Welcome to our city, Your Highness. I hope you will be as happy here with us as we are to have you among us.' He spoke in Maritzian then English and the crowd cheered.

She looked sexy as hell. No trace now of the androgynous mud-spattered farmer. Raul imagined unbuttoning her jacket as he'd undone her wedding gown last night and—

'Thank you so much. It's a pleasure to be here.' To Raul's amazement Luisa spoke in slow but clear Maritzian as she turned towards the people lining the square. 'It's kind of you all to come and welcome me to your lovely city. I'll look forward to discovering it for myself.'

The crowd roared.

It didn't matter that Luisa had turned from the microphone so the sound blurred, or that her accent wasn't perfect. The fact that she made the effort to speak Maritzian, when everyone knew from the press release that she wasn't fluent, endeared her to them.

The mayor beamed. Streamers waved and a ripple of applause rose.

Pride surged as Raul watched her smile at the throng. Only he, beside her, saw the stiff set of her jaw and how her hands shook as she clasped the heavy key.

Only he, the man who'd forced her into leaving everything she knew and adopting a role she'd rejected time and again, guessed what it cost her to put on this façade.

Razor-sharp pain speared through him. He'd done what he must for his nation and Luisa had been the one to suffer.

A memory flashed of her pain last night as she'd spoken of her grandfather's manipulation. Raul's hands balled to fists. His own demands must have been like an echo of that dreadful time. The knowledge stirred an uncomfortable, unfamiliar sensation. *Guilt.*

He'd plucked her from her world, one where she was loved and appreciated, and dropped her into an alien place. Into a role even those born to it found challenging.

Last night they'd shared physical pleasure. But he'd persuaded and challenged her into it. Would she have come to him of her own volition?

'Here, let me.' He took the key, disturbed at the shame he felt. He wasn't used to questioning his actions. He'd spent so long sure in the knowledge he acted for the public good.

'It's almost over,' he murmured. 'Just back to the car and that's it.'

Finally Luisa met his eyes and shock sucker-punched him. Gone was the wonderment and warmth that, despite his attempts to rationalise, had turned last night into something remarkable. Something he refused to analyse.

For the first time since she'd agreed to marry, Luisa's gaze was coolly remote.

Inexplicable loss filled him. He'd thought they'd begun to share something more than an acceptance of duty. Instinctively Raul reached for her but she moved away.

At the last moment he remembered to thank the mayor. By the time he'd finished Luisa was ahead of him, her spine erect and poise perfect. That hadn't been learned in the last week. Her mother's teaching?

He followed, his gaze drawn to the slim skirt that shifted over her curves with every step. That was why he didn't see the bustle on the edge of the crowd. The next thing he knew, one of the security staff lunged across the open space while another hurried forward. Instantly alert, Raul raced across the cobbles, adrenalin pumping, ready to protect her.

He skidded to a halt beside her as she bent. That was when he saw the ragamuffin dog, all hair and lolling tongue, gambolling at her feet.

Raul's heart crashed against his ribs. When he'd seen the security men swing into action he'd feared the worst. If anything had happened to her…

'Luisa, he's filthy.' The words were brusque, sharper than he'd intended as relief flared. His wife gave him a wide-eyed stare.

His wife! The world shifted beneath his feet and Raul couldn't tell if it was from shock or reaction to the reproach in her eyes.

'He's just a harmless puppy.' She cradled the mongrel, looking down and murmuring in a soft tone that made the beast wriggle in ecstasy.

If Luisa smiled at him that way, whispering and rubbing his belly, Raul would lap it up too. His groin tightened. Damn it! This was ridiculous. She only had to smile and he got as hard as a randy teenager. He didn't understand it.

A commotion caught his eye. A small boy was trying to get past Raul's staff. Raul nodded to them to let him pass.

The kid cast a fearful glance over his shoulder then hurried forward. Raul saw a scowling red-faced man in the crowd where the boy had been.

For an instant memory side-swiped Raul. Of his own father wearing that same expression on one of the few occasions he'd deigned to spend time with his young son. Raul couldn't remember what he'd done to earn his father's wrath. Scuffed his shoes perhaps or earned a less than perfect mark in his studies. It hadn't taken much to disappoint the old man.

Bitterness welled on his tongue and his eyes narrowed.

The boy stopped before them, his head sinking low.

'Is this your dog?' Raul had to wait for a silent nod and felt Luisa's hand on his arm.

What? Did she think he'd rip into the kid?

'Yes, sir. He means no harm, sir. The cord broke and—'

'Completely understandable,' Raul said. 'With all that noise it's not surprising he got overexcited.'

The boy raised his head and stared, as if unable to believe his ears.

'He must have sensed the Princess likes dogs.' Raul found himself talking just to reassure. He'd had no idea Luisa liked dogs till he saw her cuddle this one. She smiled at the boy and crouched down to his level.

Good with children and dogs. Raul watched the boy's nervousness disappear under the warmth of Luisa's approval and realised she was a natural with both. She'd make a great mother—warm and affectionate. He watched her hand the pup over and pat the kid reassuringly.

Raul could imagine her with an unruly brood, unfazed by soccer in the gloomy royal portrait gallery on a wet winter's day or kids who wanted to run outdoors instead of perfecting their Latin before they were allowed dinner.

Something scooped a hollow deep in Raul's belly at the thought of Luisa with children. *They'd be his children.*

For the first time the idea of fatherhood appealed, even though he had no experience of real family life.

He tried to imagine Luisa carrying his child and found the notion strangely satisfying. Though not as pleasurable as having her to himself, naked and needy.

'It's time to go.' He took her arm and helped her rise. Then he steered his wife and the boy towards the beet-faced man at the front of the crowd.

He wanted his wife to himself, had wanted her since he'd forced himself to leave her this morning. But first he had business to attend to.

Luisa raised a hand to wave at the crowd pressed close to the road. Safer to look at them than the man beside her who continually bewildered her.

Self-conscious, she crossed her legs over the ladder creeping up her stockings where the pup had scratched. Then she wiped at the muddy stains on her designer suit.

'Don't fidget with your clothes. No one else can see the dirt.'

Startled, she turned. She'd thought Raul focused on the crowd on the other side of the road. Even now he didn't turn. She had a perfect view of his austere profile as he waved. Luisa found her gaze lingering on his full lower lip as she remembered the way he'd kissed her last night.

Heat spiralled inside and she swallowed hard. It didn't do any good. She couldn't quench the need he'd ignited.

Obviously Raul wasn't similarly bothered. He was utterly composed. No doubt displeased by her behaviour in picking up a grubby little dog that was anything but pedigree. Her eyes shut as she imagined the press pictures. Raul looking regal and she with a ladder in her stockings.

Well, tough! She hadn't asked to be princess. He'd stampeded her into it. Now he could put up with the fact that she didn't fit the mould.

She'd read his stern demeanour through the ceremony today. As if waiting for her to embarrass herself. Not even her carefully rehearsed lines, learned with Lukas' help, had softened Raul's severe countenance.

Had she really sought his approval? The notion of such neediness disturbed her.

Only once in the whole proceedings had his face softened. With the boy.

'Why did we go over to that man in the crowd?' She hadn't even been aware of the question forming in her head.

Raul turned and a sizzle shot through her as their gazes collided.

Luisa slumped back against her seat, heart pounding as fire roared through her veins. How did he do that? Was it the same for all the women he bedded?

The idea was pure torture.

'I wanted to make sure there was no trouble.'

'Trouble?' Luisa scrabbled for coherent thought.

'He was complaining loudly about his son being uncontrollable. And about what a nuisance the dog was.'

'You're kidding!' Luisa straightened. 'Peter was a darling, but so serious, not uncontrollable. If anything he seemed too old for his years.' She hadn't understood everything he'd said but his gravity had struck her.

Raul shrugged but the movement seemed cramped. 'Living with a judgemental parent will do that.'

It was on the tip of Luisa's tongue to question Raul's assessment, till she read a bleakness in his eyes that made her back off.

'What did you say to his father?' Raul had looked every inch the monarch, full of gracious condescension.

Again that shrug. A little easier this time. 'I congratulated him on his fine son.'

'Good on you!'

Startled green eyes met hers and for a moment Luisa lost the thread of the conversation.

'And I invited both boy and dog to visit the castle, to renew the acquaintance.'

Luisa tried but couldn't read Raul's expression. Yet instinct told her why he'd done it. 'You wanted to make sure he didn't get rid of the pup?'

For an instant longer Raul held her gaze before turning back to the window and raising his hand in acknowledgement of the people thronging the road.

'A boy should be allowed a dog for companionship. Don't you think?'

His tone indicated the matter was of no importance. Yet she remembered Peter's trembling fear and the nervous way he'd eyed his father. Raul had gone out of his way to speak to them when he hadn't made time to glad-hand anyone else in the crowd, preferring to wave from a distance.

Luisa sensed the matter was anything but unimportant to Raul. The scenario had struck a chord with him.

Frowning, she realised she knew almost nothing about the man she'd married.

CHAPTER TEN

RAUL'S mother had died in childbirth, his father had been impatient with children and Raul didn't have siblings. That was all Luisa knew, apart from the fact that he distanced himself behind a formidable reserve.

What did that say about him?

'Did you have a dog when you were a boy?'

Raul shot her a surprised look as they drove through the castle gates.

'No,' he said finally, his expression unreadable. 'Dogs and antique heirlooms aren't a good mix.'

Luisa surveyed the enormous courtyard and thought of the labyrinth of terraces, walled gardens and moats around the castle. 'There's room enough outside.'

If *she* had a child she'd let him or her have a pet or three and find a way to protect the antiques.

Shock grabbed her throat as she realised she was imagining a sturdy little boy running across the courtyard with black hair and eyes as green as emeralds. Eyes like—

'Are you ready, Luisa?' She looked up to find Raul already standing beside the limousine, offering his hand. No way to avoid touching him without being pointedly rude. Yet, even braced for it, the shock that sparked from his touch and ran up her arm stunned her.

Raul gave no sign of anything untoward, which left her wondering again if it were she alone overreacting to last night's intimacy. Sternly she told herself it was natural she'd respond to the touch of her first ever lover. But when he tucked her arm through his and led her through the cavernous entrance, it was all she could do to repress the shivers of excitement running through her body. Being this close set desire humming through her.

'Who did you play with?' She sought distraction.

One dark brow winged up towards Raul's hairline, giving him a faintly dangerous air.

'I had little time for play. Princes may be born but they need to be moulded for the role too.'

Luisa stared, horrified. But his cool tone signalled an end to the subject and he picked up his pace, leading her swiftly towards the lift.

'But when you were little you must have played.'

He shrugged, the movement brushing his arm against her. She breathed in the subtle scent of warm male skin.

'I don't recall. I had tutors and lessons from the age of four. Playtime wasn't scheduled, though later sports were included in the curriculum.'

'That sounds…regimented.' She smothered her outrage and distress. Surely they could have allowed him some time to be a child! It reinforced her resolve not to risk having a baby. No child of hers would be treated so.

Raul punched the button for the lift. 'My days were busy.'

Busy, not happy. The ancient castle was perfect for hide and seek and the fantasy games young children revelled in. Had he ever played them? Her heart went out to the little boy he'd been, so lonely, she suspected now.

Did that loneliness explain his aloof attitude? His formidable self-possession?

'Did you see much of your father?' She recalled him saying his father had been impatient with children. How had that impacted? She had no idea how royal households worked but she guessed no man became as ferociously self-sufficient as Raul without reason.

Her husband shot a warning look that shivered her skin. Luisa looked straight back.

The lift rose smoothly, so smoothly she knew it hadn't caused the dropping sensation in her stomach that came with the word *husband*.

'My father was busy. He had a country to run.'

Luisa bit down hard rather than blurt out her sympathy. The doors slid open but Luisa didn't move.

'Do you mean he didn't have time for you?'

She could almost see the shutters come down over Raul's face, blanking out all expression. The suddenness of it chilled her. Yet, far from blanking her out, it made her want to wrap her arms around him. The image of Peter, the little boy in the market square, so quaintly formal, tugged at her heart. Had Raul been like that as a child?

Her own glorious childhood, filled with laughter and love, happy days on the river or riding the tractor with her dad, running riot with a couple of dogs and even a pet lizard were halcyon by comparison.

'Why do you want to know?'

'Why don't you want to tell me? I'm your wife.' She didn't even stumble over the word. 'It's right I know you better.' Yet it was like pulling teeth, trying to get him to open up even a little.

Raul stood still, his face taut and unreadable. Then she caught a flicker in his eyes that made her thighs quiver and her stomach tighten.

'Just what I had in mind.' His voice lowered to a deep resonance that caressed her skin. 'Getting to know each other better.' Raul tugged her into the carpeted hallway and she realised they stood in front of his suite.

The glint in his eyes was unmistakable. Desire, raw and hungry. Something feral and dangerous sent delicious excitement skimming through her.

Her eyes widened. No mistaking what he meant.

Sex.

It was in his knowing look. In the deep shuddering breath that expanded his wide chest, as if he had trouble filling oxygen starved lungs.

Luisa waited for outrage to take hold. For pride to give her the strength to shove him away. Indignation didn't come. It was excitement that knotted her stomach. Desire that clogged her throat.

He'd introduced her to pleasure and she was too inexperienced to hide the fact that she craved more.

Raul must have read her feelings for his lips curved in a smile that made her pulse jitter. Wordlessly he shoved open the door, pulled her in and against him as he leaned back, closing the door with his body.

Fire exploded in her blood. Last night she'd loved the heavy burden of him above her. Now she wanted to arch into him and revel in the hard solidity of his big frame. It was weak of her but she couldn't get enough of him.

She shoved aside the memory of this morning's desolation, and the suspicion that his desire now masked a determination to stop her prying into his past.

At this moment it was Raul's passion she wanted. Perhaps because of the emptiness she'd glimpsed in his eyes when he'd spoken so casually about a childhood that to her sounded frighteningly cold. Did she doom herself to a similar loneliness, marrying him?

Yet it wasn't fear that drove her. Or simple lust.

Her heart twisted as she realised she wanted to give herself to her husband in the hope of healing some of the deep hurt she'd seen flicker for a moment in his eyes.

'Luisa? Do you want this?'

'Yes.' She didn't try to hide from his searching gaze.

When he lowered his head to graze the side of her neck with his teeth the air sucked straight out of her lungs. Thought disintegrated as she sank into pleasure.

She opened her eyes and groaned as he bit into the sensitive flesh at the base of her throat. Her hands clenched at his shoulders as his hands skimmed her jacket, undoing it and her shirt and spreading the open sides wide.

'You were magnificent this morning.' His voice was a low, throaty purr as he stripped off her jacket then kissed the upper slope of her breasts as he shoved her blouse off. Her skirt followed moments later and she shivered in sensual delight as he ran his big hands over her hips.

'I just did what was expected.' Yet she felt a tiny burst of pleasure at his words. Having accepted her new role, she was determined to do it well.

She sighed as he fastened his mouth on her lacy bra, sucking hard till the nipple stood erect and darts of liquid fire shot to her core.

Convulsively she shuddered, cradling him close, overwhelmed by the sudden need to embrace him and comfort him. This big man who needed no one.

He lifted his head and met her eyes. His own were shadowed, as if he veiled his thoughts. The knowledge pained her. He worked so hard to maintain his distance. Had he never learned to share anything? Was she crazy to think they could make this work?

Then his mouth descended and he swung her up in his embrace. Heat surrounded her. Hard-packed muscle. The steady beat of his heart.

By the time he lowered her to the bed and stripped both their clothes with a deftness that spoke of practice and urgency, Luisa's thoughts had almost scrambled.

'Contraception!' she blurted out as she sank beneath him. 'I don't want to get pregnant.'

His brows rose. 'We're married, Luisa. Having a child is a natural outcome.'

She shook her head. Despite the wonderful weighted feeling of his lower body on hers, this was too important.

'No. I'm not ready.' She gulped down air and tried to order her thoughts. 'It's been too fast.'

For what seemed an eternity Raul stared, as if seeing her for the first time. Finally he nodded and rolled away, reaching for the bedside table.

When he turned back he didn't immediately cover her body with his.

For a man who'd married her out of necessity he had a

way of making her feel the absolute focus of his world. As if
nothing existed but her. His total concentration, the intensity
of his gaze, the knowing, deliberately seductive touch of his
hands on her body, were exhilarating.

Raul's gaze softened with each circling stroke and she felt
something shift deep inside. She arched into his touch and her
pulse pounded in her ears. When he leaned close his breath
was an erotic caress of her sensitive ear lobe that sent sparks
of heat showering through her.

'Come for me, Luisa.' His fingers delved and a ripple of
sensation caught her. 'Give yourself up to it.'

Gasping, she focused on him, feeling the dip and wheel
of excitement while the intense connection sparked between
them. His set face, his mouth, no longer smiling but stretched
taut in concentration. The furrow on his brow, his eyes…

Out of nowhere the orgasm hit, jerking her body and steal-
ing her breath. Heat flared under her skin as he dipped his
head to take her mouth in a long, languorous kiss that somehow
intensified the echoing spasms.

Spent at last, she sank back into the bed.

Now he'd come to her. Dreamily she smiled, her inner
muscles pulsing in readiness. Despite her exhaustion, it was
Raul she wanted. The hollow ache inside was proof of that.

He moved, but not as she'd expected. Shocked, she saw him
settling himself low, nuzzling her inner thighs.

'No! I want—'

His kiss silenced her. She shouldn't want more after the
ecstasy that still echoed through her, but the caress of Raul's
tongue, his lips, sent need jolting through her.

That was only the beginning.

Dazed, Luisa gave herself up to new caresses, new sensations that built one on the other till all she knew was Raul and
the pleasure he wrought in her malleable, ever eager body. The
taste of him was on her tongue, his scent in her nostrils as she
grew attuned to his touch and the deep approving rumble of
his voice.

Blindly she turned to him as finally he took her for himself, his rampant hardness a contrast to her lush satiation. She breathed deep, taking his shuddering, powerful body into hers as she seemed to absorb his essence into her pores.

Raul cried out and pleasure drenched her at the sound of her name in that raw needy voice. Instinctively she clutched him protectively close.

Raul lay completely spent, only enough strength in his body to pull Luisa close, her body sprawled over him.

He told himself the post-coital glow was always this intense, but he knew he lied. From the moment he'd bedded his wife he'd known the sex was different.

Why? His brain wouldn't leave the question alone.

Because she didn't meekly comply with his wishes? Because, despite agreeing to marry, she was still her own woman, not like the compliant lovers who gave whatever he wanted because of what he could provide in return?

With Luisa he had the thrilling, faintly disturbing sense that he held a precious gift in his arms.

She was far more than a warm body to sate his lust.

This was unknown territory. Or, if he were honest with himself, a little too like the feelings he'd discovered in his youth, when he'd believed in love. The thought should terrify him. He was well past believing in such things.

His lips quirked ruefully. That was why he'd seduced his wife as soon as they'd got back from the civic ceremony. Not just because he wanted her, but to stop himself puzzling over what she made him feel.

And to stop her questions. His hand clenched in the silk of her hair and she shifted delectably, soft flesh against his. Was it possible he'd used sex to avoid talking about his past? Even something as simple as his childhood?

Was he really such a coward?

His life was an open book. It had been pored over and dissected by the media for years. Yet the discomfort he'd felt answering Luisa's questions surprised him.

As did the unfamiliar need to open up to her. To share a little of himself.

He frowned. It was absurd. He didn't need a confessor or a confidante. There was no need for conversation. Yet deep down he knew he lied.

Perhaps because of the sense that he owed her for agreeing to marry?

Whatever the reason, when she shifted as if to move away, he slipped a restraining arm around the curve of her waist and cleared his throat.

'My father was interested in me only as heir to the throne.' His voice sounded husky. Raul told himself it was the aftermath of that stunning climax.

'That's awful.' Her words were murmured against his chest. She didn't look up. Somehow that made it easier.

He shrugged. 'Staff raised me. That's the way it's always been in the royal household. He dropped by just enough to remind me I had to excel to be ready to wear the crown one day.'

'And you wonder why I'm not ready for children!'

Shock smote him. He'd spoken blithely about the possibility of pregnancy, but the reality hadn't sunk in. Luisa, pregnant with his child...

'No child of ours would be raised like that.' Certainty firmed on the words.

'Really?'

Raul nodded. He'd spent years adhering to tradition as he fought to stabilise the monarchy and the nation, working behind the scenes as his father's focus narrowed to pleasing his capricious young wife. It had been Raul who'd tried to redress the damage after the fiasco with Ana.

But some traditions needed change.

'You have my word.'

He might not be a success as a father. Certainly his father's model of paternal love had been distant and unemotional. He thought of Peter, the boy with his dog. At least Raul knew what *not* to do. And Luisa would make up for his shortcomings. She'd be a natural.

He smiled, satisfied at the prospect.

'Tell me…' She hesitated.

'Yes?'

'Yesterday at the reception. Why did everyone watch you and your stepmother as if they expected a scene?'

Raul drew a heavy breath, satisfaction dissipating in an instant. But Luisa had a right to know. As she'd pointed out, she was his wife. Better to learn the facts from him than from some gossip sheet.

'Because they know I don't like her.' He stroked Luisa's hair then down her back, distracting himself just a little by the way she arched into his caress.

'Why not?' Luisa's question was a breath of sound. 'Why don't you like her?'

Raul clenched his jaw, forcing himself to answer.

'She pretended to marry him for love. He was proud and arrogant and he'd never been in love before, but he didn't deserve what he got.' Even though at first Raul had wished them both to the devil. He'd found no satisfaction seeing his father, weighed down by regret, dwindle into a shadow of the man he'd been.

'He was duped by a gold-digger half his age who wanted wealth and royal prestige. She spent most of her time with other men. His last years were hell.'

Even in his anger Raul felt a weight slide off his chest. He'd kept his views to himself so long, knowing an unguarded word would inflame the gossip and speculation he'd tried so hard to quash. The truth of his father's marriage had been guessed by many but never proven.

He'd worked tirelessly to protect his family's reputation, covering for his father as he grew erratic and less able to control his kingdom. Overcoming a desire to expose Ana for the witch she was. His country needed faith in the monarchy that kept it stable.

'There's more, isn't there? More you're not telling?'

Raul felt movement and looked down to see Luisa's bright eyes surveying him. She looked troubled.

Briefly he hesitated. But there was no point refusing to tell her. She could find out easily enough. He looked up at the wood-panelled ceiling, away from her searching gaze.

'I met Ana in my early twenties. She was my age but unlike any of the girls I knew. She wasn't aristocratic. She didn't simper or talk in platitudes. She didn't talk politics and she didn't care about court gossip.'

His lips twisted at the memory.

'She was a breath of fresh air. Vibrant, outspoken, fun. She wasn't afraid to get her hair messed riding in a convertible, or enjoy a picnic out in the open instead of dinner at a chic restaurant.' Or so it had seemed.

'I was smitten.' Raul halted, drawing a searing breath. It was the first time he'd admitted it. Strange how the memory seemed less shattering. Maybe because he saw his youthful folly clearly since he no longer believed in love.

'Oh, Raul!' No mistaking Luisa's distress. Or the tension in her body. The story wasn't a pretty one. Suddenly he wanted it over as quickly as possible.

'It turned out I was wrong about her. She seemed fresh and innocent, uncomplicated and appealing. But she wasn't what she appeared.' His mouth twisted.

'I wasn't the only one taken in. I introduced her to my father and he fell for her with all the force of an old fool for a very beautiful, very clever young woman.'

Raul remembered those days vividly. Ana had played him, holding him at arm's length once she got his father in her sights. After all, what price a prince when a king was available, with a kingdom's wealth at his disposal?

'My father married her four months later.'

Raul had thought his world had ended. He'd retreated into duty, throwing himself into anything that would dull the pain of betrayal. It had become habit to direct all his passion, all his energies into his royal obligations.

It had worked. Over the years he'd dispensed with the need for emotional ties.

'Raul, I'm so sorry. That must have been soul-destroying.'

Luisa didn't know the half of it. But it had made him stronger. He was self-sufficient and glad of it.

So why did he feel stripped naked in a way that had nothing to do with his lack of clothes?

'Do you still…care for her?'

Blindly Raul turned towards Luisa's voice, finally focusing on her troubled gaze.

'Care?' He almost spat the word. 'For the woman who deceived me and incited my own father to betray me?' A laugh tore, savage and rough, from his throat. 'For the woman who made me a laughing stock? She damned near destroyed the monarchy with her scandalous behaviour. She did destroy my father's pride and honour with her affairs.'

Raul shook his head. 'I learned a valuable lesson from her. Never to trust. Never to be gullible again. Love is a trap for the unwary.'

It struck him that what had drawn him to Ana all those years ago was what attracted him to Luisa. Her innocence in a world of political machinations. Her directness and honesty. Her beauty. Except in Luisa it was real. In Ana it had been false, designed to snare.

Ana had come to this apartment one morning just months after her wedding. She'd worn sheer black lace and even sheerer audacity and she'd expected Raul to satisfy her as his father hadn't been able to.

Rancid distaste filled his mouth. It had taken him a long time to banish the taint of that memory, even though he'd spurned her, avoiding her whenever he could.

In the long run Ana had done him a favour. Never again would he fall for the fantasy of love.

Luisa reeled from the shocking truth. The harsh light in his eyes as he'd spoken of his stepmother made her shiver.

Or was that because of the revelation that he'd once loved Ana?

Did he love her still? Despite his vehement denial, it was clear she still evoked strong emotion in him.

Nausea rose, threatening to choke Luisa. Raul had taken her with the compulsion of a man staking his claim.

Or a man intent on obliterating the past.

Had he really wanted *her*? Or had his pent-up passion been for the woman who'd rejected him yet still had a place in his life? Was Luisa a stand-in?

She bit her lip.

He'd said he didn't believe in love. Had he already fallen so hard for Ana he couldn't escape his feelings?

And if not, why did the idea of Raul, deprived of love as a child and now rejecting it as an adult, fill Luisa with sadness?

CHAPTER ELEVEN

LUISA peeked through slitted eyes as Raul dressed. She'd fallen into an exhausted sleep despite the swirl of disturbing thoughts his revelations had produced.

Hours ago they'd scaled the heights of bliss and she'd felt absurdly as if she'd found the other half of her soul in his arms, especially when he'd then begun to open up a little about his life.

But his later revelations about Ana had poisoned that heady pleasure and made her doubt.

What did Raul feel? Would she ever know?

She swallowed a knot of distress. The best she could do for herself, and the man she feared she was coming to care too much for, was be sensible—take a day at a time and try to build a workable marriage.

Easier said than done when just looking at him made her heart clench.

Hair slicked back from the shower, strong hands knotting his tie, Raul looked more potently sexy than any man had a right to.

Was this how his other lovers felt when he left them? She breathed through the hurt.

There could never be love between them.

Raul had closed himself off from that possibility. His bitterness over his father's wife skewed his emotions so much he'd admitted he'd never trust a woman, or love, again.

Who could blame him, after the devastating betrayal he'd

suffered? Pain seared her as she recalled the stoical way he'd revealed the bare bones of the awful story. But her imagination filled in some of the blanks.

What had it been like seeing the woman he'd loved living with another man—his own father? Adopting an air of unconcern in public and riding out the storm of speculation that surely must have howled around them all? She cringed thinking of the salacious gossip that must have circulated.

And facing his father—staying loyal and supporting him both publicly and, from what she'd heard, privately too, taking the brunt of responsibility for the kingdom.

She could barely imagine how bereft Raul must have felt at his father's lack of loyalty or caring.

Luisa had been scarred by her grandfather's actions, but at least she'd had the unquestioned support and love of her parents. Raul hadn't had that!

No wonder he closed himself off behind duty and a work schedule that would tax any workaholic. No wonder he found no difficulty marrying without emotion.

Was it possible he could ever learn to trust? To love?

'You're awake.' Dark eyes snared hers and something melted inside.

'You have to go?' Where had that come from? She sounded so needy.

'I'd hoped to stay here.' Heat flickered in his eyes as he took in the shape of her under the sheet. His nostrils flared and suddenly Luisa felt that now-familiar spark of desire flicker into life. Stupid to feel pleased that he obviously didn't relish leaving. It only meant her husband was virile, with an appetite for sex.

A very healthy appetite.

'There was a phone call.' He turned away to pick up his jacket. 'Urgent business.'

It was on the tip of Luisa's tongue to ask what business was so important it interrupted a honeymoon, when she remembered they weren't sharing one. Even the day after the wedding they'd been out and about on public show.

They didn't have that sort of marriage. Theirs was a convenient union. Remember?

She turned away, battling deep sadness.

'I'm sorry, Luisa.' He startled her, speaking from beside the bed. 'This is one matter I can't ignore.' She stared up into his brooding face. 'It's to do with the unrest I mentioned. I'm needed.'

She nodded. He had a country to run. That would always be his priority. Only now did she begin to understand how important that was to him. Through personal crises, his royal responsibilities at least had remained constant. No wonder he was so focused on them. Had they provided solace when he'd most needed it?

'You have a heavy schedule,' she said to fill the silence.

'You get used to it. I've been preparing for the work since I was four.'

The reminder sent a shiver down her spine. Raul had said any child of his would be brought up differently and she'd fight tooth and nail to ensure no child of hers was 'moulded' in that heartless way. She had to make a stand—for herself and for her family if she ever had one.

Luisa sat up against the headboard, drawing the sheet over her breasts and trying to ignore the flash of interest in Raul's eyes.

'I'll get up too. I have plans for this afternoon.'

'Plans? There are no appointments scheduled.'

'I want to meet with Gregor and the other gardeners. You have no objection to the parterre garden and some of the other spaces being renewed, do you?' It was a spur of the moment decision but she refused to spend the afternoon here, pining over the state of her marriage.

'No, of course not. It's overdue. But I can detail one of my staff to oversee it. It will need consultation, not just with the ground staff but with the castle historian, as well as kitchen and event staff. It's not just a matter of gardening.'

'That will be a good way to get to know them.' Luisa needed something to sink her teeth into, something to focus on other than Raul. She didn't want to think about the emotions he inspired for fear of what she'd discover.

'You don't *need* to work, Luisa.'

Her brows rose. 'You expect me to loll in the lap of luxury while you work the day after your wedding?'

'I regret that. I'd much prefer to stay.' The glint in his eyes made her pulse hammer erratically but she ignored it.

'I need something to *do*. A purpose. I'd go crazy without that. I'm used to working.'

Raul lifted a hand to his already perfectly knotted tie and for a split second she'd have said he looked uncomfortable.

'Your lessons don't keep you busy?'

'That's not enough.' She'd never been good at formal lessons. Her language skills were improving but if she had to learn about one more Maritzian monarch or the correct way to greet a grand duke, she'd scream.

Besides, the intensive lessons evoked memories of her long ago stay in Ardissia. The rigid discipline and the judgemental faces were missing, but she couldn't shake the notion she'd never live up to expectations.

Raul surveyed her, his face unreadable. 'Soon you'll be busy with official duties. As my consort there'll be plenty of events where you're required.'

'Being seen at openings and fetes?' She shook her head and sat straighter. 'That's not me.' Despite the makeover, she'd never be the glamorous clothes horse people liked to stare at in magazines. Wearing those stunning couture clothes, she felt like a fraud. Not like herself.

It didn't help, remembering Raul had bought her just as he'd bought them.

'I'll make a start this afternoon.' She met his unblinking gaze, almost challenging him to protest.

When he merely nodded Luisa took a slow breath.

If she was making a new start there was something else she had to face.

'I'm planning to visit Ardissia too.' It was time to lay her grandfather's ghost. Maybe going there, confronting the place that had meant so much to him, and held such dreadful memories for her, would help her bury her hatred.

He frowned. 'My schedule's too full right now.'

Luisa drew herself up. 'Do I need to wait for you? Aren't I Princess of Ardissia?' Much as she disliked the title, it was the one thing she'd got out of this devil's bargain: her inheritance. In her absence the province had become the responsibility of the monarch, but she was here now. 'It's time I shouldered my responsibilities.'

Raul paced towards the bed, his brows arrowing down. 'It's logical we go together. People will expect that.'

'But you're tied up every day. You just said you're not free.' A little breathing space, time to regroup after the massive changes in her life, beckoned. She'd been on a roller coaster of emotion these last weeks.

'There are matters of protocol and plans to be made. Royalty doesn't just stop by.'

Why was he against her going? No mistaking the tension in his big frame. The tantalising idea surfaced that he'd miss her. She dismissed it instantly.

'It's not dangerous, is it?'

He shook his head. 'Ardissia is safe.'

'Good. I'm sure I'll be welcome. I'll give notice I'm coming. A couple of days. Would that be enough?'

She stared into his set face, suddenly relishing the challenge of standing up to the man who'd taken over her life in more ways than she'd ever bargained for.

She needed to stake a claim as her own person lest he subsume her totally. Even now she longed for him to haul her close and forget the so important appointment that called him away. How was that for needy?

'Surely it's the right thing to do?' She worked to keep a cajoling note from her voice. 'It's only polite to visit now I've accepted my inheritance.'

Raul's lowering brows told her he didn't see it that way. The sight of tension in his jaw sent dangerous excitement zigzagging through her. As if she felt pleasure knowing she got under his skin, even in such a way as this.

Surely she wasn't that desperate for his attention?

'The timing's not ideal, but you're right. A visit makes sense. Leave it with me.'

Why did Luisa feel as if she'd lost the argument when he nodded, turned and strode out of the room, his mind obviously occupied with matters of business?

She hadn't expected him to kiss her, had she?

'This way, Your Highness.' The chamberlain ushered Luisa into her grandfather's study. She'd left it to last on her tour of the Ardissian royal palace.

She pictured the old man here, seated at the massive desk awash with opulent gilt scrollwork. Even in his towering rages he hadn't deigned to rise. Always he'd remembered his position as prince and hers as unsatisfactory, low-born grandchild.

Her teeth clenched as she recalled his poisonous words. Not merely his diatribe on her incompetence and ingratitude but his slashing vitriol at her parents.

'Thank you.' She nodded to the chamberlain, smiling despite his haughty rigidity. 'That's all.'

As he withdrew she considered the portraits lining the walls. Ancestors with remote expressions stared down their noses at her. She lifted her head, surveying the portrait of the man who'd cut off his daughter and his granddaughter when they wouldn't kowtow to his domineering ways.

'The last laugh's on you, Grandad. The farmer's daughter is Princess, soon to be Queen.'

Yet there was no pleasure in the shallow triumph. She hadn't come to gloat, but to see if she could put the past behind her and move on.

She wrapped her arms around herself, suppressing a shiver. Despite her determination to accept her lot, to dress the part and learn protocol and all the other things they foisted on her, Luisa couldn't imagine the future.

What would it hold?

Endless, empty years of public receptions and meaningless small talk? Breathtaking moments of delight when Raul treated her to mind-blowing sex? Heat curled inside at the memory of his loving.

Would she hang onto those moments, desperate for the little Raul could give her when she wanted so much more?

Would her life be sterile of friends and family?

If she had children, how could she protect them from the world that had produced a monster like her grandfather? And Raul had turned into a man of such emotional reserve she wondered if she'd ever build a relationship with him.

She paced to the window, seeking the warmth of the sun streaming in on the luxurious carpet.

Only the best for the Ardissian prince! She'd seen the run-down sections of the city and the bare amenities provided for the palace servants when she'd insisted on seeing *all* the premises. Her grandfather had spent money on his own comfort rather than his people.

Movement caught her eye. A group of young people made their way across the courtyard. On impulse Luisa opened the window. Laughter, bubbling and fresh, washed around her before they entered a door on the far side of the yard.

Wherever they were going, it appealed more than this place. She closed the window and headed for the door.

Raul drummed his fingers on the car seat as the limo purred towards the Ardissian palace. He lifted a hand to the people lining the street.

He was eager for a break after this intense week. He'd planned to come days ago, but political developments had made it impossible. Now he could please himself.

It pleased him to see his wife.

Five days she'd been away. It seemed far longer. His bed felt empty. His days regimented and predictable, despite the political crisis they'd averted.

Life seemed…less without Luisa.

His lips flattened as he thought of the day she'd announced

she'd come here. He'd only just dragged himself from the temptation of her. He'd reeled from an ecstasy unlike any he'd known. And from the unique sense of peace that came from sharing the story of his past.

Was it simply that he'd needed to unburden himself after years keeping it to himself? He couldn't shake the suspicion that the sensations of release and relief had more to do with the fact it was Luisa he shared with.

Only the most urgent crisis had forced him away, still stunned by the unprecedented sense of peace and pleasure he'd found with her.

And she'd sat there, her sweet mouth a taut line, demanding occupation. *Demanding more.*

Clearly he hadn't been enough to satisfy her!

Male pride smarted from the fact she'd been unaffected by what had passed between them, while it had knocked him completely off balance. It had been on the tip of his tongue to beg her not to leave.

Because he *needed* her! Not just sexually.

He couldn't remember feeling this way about a woman. Even Ana, at the height of her appeal, hadn't invaded his thoughts like this.

Raul smoothed his hand over the seat. At night he found himself reaching for Luisa. He felt bereft when she wasn't there.

Worse was his gut-deep sense of culpability. As the limo pulled up before her ancestral palace, her words came back to haunt him. How desperate she'd been for work to occupy her. Yet another reminder that, despite his attempts to help her adjust, this wasn't the life she'd chosen.

It was the life he'd demanded so he could inherit.

Yes, Maritz needed a strong monarch to see it through difficult times and, with the support of a democratic government, steer it clear of civil war.

But wasn't it also true he'd *needed* to be king? The monarchy had been his salvation as well as his burden as he'd worked to drag himself and his country out of the pit his father's hasty marriage had plunged them into.

And for that he'd bullied Luisa into his world.

He'd wanted to believe she'd find a fulfilling life by his side. These last weeks he'd seen glimpses of a woman who could make the role of consort her own and make a huge difference to his people, even if her way was not the traditional one.

Could she be happy here?

If he'd thought she'd be eager, waiting at the grand staircase to greet him, he was mistaken. Instead it was Lukas, whom he'd sent to support Luisa.

'Your Highness, welcome. And congratulations on the results of your recent negotiations.'

Raul smiled, allowing himself to enjoy anew a sense of relief. 'Thank you, Lukas. Hopefully it will mean peace at last.' He looked around but still no sign of Luisa.

'Her Highness planned to be here. She's delayed but shouldn't be long.' As he spoke he turned, walking with Raul inside the palace.

It was as grand and gloomy as Raul remembered.

He shuddered at the thought of Luisa here, a trusting, innocent teenager, at the mercy of the venomous old man who'd treated her and her mother so appallingly.

'Sorry?'

'I said the chamberlain has requested an audience.'

Raul stopped. 'Surely his business is with my wife. This is her property.'

One look at Lukas' face told Raul there was trouble ahead. He sighed. Days without sleep took their toll. All he wanted was his wife and a bed, in that order.

'Raul!' Luisa slammed to a stop in the doorway to her suite. She'd planned to be back earlier. Groomed and presentable, ready to greet him with calm courtesy.

One look at him, framed by the arched window, and her breath sawed out of control. Her heart kicked into a frantic rhythm. So much for calm. Just being in the same room with him shattered her composure.

She'd been so busy these last days. It was ridiculous she should miss him, but she had. More than she'd expected.

If things were different, if *they* were different, she'd run over and plant a kiss on his tense mouth until it softened in that sulky, sexy way it did when they were intimate. He'd put his arms around her and…

This was no fantasy. One look at his cool expression scotched that notion.

'Luisa.' He inclined his head but he didn't approach. Something inside her sank. 'How are you?'

'Fine, thanks.' She pushed back the hair that fell over her cheek and surreptitiously straightened her collar. She'd yanked her jacket on in a hurry. 'How was your trip?'

'Excellent.' He paused and she felt tension vibrate between them. 'Though as soon as I arrived your chamberlain came to me.'

Luisa frowned. Now she understood his disapproval. No doubt the official had poured out a litany of complaints. The man had been negative since she'd arrived.

'I see.' She breathed deep. She supposed she'd broken all sorts of rules. Now she had to face the music. But she refused to be intimidated. These were her decisions to make and she'd stick by them.

She closed the door and walked into the room. She gestured to an armchair. Raul ignored it.

'He voiced a number of concerns.'

'I'm sure he did. What did he start with? The proposal to open the state reception rooms for public functions?'

Raul shook his head, his saturnine eyebrows tilting down. 'No. It was your plan to turn the Prince's private apartments into a museum.'

Luisa's chin jerked up. 'I'm never going to use them so they might as well be put to some use.' She swept out a hand that encompassed her bright modern room with its view to the Alps. 'This is more suitable for when I visit.' She shuddered.

'All that overdecorated pomposity downstairs is too much for me.' Besides, the thought of bunking in her grandsire's bed curdled her blood.

'For us.' Raul paced closer.

'Sorry?'

'We'll visit together in future.'

What? He didn't trust her now to come here without him? She drew herself up to her full height.

'What else did he object to?' Might as well get it over, though it stuck in her craw to defend her plans.

Raul spread his arms in a gesture that drew her eyes to the expanse of his chest. She remembered his strength as he'd pulled her into his arms and taken her to heaven.

Despite her anger, heat snaked through her belly.

'He had a list. He was concerned about the plans for a children's playgroup in the eastern annexe.'

Luisa's mouth tightened. 'The premises are perfect and easily accessible from the main square. You might not know but in this part of the city there's virtually no provision for community groups. It's not like central Maritz where that's well catered for.'

It seemed her grandfather had stymied local plans to support the community, especially young people. His mindset had been rooted in the past.

'And the cooking school?'

She put her hands on her hips. 'I found students visiting the old kitchens. Their premises had been damaged when the old wiring caused a fire. The palace chef offered temporary use of the kitchens here.' Her lips firmed. 'It's a perfect match. The facilities are here, and the expertise for that matter. It's not as if there are lots of state banquets since I'm not here permanently.'

'And the same for the mechanics?'

She stared. 'How do you know about that?' She'd just come from a meeting of vocational teachers in what had been the stables but now housed an automotive workshop.

Raul stepped towards her and she read a flicker of something in his eyes that made the heat in her belly spread low and deep.

He raised a hand to her cheek. Luisa shuddered as delicious sensation stirred. She didn't want this distraction, this sweet reminder of the magic he wrought!

'It was a guess.' He held up his hand so she saw a dark stain. 'Motor oil?'

Her tongue thickened at his nearness. He was so close his body heat invaded her space.

'We were checking the facilities and I got a little...involved.'

Raul's eyes narrowed. 'I see. Like you got *involved* when you were presented with that cow?'

Luisa clenched her hands rather than spread them in a pleading gesture. The press had had a field day with that and she'd avoided reading the paper for days since. One paper in particular delighted in portraying her as wilful and disrespectful, though most seemed positive.

The animal had been beautiful, with garlands of flowers round its neck and horns and a huge alpine bell.

'It was part of the official welcome to Ardissia. Lukas explained it was a sign of great respect from the rural population. I couldn't refuse it!'

'But did you have to milk it?' His mouth tightened till the strain showed at his jaw.

She shrugged, feeling hemmed in by his disapproval. 'OK, so it wasn't proper protocol. I know real princesses wouldn't dream of it. But we got talking about dairy cattle and suddenly they offered me a milking stool and a bucket and...' She threw up her hands. 'So sue me! You insisted I do this. Don't complain now that I'm unorthodox. I'm trying. And—' she jabbed a finger into his pristine shirt '—while I'm happy to hear suggestions about these ideas for the palace, it's ultimately *my* decision. No one else's!'

'Exactly what I told your chamberlain.'

'Sorry?' Luisa was so dazed she barely noticed Raul had closed his hand around her prodding finger.

'I told him to keep his thoughts to himself until he had a chance to share them with you.'

Luisa stared. 'You don't mind?'

His nostrils flared. 'I mind very much being accosted by a jumped-up official who bad-mouths his employer behind her back. And I'm furious.'

Her shoulders sank. Here it came.

'Furious I didn't have the right to fire the troublemaker on the spot. He's your employee but he's more concerned about his own prestige than his job!'

'Raul?' Only now did she notice his other arm had slipped round to drag her close. She inhaled his intoxicating scent. It was like reliving those intense dreams that had haunted her ever since she'd come here.

'It's your decision, Luisa. But you need to consider finding someone better. Someone who can work with you on your plans rather than thwart them.'

She locked her knees against the trembling that started somewhere near her heart and spread to her limbs.

'You don't *mind* what I've been doing?' She'd been so sure of his disapproval her brain struggled with any other explanation for his tight-lipped expression.

'Why should I mind?' He rubbed her back in a circling motion that eased muscles drawn to breaking point. 'It's good to see you getting involved and listening to your people. I'm proud of what you've tackled in such a short space of time. But you're sensible enough to take advice and not rush into anything without due consideration.'

She blinked, staring up into dark green eyes that glimmered with warmth. The shock of it nearly undid her.

After the chamberlain's starchy disapproval and the knowledge her grandfather would roll in his grave at her plans for his precious palace, she hadn't been surprised to read criticism in Raul's expression.

Except now she couldn't find it.

A wave of warmth crashed over her that had nothing to do

with Raul's nearness. It stemmed from an inner glow, knowing he'd stood up for her with the chamberlain.

That he was ready to support her.

That he seemed to care.

She put out another trembling hand to his chest, spreading her fingers to capture the steady beat of his heart. His arm tightened around her and he leaned close.

'But what I most want to know, wife, is what the mayor said when you presented him with a bucket of warm milk.'

Again she caught that flicker in his eyes, the tightening of his lips. This time she realised what it was.

Raul trying not to laugh.

'He was very impressed and told me I had hidden talents.' Her mouth twitched. 'Then he showed me an old local technique he reckons gives you a better grip.'

Raul's face creased into a smile, then a grin. He tipped his head back and released a deep infectious laugh that made her lips curve and her heart dance.

Deep within Luisa something relaxed, unfurled and spread.

Happiness.

CHAPTER TWELVE

THAT happiness stayed. It was like a glowing ember, warming her from the inside and thawing the chill that had gripped her so long.

With each week Luisa found herself more content. She grew fond of her new home and its people. The nation of Maritz and even its tiny principality of Ardissia that she'd recalled as a nightmare place from her youth were growing more like home. She could be happy here.

Then there was Raul. He could be gentle and tender but there was always an undercurrent of explosive passion between them that left her breathless. Luisa shivered as erotic memories surfaced. Their physical intimacy was out of this world, and she always felt she got close then to the real man behind the façade.

The man she wanted to know better.

Raul was a loner. No wonder, with such a regimented childhood, brought up by staff rather than doting parents. Then there was his father's betrayal with the woman Raul had fallen for.

He'd spent so long cutting himself off from emotional connections; the moments when he let down his guard with her were special, poignantly precious.

More and more, Raul shared his wry wit, surprising her into giggles of shock or delight. The last thing she'd expected from the man who'd married her to claim the crown.

But as she watched him work tirelessly for his country,

every day and into the night, and saw his people respond to him, she knew he was the right man for the job.

Luisa's anger over his ruthless actions was now strangely muted. She knew Raul wasn't the unfeeling villain she'd once painted him. In some ways he was as much a victim of circumstance as she. A wounded man who hid his vulnerability behind a façade.

She felt melancholy. For, despite the way he stood up for her, supporting her sometimes unorthodox approach to her royal duties, she could never forget that for him she was an unwanted wife.

The wife he had to have.

A sweet ache pierced her and she pressed a hand to her chest. She hitched a breath and stared blindly at the newspaper on the desk before her.

It hurt because, even knowing Raul made the best of their convenient marriage, Luisa had done the unthinkable.

She'd fallen in love.

Despite the pain, happiness bubbled. Ripples of delight shivered through her till she trembled.

Love was such a big emotion. It overcame the fears plaguing her.

Surely there was a way she could make this marriage work? Make him care for her the way she cared for him?

'Sitting alone, Luisa?' Raul's voice made her jump and turn. Her heart kicked as she took in his tall frame, his sculpted features and the flare of heat in his eyes.

She yearned to throw herself into his embrace. Declare her feelings and demand he love her too.

If only it were that simple.

She sat where she was, limbs stiffening as she strove not to give herself away. He'd be horrified if he guessed her feelings. She had to be calm while inside she was a nervous jumble of joy and fear and tentative hope.

'My language lesson's over and I was trying to read the paper.' She twisted her fingers together and looked down, choosing an article at random. 'There's a picture of you but the words are too difficult.'

He stood behind her. She knew from the way her flesh prickled. Her body possessed radar tuned solely to Raul. Whenever he approached, even when he watched her from the other side of a crowded reception, Luisa felt it.

'It's a court report. Why not try something simpler?' His words were a puff of warmth at her ear as he leaned in.

Luisa shut her eyes, willing him to forget the paper and slide his arms around her.

'Luisa?'

She snapped her eyes open. 'What's the article about?' She didn't care but she had to say something.

'Just the trial of people illegally stockpiling banned weapons. Why don't we—'

'But why were you a witness?' She'd finally made sense of the caption.

'It's not that exciting.'

She frowned, finally concentrating on the piece. 'It says something about an armed raid. And a plot. A coup.' That word was familiar. She pointed at the next paragraph. 'What's that word?'

A sigh riffled her hair. He hesitated so long she wondered if he'd answer. 'Assassination.'

Luisa swung round, shock widening her eyes.

'Who did they want to assassinate?' Ice froze her feet, her legs, creeping upwards as she read resignation in Raul's expression.

Surely it couldn't have been...

'The cabinet. As many government officials as they could.' He straightened and stepped away and she felt bereft. She pushed back her chair and stood on shaky legs.

'And the Prince?' The words were a brittle rasp from her constricting throat. 'They wanted to kill you?'

To her horror he didn't deny it, merely lifted his shoulders. 'Don't worry, Luisa, it was over weeks ago, when you went to Ardissia.'

The glacial frost encroached to her heart and she wrapped her arms around herself. 'You didn't tell me.'

He strode to her and rubbed his hands over her rigid arms. 'You have nothing to fear, honestly. It's all over.'

'You think I'm worried for myself?'

Raul's eyes widened and for an instant she saw a flicker of shock. Then he drew her close. Beneath her ear she heard the strong beat of his heart. Her hands slid under his jacket, palming the muscled heat of his torso.

He was so alive. So vibrant. If anything happened to him…

Terror was a jagged blade, slicing through her.

This was the downside of love. She cared so much for Raul the thought of losing him was impossible to bear.

He moved to step back but she burrowed closer. His arms tightened till she felt cocooned and safe.

'Listen, Luisa. It really is over. These were just a handful of the lunatic fringe. The police had monitored them for some time so there was no danger. In fact their schemes have done everyone a favour.'

'How?' She arched back to meet his eyes.

'I told you there'd been unrest. It got worse in the final stages of my father's reign.' Raul paused before finally continuing.

'There were limits to what I could achieve as prince. In the last years as his marriage deteriorated, he became…erratic. He let his cronies grab too much power and didn't think strategically about the nation's well-being. Power blocs have been vying for position.'

'Lukas said you'd worked to keep the peace.'

'Did he? It looked at one stage as if the various parties might tear the country apart. The news that unstable elements saw that as an opportunity for a bloodbath made them all rethink and realise how important our peace and democracy are. It's brought them back to the negotiating table.' He smoothed his hand over her hair in a gentle caress.

'When the coronation takes place and parliament resumes, we'll be working together.'

'But what about—'

A finger against her lips stopped her words. 'It's nothing to concern you.' He turned to the newspaper. 'Let me find you something easier to read.'

Luisa's mind whirled. Raul had been in danger for his life. She'd assumed his talk of protecting the country was exaggerated to cover his desire to inherit.

Her stomach hollowed, realising how serious the situation had been. That she might have lost him.

That he hadn't considered sharing even a little of the truth with her. Even now he didn't want her to know.

And she'd thought they'd been building a rapport!

Raul might support her attempts to become a princess. He might take her to paradise with his body. But as for sharing anything more significant… How could she pretend it was possible when he kept so much from her?

Pain twisted to raw anguish in Luisa's heart. Even if he didn't carry a torch for Ana, his distrust was so ingrained Luisa saw now her chances of truly connecting with him were doomed.

He was a man she could love. The man she *did* love—strong, caring, capable and tender. But she knew no way to breach the final brittle shell of reserve he wore like armour. The shell that kept them apart even when she'd imagined they shared more and more.

She'd fooled herself, believing that after their time together he'd begun to feel something for her too.

He wouldn't want to hear her declaration of love.

He didn't want to share himself.

How would he react if she told him she suspected he'd shared enough of himself to create a child with her?

CHAPTER THIRTEEN

'This way, Your Highness.'

Raul followed the urban planner across waste ground, listening to him extol the virtues of the site that would become a community garden. Another of Luisa's projects.

It had merely taken mention of unused public land in a disadvantaged area for Luisa to find a use for it. Castle staff lent expertise to help the community build a place to meet, play and grow food. But it was Luisa, with Lukas' help, who'd checked zoning restrictions, negotiated with the council and met with residents.

His wife had extraordinary organisational skills, honed keeping a struggling business afloat. He'd seen with pleasure how she put those skills to use in Ardissia and here in the capital.

Raul admired her practicality, her drive to make things better.

Who'd have thought a girl off the farm would be such a success? She was a breath of fresh air, cutting through hidebound protocol with a smile, yet sensitive enough to see when tradition was necessary.

People loved her, drawn by her charm and warmth, and the royal fairy tale romance was a source of real pleasure after difficult political times.

Raul urged the planner towards the group at the centre of the site. Luisa was there, wearing her trademark casual chic clothes. He stifled a smile, seeing a couple of girls in almost matching gear.

Luisa's couture gowns were seen now only at formal functions. Instead she'd set her own trend, the first Maritzian royal to wear casual clothes to meet the people. But on Luisa casual looked so good. Today she wore slim-fitting jeans, low-heeled boots of supple scarlet and a matching jacket over a white top.

Only this time she hadn't shoved up her sleeves so she could take a hands-on role. Her boots were pristine, not even a fleck of dirt. Her face wasn't flushed with exertion and she didn't have a hair out of place as when she'd cuddled some toddler in a crowd.

He liked it when she looked a little flushed and rumpled. It reminded him of Luisa naked in his bed.

Now she looked elegant with her stylish clothes and pale, fine-boned features.

Raul's eyes narrowed. Too pale, surely?

Usually Luisa was a golden girl with her colouring and her tan. It complemented her infectious smile as she chatted with anybody and everybody.

Now, though surrounded by people as usual, she stood a little aloof, hanging back from the discussion. She looked peaky and the smile she wore wasn't the grin he'd become accustomed to.

No one else seemed to sense anything wrong.

But he'd come to know his wife.

He tensed, premonition skating down his nape as he recalled recent changes he'd preferred not to dwell on. Times when Luisa's warm impulsiveness had grown strained, appearing only in the heights of passion.

Then she was all his, just as he wanted her.

He repressed a scowl. Did he imagine she'd grown cooler? The suspicion had hit several times that she no longer wanted to share herself. As if she tried to hide the woman he'd come to think of as the real Luisa. Open, honest and exuberant.

Or as if that Luisa had ceased to exist.

An icy hand gripped his innards as he fought a rising tide of tension. A sense of déjà vu.

He squashed the thought. Luisa was *not* Ana. Only Raul's youth and the blindness of so-called love had ever convinced him Ana was the sort of woman he could trust.

Yet still he couldn't shift a sense of foreboding.

'Is everything OK?'

Luisa swung round, away from people waving goodbye. Raul had moved across the limo's wide seat to settle beside her. He'd raised the privacy screen.

Excitement zinged through her veins and drew the skin of her breasts and stomach tight. Her body betrayed her. She couldn't resist Raul, even knowing their relationship was tragically one-sided. Lately too, the more she tried to pull back and develop some protective distance, the more determined he seemed to invade her space.

Yet there was no gleam in his eyes now, just the shadow of a frown.

'Of course. Everything's fine.' With a supreme effort Luisa pasted a smile on her lips as she lied.

She teetered on a knife-edge of despair. She'd given her heart to a man who couldn't reciprocate her feelings. And now it seemed possible there'd be a child.

Her emotions were like a seesaw. One moment she was thrilled at the idea of carrying Raul's baby, at the new life she hoped she cradled in her womb. The next chill fear gripped her at the idea of bringing a child into this tiny family so unlike anything she'd dreamed of. Love was anathema to Raul yet it was her hidden secret. What sort of world was that in which to raise a child?

That was when she hoped against hope the pregnancy was a false alarm and guilt ate her, for wishing away such a precious gift.

She couldn't blame Raul. With his past it was no wonder he'd cut himself off from the deepest of emotions. She didn't even know if he believed in love!

As for his unswerving dedication to his country, putting it ahead of personal relationships, she could understand that too.

When she'd translated the papers about that trial she'd been stunned to learn the key role Raul had played in the investigation, as well as the political ramifications of the plot. Maritz needed Raul even more than Raul needed the satisfaction of fulfilling the role he was born to.

'Luisa?'

'Yes?' She looked over his shoulder and waved. 'What did you think of the garden site? It's got potential, don't you think? And the locals are very enthusiastic.' Great. Now she was babbling.

'The site is excellent.' He paused and she sensed he chose his words carefully. 'You seem…not as exuberant as usual.'

Luisa darted a glance at him then away, her stomach churning. 'I didn't think exuberance in a princess was a good thing.' She clenched nervous hands and searched for a neutral topic. 'The project's going well, don't you think?' Or had she already said that? Her brain was scrambled.

'Very well. You should be pleased.'

'I am. The volunteers have worked so hard.'

'You've worked hard too.' His brows puckered. 'You haven't been overdoing it, have you?'

Luisa's breath snagged. Had he guessed? She'd been forced from bed earlier and earlier by what she suspected was morning sickness. She didn't want Raul to see her white, nauseous and bedraggled. Especially when she didn't know how he'd react to the news.

It was one thing for him to say he'd break with tradition in bringing up a child. Another to welcome their baby with the whole-hearted love it deserved.

In that moment she decided. The idea of a trip home to see Mary and Sam had lurked in the back of her mind for days. Now the need for their warmth and unquestioning support was too much to resist. She'd visit them and discreetly schedule a doctor's appointment, something that was impossible here.

Imagine even visiting a pharmacy in Maritz to buy a pregnancy test kit! The news would be in the press before nightfall.

Luisa needed time and space to come to grips with the changes in her life. She'd go as soon as the coronation was over.

'Of course I haven't overdone it. I'm fit as ever.'

He placed his hands over hers. Instantly she froze. She hadn't realised she'd been wringing them. His warmth flowed into her and for a moment her racing brain calmed. Perhaps after all she could—

'You didn't cross the site to say hello to the people on the far side of the block.'

Luisa drew a steadying breath. 'We'd run out of time. I know you have a meeting and I'd already been there a while before you arrived.'

'Still—' his gaze pierced hers '—normally you make time for everyone.'

'You wanted to see them?' She'd been so eager to get away, to find quiet in which to think.

'No, you're right.' He shook his head. 'I'd run out of time. It just seemed...unlike you.'

Luisa flexed her fingers and instantly he released his grip and moved away.

Pain gripped her chest.

See? It wasn't that he wanted to hold her. Except of course when they had sex. He was just making sure she was well enough to carry out her duties.

Raul's meeting had been endless. Time and again he'd caught himself staring at his watch, calculating how long before he could get away.

He should be pleased. All was set for the coronation next week and negotiations with formerly difficult local leaders had proved fruitful.

Yet he couldn't concentrate. Luisa had seemed strained earlier this afternoon. This morning he'd woken to find she'd slipped from his bed again. What had begun as an occasional irritation was now a worrying habit.

He felt unsettled when she wasn't there. He liked waking with her. Not only for the physical satisfaction of early morning sex. But because she made him feel good. Relaxed. Content.

Strange, when in the past he'd preferred to sleep alone. But so many things about his marriage were unusual.

Like the way he watched Luisa. She was vibrant and attractive, though not as gorgeous as some women he'd known. Yet he found himself watching her all the time, smiling when she smiled, enjoying her interactions with others and her combination of spunk and intelligence during their own discussions.

Though there hadn't been many of those lately. His fingers tightened on the neck of the chilled champagne bottle. Tonight would be different.

He put his head in the outer office before leaving for the private apartments.

'Clear my calendar for the fortnight after the coronation, can you?' He was determined to spend time alone with Luisa. Now things were stable he'd take time off and give her a honeymoon they'd both enjoy.

He couldn't think of anything he enjoyed more than being with his wife.

'Yes, sir.' The junior secretary took a note.

'Don't book anything else in my wife's diary either. I'll talk to her about clearing her dates as well.'

He smiled. A couple of weeks at his secluded lakeside retreat. It would be beautiful at this time of year. Luisa would love it and they could be alone.

'I'm sorry, sir.' The girl frowned. 'The princess is booked on a flight the day after the coronation.'

'A flight? It must be a mistake.'

'No, sir. I organised it myself just hours ago.'

Raul felt a curious hollow sensation deep in his chest. He strode to the computer.

'Show me.'

Silently she found the booking then turned the screen towards him. A flight to Sydney, no stopovers. No return.

The void in Raul's chest expanded and the breath seared from his lungs.

'Was there a call from Australia?' It might be sickness in the family. Luisa was close to her aunt and uncle.

But she hadn't mentioned it to him.

'Not that I know of, Your Highness.'

She bit her lip and Raul realised he was looming over her, glowering. He took a step back and forced a smile.

'That's fine. I'll talk to her about it myself.' He turned on his heel. A sixth sense chilled his flesh.

A one-way ticket to Sydney. Alone.

He forced down the instant thought that she'd had enough. That Luisa couldn't stand it here, had never forgiven him for bringing her to Maritz and planned to leave for good. *Leave him.*

His skin prickled and he lengthened his stride.

There would be an explanation. Yet his belly was a hard twist of tension as he headed for the royal apartments.

Raul tapped on the door of her suite and waited.

Strange. According to the secretary, Luisa had come here an hour ago to rest.

He knocked again and turned the handle. Perhaps she'd fallen asleep on the bed. Despite his concern, Raul's mouth kicked up at the idea of Luisa, tousled and soft from sleep.

He stepped in and slammed to a stop.

Time splintered.

He stood frozen, bile rising as his numb mind absorbed details. Déjà vu smote him and he reeled.

Yet this was worse. Far worse. This was Luisa…

Luisa and Lukas.

This clearly was no business meeting but something far more intimate.

Luisa wore a tight tank top and flirty skirt, her hands curled round Lukas' shoulders. Lukas, the man he would have trusted with his life! *The man he'd trusted with Luisa.*

Lukas held her close in his embrace, arms wrapped possessively round her slim form. Their blond heads were just a kiss apart.

Raul recalled his wife's recent coolness, the way she left his bed and tried to distance herself. Had Raul been a coward, ignoring signs he didn't want to see? Could Luisa have betrayed him as Ana had?

It felt as if someone had reached in and ripped his heart out.

Lukas had removed his jacket and tie. His collar was undone. Had Luisa done that? Had she used her nimble fingers to begin undressing him?

Roaring pain blasted Raul. It battered like a mountain avalanche till he could barely stand upright. It clamped his chest in a vice so tight he couldn't draw breath.

An explosion of shattering glass at his feet roused him from sick shock. The couple before him whipped their heads round and noticed him.

Fiery colour washed Luisa's face and her hands dropped. Lukas straightened and released her, adjusting his collar.

Raul's brain filled with an image he couldn't thrust away. Of Ana and his father, emerging from a state bedroom after his old man had taken Raul's visitor on a personal tour. Ana had coloured and looked away. His father had stood straighter, fiddling with his cuffs.

The beginning of their betrayal.

Raul breathed deep. With an effort he cleared his whirling thoughts.

This was Luisa and Lukas. Not Ana and his father.

His heart thundered and adrenalin pumped in his blood, but sanity prevailed. He forced his stiff legs to move. Ignoring the churning in his belly, he prowled into the room.

Raul watched Luisa's bright flush fade and her skin pale to bone-white.

'Luisa.' His voice sounded unfamiliar.

'Your Highness.' Lukas hurried into speech. 'I know this must look—'

Raul slashed one silencing hand through the air. It was Luisa he needed to talk with.

'But Your Highness…Raul…'

Raul swung round, focusing on his secretary. Through all the years they'd worked together Lukas had been a stickler for formality, refusing Raul's suggestion more than once that in private Lukas call him by name.

Fear churned in Raul's belly that Lukas should choose this moment to bridge that gap. To put them on equal footing.

Why? Because he and Luisa…?

No! Raul refused to let himself think it.

Yet, like a spectre, the possibility hovered in the recesses of his brain, waiting to swamp him in a moment of weakness.

'Leave us, Lukas.'

His voice was harsh with shock and a fear greater than anything he'd known.

Still Lukas didn't move, but looked to Luisa who stood, fingers threading nervously before her.

'Go, Lukas,' she whispered. 'It will be all right.'

Finally, with lagging steps he left. Raul heard the door click quietly behind him. Yet still Luisa didn't meet his eyes.

Anxiety stretched each nerve to breaking point. He clenched his hands, forcing himself to wait till she was ready to talk.

'It's not what you think.'

'You don't know what I'm thinking.' At this moment rational thought was almost beyond him. He was a mass of churning emotions. Only the voice that told him over and over that Luisa was *different*, was *his*, kept him sane.

She lifted her head and met his gaze and the familiar sizzle in his veins eased a fraction of the desperate tension in his body.

This was his Luisa. He refused to believe the worst.

'Aren't you going to ask about Lukas?'

'I know you'll tell me.' He just prayed he was man enough to hear the truth.

She paced away, her steps short, her eyes averted as if she couldn't bear to look at him. Fear knotted his brain.

'He was helping me.'

'Go on.'

'He was teaching me to dance.'

'Sorry?' Raul stared, flummoxed by the unexpected response.

'Teaching me to waltz, ready for the coronation ball.' Luisa flashed him a challenging look. 'At home our local dance was a disco in the school hall and I never learnt anything formal.' She looked at a point over his shoulder. 'It didn't matter at our wedding because the country was in mourning and there was no dancing at the reception, but this time...' She shrugged stiffly. 'I didn't want to disgrace you on your big day.'

Raul frowned. There was something so intimate about the idea of teaching Luisa to waltz. Holding her in his arms and showing her how to move her body with his.

'You could have asked me.' Surely that was the sort of thing husbands did? He'd have revelled in it.

What did it say about their marriage that she'd turned to his *secretary* to help her?

Colour washed her throat and her mouth pursed. 'And make it obvious there was another simple thing I couldn't do? You have no idea how hard it's been to try to get everything right—the protocol and customs and language—and still I make so many mistakes. Besides—' she drew a shaky breath '—it's so basic. How embarrassing not even to know how to waltz.'

She blinked quickly and his heart compressed.

'I don't care if you can't dance.' His voice was rough as he stepped closer.

'But I do. I wanted...' She chewed her lip.

'You thought anyone would care about your dancing ability? That I'd care? That's absurd!' Not after they'd shared so much. More than he'd shared with any other woman.

'Absurd?' She shook her head and spun away to pace the room again.

Raul wanted to tug her into his arms but the way she wrapped her arms round her torso and her strained expression told him this wasn't the time.

'What's really absurd is marrying someone you don't know. Giving yourself to someone who'll never care for you. Can never care for you because he never got over the woman who hurt him years ago.'

Shock held Raul mute as her words lashed him. He couldn't credit what he heard. Luisa believed he hadn't got over Ana?

'That's not true!'

He reached for her, took her arm, but she shrugged out of his grasp.

Anguish lacerated him at her rejection.

'Do you know how it feels knowing I wasn't your first choice of wife, not even your second? That you married me because of who my grandfather was?'

She drew a huge shuddering sigh and Raul felt the full weight of regret bear down on him for all he'd done to this vibrant, special woman.

All through their relationship his needs had come first. She'd given him what he wanted, more than he'd ever dreamed possible, and all the time she'd suffered.

He'd known it, had felt pangs of guilt but never before had he truly faced the full magnitude of Luisa's distress and loss. He'd conned himself into believing she'd begun to feel some of the pleasure he did in their union, shared some of his hopes for the future.

Reality hit him like a sledgehammer to the heart.

Raul shoved trembling hands into his pockets rather than reach for her. Clearly she didn't want his touch. The knowledge burned like acid.

'Is that why you've booked a flight to Sydney next week?'

Luisa's mouth gaped then shut with a snap. 'You know about that?'

'I just found out.' He waited. When she remained silent he prompted, hoping against hope there was another reason for her trip. 'Is there a family emergency?'

She shook her head and he felt hope flicker and fade.

'I wanted to go home.' Her voice cracked and it was all Raul could do not to scoop her close.

'This is your home.' His voice was rough, emotion scouring each word.

She shook her head so fervently fine gold hair whirled around her face and he'd have sworn her eyes shimmered with tears. His stomach clenched as from a crippling blow.

'I need time. Time away from here.'

Time away from him.

Something withered in Raul's breast. Something he couldn't put a name to. He'd hoped eventually she'd be happy with him, forget how he'd forced her to come here. Had he deluded himself, believing she'd come to care for him? That they'd begun to share something special?

But he couldn't give up.

'You belong here now, Luisa.'

He cut himself off before he could say she belonged to *him*.

'Do I?' She spun away, her arms wrapped over her chest. She drew a shuddering breath. 'I think it would be wise if I went away for a while. You see—'

'Running away, Luisa?' He couldn't be hearing this. Only yesterday she'd snuggled, naked in his embrace, and he'd felt... he'd hoped...

She shook her head. 'You'll be crowned. You'll have what you want.' Her voice sounded muffled.

And what if it was *her* he wanted? It struck him with the force of absolute truth that he wanted nothing more than to spend his life with Luisa.

Why had he not seen it so clearly before?

The crown, even his country, meant nothing without Luisa.

Had he lost her for good?

Unbidden, an image rose of her and Lukas. Would they meet in Australia?

He refused to consider the possibility.

'You can't leave the day after the coronation. At least put off the trip for a while.' He needed time to make her see reason. Time to convince her to stay.

She stiffened. 'I thought I should be there for the ceremony. But maybe it would be better if—'

She stopped as his mobile phone beeped insistently. With an impatient click of his tongue Raul reached into his pocket and switched it off.

'That's your private line. It's probably important.'

He stalked towards her, in no mood to be distracted. '*This* is important, Luisa.'

The sound of Luisa's landline ringing cut across his words. Before he could prevent her, she'd lifted the receiver, as if eager for the interruption.

'It's for you.' She held out the receiver to him. 'The government's legal counsel says he has to speak with you.'

Raul hesitated. They needed to discuss this now. But the matter he'd had the lawyers working on would surely help his cause with Luisa. He was desperate enough to clutch at anything that would help.

He reached for the phone.

Luisa watched Raul, so intent on the lawyer's news.

See? She'd been right about his priorities. As his wife she came somewhere near the bottom.

He'd challenged her about her trip to Australia and she'd waited, half dreading, half hoping he'd decree she couldn't go, say she had to remain, not for reasons of state but because he couldn't bear to be parted from her.

She'd imagined being swept into his arms, hauled against his hard torso and imprisoned there. Because he loved her as she loved him and he refused to release her.

Reality was so different.

'There's something I need to attend to.'

Wearily she nodded. There'd always be something more important than the state of their marriage. Dejectedly she wondered if perhaps it would be better if she left and didn't return.

'Luisa, did you hear me?'

'Sorry?' She looked up to find him already reaching for the door.

'I said we need to talk, *properly*. I'll be back as soon as I can.'

Luisa nodded, donning the mask of composure that now felt brittle enough to crack. Or was that her heart? Her last hope for a real marriage had just shattered.

CHAPTER FOURTEEN

'THANK YOU, everyone.' Raul nodded to the High Court judges, the Attorney General and the other witnesses who'd been urgently summoned two hours ago on his orders to witness this history-altering event.

In other circumstances he'd be excited at the prospect of initiating such significant change. But it was all he could do to wait patiently while they filed slowly from the chamber, leaving him alone.

So alone.

His mind snagged on the image of Luisa just hours ago in her room, pale and strained as she spoke of the need to get away. The hurt she'd felt at her place in his life.

How deeply he'd injured her, forcing her into his world.

Was he doing the right thing now, trying to tie her to him more strongly than ever? He looked at the parchment on the desk, checked, signed, countersigned and witnessed. The document he'd long planned as a surprise for Luisa, a testament of his regard for her.

The document that now represented his last-ditch, desperate effort to convince her to stay.

Did he have the right to try to hold her when life with him had made her so patently unhappy?

Until today he'd thought her content. More than content: happy.

Was he doomed never to find that emotional closeness Luisa

had spoken of so longingly? Was he simply not the right man to make her happy?

Pain seared through his clenched jaw at the notion of letting her go.

Terror engulfed him at the thought of life without her.

But who could blame her? He'd never experienced real love and surely that lack had left him emotionally flawed. Was he incapable of providing what she needed in a husband?

If she wanted to be here it would be different. Together they could face anything. If she cared for him...

His bark of raw laughter was loud in the silence. How could Luisa care for him after what he'd done to her? He'd deluded himself, believing things had changed between them these past weeks. The way she'd shied from his touch this evening said it all.

He turned to the window and looked at the glitter of city lights below. Normally he enjoyed the view of the capital he loved, the valley that had been home to his family for centuries. That sense of place, of belonging, always brought comfort.

Not now. Now all he felt was the terrible aloneness.

Life without Luisa.

He couldn't conceive it. His brain shut down every time he thought about it and a terrible hollow ache filled him. His very hands shook at the idea of her on a plane to Australia without him.

He should do the honourable thing and let her go. Release her from this life she'd never desired.

Yet he wanted to throw back his head and howl his despair at the idea of losing her. His pulse raced and his skin prickled with sweat at the thought of never seeing her again. Never holding her.

Never telling her how he felt.

Excruciating pain ripped at him, giant talons that tore at his soul.

It was no good, try as he might to be self-sacrificing, this was more than he could bear. It was asking too much.

He grabbed the parchment and rolled it quickly, heedless of the still drying wax seals. Turning on his heel he strode to the door.

Luisa woke slowly, clinging to a surprisingly wonderful dream.

After hours pacing the floor she'd retreated to bed. And still she'd tortured herself reliving the blank look on Raul's face as he'd left her, already intent on other business. The fact that he hadn't countermanded her trip to Sydney. That he didn't care.

Now she felt…safe, cocooned in a warm haven that protected her from everything. She didn't want to move.

But she had no choice. Even in her half aware state she registered the sick feeling, the rising nausea. She breathed deep, trying to force it back but it was no good.

With a desperate lurch she struggled upright, only to find her movements impeded by the large man wrapped around her back. His legs spooned hers, his palm on her stomach.

'Raul!' It was a raw croak. What was he doing here? When had he—?

Her stomach heaved and she thrust his confining arm away, swinging her legs off the bed.

'Luisa!' His voice was sharp. 'What's wrong?'

She had no time for explanations. She stumbled across the room, one hand to her stomach, the other clamped to her mouth as she tasted bile.

Miraculously the bathroom door swung open and she dived in just in time to brace herself as her last meal resurfaced. Her legs wobbled so much her knees folded and she almost crumpled to the floor.

But an arm lashed round her, keeping her upright with all Raul's formidable strength. Behind her she felt his body, hot and solid, anchoring her.

Then she bent, retching as the paroxysm of nausea overcame her. Her skin prickled horribly and searing bitterness filled her as her stomach spasmed again and again till there was nothing more to bring up.

She slumped, trembling and spent, eyes closed as she tried to summon strength to move.

Her head spun, or did she imagine movement? Next thing she knew she was seated on the side of the bath and she sighed her gratitude as every muscle melted. Raul supported her and she couldn't summon the energy to order him out. Not when he was all that kept her upright.

Then, like a blessing, a damp cloth brushed her forehead, her cheeks and throat, her dry lips. She turned her face into it gratefully.

'Drink this.' A glass nudged her mouth. Gratefully she sipped cool water. The damp cloth wiped her forehead again and she almost moaned in relief. She was weak as a kitten.

How could she face Raul now? Why was he here?

Tears stung as exhaustion and self-pity flooded her.

'You're ill. I'll call a doctor.' She opened her eyes to meet a worried dark green gaze. Raul looked grim.

She wanted to sit, basking in her husband's concern, pretending it meant more than it surely did.

'No. I'm not ill. It's perfectly normal. A doctor won't help with this.'

Belatedly she realised what she'd said as Raul's brows arched. Shock froze his features as he read the implications of her nausea.

She'd meant to tell him soon. But not like this.

'Please,' she said quickly. 'I need privacy to freshen up.' She refused to have this conversation on the edge of the bath, with her hair matted across her clammy brow.

Luisa turned away, not wanting to see suspicion darken his gaze. Pain welled and she bit her lip. After seeing her with Lukas it would be no surprise if Raul questioned the baby's paternity. He hadn't said he believed her explanation of why she'd been in Lukas' embrace.

Raul left the room without a word.

She should have been grateful but felt only despair that he'd been eager to go. So much for her fantasy of them bonding over their child!

Luisa took her time in the bathroom, but when she opened the door Raul was there. To her astonishment he swooped, scooping her into his arms.

'I can walk.' But her protest was half-hearted. His embrace was magic, even knowing it didn't mean anything. Raul was a man for whom duty was paramount. Tending to a pregnant female would come naturally.

He deposited her on the bed, where plumped up pillows sat against the headboard. He drew the coverlet over her and reached for something on the bedside table.

'Here. Try this.' It was a plate of salted crackers. He must have ordered them while she was in the bathroom.

'I'm not an invalid.' Luisa pushed them aside and fought not to succumb to the sweet delight of being cared for. Absurdly, the thoughtful gesture made her eyes swim, despite her anger and distress.

It didn't help that Raul looked wonderful. Faded denim stretched across his taut, powerful thighs. He wore a black pullover, sleeves bunched up to reveal strong, sinewy forearms. He was even more gorgeous than in one of his suave suits. Would she ever see him like this again? Her throat closed as she realised the answer was probably no.

The bed sank as he sat, facing her. Luisa's heart squeezed.

'You're pregnant.' It was a statement.

'I think so. But if I am it's your child.' She met his impenetrable gaze defiantly. 'It's got nothing to do with Lukas.'

He reached out and smoothed a lock of hair off her brow. Luisa's breath caught at the seeming tenderness of the gesture. She told herself she was a fool.

'I didn't think it had.'

'Oh.' She sank back, stunned.

'Have you seen a doctor?'

'No. It's still early.' She knew exactly when their baby had been conceived: that first tempestuous night of marriage, when she'd learned about ecstasy and heartache.

But Raul's calm acceptance surprised her. 'So you never thought—?'

He shook his head. 'I can't lie and say it didn't occur to me.' His eyes slid from hers. 'But when would you have time for an affair? It's *my* bed you share? *My* sofa. *My* desk.'

'You've made your point!' He didn't have to remind her how needy she was for him. How he only had to tilt one dark eyebrow in delicious invitation for her pulse to thrum with anticipation.

She stared hard into his face, trying to decipher his thoughts. Bewildered, she shook her head. 'I thought you'd believe—'

'That my wife was having an affair with my secretary?' Raul grimaced and placed has hand over hers. She felt heat, power and solidity, and she couldn't bring herself to dislodge his hand.

'I admit it was an unpleasant shock.' He tightened his hold and drew a deep breath that expanded his chest mightily. 'But I've come to know you, Luisa. You'd never go behind my back with another man. You're honest, genuine and caring. You wouldn't behave like that.' The words fell like nourishing rain in her parched soul.

He believed in her?

Her hands trembled with the shock of it.

'I know Lukas too,' he continued. 'We've worked together for years. How could I believe the worst, knowing you both?'

'I—' Words failed her. Such trust, when Raul had been so badly hurt before, and in the face of such evidence, stunned her. She'd expected a myriad of questions at the very least. Her heart swelled.

'I thought after Ana—'

'Forget Ana. I was a fool ever believing myself in love with her. But I got over her years ago. This is about you and me, Luisa. No one else.'

Raul's intense stare pinioned her, even as relief flared deep

inside at the knowledge the other woman was no rival for
Raul's affection. She'd worried about that so long! A burgeon-
ing sense of lightness filled her.

'Luisa.' Her name was a sudden hoarse rasp that startled
her. 'I want you to stay. Here, with me. Don't go to Sydney.'

The trembling in her hands intensified as tenuous joy rose.
He believed in her! He wanted her!

It took a moment to realise why.

Disillusionment was bitter on her tongue. She tried to pull
away but his grasp tightened.

'Because of the baby! You want your heir.' That was why
he'd changed his mind about her going. This was about bloodlines. How could she have thought otherwise? She knew to her
cost how important royal blood was in this place. Her heart
spasmed in distress.

'Of course I want to be with the baby and you.'

She shook her head, a lead weight settling on her chest. The
pain was worse now, more intense after that single moment of
hope. She almost cried out.

Despite her efforts to make a place for herself here, Luisa
knew she was too impulsive, too casual, too ready to bend the
rules to make a good monarch's wife.

It wasn't Luisa he wanted, just her unborn child.

'Please let go of me. This won't work.' She didn't know how
she summoned the strength to speak calmly, when inside it
felt as if she were crumbling.

For what seemed an age he held her, his gaze sharp on
her face. Then finally, when she'd almost given up on him
responding, he released her and turned away, his shoulders
hunching.

Instantly Luisa missed his warmth, his strength. She looked
at her hands, where he'd gripped her so tightly, and it hit her
she wasn't trembling any more.

Stunned, she looked to Raul, the distracted way he shoved
a hand through his hair. She stared, not believing what she
saw.

It was *him*. He was shaking all over.

'Raul?' Luisa's voice sounded hollow, as if it came from far away. She didn't understand what was going on. Her big, strong husband shook like a leaf.

'Raul! What is it?'

He didn't answer and she reached out a tentative hand to his shoulder. She felt the tremors running through his large frame.

'Raul!' Fear welled. Was he ill?

'I can't. I…' His head sank between his shoulders.

Frantically Luisa tugged at his upper arm, turning him towards her. She rose onto her knees and shuffled closer.

'What is it? Please, tell me.'

Finally he swung his head towards her. He was haggard as she'd never seen him, his flesh drawn too tight across the bones. Only his eyes looked alive in that spare face. They glittered, overbright.

'I can't lose you, Luisa.' His voice was a whisper of anguish that tore at her. 'God help me, I can't let you go. When you said you had to get away I knew I couldn't force you to stay any longer. But…'

'Raul?' She gulped. 'I don't understand. What are you saying?'

Luisa stared, dumbfounded, at the man she'd heard give speeches in four languages, charming, persuasive Raul, struggling to get his words out. Her grip eased on his arm and her hand slid up in a soothing caress.

'I need to look after you, Luisa. You and our baby.' Her heart somersaulted at the sound of those words: *our baby.*

'We'll come to some arrangement.' Much as the idea of part-time parents pained her, she knew their baby needed them both.

'I don't want *an arrangement.*' He lifted his head, the glitter in his eyes different, almost dangerous. 'I want my wife and child. Here.' He reached out to grab a rolled up paper from the foot of the bed. 'This will prove how much I want you here.'

With fumbling hands he thrust it at her, almost ripping the thick parchment as he hastened to unroll it.

'It's all in Maritzian.' Despairingly she skimmed the document, too distracted to concentrate properly. All she took in was the column of seals and signatures at the bottom, beginning with the flourish of Raul's formal signature and the royal dragon seal.

'What is it, Raul?' She'd never seen him like this, so agitated she wanted to cradle him close.

'It authorises a change in the royal succession from the moment I'm crowned. On that day you'll become Queen.'

She frowned. 'That's no change.'

He shook his head. 'Queen, not royal consort. You'll be my equal, my partner in ruling the kingdom.' His gleaming gaze met hers and the force of it warmed her very soul. 'How else can I prove what you mean to me? How much I need and trust you?'

Her eyes widened. 'But you can't do that! I'm not…not…I don't have the experience. I wouldn't know what to do. I—'

He grabbed her hands and held them tight. 'You'll learn. I'll teach you.' He kissed her palm and shivers of delight ran through her.

'But Maritz isn't ready for this. I'm not good at—'

'Maritz will adapt. You're capable and honest and caring. You'll make a perfect queen. For my country. For me. For our child.' His gaze dipped to her belly and heat sizzled through her.

'But I break all the rules.'

'Sometimes they need to be broken. There's more to life than protocol, you know.' He smiled, a slow, devastating smile that heated her from the soles of her feet to the top of her head.

'You're a princess to make anyone proud. Already our people respect and care for you, because they see how you care about them. You've helped them when it counted. You've helped *me*. You've changed my life and taught me hope.'

Luisa's brain whirled. It was too much to comprehend.

'Can you forgive me, Luisa? Enough to stay and give me another chance?'

She watched him swallow hard and searched her heart for a response. She loved him but was that enough to face the future? To build a life together even in the light of this momentous gesture of faith?

If he hauled her into his arms and swept her away on a tide of passion it would be easy to say yes. She yearned for that. But life wasn't so simple.

'It's not about forgiving the past. It's about the future.' She drew a difficult breath, wondering if he'd understand. 'I want a real marriage. A happy family. I want my child to enjoy being a child, with parents who really care. I want—'

'Love,' he finished for her on a husky whisper that pierced her. 'And trust and respect.' He nodded. 'You deserve it, Luisa. That's what I want to give you. If you'll let me try.'

Her breath caught in her throat at the look in his eyes.

'I love you, Luisa. I want you by my side.'

Dazed, Luisa stared into his tense face. A pulse jerked at the base of his neck and another beat at his temple. He looked like a man on the edge.

'It can't be,' she whispered, stunned into immobility.

'It's true.'

Silently she shook her head, afraid to believe.

'I didn't realise it myself.' His mouth twisted in a lopsided grimace that made her want to cuddle him close. 'I'd spent so long explaining away my feelings because the alternative was too terrifying. All my adult life I've worked to shut off my emotions. Then you came along. You made me *feel* so much, so intensely.'

Raul threaded his fingers through hers and tingling heat spread through her bloodstream. 'I've been torn, regretting the way I forced you here, forced you to marry me.' His eyes flashed. 'Yet knowing that in my heart I couldn't be truly sorry because it brought you to me and I couldn't let you go. How selfish is that?'

He thrust his other hand through his glossy hair in a

distracted gesture that made her want to wrap her arms around him. 'I'd told myself for so long that love was a fool's game. And here I was falling for a woman who had every reason to hate me.'

'I don't hate you.' The admission slipped out. She was numb, dazed.

'Really?' Hope blazed in his eyes. 'Then it's far more than I deserve.' His hand moved up to stroke her cheek and thread into her hair. Hope whispered through her.

'I've been torturing myself, telling myself I should find the strength to let you walk away and be happy.' His hold tightened.

He brought their joined hands up so he could kiss her wrist. 'But I can't do it. I have to fight for you.'

'Tell me again,' she whispered, her voice uneven. 'Tell me you love me.'

Raul lifted both hands, tenderly bracketing her face.

'I love you, Luisa. Never doubt it. I want to be by your side always. To share with you, be the one you turn to. Teach you to waltz and whatever else you want if you'll share your warmth and your laughter with me.'

Something shifted deep inside her. A tightness eased and Luisa drew breath, it seemed for the first time in an age.

'Oh, Raul!' She choked with emotion. 'I've loved you so long. I never thought…' She blinked furiously as tears welled.

'Truly?' His voice was husky with awe.

She nodded and gentle fingers wiped the wetness from her cheeks. 'Truly. Desperately.'

'My darling!' His forest-dark eyes meshed with hers. 'I didn't mean to make you cry, sweetheart. I only want to make you happy. Always.'

'You do.' She blinked and smiled. 'I've been happy here with you.'

She saw doubt and fear etched across his features. Uncertainty in the man who'd strode into her life and grabbed her destiny in his strong hands. Who ruled a kingdom with an ease anyone would envy.

'I'll make mistakes,' he admitted. 'This is all new to me. I've never felt like this.' He swallowed hard and she read a flicker of anxiety in his eyes. 'I'm not a good risk, I know. I don't have your gift of closeness and warmth. I have no experience of real family life. No role model of how to be a good father—'

Luisa's fingers on his lips stopped his words. Her heart contracted, seeing the man she loved unsure of himself.

Seeing his self-doubt, Luisa knew the truth. She had to cast off her own fear. She had to trust, in him and in herself and put the past behind her.

'I'm willing to try if you are,' she whispered in a voice croaky with emotion. It welled inside, making her whole being tremble.

Dark eyes met hers and the love she read there made her poor bruised heart squeeze tight.

'Luisa!' He gathered her close, kissing her neck, her cheeks. He held her as if she was the most precious thing in the world.

It was glorious, but it wasn't enough. Not when her heart soared with wonderment.

She cupped his hard jaw and pressed her lips full on his mouth. Instantly he responded, his mouth hungry, as if it had been a lifetime since they'd kissed. As if they'd never kissed.

Not really.

Not like this.

Raul's kiss healed. It was demanding, possessive, yet poignantly sweet. A giving and receiving, not just of physical delight but of love. True love.

Eventually they pulled apart, enough to gulp in much needed air. But Raul's arms were locked close around her and Luisa's hands were clamped tight at his shoulders.

Happiness surged so strongly she felt incandescent with it.

'I can't believe this is real.'

His shining eyes met hers and her heart somersaulted when she read the tenderness there. 'Let me show you how real, my sweet.' He gathered her close and kissed her till the world fell away.

EPILOGUE

THE ballroom was packed. Out in the courtyard more people gathered beneath fluttering royal banners, garlands and gilded lanterns.

Cheers reverberated off the antique mirrors and frescoed ceiling as the crowd applauded their new rulers: King Raul and Queen Luisa. The first joint monarchs in Maritzian history.

Goosebumps rose on Luisa's bare arms as she heard their names shouted once, twice, three times, first by the herald and then by the swelling voices of the throng.

On her head sat a delicate diadem of pure gold and dazzling brilliant cut diamonds. In her hand rested the mediaeval bejewelled orb and in Raul's, seated beside her, the engraved golden sceptre.

She breathed deep, hardly daring to believe this moment was real. But then a warm hand enfolded hers and squeezed. She turned and fell into the warm green depths of Raul's loving gaze.

It was real. The ceremony, the crowd, but most important of all, Raul's love.

He raised her hand and pressed a fervent kiss there. Instantly excitement shot through her. And anticipation.

He smiled, a devilish light in his eyes and she knew her expression gave her away. He read her feelings for him on her face. She didn't care. She revelled in their love.

And this was only the beginning...

Raul laughed and through the haze of well-being she heard the crowd applaud again.

She turned and looked down from her throne. There was Lukas standing with Luisa's new secretary, Sasha. From this angle it looked like they held hands. Then there were Tamsin and Alaric, their smiles conspiratorial. Mary and Sam were in the front row, in places of honour, beaming at Luisa as if it were the most natural thing that she should marry a king and rule a country.

She shook her head in wonderment.

'Are you ready, sweetheart?'

Raul rose and drew her to her feet. Officials appeared to take the precious orb and sceptre.

'Ready as I'll ever be.' He led her down from the dais to the polished floor where space was made for them.

'You'll be fine,' he murmured and pulled her into his arms. 'If there's a problem, blame it on your teacher.'

She gazed into his eyes, ablaze with love, felt him swing her into a waltz and smiled. The music soared and she whirled in the arms of the man she adored. She was home.

A BREATHLESS
BRIDE

FIONA BRAND

For the Lord. Thank you.
"On finding one pearl of great value, he went
and sold all that he had and bought it."
Mathew 13:46

One

With a wolf-cold gaze, Constantine Atraeus scanned the mourners attending Roberto Ambrosi's funeral, restlessly seeking…and finding.

With her long blond hair and dark eyes, elegantly curved body and rich-list style, Roberto's daughter Sienna stood out like an exotic bird among ravens.

His jaw compressing at the unmistakable evidence of her tears, Constantine shook off an unwilling surge of compassion. And memories. No matter how innocent Sienna looked, he couldn't allow himself to forget that his ex-fiancée was the new CEO of her family's failing pearl empire. She was first and foremost an Ambrosi. Descended from a once wealthy family, the Ambrosis were noted for two things: their luminous good looks and their focus on the bottom line.

In this case, his bottom line.

"Tell me you're not going after her now."

Constantine's brother Lucas, still jet-lagged from a long-haul flight from Rome to Sydney, levered himself out of the Audi Constantine had used to pick up both of his brothers from the airport.

In the Sydney office for two days of meetings, Lucas was dressed for business, although he'd long since abandoned the jacket and tie. Zane, who was already out of the car and examining the funeral crowd, was dressed in black jeans and a black shirt, a pair of dark glasses making him look even more remote.

Lucas was edgily good-looking, so much so that the media dogged him unmercifully. Zane, who was technically their half brother, and who had spent time on the streets of L.A. as a teenager before their father had found him, simply looked dangerous. The outer packaging aside, Constantine was confident that when it came to protecting his family's assets both of his brothers were sharks.

Constantine shrugged into the jacket he'd draped over the back of the driver's seat as he watched Sienna accept condolences, his frustration edged by a surge of emotion that had nothing to do with temper.

Grimly, he considered that the physical attraction that had drawn him away from The Atraeus Group's head office on Medinos, when his legal counsel could have handled the formalities, was clouding his judgment.

No, that wasn't it. Two years ago Constantine had finally learned to separate sexual desire from business. He was no longer desperate.

This time if and when Sienna Ambrosi came to his bed, it would be on his terms, not hers.

"I'm not here to put flowers on Roberto's grave."

"Or allow her to grieve. Ever heard of tomorrow?" Lucas shrugged into his jacket and slammed the door of the Audi.

Constantine winced at Lucas's treatment of the expensive car. Lucas hadn't been old enough to remember the bad old days when the Atraeus family had been so poor they hadn't been able to afford a car, but Constantine could. His father's discovery of a rich gold mine on the Mediterranean island of Medinos hadn't altered any of his childhood memories. He would never forget what it had felt like to have nothing. "When it comes to the Ambrosi family, tomorrow will be too late." Resignation laced his tone as he eyed the press gathering like vultures at a feast. "Besides, it looks like the story has already been leaked. Bad timing or not, I want answers."

And to take back the money Roberto Ambrosi had conned out of their dying father while Constantine had been out of the country.

Funeral or not, he would unravel the scam he had discovered just over a week ago. After days of unreturned calls and hours of staking out the apparently empty residences of the Ambrosi family, his patience was gone, as was the desire to finish this business discreetly.

Lucas fell into step beside Constantine as he started toward the dispersing mourners. Grimly, Constantine noted that Lucas's attention was fixed on the younger Ambrosi daughter, Carla.

"Are you certain Sienna's involved?"

Constantine didn't bother to hide his incredulity.

Just what were the odds that the woman who had agreed to marry him two years ago, knowing that her father was leveraging an under-the-table deal with his, hadn't known about Roberto's latest scam? "She knows."

"You know what Roberto was like—"

"More than willing to exploit a dying man."

Constantine made brief eye contact with the two bodyguards who had accompanied them in a separate vehicle. The protection wasn't his choice, but as the CEO of a multibillion-dollar corporation, he'd had to deal with more than his share of threats.

As they neared the graveside, Constantine noted the absence of male family members or escorts. The wealthy and powerful Ambrosi family, who had employed his grandfather as a gardener, now only consisted of Margaret—Roberto's widow—the two daughters, Sienna and Carla, and a collection of elderly aunts and distant cousins.

As he halted at the edge of the mounded grave, the heavy cloud, which had been steadily building overhead, slid across the face of the midday sun and Sienna's dark gaze finally locked with his. In that fractured moment, something close to joy flared, as if she had forgotten that two years ago, when it had come down to a choice between him or the money, she had gone for the cash.

For a long, drawn out moment, Constantine was held immobile by a shifting sense of déjà vu, a powerful moment of connection he had been certain he would never again feel.

Something kicked in his chest, an errant pulse of emotion, and instead of dragging his gaze away he allowed himself to be caught, entangled...

A split second later a humid gust of wind sent leaves flying. In the few moments it took Sienna to anchor the honeyed fall of her hair behind one ear, the dreamy incandescence that had ensnared him—fooled him—so completely two years ago was gone, replaced by stunned disbelief.

A kick of annoyance that, evidently, despite all of his unreturned calls, Sienna had failed to register his presence in Sydney, was edged by relief. For a moment there, he had almost lost it, but now they were both back on the same, familiar page.

Constantine terminated the eye contact and transferred his attention to the freshly mounded soil, now covered by lavish floral tributes. Reasserting his purpose, reminding himself.

Roberto Ambrosi had been a liar, a thief and a con man, but Constantine would give him his due: he had known when to make his exit.

Sienna, however, had no such avenue of escape.

Sienna's heart slammed hard as Constantine closed the distance between them. Just for a few moments, exhausted by sadness and worn-out from fighting the overwhelming relief that she no longer had to cope with her father's gambling addiction, she had let the grimness of the cemetery fade.

She'd trained herself to be a relentlessly positive thinker, but even for her, the wispy daydream had been unusually creative: a reinvention of the past, where love came first, instead of somewhere down a complex list of assets and agendas. Then she had turned and for a disorienting moment, the future she had once thought was hers—and which she had needed with a fierceness that still haunted her—had taken on dazzling life. Constantine.

The reality of his clean, powerful features—coal-black hair brushing broad shoulders and the faintly resinous male scent that never failed to make her heart pound—had shocked her back to reality.

"What are you doing here?" she demanded curtly. Since the embarrassing debacle two years ago, the Ambrosis and the Atraeuses had preserved an icy distance. Constantine was the last person she expected to see at her father's funeral, and the least welcome.

Constantine's fingers closed around hers. The warm, slightly rough, skin-on-skin contact sent a hot, tingling shock through her. She inhaled sharply and a hint of the cologne that had sent her spiraling into the past just seconds ago made her stomach clench.

Constantine was undeniably formidable and gorgeous. Once he had fascinated her to the point that she had broken her cardinal rule. She had stopped thinking in favor of feeling. Big mistake.

Constantine had been out of her league, period. He was too rich, too powerful and, as she had found out to her detriment, utterly focused on protecting his family's business empire.

Bitterly, she reflected that the tabloids had it right. Ruthless in business, ditto in bed. The CEO of The Atraeus Group was a catch. Just don't "bank" on a wedding.

He leaned forward, close enough that his cleanly shaven jaw almost brushed her cheek. For an electrifying moment she thought he was actually going to kiss her, then the remoteness of his expression wiped that thought from her mind.

"We need to talk." His voice was deep and curt—a cosmopolitan mix of accents that revealed that, his Mediterranean heritage aside, he had been educated in the States. "Five minutes. In the parking lot." Jerking her fingers free, Sienna stepped back, her high heels sinking into the soft ground.

Meet with the man who had proposed one week, then discarded her the next because he believed she was a calculating gold digger?

That would be when hell froze over.

"We don't have anything to discuss."

"Five minutes. Be there."

Stomach tight, she stared at the long line of his back as he strolled away through the ranks of marble headstones. Peripherally she noticed Lucas and Zane, Constantine's two brothers, flanking him. Two security guards kept onlookers and the reporters who inevitably hounded the Atraeus family at bay.

Tension hummed through her at the presence of both brothers and the security. The bodyguards were a reality check, underlining the huge gulf between her life and his.

She registered a brief touch on her arm. Her sister, Carla. With an effort of will, Sienna shook off the shock of Constantine's presence and her own unsettling reactions. Her father's sudden death and the messy financial fallout that followed had consumed every waking moment for the past few days. Despite that, all it had taken had been one fractured moment looking into Constantine's gaze and she had forgotten where she was and why.

Carla frowned. "You look as white as a sheet. Are you all right?"

"I'm fine." Desperate to regain her equilibrium, Sienna dug in her purse, found her compact and checked her makeup. After the tears in church and the humid heat, any trace of the light makeup she had applied that morning was gone. Her hair was tousled and her eyes were red-rimmed—the exact opposite of her usual cool, sophisticated façade.

Carla—who was far more typically Medinian than Sienna in appearance with glossy dark hair and stunning light blue eyes that stopped people in their tracks—watched the Atraeus brothers, an odd expression in her eyes. "What are they doing here? Please don't tell me you're seeing Constantine again."

Sienna snapped the compact closed and dropped it into her purse. "Don't worry, I'm not crazy."

Just confused.

"Then what did they want?"

Carla's clipped demand echoed Sienna's question, although she couldn't afford the luxury of either anger or passion. For the sake of her family and their company, she had to be controlled and unruffled, no matter how worried she felt. "Nothing."

Constantine's series of commands replayed itself in her mind. Another gust, this one laced with fat droplets of rain, snapped her numbed brain back into high gear. Suddenly she formed a connection that made her pulse pound and her stomach hollow out.

Oh, damn. She needed to think, and quickly.

Over the past three days, she had spent long hours sifting through her father's private papers and financial records. She had found several mystifyingly large deposits she couldn't match to any of the business figures. Money had come in over a two-month period. A very large amount. The money had been used to prop up Ambrosi Pearls' flagging finances and cover her father's ongoing gambling debts, but she had no idea of its source. At first she thought the money had to be winnings, but the similar amounts had confused her. Roberto Ambrosi had won large sums of money in the past, but the amounts had differed wildly.

Now Constantine wanted a conversation.

Desperate to deny the conclusion that was forming, and to distract Carla, who was still locked on the Atraeus brothers like a heat-seeking missile, she craned around, searching for their mother. "Mom needs help."

Carla had also spotted the reporter chatting to Margaret Ambrosi, who was exhausted and still a little shaky from the sedatives the doctor had prescribed so she could sleep. "Oh, heck. I'll get her. It's time we left anyway. We were supposed to be at Aunt Via's for lunch ten minutes ago."

A private family lunch at the apartment of their father's

sister, Octavia, not a wake, which Sienna had decreed was an unnecessary luxury.

The last four days since her father had collapsed and died from a heart attack had been a roller-coaster ride, but that didn't change the reality. The glory days of Ambrosi Pearls, when her grandfather had transferred the company from the disaster zone Medinos had become during World War II to Sydney, were long gone. She had to balance the need to bolster business confidence by giving the impression of wealth and stability against the fact that they were operating on a shoestring budget. Luckily, her father had had a small insurance policy, enough to cover basic funeral expenses, and she'd had the excuse of Margaret Ambrosi's poor health to veto any socializing.

Her gaze narrowed. "Tell Via I'm not going to be able to make it for lunch. I'll see you at home later on."

After she had gotten rid of Constantine.

Constantine sent a brooding glance at the sky as he unlocked the Audi and settled in to wait for Sienna.

From the backseat Zane crossed his arms over his chest and coolly surveyed the media who were currently trying to bluff their way past Constantine's security. "I can see she still really likes you."

Constantine stifled his irritation. At twenty-four, Zane was several years his junior. Sometimes the chasm seemed much wider than six years. "This is business." Not pleasure.

Lucas slid into the passenger-side seat. "Did you get a chance to discuss the loan with Roberto?"

The words *before he died* hung in the air.

Constantine dragged at his tie. "Why do you think he had the heart attack?"

Apparently Roberto had suffered from a heart condition. Instead of showing up at Constantine's house, as arranged for the meeting that he himself had requested, he had been seated at a blackjack table. When he hadn't shown up, Constantine had made some calls and found out that Roberto had gone directly to the casino, apparently feverishly trying to win the money he needed.

Constantine had sent his personal assistant Tomas to collect Ambrosi, because going himself would have attracted unwanted media attention. Tomas had arrived to find that seconds after a substantial win the older man had become unwell. Tomas had called an ambulance. Minutes later Roberto had clutched at his chest and dropped like a stone.

Constantine almost had a heart attack himself when he had heard. Contrary to reports that he was ruthless and unfeeling, he had been happy to discuss options with Roberto, but it was not just about him. He had his family and the business to consider and Roberto Ambrosi had conned his father.

Lucas's expression was thoughtful. "Does Sienna know that you arranged to meet with her father?"

"Not yet."

"But she will."

"Yep." Constantine stripped off his tie, which suddenly felt like a noose, and yanked at the top two buttons of his shirt.

He wanted to engage Sienna's attention, which was the whole point of him dealing with the problem directly.

It was a safe bet that, after practically killing her old man, he had it by now.

Thunder rumbled overhead. Sienna walked quickly toward her car, intending to grab the umbrella she had stashed on the backseat.

As she crossed the parking lot a van door slid open. A reporter stepped onto the steaming asphalt just ahead of her and lifted his camera. Automatically, her arm shot up, fending off the flash.

A second reporter joined the first. Spinning on her heel, Sienna changed direction, giving up on the notion of staying dry. Simultaneously, she became aware that another news van had just cruised into the parking lot.

This wasn't part of the polite, restrained media representation that had been present at the beginning of the funeral. These people were predatory, focused, and no doubt drawn by the lure of Constantine and the chance to reinvent an old scandal.

The disbelief she'd felt as she'd met Constantine's gaze across her father's grave increased. How dare he come to the funeral? Did he plan to expose them all, most especially her mother, to another media circus?

With an ominous crash of thunder, the rain fell hard, soaking her. Fingers tightening on her purse, she lengthened her stride, breaking into a jog as she rounded the edge of a strip of shade trees that bisected the parking lot. She threw a glance over her shoulder, relieved that the rain had beaten the press back, at least temporarily. A split second later she collided with the solid barrier of a male chest. Constantine.

The hard, muscled imprint of his body burned through the wet silk of her dress as she clutched at a broad set of shoulders.

He jerked his head at a nearby towering oak. "This way. There are more reporters on the other side of the parking lot."

His hand landed in the small of her back. Sienna controlled a small shiver as she felt the heat of his palm, and her heart lurched because she knew Constantine must have followed her with the intent of protecting her. "Thank you."

She appreciated the protection, but that didn't mean she was comfortable with the scenario.

He urged her beneath the shelter of the huge, gnarled oak. The thick, dark canopy of leaves kept the worst of the rain off, but droplets still splashed down, further soaking her hair and the shoulders of her dress.

She found a tissue in her purse and blotted moisture from her face. She didn't bother trying to fix her makeup since there was likely to be very little of it left.

Within moments the rain slackened off and a thin shaft of sunlight penetrated the watery gloom, lighting up the parking lot and the grassy cemetery visible through the trees. Without warning the back of her nose burned and tears trickled down her face. Blindly, she groped for the tissue again.

"Here, use this."

A large square of white linen was thrust into her hand. She sniffed and swallowed a watery, hiccuping sob.

A moment later she found herself wrapped close, her face pressed against Constantine's shoulder, his palm hot against the damp skin at the base of her neck. After a moment of stiffness she gave in and accepted his comfort.

She had cried when she was alone, usually at night and in the privacy of her room so she wouldn't upset her mother, who was still in a state of distressed shock. Most of the time, because she had been so frantically busy she'd managed to contain the grief, but every now and then something set her off.

At some point Constantine loosened his hold enough that she could blow her nose, but it seemed now that she'd started crying, she couldn't stop and the tears kept flowing, although more quietly now. She remained locked in his arms, his palm massaging the hollow between her shoulder blades in a slow, soothing rhythm, the heat from his body driving out the damp chill. Drained by grief, she was happy to just be, and to soak in his hard warmth, the reassurance of his solid male power.

She became aware that the rain had finally stopped, leaving the parking lot wreathed in trailing wisps of steam. In a short while she would pull free and step back, but for the moment her head was thick and throbbing from the crying and she was too exhausted to move.

Constantine's voice rumbled in her ear. "We need to leave. We can't talk here."

She shifted slightly and registered that at some point Constantine had become semi aroused.

For a moment memories crowded her, some blatantly sensual, others laced with hurt and scalding humiliation.

Oh, no, no way. She would not feel this.

Face burning, Sienna jerked free, her purse flying. Shoving wet hair out of her face, she bent to retrieve her purse and the few items that had scattered—lip gloss, compact, car keys.

Her keys. Great idea, because she was leaving now.

If Constantine wanted a conversation he would have to reschedule. There was no way she was staying around for more of the same media humiliation she'd suffered two years ago.

"Damn. Sienna…"

Was that a hint of softness in his eyes? His voice?

No. Couldn't be.

When Constantine crouched down to help gather her things, she hurriedly shoveled the items into her bag. The rain had started up again, an annoying steamy drizzle, although that fact was now inconsequential because every part of her was soaked. Wet hair trailed down her cheeks, her dress felt like it had been glued on and there were puddles in her shoes.

Constantine hadn't fared any better. His gray suit jacket was plastered to his shoulders, his white shirt transparent enough that the bronze color of his skin showed through.

She dragged her gaze from the mesmerizing sight. "Uh-uh. Sorry." She shot to her feet. She was so not talking now. His transparent shirt had reminded her about her dress. It was black, so it wouldn't reveal as much as white fabric when wet, but silk was silk and it was thin. "Your conversation will have to wait. As you can see, I'm wet."

She spun on her heel, looking for an avenue of escape that didn't contain reporters with microphones and cameras.

His arm snaked around her waist, pulling her back against the furnace heat of his body. "After four days of unreturned calls," he growled into her ear, sending a hot shiver down her spine, "if you think I'm going to cool my heels for one more second, you can think again."

Two

Infuriated by the intimacy of his hold and the torrent of unwanted sensation, Sienna pried at Constantine's fingers. "Let. Me. Go."

"No." His gaze slid past hers.

Movement flickered at the periphery of Sienna's vision, she heard a car door slam.

Constantine muttered something curt beneath his breath. Now that the torrential downpour was over, the media were emerging from their vehicles.

He spun her around in his arms. "I wasn't going to do this. You deserve what's coming."

Her head jerked up, catching his jaw and sending a hot flash of pain through her skull, which infuriated her even more. "Like I did last time? Oh, very cool, Constantine. As if I'm some kind of hardened criminal just because I care about my family—"

Something infinitely more dangerous than the threat of

unwanted media exposure stirred in his eyes. "Is that what you call it? Interesting concept."

His level tone burned, more than the edgy heat that had invaded her body, or the castigating guilt that had eaten at her for the past two years. That maybe their split had been all her fault, and not just a convenient quick exit for a wealthy bachelor who had developed cold feet. That maybe she had committed a crime in not revealing how dysfunctional and debt-ridden her family was.

Her jaw tightened. "What did I ever do to truly hurt you, Constantine?"

Grim amusement curved his mouth. "If you're looking for a declaration, you're wasting your breath."

"Don't I know it." She planted her palms on his chest and pushed.

He muttered a low, rough Medinian phrase. "Stay still."

The Medinian language—an Italian dialect with Greek and Arabic influences—growled out in that deep velvet tone, sent a shock of awareness through her along with another hot tingling shiver.

Darn, darn, darn. Why did she have to like that?

Incensed that some crazy part of her was actually turned on by this, she kept up the pressure, her palms flattened against the solid muscle of his chest, maintaining the bare inch of space that existed between them.

An inch that wasn't nearly enough given that explosive contact.

Maybe, just maybe, the press would construe this little tussle as Constantine comforting her instead of an undignified scuffle. "Who called the press?" She stabbed an icy glare at him. "You?"

He gave a short bark of laughter. "*Cara,* I pay people to keep them off."

She warded off another one of those hot little jabs of response. "Don't call me—"

"What?" he said. "Darling? Babe? Sweetheart?"

His long, lean fingers gripped her jaw, trapping her. He bent close enough that anyone watching would assume their embrace was intimate, that he was about to kiss her.

A bittersweet pang went through her. She could see the crystalline depths of his eyes, the tiny beads of water clinging to his long, black lashes, the red mark on his jaw where her head had caught him, and a potent recollection spun her back to the first time they had met, two years ago.

It had been dark but, just like now, it had been raining. Her forward vision impeded by an umbrella, she had jogged from a taxi to the front door of a restaurant when they had collided. That time she had ended up on the wet pavement. Her all-purpose little black dress had been shorter, tighter. Consequently the sexy little side split had torn and her umbrella and one shoe had gone missing in action.

Constantine had apologized and asked if anything was broken. Riveted by the low, sexy timbre of his voice as he had crouched down and fitted the shoe back on her foot, she'd had the dizzying conviction that when she had fallen she had landed in the middle of her favorite fairy tale and Prince Charming had never looked so good. She had replied, "No, of course not."

Although, she had whimsically decided, when he left her heart could be broken.

The pressure of Constantine's grip on her arms zapped her back to the present. A muscle pulsed along the side of his jaw and she was made abruptly aware that, his mystifying anger aside, Constantine was just as disturbed as she.

"*Basta*," he growled. Enough.

Constantine jerked back from the soft curve of Sienna's mouth and the heady desire that, despite all of his efforts, he had never been able to eradicate. "You're wearing the same dress."

"No," she snapped back, informing him that in the confusion of the collision she had been as caught up by the past as he. "That was a cocktail dress."

"It feels the same." Wet and sleek and almost as sensual as her skin.

"Take your hands off me and you won't have to feel a thing."

Her voice was clipped and as cool as chipped ice, but the husky catch in her throat, her inability to entirely meet his gaze, told a different story.

He should let her go. She was clearly shaken. Lucas had been right—on the day of her father's funeral he should show compassion. But despite the demands of common decency, Constantine was unwilling to allow her any leeway at all.

Two years ago Sienna Ambrosi had achieved what no other woman had done. She had fooled him utterly. Touching her now should be repugnant to him. Instead, he was riveted by the fierce challenge in her dark eyes and the soft, utterly feminine shape of her body pressed against his. And drawn to find out exactly how vulnerable she was toward him. "Not until I have what I came for."

Her pupils dilated with shock, and any lingering uncertainty he might have entertained about her involvement in her father's scam evaporated. She was in this up to her elegant neck. The confirmation was unexpectedly depressing.

She blushed. "If it's a discussion you want, it will have to wait. In case you hadn't noticed, we're both wet and this is my father's funeral." She shoved at his chest again.

His hold on her arms tightened reflexively. The sudden full-body contact sent another electrifying shock wave of heat through Constantine, and in that moment the list of what he wanted, and needed, expanded.

Two years ago passion had blindsided him to the point that he had looked past his parents' stormy marital history and the tarnished reputation of the Ambrosi family in an attempt to grasp the mirage. He didn't trust what he had felt then, and he trusted it even less now. But he knew one thing for sure: one night wouldn't be enough.

Sienna threw a glance over her shoulder. "This media craziness is all your fault. If you hadn't turned up, they wouldn't have bothered with us."

"Calm down." Constantine studied the approaching reporters. "And unless you want to be on the six o'clock news, stay with me and keep quiet. I'll do the talking."

The two dark-suited men who had been flanking Constantine earlier materialized and strolled toward the reporters.

In that moment Sienna realized they had been joined by a television crew.

The barrage of questions started. "Ms. Ambrosi, is it true Ambrosi Pearls is facing bankruptcy?"

"Do you have any comment to make about your father allegedly conning money out of Lorenzo Atraeus?"

Several flashes went off, momentarily blinding her. An ultraslim, glamorous redhead darted beneath one of the bodyguard's arms and shoved a mike in her face. Sienna recognized the reporter from one of the major news channels. "Ms. Ambrosi, can you tell us if charges have been brought?"

Shock made Sienna go first hot then cold. "Charges—?"

"Unless you want a defamations suit," Constantine interjected smoothly, "I suggest you withdraw those questions. For the record Ambrosi Pearls and The Atraeus Group are engaged in negotiations over a business deal. Roberto Ambrosi's death has complicated those negotiations. That's all I'm prepared to say."

"Constantine, is this just about business?" The red-headed reporter, who had been maneuvered out of reach by one of the bodyguards, arched a brow, her face vivid and charming. "If a merger of some kind is in the wind, what about a wedding?"

Constantine hurried Sienna toward a sleek black Audi that had slid to a halt just yards away. "No comment."

Lucas climbed out of the driver's seat and tossed the keys over the hood.

Constantine plucked the keys out of midair and opened the passenger-side door. When Sienna realized Constantine meant her to get into the car, with him, she stiffened. "I have my own—"

Constantine leaned close enough that his breath scorched the skin below her ear. "You can come with me or stay. It's your choice. But if you stay you're on your own with the media."

A shudder of horror swept through her. "I'll come."

"In that case I'm going to need your car keys. One of my security team will collect your car and follow us. When we're clear of the press, you can have your little sports car back."

Suspicion flared. "How do you know I have a sports car?"

"Believe me, after the last few days there isn't much I don't know about you and your family."

"Evidently, from the answers you gave the press, you know a lot more than I do." She dug her keys out of her purse and handed them over. As badly as she resented it, Constantine's suggestion made sense. If she had to return to the cemetery to pick up the car later on, it was an easy bet she'd run into more reporters and more questions she wasn't equipped to answer.

Seconds later she was enclosed in the luxurious interior of the Audi, the tinted windows blocking out the media.

She reached for her seat belt. By the time she had it fastened, Constantine was accelerating away from the curb. Cool air from the air-conditioning unit flowed over her, raising gooseflesh on her damp skin.

Nerves strung taut at the intimacy of being enclosed in the cab of the Audi with Constantine, she reached into her purse and found her small traveling box of tissues. Pulling off a handful, she handed them to Constantine.

His gaze briefly connected with hers. "*Grazie.*"

She glanced away, her heart suddenly pounding. Hostilities were, temporarily at least, on hold. "You're welcome."

She pulled off more tissues and began blotting moisture from her face and arms. There was nothing she could do about her hair or her dress, or the fact that the backs of her legs were sticking to the very expensive leather seats.

She glanced in the rearview mirror. Her small sports car was right behind them, followed by the gleaming dark sedan, which contained the second of Constantine's bodyguards and his brothers. "I see you still travel with a SWAT team."

Constantine smoothly negotiated traffic. "They have their uses."

She flashed him a cool look. There was no way she would thank him yet, not when it was clear that Constantine's presence had attracted the press. Until he had showed up, neither she nor any member of her family had been harassed. She studied the clean line of his profile, the inky crescents of his lashes and the small scar high on one cheekbone. Unbidden, memories flickered—the dark bronze of his skin glowing in the morning light, the habit he'd had of sprawling across her bed, sheets twined around his hips, all long limbs and sleek muscle.

Hot color flooded her cheeks. Hastily she transferred her gaze to the traffic flowing around them. "Now that we're alone you can tell me what that media assault was all about." The very fact that Constantine had interceded on her behalf meant something was very wrong. "Conned? Charges? And what was that about negotiating a deal?"

With her background in commercial law, Sienna was Ambrosi Pearls' legal counsel. At no point in the past two years had her father so much as mentioned The Atraeus Group, or any financial dealings. After the loan Roberto had tried to negotiate had fallen through, along with her engagement, the subject had literally been taboo.

Constantine braked for a set of lights. "There is a problem, but I'm not prepared to discuss it while I'm driving."

While they waited in traffic her frustration mounted. "If you won't discuss it…" her fingers sketched quotation marks in the air, "then at least tell me why, if Ambrosi Pearls is supposed to have done something so wrong, you're helping me instead of throwing me to the media wolves?"

"In an instant replay of the way I treated you two years ago?"

The silky edge to his voice made her tense. "Yes."

The lights turned green. Constantine accelerated through the intersection. "Because you're in shock, and you've just lost your father."

Something about the calmness of his manner sent a prickle of unease down her spine, sharpened all of her senses.

His ruthless business reputation aside, Constantine was known to be a philanthropist with a compassionate streak. He frequently gave massive sums to charities, but that compassion had never been directed toward either her or her family.

"I don't believe you. There's something else going on." During the short conversation during which he had broken their engagement, Sienna had tried to make him understand the complications of her father's skyrocketing gambling debts and the struggle she had simply to support her mother and keep Ambrosi Pearls afloat. That in the few stressful days she'd had before Constantine had discovered the deal, the logic of her father asking Lorenzo Atraeus for a loan had seemed viable.

She had wasted her breath.

Constantine had been too busy walking out the door to listen to the painful details of her family's financial struggle.

"As you heard from the reporters, there is very definitely 'something else going on.' If you'll recall, that was the reason our engagement ended."

"My father proposed a business deal that your father wanted."

"Reestablishing a pearl facility on Medinos was a proposal based on opportunism and nostalgia, not profit."

Her anger flared at the opportunism crack. "And the bottom line is so much more important to you than honoring the past or creating something beautiful."

"Farming pretty baubles in a prime coastal location slated for development as a resort didn't make business sense then and it makes no sense now. The Atraeus Group has more lucrative business options than restoring Medinos's pearl industry."

"Options that don't require any kind of history or sentiment. Like mining gold and building luxury hotels."

His gaze briefly captured hers. "I don't recall that you

ever had any problem with the concept of making money. As I remember it, two years ago money came before 'sentiment.'"

Sienna controlled the rush of guilty heat to her cheeks. "I refuse to apologize for a business deal I didn't instigate." Or for being weak enough to have felt an overwhelming relief that, finally, there could be an answer to her family's crippling financial problems. "My only sin was not having the courage to tell you about the deal."

She stared out of the passenger-side window as Constantine turned into the parking lot of a shopping mall. It was too late now to admit that she had been afraid the impending disgrace of her father's gambling and financial problems would harm their engagement.

As it turned out, the very thing she had feared had happened. Constantine believed she had broken his trust, that her primary interest in him had always been monetary. "I apologized for not discussing the deal with you," she said, hating the husky note in her voice, "but, quite frankly, that was something I would have assumed your father would have done."

Constantine slotted the Audi into a space. She heard the snick as he released his seat belt. He turned in his seat and rested an arm along the back of hers, making her even more suffocatingly aware of his presence.

"Even knowing that my father's lack of transparency indicated he was keeping the deal under wraps?"

A dark sedan slid into a space beside the Audi. One of Constantine's bodyguards, with Lucas in the passenger seat and Zane in the rear. A flash of cream informed her that her sports car, driven by the second bodyguard, had just been parked in an adjacent space.

Feeling hemmed in by overlarge Medinian males, Sienna released her seat belt and reached for her purse. "I didn't understand that you were so against the idea of re-establishing a pearl industry on Medinos."

Stupidly, when she hadn't been frightened that she would lose Constantine and burying her head in the sand, she had been too busy coping with the hectic media pressure their engagement had instigated.

Life in a fish tank hadn't been fun.

"Just as I couldn't understand why you failed to discuss the agreement, which just happened to have been drawn up the day following our engagement announcement."

Her gaze snapped to his. "How many times do I have to say it? I had nothing to do with the loan. Think about it, Constantine. If I was that grasping and devious I would have waited until after we were married."

A tense silence stretched, thickened. Now she really couldn't breathe. Fumbling at the car door, she pushed it wide.

Constantine leaned across and hauled the door shut, pinning Sienna in place before she could scramble out. The uncharacteristic surge of temper that flowed through him at the deliberate taunt was fueled by the physical frustration that had been eating at him ever since he had decided he had to see her again.

The question of just why he had taken one look at Sienna two years ago and fallen in instant lust, he decided, no longer existed. It had ceased to be the instant he had glimpsed her silky blond head at the funeral. Even wet and bedraggled, her eyes red-rimmed from crying, Sienna was gorgeous in a fragile, exotic way that hooked into every male instinct he possessed.

The combination of delicacy paired with sensuality, in Anglo-Saxon terms, was crazy-making. He was at once caught between the desire to protect and cushion her from the slightest upset and the desire to take her to bed and make love to her until she surrendered utterly.

It was an unsettling fact that he would rather argue with Sienna than spend time with any other woman, no matter how gorgeous or focused on pleasing him she might be.

"Now that's interesting. I assumed that the reason you stayed quiet about the loan was that your father needed the money too badly to wait."

Her face went bone-white and he knew in that instant that he had gone too far.

Then, hot color burned along her cheekbones and the aura of haunted fragility evaporated. "Or maybe I was simply following orders?"

His gaze shifted to her pale mouth, the line of her throat as she swallowed. "No," he said flatly.

Sienna had been Roberto's precocious second-in-command for the past four years. She had run the family's pearl house with consummate skill and focused ambition while her father had steadily gambled the profits away at various casinos. The last time she had taken an order from Roberto, she had been in the cradle. If she had a weakness, it was that she needed money.

His money.

And she still did.

She pulled in a jerky breath. He felt the rise and fall of her breasts against his arm, the feathery warmth along his jaw as she exhaled. The light, evocative scent she wore teased his nostrils as flash after flash of memory turned the air molten.

A tap on the passenger-side window broke the tension. One of his security guards.

Constantine released his hold on the door handle, his temper tightly controlled as he watched Sienna climb out and collect her car keys.

Levering himself out of the Audi into the now blistering heat of early afternoon, Constantine gave the guard his instructions. For the past four days he had seldom been without an escort but for the next hour he required absolute privacy.

Peeling out of his damp jacket, he tossed it behind the driver's seat. He frowned as he noticed Lucas speaking with Sienna. From the brevity of the exchange he was aware that his brother had simply offered his condolences, but Sienna's smile evoked an unsettling response.

The fact that Lucas was every inch a dangerous Atraeus male shouldn't register, but after the charged few moments in the Audi, the knowledge of just how successful his brother was with women was distinctly unpalatable.

Constantine strolled toward Sienna as she slid her cell phone out of her purse and answered a call.

Lucas waylaid him with a brief jerk of his chin. "Are you sure you know what you're doing?"

"Positive."

"It didn't look like a business discussion back at the cemetery, and it sure as hell didn't look like a business discussion just then."

Constantine knew his gaze was cold enough to freeze. "Just as long as you remember that Sienna Ambrosi is my business."

Lucas lifted a brow. "Message received."

Jaw tight, Constantine watched as Lucas climbed into the passenger-side seat of the dark sedan. He lifted a hand as the car cruised out of the parking lot. Maybe he hadn't needed to warn Lucas off, but the instinct to do so had been knee-jerk and primitive. In that moment he had acknowledged one clear fact: for the foreseeable future, until he had gotten her out of his system, Sienna Ambrosi was his.

While he waited for Sienna to terminate her call, he grimly considered that fact, sifting through every nuance of the past hour. The tension that had gripped him from the moment he had laid eyes on Sienna at the funeral tightened another notch.

Constantine knew his own nature. He was focused, single-minded. When he fixed on a goal he achieved it. His absolute commitment to running the family business was both a necessity and a passion and he had never flinched from making hard choices. Two years ago, severing all connection with Sienna and the once pampered and aristocratic Ambrosi family had been one of those choices.

Sliding dark glasses onto the bridge of his nose, Constantine crossed his arms over his chest and studied the pure line of Sienna's profile, the luscious combination of creamy skin and dark eyes, her soft pale mouth.

Until he had been handed an investigative report he had commissioned on Ambrosi Pearls and had discovered that Sienna had been linked on at least three occasions with Alex Panopoulos, a wealthy retailer.

He still remembered the moment of disorientation, the grim fury when he'd considered that Panopoulos could be Sienna's lover.

He had soon eliminated that scenario.

According to the very efficient private eye employed by the security firm, Panopoulos was actively hunting but the Greek hadn't yet managed to snare either of the Ambrosi girls.

Sienna registered Constantine's impatience as she ended her conversation with Carla, who had been concerned that she had been caught up in the media frenzy in the parking lot.

Constantine lifted a brow. "Where do we talk? Your place or mine?"

Sienna dropped her phone back into her purse. After the tense moments in the car and the sensual shock of Constantine invading her space, she couldn't hide her dismay at the thought of Constantine's apartment. Two years ago they had spent a lot of time there. It had also been the scene of their breakup.

The thought of Constantine in the sanctuary of her own small place was equally unacceptable. "Not the apartments."

"I don't have the apartment anymore. I own a house along the coast."

"I thought you liked living in town."

"I changed my mind."

Just like he had about her. Instantly and unequivocally.

He opened the door of her small soft-top convertible. Feeling as edgy as a cat, her stomach tight with nerves, she slipped into the driver's seat, carefully avoiding any physical contact. "Carla's taken Mom to a family lunch at Aunt Via's apartment, so they'll be occupied for the next couple of hours. I can meet you at my parent's beach house at Pier Point. That's where I've been staying since Dad died."

Constantine closed her door. Bracing his hands on the window frame, he leaned down, maintaining eye contact. "That explains why you haven't been at your apartment, although not why you haven't been returning my calls at work."

"If you wanted to get hold of me that badly you should have rung my mother."

"I got through twice," he said grimly. "Both times I got Carla."

Sienna could feel her cheeks heating. After Sienna's breakup with Constantine, Carla had become fiercely protective. Constantine hadn't gotten through, because Carla would have made it her mission to stop him.

"Sorry about that," she said, without any trace of sympathy in her voice. "Carla said there had been a couple of crank calls, then the press started bothering Mom in the evenings, so we went to stay at the beach house."

Constantine had also left a number of messages at work, which, when she had been in the office at all, Sienna had ignored. She had been feverishly trying to unravel her father's twisted affairs. Calling Constantine had ranked right up there with chatting to disgruntled creditors or having a cozy discussion with IRD about the payments Ambrosi Pearls had failed to make.

"If Pier Point is hostile territory, maybe we should meet on neutral ground?"

Was that a hint of amusement in his voice?

No, whatever it was Constantine was feeling, it wasn't amusement. There had been a definite predatory edge to him. She had seen a liquid silver flash of it at the gravesite, then been burned by it again in the parking lot.

The foreboding that had gripped her at the cemetery returned, playing havoc with her pulse again.

Suddenly shaky with a combination of exhaustion and nerves, she started the car and busied herself with fastening her seat belt. "The beach house is far enough out of town that the press isn't likely to be staking it out. If this conversation is taking the direction I think it is, we'd better meet there."

"Tell me," he said curtly. "What direction, exactly, do you think this conversation will take?"

"A conversation with Constantine Atraeus?" Her smile was as tightly strung as her nerves. "Now let me see… Two options—sex or money. Since it can't possibly be sex, my vote's on the money."

Three

Money was the burning agenda, but as Sienna drove into Pier Point, with Constantine following close enough behind to make her feel herded, she wasn't entirely sure about the sex.

Earlier, in the Audi, Constantine's muscular heat engulfing her, she had been sharply aware of his sexual intent. He had wanted her and he hadn't been shy about letting her know. The moment had been underscored by an unnerving flash of déjà vu.

The first time Constantine had kissed her had been in his car. He had cupped her chin and lowered his mouth to hers, and despite her determination to keep her distance, she had wound her arms around his neck, angled her jaw and leaned into the kiss. Even though she had only known him for a few hours she had been swept off her feet. She hadn't been able to resist him, and he had known it.

Shaking off the too-vivid recollection, she signaled and

turned her small sports car into her mother's driveway. Barely an hour after the unpleasant clash across her father's grave, those kinds of memories shouldn't register. The fact that Constantine wanted her meant little more than that he was a man with a normal, healthy libido. In the past two years he had been linked with a number of wealthy, beautiful women, each one a serious contender for the position of Mrs. Constantine Atraeus.

He turned into the driveway directly behind her. As Sienna accelerated up the small, steep curve, the sense of being pursued increased. She used her remote to close the electronic gates at the bottom of the drive, just in case the press had followed. After parking, she grabbed her handbag and walked across the paved courtyard that fronted the old cliff-top house.

Constantine was already out of his car. She noticed that in the interim he'd rolled his sleeves up, baring tanned, muscled forearms. She unlocked the front door and as he loomed over her in the bare, sun-washed hall, her stomach, already tense, did another annoying little flip.

He indicated she precede him. She couldn't fault his manners, but that didn't change the fact that with Constantine padding behind her like a large, hunting cat, she felt like prey.

"What happened to the furniture?"

The foreign intonation in his deep voice set her on edge all over again. Suddenly, business agenda or not, it seemed unbearably intimate to be alone with him in the quiet stillness of the almost empty house.

Sienna skimmed blank walls that had once held a collection of paintings, including an exquisitely rendered Degas. "Sold, along with all the valuable artwork my grandfather collected."

She threw him a tight smile. "Auctioned, along with

every piece of real jewelry Mom, Carla and I owned—including the pearls. Now isn't that a joke? We own a pearl house, but we can't afford our own products."

She pushed open the ornate double doors to her father's study and stood aside as Constantine walked into the room, which held only a desk and a couple of chairs.

His gaze skimmed bare floorboards and the ranks of empty built-in mahogany bookshelves, which had once housed a rare book collection. She logged the moment he finally comprehended what a sham their lives had become. They sold pearls to the wealthy and projected sleek, rich-list prosperity for the sake of the company, but the struggle had emptied them out, leaving her mother, Carla and herself with nothing.

He surveyed the marks on the wall that indicated paintings had once hung there and the dangling ceiling fitting that had once held a chandelier. "What didn't he sell to pay gambling debts?"

For a split second Sienna thought Constantine was taking a cheap shot, implying that both she and Carla had been up for auction, but she dismissed the notion. When he had broken their engagement his reasons had been clear-cut. After her father's failed deal he had made it plain he could no longer trust her or the connection with her family. His stand had been tough and uncompromising, because he hadn't allowed her a defense, but he had never at any time been malicious.

"We still have the house, and we've managed to keep the business running. It's not much, but it's a start. Ambrosi employs over one hundred people, some of whom have worked for us for decades. When it came down to keeping those people in work, selling possessions and family heirlooms wasn't a difficult choice."

Although she didn't expect Constantine with his reputation for being coldly ruthless in business to agree. "Wait here," she said stiffly, "I'll get towels."

Glad for a respite, she walked upstairs to her room. With swift movements she peeled off her ruined shoes, changed them for dry ones then checked her appearance in the dresser mirror. A small shock went through her when she noted the glitter of her eyes and the warm flush on her cheeks. With her creased dress and tousled hair, the look was disturbingly sensual.

Walking through to the bathroom, she towel-dried her hair, combed it and decided not to bother changing the dress, which was almost dry. She shouldn't care whether Constantine thought she was attractive or not, and if she did, she needed to squash the notion. The sooner this conversation was over and he was gone, the better.

She collected a fresh towel from the linen closet and walked back downstairs.

Constantine turned from the breathtaking view of the Pacific Ocean as she entered the study, his light gaze locking briefly with hers.

Breath hitching at the sudden pounding of her heart, Sienna handed him the towel, taking care not to let their fingers brush. She indicated the view. "One of the few assets we haven't yet had to sell, but only because Mom sold the town house this week. Although this place is mortgaged to the hilt."

It would go, too. It was only a matter of time.

He ran the towel briefly over his hair before tossing it over the arm of a chair. "I didn't know things had gotten this bad."

But, she realized, he had known her father's gambling had gotten out of hand. "Why should you? Ambrosi Pearls has nothing to do with either Medinos or The Atraeus Group."

His expression didn't alter, but suddenly any trace of compassion was gone. Good. Relief unfolded inside her. If anything could kill the skittish knowledge that not only was she on edge, she was sexually on edge, a straightforward business discussion would do it.

She indicated that Constantine take a seat and walked around to stand behind her father's desk, underlining her role as Ambrosi Pearls' CEO. "Not many people know the company's financial position, and I would appreciate if you wouldn't spread it around. With the papers speculating about losses, I'm having a tough time convincing some of our customers that Ambrosi is solid."

Constantine ignored the chair in favor of standing directly opposite her, arms crossed over his chest, neutralizing her attempt at dominance.

Sienna averted her gaze from the way the damp fabric of his shirt clung to his shoulders, the sleek aura of male power that swirled around Constantine Atraeus like a cloak.

"It must have been difficult, trying to run a business with a gambler at the helm."

As abruptly as if an internal switch had been thrown, Sienna's temper boiled over. Finally, the issue he hadn't wanted to talk about two years ago. "I don't think you can understand at all. Did your father gamble?"

Constantine's gaze narrowed. "Only in a good way."

"Of course." Lorenzo Atraeus had been an excellent businessman. "With good information and solid investment backing so he could make money, then more money. Unlike my father who consistently found ways to lose it, both in business and at the blackjack table." Her heart was pounding; her blood pressure was probably off the register. "You don't know what it's like to lose and keep on losing because you can't control someone in your family."

"My family has some experience with loss."

His expression was grim, his tone remote, reminding her that the Atraeus family had lived in poverty on Medinos for years, farming goats. Constantine's grandfather had even worked for hers, until the Ambrosis had lost their original pearl business when it had been bombed during the war. But that had all been years ago. This was now.

She leaned forward, every muscle taut. "Running a business with a gambler at the helm hasn't been easy."

He spread his palms on the desk and suddenly they were nose to nose. "If it got that bad why didn't you get out?"

And suddenly, the past was alive between them and she was taking a weird, giddy delight in fighting with Constantine. Maybe it was a reaction, a backlash to the grief and strain of the funeral, or the simple fact that she was sick of clamping down on her emotions and tired of hiding the truth. "And abandon my family and all the people who depend on our company for their livelihood?" She smiled tightly. "It was never an option, and I hope I never arrive at that point. Which brings us to the conversation you want so badly. How much do we owe?"

"Did you know that two months ago your father paid a visit to Medinos?"

Shock held her immobile. "No."

"Are you aware that he had plans to start up a pearl industry there?"

"Not possible." But blunt denial didn't ease the cold dread forming in her stomach. "We barely have enough capital to operate in Sydney." Her father had driven what had been a thriving business into the ground. "We're in no position to expand."

Something shifted in Constantine's gaze, and for a

fleeting second she had a sense that, like it or not, he had reached some kind of decision.

Constantine indicated a document he must have dropped on the desk while she'd been out of the room. Sienna studied the thick parchment. Her knees wobbled. A split second later she was sitting in her father's old leather chair, fighting disbelief as she skimmed the text.

Not one loan but several. She had expected the first loan to date back to the first large deposit she had found in her father's personal account several weeks ago, and she wasn't disappointed.

She lifted her head to find Constantine still watching her. "Why did Lorenzo lend anything to my father? He knew he had a gambling problem."

"My father was terminally ill and clearly not in his right mind. When he died a month ago, we knew there was a deficit. Unfortunately, the documents confirming the loans to your father weren't located until five days ago."

Her jaw clenched. "Why didn't you stop him?"

"Believe me, if I had been there I would have, but I was out of the country at the time. To compound the issue, he bypassed the usual channels and retained an old friend, his retired legal counsel, to draw up the contracts."

Constantine ran his fingers around his nape, his expression abruptly impatient. "I see you're now beginning to understand the situation. Your father has been running Ambrosi Pearls and his gambling addiction on The Atraeus Group's money. An amount he 'borrowed' from a dying man on the basis of a business he had no intention of setting up."

Fraud.

Now the questions fired at her by the reporters made sense. "Is that what you told the press?"

"I think you know me better than that."

She felt oddly relieved. It shouldn't matter that Constantine hadn't been the one who had leaked the story, but it did.

Someone, most likely an employee, would have sold the information to the press.

Sienna stared at the figure involved and felt her normal steely optimism and careful plans for Ambrosi Pearls dissolve.

Firming her chin, she stared out at the bright blue summer sky and the endless, hazy vista of the Pacific Ocean, and tried to regroup. There had to be a way out of this; she had wrangled the company out of plenty of tight spots before. All she had to do was think.

Small, disparate pieces of information clicked into place. Constantine not wanting to talk to her at the funeral or in the car, the way he had remained standing while she had read through the documents.

He had wanted to watch her reaction when she read the paperwork.

Her gaze snapped to his. "You thought I was part of this."

Constantine's expression didn't alter.

Something in her plummeted. Sienna pushed to her feet. The loan documents cascaded to the floor; she barely noticed them. When Lorenzo Atraeus had died, he had left an enormous fortune based on a fabulously rich gold mine and a glittering retail and hotel empire to his three sons, Constantine, Lucas and Zane.

It shouldn't be uppermost in her mind, but it suddenly struck her that if Ambrosi Pearls was in debt to The

Atraeus Group, by definition—as majority shareholder—that meant Constantine.

Constantine's gaze was oddly bleak. "Now you're getting it. Unless you can come up with the money, I now own Ambrosi Pearls lock, stock and barrel."

Four

The vibration of a cell phone broke the electrifying silence.

Constantine answered the call, relieved at the sudden release of tension, the excuse to step back from a situation that had spiraled out of control.

He had practically threatened Sienna, a tactic he had never before resorted to, even when dealing with slick, professional fraudsters. In light of the heart-pounding discovery that Sienna hadn't known about her father's latest scam, his behavior was inexcusable. He should have stepped back, reassessed, postponed the meeting.

Gotten a grip before he wrecked any chance that she might want him again.

Unfortunately, Sienna doing battle with him across the polished width of her father's desk had put a kink in his strategy. Her cheeks had been flushed, her eyes fiery, shunting him back in time to hot, sultry nights and tangled sheets. It was hard to think tactically when all he wanted to do was kiss her.

She had never been this animated or passionate with him before, he realized. Even in bed he had always been grimly aware that she was holding back, that there was a part of her he couldn't reach.

That she was more committed to Ambrosi Pearls than she had ever been to him.

To compound the problem, he had mentioned the bad old days when the Atraeus family had been dirt-poor. Given that he wanted Sienna back in his bed, the last thing he needed was for her to view him as the grandson of the gardener.

Jaw tight, he turned to stare out at the sea view as he spoke to his personal assistant. Tomas had been trying to reach him for the past hour. Constantine had been aware he had missed calls, something he seldom did, but for once, business hadn't been first priority.

Another uncharacteristic lapse.

Constantine hung up and broodingly surveyed Sienna as she gathered the pages she had knocked onto the floor and stacked them in a precise pile on the desktop. Even with her dress crumpled and her makeup gone, she looked elegant and classy, the quintessential lady.

A car door slammed somewhere in the distance. The staccato of high heels on the walkway was followed by the sound of the front door opening.

Constantine caught the flare of desperation in Sienna's gaze. Witnessing that moment of sheer panic was like a kick in the chest. He was here to right a wrong that had been done to his father, but Sienna was also trying to protect her family, most specifically her mother, from him. It was a sobering moment. "Don't worry," he said quietly. "I won't tell her."

Sienna stifled a surge of relief and just had time to send Constantine a grateful glance before Margaret Ambrosi stepped into the room, closely followed by Carla.

"What's going on?" her mother demanded in the cool, clear tone that had gotten her through thirty years with a husband who had given her more heartache than joy. "And don't try to fob me off, because I know something's wrong."

"Mrs. Ambrosi." Constantine used a tone that was far gentler than any Sienna could ever remember him using with her. "My condolences. Sienna and I were just discussing the details of a business deal your husband initiated a few months ago."

Carla's jaw was set. "I don't believe Dad would have transacted anything without—"

Margaret Ambrosi's hand stayed her. "So that's why Roberto made the trip to Europe. I should have known."

Carla frowned. "He went to Paris and Frankfurt. He didn't go near the Mediterranean."

An emotion close to anger momentarily replaced the exhaustion etched on her mother's face.

"Roberto left a day earlier because he wanted to stop off at Medinos first. He said he wanted to visit the site of the old pearl facility and find his grandparents' graves. If anything should have warned me he was up to something that should have been it. Roberto didn't have a sentimental bone in his body. He went to Medinos on business."

"That's correct," Constantine said in the same gentle tone, and despite the antagonism and the towering issue of the debt, Sienna could have hugged him.

One of the qualities that had made her fall so hard for Constantine two years ago had been the way he was with his family. Put simply, he loved and protected them with the kind of fierce loyalty that still had the power to send a shiver down her spine. After years of coping with a father who had always put himself first, the prospect of being included in Constantine's family circle, of being the focus of that fierce protective instinct, had been utterly seductive.

That had been the prime reason she had frozen inside when she had found out that her father had done an under-the-table deal with Roberto Atraeus. She hadn't been able to discuss it; she had been afraid to even think about it. She had known how Constantine would react and when the details of the loan had surfaced, the very thing she had feared most had happened. He had shut her out.

She blinked, snapping herself out of a memory that still had the power to hurt.

Constantine checked his watch. "If you'll excuse me, I have another appointment. Once again, my apologies for intruding on your grief."

His cool gray eyes connected with hers, the message clear. They hadn't finished their discussion.

"I'll see you out." Shoving the loan documents out of sight in a drawer, she followed Constantine out into the bare hallway. As much as she didn't want to spend any more time with him, she did want to get him out of the house and away from her mother before she realized there was a problem.

The bright sunlight shafting through the open front door was glaring after the dim coolness of the study.

"Watch your step."

Constantine's hand cupped her elbow, the gesture nothing more than courtesy, but enough to reignite the humming awareness and the antagonism that had been so useful in getting her through the last hour and a half.

Pulse pounding, she lengthened her stride, moving away from the tingling heat of his touch and her growing conviction that Constantine wasn't entirely unhappy with the power he now wielded over Ambrosi Pearls, and her. That behind the business-speak simmered a very personal agenda.

Her stomach tightened at the thought, her mouth going dry as the taut moments in his car replayed themselves. Barely two hours ago Constantine Atraeus, the man, hadn't registered on her awareness. She had blanked him out, along with everything else that was not directly involved with either Ambrosi Pearls or her father's funeral arrangements. Now she couldn't seem to stop the hot flashes of memory and an acute awareness of him. "Thank you for not saying anything about the debt to Mom."

"If I'd thought your mother was involved, I would have mentioned it."

"Which means you do think I'm involved."

Suddenly the whole idea that she could be crazily attracted to Constantine again was so not an issue.

Constantine followed her out into the courtyard and depressed the Audi's key. The sleek car unlocked with an expensive thunk. "You've been running Ambrosi single-handedly for the past eighteen months. And paying Roberto's debts."

She grabbed a remote control from her car and opened the gate at the bottom of the driveway. As far as she was concerned, the sooner he left the better. "By selling family assets, not trying to take more loans when we're already overcommitted."

Constantine's phone buzzed. He picked up the call and spoke briefly in Medinian. She heard Lucas's name and mention of the company lawyer, Ben Vitalis. Business. That explained all three Atraeus brothers being in Sydney at the same time, no matter for how short a period. It also emphasized the fact that Constantine might be here to deal with the mess her father had entangled them both in, but on The Atraeus Group's global radar, Ambrosi Pearls was only a blip.

The tension that gripped her stomach and chest tightened another notch. Which, once again, pointed to the personal agenda.

Constantine terminated the call. "We have a lot to discuss, but the discussion will have to wait until tonight. I'll send a car for you at eight. We can talk over dinner."

She stiffened. Dinner definitely sounded more personal than business, which didn't make sense.

He had been gone for two years. In that time he hadn't ever contacted her. For the first couple of months, she had waited for him to call or to turn up on her doorstep and say he was sorry and that he wanted to try again. The fact that he never had had been an unexpected gift.

She had gotten over him. If he thought she was going to jump feetfirst into some kind of affair with him now, he could think again. "In case you didn't notice, I buried my father today. We have to talk, but I need a couple of days."

Which would give her time to consult their accountant and investigate options. The chance that she could either raise the loan money or make a big sale that quickly was slim, but she had to try. It would also give her time to step back from the mystifying knee-jerk reactions she kept having toward Constantine. She no longer loved him and she certainly did not like him. She could not want him.

Constantine opened the car door. "A few days ago that could have been arranged, but you chose to avoid me. I'm flying out at midnight tomorrow. If you can't find time before then, tomorrow there's a cocktail party at my house, a business meet and greet for The Atraeus Group's retail partners."

"No." As imperative as it was to come to grips with the looming financial disaster, the last thing she wanted was to attend a reception with Constantine, informal or not, at his house. "We'll have to reschedule. In any case I would prefer to talk during business hours."

In a neutral, business setting where the male/female dynamic could be neatly contained.

The businesslike gleam in Sienna's gaze sent irritation flashing through Constantine.

None of this was going as he had envisioned. Not only did he feel like a villain, but she was now trying to call the shots and he was on the verge of losing his temper again, something else that never happened. "We need to talk. When is the reading of the will scheduled?"

"This afternoon, at four."

He saw the moment the reality of her position sank in. If she didn't agree to a meeting he could conceivably send a representative to the reading of the will with the loan documents. It was something he had no intention of doing, specifically because it would frighten her mother.

"You're out of options, Sienna." Constantine slid behind the wheel of the Audi before he caved and started hemorrhaging options that would leave him out of her life altogether.

The engine started with a throaty purr. "Be ready tomorrow at eight."

The following morning, Constantine walked into The Atraeus Group's Sydney office. He was ten minutes late, not quite a first, but close. He had been late once before; two years ago to be exact.

Lucas and Zane, who were both gym freaks, were already there, looking sharp and energized against the clinical backdrop of chrome and leather furniture and executive gray walls. Constantine preferred to jog on the beach or swim rather than subject himself to a rigid workout program. Watching the sunrise and getting sand in his cross trainers was the one break he cut himself in a day that was already too regimented. After a near sleepless night spent pacing, however, this morning he had figured he could forgo his normal dawn run.

He zeroed in on the take-out coffee sitting on his desk and frowned in the direction of his brothers who were both regarding him with the kind of interested gaze that made him wonder if he'd grown an extra head or put his shirt on backward. "What?"

Zane ducked his head and stared hard at the glossy business magazine he was reading, which was odd in itself. His usual reading material involved fast boats, even faster cars and art installations that Constantine didn't pretend to understand. Lucas, meanwhile, hummed snatches of something vaguely familiar under his breath.

His temper now definitely on a short fuse, Constantine drank a mouthful of the coffee, which was lukewarm.

Lucas dropped a section of the morning paper on his desk. "Now that you've had some caffeine you'd better take a look at this."

Even though he had expected it, the photo taken at Roberto Ambrosi's funeral took his breath away. He remembered holding Sienna so she wouldn't walk into the barrage of cameras, but the clinch the reporter had snapped didn't look anything like protective restraint. His gaze was fused with hers, and he looked like he was about to kiss her. From memory, that was exactly how he had felt.

He skimmed the short article, going still inside when he read the statement that he had arrived in Sydney the day before Roberto Ambrosi had dropped dead from a heart attack for the specific purpose of arranging a meeting with the head of Ambrosi Pearls.

The article, thankfully, didn't go so far as to say he had

caused Ambrosi's fatal heart attack, but it did claim a wedding announcement was expected. The tune Lucas had been humming was suddenly recognizable; it had been the *Wedding March*.

He cursed softly. "When I find out who leaked the story to the press—"

"You'll what?" Lucas crumpled his own empty take-out cup and tossed it in the trash bin. "Give them a pay raise?"

Constantine dropped the newspaper on his desk. "Is it that obvious?"

"You're here."

Zane pushed to his feet, the movement fluid. "If you want to step back from the negotiations, Lucas and I can delay the New Zealand trip. Better still, let Vitalis handle the loan."

"No." Constantine's reply was knee-jerk, his gaze suddenly cold enough to freeze, despite the fact that he knew both Lucas and Zane were only trying to protect him.

Zane shrugged, his shoulders broad in his designer jacket. "Your choice, but if you stay in Sydney the press is going to have a field day."

Constantine studied the grainy newspaper photo again. "I can handle it. In any case I'm flying out tomorrow night."

A cell phone vibrated. Lucas's expression was grim as he took his phone out of his pocket. "The sooner the better. You don't need this."

Jaw tense, Constantine stalked over to the glass panels that took up one entire wall of his office, drinking his coffee while Lucas answered his cell.

From here he could see one corner of the Ambrosi building. The office block, dwarfed as it was by the skyscrapers that sprouted near the heart of the Central Business District, clearly undercapitalized one of the more valuable pieces of real estate in town.

Although the monetary value of anything Ambrosi was fast ceasing to hold any meaning for him.

He couldn't stop thinking about the way Sienna had tried to protect her mother yesterday. If she had read the newspaper story, she would hold an even worse opinion of him now, despite the fact that in his own way he had been trying to help her family by keeping the location of her father's heart attack quiet. The furor of Roberto dropping dead in a casino would not help the grieving family or do Ambrosi Pearls any favors.

Not that Sienna was likely to attribute any honorable motivations to his actions.

Lucas terminated his call. "That was one of our security guys. Apparently a news crew has found the location of the Pier Point house. Sienna's down on the beach sunbathing."

Constantine went cold inside. "They must have followed me yesterday." He dropped his now empty take-out cup in the trash.

This morning's story had been buried in the social pages of the paper. If he wasn't fast enough, Sienna could be a lead story by tomorrow morning.

In Sienna's eyes, he was certain that somehow, that, also, would be his fault.

Lucas looked concerned. "Do you want company?"

Constantine barely spared Lucas and Zane a glance. "Catch your flight out. Like I said, I can handle this."

Five

Sienna saw the reporter while he was negotiating the narrow track down to the tiny bay below the Pier Point house. Annoyance flashed through her at the intrusion, and the realization that the reporters had found her family hideaway. No surprises how that had happened, she thought grimly.

To leave the beach she would either have to swim out or climb past the reporter, which meant he would be snapping pictures of her in a bikini all the way. Not good.

She jogged into the water. A leisurely swim later, she pulled herself up onto a small diving pontoon anchored out in the bay.

Slicking wet hair back from her face, she checked out the reporter who was now standing with a forlorn air at the edge of the water. Satisfied that he didn't have a telescopic lens, because if he did he would have had it trained on her by now, Sienna sat down on the bobbing platform and waited for him to leave. If necessary, she could swim to the other end of the bay, climb the rocky slope and walk back to the house.

Long minutes ticked by. She checked her waterproof watch. If he decided to wait her out on the beach, she would have to consider the swim because she was expecting a call in just under an hour back at the house.

She lay down on her back, making herself an even smaller target for the reporter's lens, and forced herself to relax. All last night her stomach churned from the discovery she'd made the previous afternoon that Constantine had been in town when her father had died.

She had spent the night tossing and turning, alternately furious with Constantine because he seemed to be at the center of her entire financial mess, then paralyzed with fear because there didn't seem to be a thing she could do to stop him from taking everything.

As satisfying as it would be to blame Constantine, though, she knew that wasn't fair. Her father, who had been a charming, larger-than-life rogue, had had a number of minor heart attacks over the years. Just recently he had been scheduled for a bypass operation, because his health had gone rapidly downhill. His doctor had specifically told him to stay away from casinos because the stress and excitement were detrimental to his health.

She shielded her eyes from the sun with the back of her hand and smothered a yawn. She allowed her lids to close, just for a few seconds. When she opened them, she was abruptly aware that more than a few seconds had passed.

Cautiously, she scanned the beach, which was empty. The sound that had jerked her out of sleep suddenly fell into its correct context. It wasn't the rhythmic splash of waves against the pontoon. A swimmer, large, male and muscular, was cutting through the water, heading straight for her.

It wasn't the reporter, who appeared to have left the beach. She recognized that smooth, effortless crawl. It was Constantine.

Slipping into the water, she struck out away from the pontoon. If she swam in a semicircle she would be able to avoid Constantine and hopefully get back to the beach before he did. With any luck he would stay aimed at the pontoon and wouldn't realize that she had gone.

Maybe the fight-or-flight reaction was overkill, but dressed in a skimpy pink bikini she preferred to go with the unreasoning panic. If she was going to talk to a mostly naked and wet Constantine, she wanted to be wearing clothes.

Turning her head as she swam, she checked out the pontoon and saw Constantine swimming directly behind her. Her heart pounded out of control. She was good in the water, but Constantine was a whole lot better. When they had been dating he had encouraged her to take a scuba diving course because he had wanted her to share his passion for the sport. After she had qualified he had taken her out a couple of times before they had broken up, making sure she was water fit and proficient with the complex array of scuba gear. She knew firsthand how powerful he was in the water.

The sandy bottom appeared below. She swam a few more strokes then began to wade. The world spun as Constantine swung her into his arms, which was no easy feat. Apart from the fact that he had just swum a good distance, she was not small. She was five foot seven, and lean and toned because she regularly put in time at the pool, swimming laps. She also lifted weights and had progressed to the point where she could almost bench her own body weight, which, according to her gym instructor, was very cool. That all meant that she was a lot heavier than she looked.

She stiffened and tried to shimmy out of his grasp. And tried not to like that he was carrying her. In response, his arms tightened, holding her firmly against his chest.

Avoiding his interested gaze and the fact that he was barely out of breath, she shoved at his slick shoulders. "Okay, tough guy, you can let me go now."

Somewhere it registered that she had said at least some of those words before, the previous day. They hadn't done the trick then, either. She spied batteries and what looked like a camera memory stick scattered on her beach towel. There were some interesting scuffle marks in the sand. "What did you do with the reporter?"

"If you're looking for a shallow grave you won't find one. Although I admit I was tempted."

Constantine let her down on the sand. "Honey, I wasn't there when your father had the heart attack," he said quietly. "I didn't know he had a heart condition. He was at a casino instead of attending the meeting he had requested with me when he had the attack. One of my men, Tomas, got him out of there before the newspapers could get hold of the story. Unfortunately, someone leaked details. Probably the same person who went to the newspapers about the loan."

He had tried to protect them. For a moment Sienna's mind went utterly blank. She was so shocked by what he had done that his calling her "honey" barely registered.

She sucked in a deep breath, but the oxygen didn't seem to be getting through. It registered that the fast swim after an almost sleepless night had not been a smart move, her head felt heavy and pressurized, her knees wobbly. When her vision started to narrow and fade she knew she was going to faint for the first time in her life.

"This is not happening." Her hand shot out, automatically groping for support.

Constantine's arm was suddenly around her waist, holding her steady. The top of her head bumped his chin. The scrape of his stubbled jaw on the sensitive skin of her forehead sent a reflexive shiver through her, and suddenly she had her sight back. She inhaled. His warm male scent, laced with the clean, salty smell of the sea, filled her nostrils.

As if a switch had been thrown, she was swamped by memories, some hot and sensuous, some hurtful enough that her temper roared to life. She stiffened, lurching off balance despite the support.

Constantine said something curt beneath his breath. His arm tightened, an iron bar in the small of her back. When she next focused on him, she was sitting on the sand with Constantine holding her head down between her knees.

"I'm okay now," she told him.

The pressure on her neck disappeared. She lifted her head and blinked at the brilliance of sun and sand. Constantine was sitting beside her, his arms resting on his drawn-up knees. The moment seemed abruptly surreal. It suddenly occurred to her how different Constantine was at the beach, almost as if when he walked onto the sand he shed his responsibilities along with his clothes.

A vibrating sound caught her attention, a cell phone ringing. She looked around and spotted his clothes, an expensive suit, shirt and tie and designer shoes lying in an untidy pile on the sand. She made a covert study of Constantine. He wasn't wearing swimming trunks, just dark gray boxers, the wet fabric hugging the powerful muscles of his thighs.

Constantine made no move toward his phone.

"Aren't you going to answer that?"

His expression was surprisingly relaxed, almost content. "No."

"Why not?"

His mouth kicked up at the corner. "I don't answer phones at the beach."

She found herself smiling back at him. In this, at least, they were the same. She regularly "ran away" to the beach, needing the uncomplicated casualness of sun and sand, the feeling of utter freedom the water gave her.

She hadn't ever applied those needs to Constantine, but she did now and a sharp tug of grief for everything they had lost pulled at her. Since the breakup she had been so focused on the things that had gone wrong, she hadn't wanted to remember the wonderful moments.

She sifted sand between her fingers. "Then you should probably go to the beach more often."

His gaze rested on hers with an odd, neutral look. For the first time she acknowledged that when Constantine had walked away from her, his emotional cut-off hadn't been as clinical as she had imagined. He had lost, too.

With a final twitch the phone stopped vibrating.

"Why would you even consider helping my father?" Instead of avoiding his gaze, Sienna let herself be pinned by it. Not because she wanted the contact, but because she needed to establish that Constantine was telling the truth about what had happened.

"I'm not a monster. I was willing to talk."

"You were there to collect." She didn't come right out and say he had killed her father, but the thought loomed large in her mind.

"Now that's where you're wrong." Constantine's gaze was unnervingly direct. "Your father contacted

me and made the arrangement to meet. I wasn't there
to collect. He wanted another loan."

A few minutes before eight, Sienna stepped into an
ankle-length, midnight blue silk shift and ruthlessly
squashed the heady sense of anticipation that had been
building ever since those few minutes on the beach. She
had to keep reminding herself that Constantine was forcing her to meet him at a social event; this wasn't a date.

She checked her makeup, which she'd spent several
minutes applying. Her hair was coiled in a classic knot.
The Ambrosi pearls she was wearing were the only lavish
note. Part of a sample collection they were using to woo
a European retail giant, de Vries, the flowerlike cluster of
pearls at each lobe and the choker, made from a string of
pearl flowers, looked both modern and opulent.

She was attending Constantine's cocktail party at his
command, but that didn't mean she couldn't use the opportunity to promote her company. An Atraeus Group meet
and greet translated to a room filled with clients and sales
contacts Ambrosi Pearls desperately needed.

The car arrived just before eight.

Carla, who had hovered in her bedroom while Sienna
had dressed discussing the loan situation, followed her
downstairs. Carla was Ambrosi's PR guru, she was also
the current Face of Ambrosi, a cost-cutting move that had
made sense because Carla was outrageously gorgeous and
photogenic.

Carla watched as Sienna checked that she had her
phone, credit card and house key. "I'll wait up for you. If
you need help, call me or text, and I'll come and get you."

Sienna pinned a determined smile on her face. "Thanks,
but that won't be necessary. Believe me, this is strictly
business."

She braced for the next confrontation with Constantine as she stepped out into the courtyard. Instead, a lean, dark man who introduced himself as Tomas, Constantine's personal assistant, opened the passenger door of a sleek sedan.

Disappointment flattened her mood as Sienna climbed into the expensive, leather-scented interior. Despite the tension, after the interlude on the beach, she had been certain Constantine had been more than a little interested in picking up where they had previously left off. Evidently, she had been wrong. If Constantine had wanted to underline the power he held, he couldn't have done it more effectively than this.

Twenty minutes later, Tomas turned into a gated drive flanked by security and parked outside an impressive colonial mansion. Sienna took in the sleek, expensive cars that lined the gravel driveway and the lush, tropical garden lit by glowing lights as she mounted the steps to the front door. A brief security check later and she was shown into a chandelier-lit room.

She glimpsed Constantine, dark and brooding in a black suit and fitted black T-shirt, at one end of the crowded room. Jaw firming, she started toward him, her eyes narrowed assessingly as she studied the wealthy, influential crowd. Her heart sped up at the thought that there could even be a de Vries representative here and she would have the opportunity to apply a little direct pressure.

Her way was abruptly blocked by Alex Panopoulos, one of Ambrosi's most prestigious clients.

Panopoulos, the CEO of an Australasian retail empire, had tried to date both her and Carla on several occasions. Since Panopoulos had a reputation as a likeable rogue and a playboy, deflecting him socially hadn't been difficult. He took the rebuffs with good humor; the only problem was he kept bouncing back.

"Sienna." Panopoulos took both of her hands in his. "I was sorry to hear about your father. I was out of the country until this afternoon, otherwise I would have attended the funeral. Did you get my flowers?"

The "flowers" were an enormous arrangement of hot-house orchids that had cost a small fortune and which Carla had given to an elderly neighbor. "Yes, thank you." She flexed her fingers, wondering when he was going to release them. Simultaneously, she sent small darting glances around the room trying to spot the de Vries rep, Harold Northcliffe, a short, plump man who had a reputation for being elusive.

Panopoulos ignored the small movements. "And…how is the business?"

Sienna held on to her professional veneer with difficulty. "We closed today, but otherwise, it's business as usual."

He released one hand and brushed the delicate skin beneath one eye. "With your usual efficiency, no doubt. It's good to take care of business, but I think you also need to take care of yourself."

For a brief moment in time, Sienna almost wished she could have felt something for Panopoulos, even though she knew this was part of his routine, as practiced and slick as his formidable management skills.

Panopoulos smiled, signaling that he was closing in for the kill. "As a matter of fact, I'm very glad we've met tonight. I was hoping you might have dinner with me next week."

Sienna stiffened. Panopoulos was canny. She suspected that he deliberately kept in touch with both her and Carla on a personal level in order to gain an inside track on acquiring Ambrosi, should the business falter. "If you're worried about what the papers are printing, don't be. Ambrosi Pearls will continue to supply your orders."

The calculating glint in his eye grew stronger, more direct. "I'm sure that is so. But it was the future I wanted to discuss."

His grip on her remaining hand tightened. With a start, Sienna realized he meant to lift her fingers to his mouth.

"Panopoulos."

He dropped her fingers as if they had suddenly become red-hot. "Atraeus."

Constantine's gaze briefly locked with hers before he turned his attention back to Panopoulos. "I hear you're joining us on Medinos for the opening of our newest resort complex."

Panopoulos's expression was carefully blank. "I appreciate the opportunity to establish a retail outlet on Medinos. Seven-star hotels are thin on the ground."

"I understand you've made a substantial bid for floor space for the second stage of the resort complex?"

"I spoke with Lucas a few minutes ago. He's set up a preliminary meeting."

"In that case, I'll look forward to seeing you on Medinos next week. Now, if you'll excuse us, Ms. Ambrosi and I have a business matter to discuss."

Panopoulos's gaze narrowed at the smooth dismissal. "Of course."

Constantine's palm landed in the small of her back, burning through the silk and sending a shock of awareness through her as he urged her past Panopoulos.

Seconds later they stepped out of the crowded reception room and onto a deserted patio. Enclosed by walls and cascading foliage, the outdoor space was lushly tropical. A tinkling fountain added an exotic note, and gardenias released their perfume into air that was still sultry from the afternoon storms.

Annoyed by the high-handed way he had dispensed with Panopoulos then marched her away, Sienna stepped back from Constantine, deliberately using a patio chair to create even more space between them. "You shouldn't have done that. I was in discussion with a client. Alex is one of Ambrosi's best custom—"

"What did he want?"

The grim register of Constantine's voice intensified the distracting, humming awareness. The potent attraction made no sense; she should have been over it long ago. "That's none of your business."

"If Panopoulos wanted to discuss Ambrosi, then that is my business."

The soft reminder of just how much power Constantine wielded over her family's company, and her, strengthened the notion that he wasn't in the least unhappy with the situation. "Our discussion was personal. As it happened, he was asking me out to dinner."

"You turned him down."

His flat assertion that she had no interest in Alex contrarily made her bristle. "As a matter of fact, I didn't." Which wasn't a lie, because Constantine had intervened before she could turn him down.

He said something curt beneath his breath. "You're aware that it's Ambrosi Pearls that Panopoulos wants?"

Annoyance exploded inside her, the burst of temper a welcome change from the uncharacteristic jittery angst that had overtaken her since the conversation at her father's gravesite. "Yes. Now, if you'll excuse me—"

"Not yet."

The soft demand froze her in place. Light washed over the sharp cut of his cheekbones, highlighting the irritable glitter of his eyes. In that moment she registered that Constantine wasn't just angry, he was furious.

She had only ever seen him furious once before—the day they had broken up—but on that occasion he had been icily cool and detached. The fact that his formidable control had finally slipped and he was clearly in danger of losing his temper ratcheted the tension up several notches.

A heady sense of anticipation gripped her. She had the feeling that they were standing on some kind of emotional precipice, that for the first time she was going to see the real Constantine and not the controlled tycoon who had a calculator in place of a heart.

Overhead, thunder rumbled; the air was close and tropically hot. In the distance an electrical storm flickered.

Great. Just what she needed, to be reminded of the previous afternoon's encounter and her complete and utter loss of composure.

"Has he proposed?"

Sienna drew in a sharp breath. If she didn't know better, she could almost swear that Constantine was jealous. "Not yet."

"And if he does?"

"If he does…" She searched for something, anything, to say that would reduce her vulnerability. "I'll have to consider saying yes. It's a fact that this time, with a family and business to care for, when it comes to marriage, business does count. Right now, as far as I'm concerned a husband with money would be win-win."

"When Panopoulos finds out how much Ambrosi owes, he won't place your relationship on a formal footing."

Sienna's heart pounded out of control when he shifted the patio chair and glided closer, looming over her in the small courtyard, his breath stirring her hair.

His gaze dropped to her mouth and she was suddenly unbearably aware that he intended to kiss her.

Six

Sienna retreated a step. Big mistake. She had allowed herself to be cornered, literally. One more step and she would come up against the courtyard wall. "I find that remark offensive."

"It would only offend if you'd slept with Panopoulos, and I don't think you have."

Her jaw firmed. She had made a mistake, dangling Panopoulos in front of Constantine, but it was too late to backtrack now. "You can't be sure of that."

"I've been in town for four days. When I wasn't trying to contact you, I made some inquiries. It wasn't difficult to obtain information."

Her stomach sank. With his resources, Constantine would have found it ridiculously easy to discover whatever he wanted to know about her, including the fact that her personal life was as arid as a desert. She seldom dated. She didn't have time to date; she was too busy trying to sell pearls. "You've got no right to pry into my private affairs."

"It's not exactly what I had planned for my leisure time, either, but whether we like it or not, for the foreseeable future, everything to do with Ambrosi Pearls and you is my business. Have you discussed the loan with Brian Chin yet?"

The sudden change from personal to business threw her even more off balance. Brian Chin was Ambrosi's accountant. "I faxed the pages to him this afternoon. He wasn't happy."

An understatement. Like her, Brian had been in a state of shock.

"I take it Chin is still the extent of your financial advice?"

"Brian's been with us for ten years; he's loyal."

"But not a player. He could never control your father."

"Who could?" Even though she felt disloyal to her bluff, charismatic father, it was a relief to finally say the words.

Impatience registered in his gaze. "Then why did you try?"

"Someone had to. Mom doesn't have a head for business. Neither does Carla. If I hadn't stepped in we would have lost everything a long time ago."

"I would have helped."

Her jaw squared. "You had your chance."

His gaze narrowed at her reference to the financial deal that had ended their engagement. "Not under those conditions."

"If you'd bothered to find out anything about me at all, you would have known how important Ambrosi is to me."

"I knew. Why do you think I walked?"

Shock reverberated through her. In a moment of clarity,

she saw herself as she had been two years ago, just seconds ago—driven, obsessed.

The fact that Constantine had ended their engagement so quickly was no longer incomprehensible. She had always known he was ruthless and uncompromising in business; she just hadn't translated that reality to his personal life. He hadn't liked being left out of the picture and he hadn't been prepared to take second place to either her father's gambling addiction or Ambrosi Pearls.

"Finally, you get it."

And suddenly he was close, too close. An automatic step back and the chill of the masonry wall, a stark contrast to the potent heat of his body, brought her up short. Lightning flickered, the display increasingly spectacular, followed by a growl of thunder.

She should shimmy out, slip past him. A quick call to a taxi firm and five minutes on the roadside and she would be on her way home. If Constantine wanted a discussion it would have to be over the phone, or with lawyers present.

His hand landed on the wall beside her head, cutting off that avenue of escape. "Why didn't you tell me what was going on two years ago?"

"And watch you walk away, like you did when you found out about the proposed loan?"

"I told you, I would have helped."

For a moment her mind went utterly blank. Until then she hadn't realized how angry she had been at Constantine for walking away, for choosing not to even try to understand her predicament when she had desperately needed his support. "And then walked? Thanks, but no thanks."

"You could have used professional help for your father and the business."

"He wouldn't accept the first, and we couldn't afford the second."

The pad of his thumb slid along the line of her jaw. Her pulse pounded out of control, her body's response to the sudden stifling intimacy of his touch intense and unsettling.

She felt caught and held by emotions she didn't want to feel: anger, frustration and, unacceptably, a heady, dizzying anticipation. Ever since those loaded moments in his car, she realized she had been waiting for Constantine to make a move on her.

He muttered a short, rough Medinian phrase. "Why are you so stubborn?"

"I guess it's an Australian trait."

Reminding Constantine that after the Second World War, the Ambrosi family had chosen to uproot themselves from Medinos and make Australia their home was a tenuous counterpunch. But in that moment she was willing to grasp at anything that separated her from Constantine.

His hold was gentle enough that she could slide away, walk away if she wanted...

She saw the moment he logged her decision, the intent in his gaze as he angled her jaw so that her mouth was mere inches from his. She also learned something else. If she was still blindly, fatally attracted to Constantine, it was an unsettling fact that he also wanted her, and suddenly there was no air.

Constantine's mouth brushed hers. Sienna jerked back in an effort to control the heat that shimmered through her. She shouldn't want to know what touching him again— kissing him—would feel like when she had spent two years working doggedly to forget. "This isn't fair."

He grinned quick and hard. "It wasn't meant to be."

His hands settled at her waist. Now was the time to pull

back, to insist that they keep their relationship on a business footing.

Instead, seduced by the mesmerizing fact that he did still want her, that if she wasn't careful she could fall for him again, she lifted up on her toes, cupped his jaw and kissed him back.

A bolt of heat seared straight to her loins. She could feel his fingers in her hair, the sharp tug as he pulled out pins, the soft slide of her hair over her shoulders.

He cupped her breast through the double layer of silk and her bra. Her stomach clenched and for a timeless moment she hung suspended. Until a masculine voice registered and she was free, cool air circulating against her overheated skin.

Constantine controlled the savage desire to dismiss Tomas, who was hovering at the entrance to the courtyard.

His PA was under strict instructions not to interrupt this interlude, or let anyone else do so, which meant that whatever Tomas had to say was urgent.

Positioning himself so that he blocked Sienna from Tomas's view, and the curious stares they were now attracting from the handful of guests who had drifted near the French doors, Constantine took the phone Tomas handed him and answered the call.

The conversation with his chief financial advisor was brief and to the point. The legal tangle his father and Roberto Ambrosi had concocted between them had resulted in an unexpected hitch. Lorenzo had signed away water rights Constantine needed for Roberto's bogus pearl enterprise. No water rights meant no marina development, which effectively froze a project in which he had already invested millions.

Constantine terminated the call and handed the phone back to Tomas. Dismissing him with curt thanks, he turned back to Sienna. He had expected that in the brief interval it had taken to deal with the phone call she would close off from him, and he wasn't wrong. Grimly, he noted that in the space of less than two minutes she had smoothed her hair back into an elegant knot, found her evening bag, which she had dropped, and recovered the cool composure that irked him so much.

A jagged flash of lightning signaled that the violent electrical storm had rolled overhead. Sienna, he noticed, didn't so much as flinch. Her gaze was already focused on his room of retailers and, no doubt, the prospect of closing a number of lucrative sales deals.

Not for the first time it occurred to him that he might have more success with Sienna if he had one of her order sheets in his hand.

When she would have strolled past him, using the avenue of an interested group of spectators who had strolled out onto the courtyard to view the pyrotechnics as an escape route, Constantine blocked her way.

"We haven't finished our discussion." He indicated the softly lit decking that encircled the ground level of the house. "We can conclude our business in the privacy of my study."

Sienna teetered on the brink of refusing, the danger inherent in a private meeting suddenly vastly more potent than the financial threat.

In the end, though, she nodded and mounted the veranda steps, eager to at least get under cover. "I take it the phone call was bad news?"

Constantine's calmness was utterly at odds with the white-hot intensity of the kiss. "Nothing that can't be handled."

The call had been bad news, but that suited Sienna. A return to animosity would be a relief, neutralizing the panicked notion that Constantine was intent on maneuvering her back into his bed.

A hot pulse of adrenaline went through her as the thought gathered momentum. She should never have kissed him back. It had been a reckless experiment. She had practically thrown herself at him. Temporarily at least, it had altered the equation between them, giving him a power over her she had vowed he would never again have.

As if to underscore her imminent danger, a deafening clap of thunder sent her wobbling off balance. One stiletto jammed in a knot in the decking timber and in that moment the lights went out, plunging them into darkness.

Constantine's arm curved around her waist. She found herself pressed against the hard outline of his body, her breasts flattened against his chest. She registered the firm shape of his arousal pressed against her stomach. Heated awareness flashed. Reflexively, she shoved at his chest and bent down to release her foot from the stuck shoe. As she straightened, her head connected solidly with Constantine's jaw in a replay of what had happened the previous day.

Constantine lurched off balance. A second white-hot flash illuminated the fact that on this particular stretch of veranda there was no railing to halt his fall, just a sculpted patch of shrubbery. In the next instant they were plunged back into pitch-blackness.

Panic burned through Sienna as she pulled off her remaining shoe, tossed it on the deck along with her evening bag, and gingerly felt her way to the edge of the decking. Hitching her dress up, she climbed into the garden, picking her way through a collection of rocks and succulents, to find Constantine. Lightning flickered again, illuminating him as he pushed into a sitting position.

"Where am I?"

She grabbed his arm. "In the garden."

He rubbed at his jaw, making her feel instantly guilty. That was the second time she had hit him in the same spot.

"Figures."

Bracing her arm around his waist she helped him up, staggering under his weight.

Her dress was catching on the spiky leaves of some tropical flower. Something both crunchy and soft squished under her bare foot. Not a plant.

They stepped onto cool, damp grass. Constantine's arm tightened around her waist, tucking her firmly against his side, until they made their way to a line of solar garden lights that illuminated a path. Seconds later they climbed a shallow series of steps back onto the veranda.

From the controlled tautness of his muscles, the smooth way he moved, Sienna had a sudden suspicion that Constantine no longer needed her support, if he had ever needed it at all.

The click of a door latch punctuated the now distant rumble of thunder. Groping for reference points in the darkness, Sienna's fingers brushed over the smooth painted surface of a doorframe.

Another step and she was inside, her bare feet sinking into thick carpet. The door slammed, cutting off sound. The darkness was warmer and hushed here, scented with the springlike freshness of flowers and a rich undernote of leather. It did not smell like a working environment. "Where are we?"

"My private suite. The study is just down the hall."

Constantine leaned back against the door. Sienna's hand shot out, landing on the taut muscles of his abdomen. His arm tightened around her waist, sealing her against the seductive heat of his chest, and she was made shiveringly aware that Constantine was showing no inclination to move.

Resisting the counterproductive urge to stay put, Sienna disentangled herself and stepped free. She was now certain that, apart from his initial dazed state, there was nothing wrong with Constantine. She peered into the stygian darkness and injected a note of briskness into her voice. "Tell me where you keep a flashlight or candles."

"There's a flashlight in the bedroom."

She was not falling for that one. "In that case you can stay here. I'm going to get help."

And right after she found one of Constantine's minions, she would call for a taxi. He would have all the help he needed. There would be no need for her to come back and check on him.

His fingers locked with hers in the darkness, anchoring her in place. "I don't need help."

Lightning flashed through the leaded sidelights on either side of the door, illuminating the darkening bruise on Constantine's jaw.

She inhaled sharply. "I did hurt you."

"Tell me about it," he murmured and drew her toward him.

His mouth came down on hers, his lips warm and unexpectedly soft. Suddenly, leaving was not an option. Lifting up on her toes, she wound her arms around his neck and returned the kiss with interest. Any idea that Constantine was truly hurt or vulnerable dissolved. If he had been stunned by the fall, clearly the effects had worn off because he was fully aroused.

Long minutes later, he lifted her into his arms, negotiated the hall and carried her into a darkened room, his night vision unerring as he located a couch and set her down on it.

As she went to work on the buttons of his shirt, she felt the zipper of her dress release, then the fastening of her bra. Another long, searing kiss and Constantine peeled both garments away.

Lightning, paler and more distant now, flickered as he jerked his tie free and shrugged out of the jacket and the shirt. His weight came down on her, the bare skin of his chest hot against her breasts. For long breathtaking moments they continued to kiss with a drugging, seducing sweetness that spun her back to long afternoons in her apartment, even longer nights in his bed.

His fingers hooked in the waistband of her panties. She lifted her hips and with one gliding movement she was naked aside from the pearls in her lobes and at her throat.

She had a brief moment to consider that she was on the verge of making a monumental mistake before deciding that after the past two years of worry and work, she could do what she wanted just this once. She could give in to the exhilarating passion she had thought had died when Constantine had walked out on her.

The feel of his trousers against her inner thighs as he came down between her legs was a faint irritation, signaling that Constantine wasn't naked. She had thought, in the brief interval that he had separated himself from her that he would have dispensed with his pants altogether. That small detail faded into insignificance as finally, achingly, they came together.

Until that moment she hadn't realized how much she had missed him, missed this. She had loved the touch, the taste, the feel of him, loved the intimacy of making love, the way he'd made her feel when they'd been together.

Constantine murmured something rough in Medinian. "I knew it. You haven't been with anyone else."

Sienna was momentarily distracted by the satisfaction

in his voice, then his mouth closed over one breast and hot pleasure zapped conscious thought, and she could only clasp his shoulders and move with him.

She heard his indrawn breath. The pressure was close to unbearable, holding her on a knife's edge of expectation, and in a moment of shock she realized he was wearing a condom. She hadn't been aware that he had put one on. Aside from the occasional distant flicker of lightning outside it was pitch-black, and for long, dizzying minutes she'd been blindly absorbed by the overwhelming sensations.

The brief span of time when she had thought he had been undressing was now explained. He had been performing a much more important task.

She should be grateful that he hadn't lost his head the way she had, that he had protected them both, but the knowledge that he had condoms with him was abruptly depressing. A man didn't carry condoms unless he expected, or planned, to make love.

He began to move and her breath hitched in her throat. With every gliding stroke the pleasure wound tighter and tighter. She coiled her arms around his neck, burying her face against his shoulder as the burning tension gathered. Her climax finally hit her in shimmering, incandescent waves. Dimly she was aware of Constantine's release just seconds after her own, the moment primal and extreme.

Soft golden light flooded the room with shocking suddenness. Constantine's gaze locked with hers and any doubt that the lovemaking had been a spur of the moment decision on his part evaporated when she saw the possessive satisfaction in his eyes. However random the events that had precipitated this interlude appeared, he *had* planned to make love to her.

She stirred beneath Constantine's weight, with an effort

of will controlling the intense emotions that had temporarily hijacked her brain, and the hurt. She had wanted to believe that Constantine had been as swept away as she had been.

She pushed at his shoulders. Obligingly, he shifted to one side, allowing her to scramble off the couch.

Feeling exposed and more than a little flustered, she found her dress. Stepping into it, she quickly fastened the zipper. Her bra was hooked over one end of the couch, and she spied her panties beneath an elegant coffee table.

Constantine was in the process of fastening his pants. Cheeks burning, she averted her gaze from his sleek, bronzed shoulders and lean hips. Instead, she snatched up the panties and made a beeline for the bathroom.

Feeling increasingly horrified at her lack of control, she stared at her reflection in the large mirror positioned over a marble vanity. Her hair was disheveled, her skin flushed, her mouth swollen. Constantine might have planned to make love to her, but that didn't change the fact that she had practically thrown herself at him—not once, but twice. And he had been quite happy to take advantage of her vulnerability.

A few minutes later, freshened up, her hair finger combed, she ventured back out into the sitting room. The dress had smoothed out against the warmth of her skin, but she was still minus her shoes and her clutch, which were both outside on the veranda.

Constantine was pacing the room talking into a cell phone, his expression taut. He had pulled on a fresh shirt, which he had left unbuttoned. Her gaze skittered away from the mouthwatering slice of tanned chest and washboard abs. The sexy casualness of his attire emphasized the intimacy of what they had just shared.

Constantine terminated the call and slipped the phone into his pocket.

"Problems?" Suddenly in a hurry to leave, she circled the room, giving the large leather sofa a wide berth as she inched toward the door.

Constantine's silvery gaze tracked her. "A hitch with the new resort."

"Which is why you're flying out tonight."

There was an oddly weighted pause. "You could come with me."

For a brief second, despite the hurt and disillusionment, dizzying temptation pulled at her. "To Medinos?"

He glanced at his watch. "I fly out in three hours. You're welcome to share the flight with me. It makes sense," he concluded smoothly. "We haven't had time to…complete our business. We can pick up where we left off."

In his bed.

Sienna squashed the wild impulse to say yes, to immerse herself even more deeply in a relationship that logic and history dictated was destined to crash and burn.

The sensible response was to refuse, to put their relationship back on a business footing.

Her fingers automatically went to the pearl choker at her throat. She forced herself to breathe, to think. This was no longer just about her.

An Atraeus Resort opening was an A-list event, by invitation only. It would be jam-packed with high-end press and industry professionals. All of the luxury retail giants would be represented, including de Vries.

Despite what had happened on the couch, going to Medinos was an opportunity she couldn't afford to pass up.

She would never have a better chance to push Ambrosi Pearls' new range and secure the sales contract they had been chasing. If de Vries signed even a one-year deal, they could pay off Constantine. They would be free and clear. "All right."

Surprise flared in Constantine's gaze and was just as quickly controlled. "Tomas will take you home so you can pack your bag."

She thought quickly. Apart from the fact that she didn't want to be closeted alone with Constantine on a luxury corporate jet, this was a business trip; she needed time to prepare. Namely to pick up the samples from the vault at the office and make an appointment to meet with the de Vries representative attending the opening. The process of arranging the meeting was a delicate business, which could take days. "I can't go to Medinos tonight. I'll need two days before I leave."

Constantine's gaze narrowed at the sudden crispness of Sienna's voice, at odds with her softly flushed cheeks and tousled hair. His mood deteriorated further as she fingered the silky pearls at her throat for the third time and counting.

When they had been making love, the pearls had seemed to glow in the dark, reminding him that he wasn't just making love to the woman he wanted, he was making love to the CEO of Ambrosi Pearls.

Now she was backing off fast—from the lovemaking and from the unspoken admission he had forced from her that, deny it as she might, she still wanted him.

But at least she had agreed to come to his country, which was progress.

The idea had crystallized when she had stated that she would consider marriage with Panopoulos, then it had set in stone when he had discovered that she hadn't slept with anyone in the two years since their break up.

The primitive surge that had gripped him when he had

realized that Sienna, who had been a virgin when they had first made love, had never belonged to anyone but him, had been profound.

The thought that she could take another lover, possibly Panopoulos, made him break out in a cold sweat. That scenario was unacceptable. "In that case, let me know a departure time and I'll make the company jet available to you."

"No." Her chin jerked up, dark eyes shooting fire at the concept of him paying for her travel, underlining the fact that she was backing off, fast. "I'll book a commercial flight."

In a room filled with soft gold light and pooling shadows, suddenly the Medinian part of her ancestry, the long line of alchemists and merchants stretching back into antiquity, was starkly evident. His jaw tightened as the fascination that had gripped him the first time he had seen her struck him anew. "You can't afford the commercial flight."

By his calculations, he had been paying for everything, including her salary for the past two months.

Her cheeks flushed a deeper shade of pink. "I have money of my own."

"Then at least let me organize your ride home." He took out his phone and dialed Tomas before she could argue.

Seconds later he hung up and followed her out onto the veranda. Sienna had found her clutch and shoes.

Constantine crouched down and gently levered the stiletto heel out of a knot in the decking timber.

She took it from him, her movements brisk. As she slipped her foot into the shoe, she gripped the frame of a nearby window for balance. He caught her studying his reflection in the glass and satisfaction curled through him.

If Sienna had been indifferent to him, he would have

expedited the paperwork, which was cut-and-dried, and walked away. But she did want him. Their chemistry was hot enough to burn.

The fact that he was jealous of Panopoulos didn't please him. The uncomfortable reality that he still wanted Sienna after she had broken his trust two years ago was even more difficult to accept.

There was nothing logical about the emotions. He didn't want the attraction, but it existed, the pull absolute and powerful.

Tomas appeared, a set of keys in one hand. Sienna shot Constantine a bright, professional smile, her gaze missing his by inches as she hurried after Tomas.

As if she couldn't wait to be gone.

Gingerly, Constantine probed at the lump that had formed on the back of his head, clearly from one of his expensive and strategically placed landscape rocks.

He studied the now floodlit grounds and the patch of crushed bromelia balansae.

Damn. He couldn't believe he had fallen into the garden.

Seven

Two days later Sienna disembarked from her commercial flight into the searing heat of Medinos. The ice-blue cotton shift she was wearing was already sticking to her skin as she strolled into the arrivals terminal and found Tomas waiting for her.

Her stomach tensed against a twinge of what was, unacceptably, disappointment. During the flight she had been too wound to sleep, anticipating seeing Constantine when she landed.

Minutes later, with her luggage loaded into the trunk, Sienna slid dark glasses onto the bridge of her nose and settled into the passenger seat of a sleek, modern sedan. While Tomas drove, she stared curiously at limestone villas, fields of olives and grapes and an endless vista of sea and sky.

She had expected Medinos, with its wild, hard country, to be fascinating and she wasn't disappointed. Constantine and his family now owned vast tracts, some in plantations and farms. The original goat farm and market garden on the island of Ambrus was now, of course, a fabulously wealthy gold mine. In fact, the entire island of Ambrus was now owned by the Atraeus family.

From her research on the internet she'd discovered that the main island was large and well populated, although, because the interior was so rugged settlement was primarily on the coast. Other islands of the group were visible as they wound along a high precipitous road, appearing to float hazily in the distance. The lyrical names were as imbued with mystery and magic as the shimmering images: Nycea, Thais, Pythea and, closer in, Ambrus.

Tomas's cell phone rang, the buzz discreet. The low timbre of his voice as he spoke in rapid Medinian briefly spun her back to the explosive interlude with Constantine at his home.

When Sienna had exited the taxi that night after refusing to be driven by Tomas, Carla had been waiting.

Predictably, she had been horrified when she'd learned Sienna had decided to go to Medinos. "Please tell me you're not going with him."

"Don't worry." Sienna kept her voice crisp and light as she struggled to control her blush. "I'm traveling separately. This is business."

Although, very little of what they had done that night had even the remotest connection to business.

Dropping her evening bag on the kitchen table, she filled the electric jug with water and set it to boil. What she wanted was a steadying dose of caffeine but, since she needed to sleep, it was going to have to be herbal tea. As she turned to lean on the table, her reflection in the kitchen window flashed back at her. Tousled hair and bare mouth, the rich luster of pearls making her look more like a courtesan than the CEO of a company.

She had let him make love to her.

Guilty heat burned through her again at the instant, vivid recall of Constantine's mouth on hers, his muscular body pressing her into the soft leather couch.

Carla's expression was taut as she leaned against the frame of the kitchen door, her feet bare, her arms wrapping her thin silk robe closely around her waist. "I knew it. He wants you again."

"No." A little desperately, Sienna searched out painkillers, drank two down with a glass of water, then found mugs and tea bags, glad for the excuse to avoid Carla's too-sharp gaze. "At least, no more or less than he wants any woman."

"So, why does he want you to go to Medinos?"

She set the mugs on the table and dropped in the tea bags. "Not because he wants a relationship."

She poured hot water over the fragrant chamomile. What had happened on the couch had nothing to do with a relationship. It had been sex, pure and simple. Planned sex. Constantine had made no bones about wanting her and she hadn't been able to resist him.

Sienna removed the tea bags and handed Carla her mug. "I'm going to Medinos because a de Vries rep will be at the opening of the new Atraeus Resort. With any luck I can stall Constantine long enough to give us a chance to secure that contract."

A glimmer of hope entered Carla's eyes. She knew as well as Sienna that if they signed with de Vries they would be able to pay off the Atraeus loan outright. They would not lose Ambrosi Pearls.

"Hallelujah," Carla murmured. "Finally some light at the end of the tunnel. I just wish you didn't have to go to

Medinos. I don't trust the Atraeus men, and especially not Constantine. He doesn't have a reputation for revisiting anything—not mistakes, and definitely not affairs. Promise me that whatever you do, you won't let him make you his mistress. Nothing's worth that. Nothing."

Stung by the knowledge that even Carla now labeled her brief engagement to Constantine as an affair, Sienna sipped her tea. "The only liaison Constantine and I will be discussing is a business one."

Carla's cheeks were flushed, her jaw set. "Good. That's what I needed to hear. Be careful."

Sienna intended to be.

She turned her attention back to the glittering Medinian sea and a fishing boat maneuvering alongside a long narrow jetty. They were driving through the outskirts of a city now and the streets were increasingly busy. Olive-skinned, dark-eyed Medinians and brightly garbed tourists mingled, enjoying the brilliant sunshine and the vibrant market-style shopping and street cafés.

Tomas pointed out *Castello* Atraeus, a fortress built on the highest point of the headland, which overlooked the city of Medinos and the bay. Constructed of the same stone that many of the villas and cottages were made of, Sienna knew the original ancient *castello* which had once belonged to a noble family that had since died out, had been almost completely destroyed during the war. Lorenzo Atraeus had bought the ruin with his newfound wealth and had painstakingly rebuilt it, following the ancient designs.

Tomas briefly pointed out other buildings of significance including a magnificent modern library, which Lorenzo had gifted to the city, before driving along a curving stretch of beach. Minutes later, he turned into the lushly planted parking bay of The Atraeus Group's newest hotel—a sleek, luxury, seven-star resort that had only recently been completed.

As Sienna exited the car, her gaze was caught by the island that floated closest to Medinos. "Is that Ambrus?"

Tomas waited for the bellhop to load her bags. "Yes. That is Ambrus."

Looping the strap of her handbag over her shoulder, she walked into the air-conditioned paradise of the hotel's signature cream-and-gold foyer, with its intricately carved frescoes and exquisite mosaics.

Her heart thumped once, hard, when she glimpsed a head of coal-black hair brushing a familiar set of broad shoulders. Constantine was dressed casually in dark pants, a black T-shirt and a loose jacket. In the lush surroundings, he seemed even more darkly masculine and exotic than she remembered. His gaze locked with hers and any idea that this was a chance meeting evaporated.

Feeling overheated and a little flustered because she hadn't expected to encounter Constantine at the front desk, Sienna busied herself signing the register and collecting her key. Constantine spoke briefly with Tomas, directed the bellhop to her suite then insisted on accompanying her.

The lavish ground-floor suite he directed her to had both internal and external access, with huge glass sliding doors that framed an achingly beautiful view of Ambrus. Constantine unlocked the doors to a private patio.

Shielding her eyes against the sun, Sienna stepped outside and stared across the limpid blue water at towering black cliffs. High, rugged hills were bleached the color of ripe wheat by the sun, and the lower slopes were dotted by flashes of white, which she assumed were goats.

She had expected to feel a connection to Medinos. For years, just the name itself had entranced her, although the villa and pearl facility her family used to own were definitely past history.

Sienna logged the moment Constantine moved to stand beside her, her stomach clenching at the faint scents of aftershave and clean male. "Ambrus looks deserted."

Her gaze connected with his. For a split second she was spun back to the interlude at his house, the moment of clarity when the lights had come on and she had seen the possession in his eyes.

He indicated the island. "The mining company operates on the eastern side. There's a construction project for a new resort complex and marina on the northern headland. Other than that, we run goats to keep the weeds down. Your family's old pearl facility is based on the northwestern side."

She stared at the high, stark cliffs, the utter absence of anything as soft and tamed as a sandy beach. She knew there were calm bays and inlets—there had to be for the pearl beds—but there was nothing remotely civilized about the southern end.

A discreet tap on her door relieved her of her tingling awareness of Constantine and the hot flashes of memory that kept surfacing. Glad for an excuse to end the unnerving tension, Sienna walked through the elegant sitting room and opened the door so the bellhop could carry her bags inside.

Relieved to see her padlocked sample case stacked on top of her luggage, she tipped the lean young man. The future of Ambrosi Pearls was literally tied up in the contents of that case.

She started guiltily as Constantine prowled up behind her.

His gaze rested broodingly on the sample case, although he couldn't possibly know its contents.

He handed her two cream-colored embossed cards. The first was an invitation to the official opening of the resort that evening, the second an invitation to a luncheon to celebrate the product launch of a new collection of Atraeus gold jewelry the following day. "We won't have time to talk about the loan details today. That discussion will have to wait until this evening."

On the back of both cards, precisely handwritten—no doubt by Tomas or another of Constantine's people—were instructions on dress, reminding her that while Medinos might be a tourist destination, it was closer to the east in its moral codes than the west.

Cheeks flushed, she slipped the cards in her handbag, which was still looped over her shoulder. "Thank you."

Constantine stepped past her and paused at the open door. "I was certain you would appreciate the opportunity to circulate."

Sienna closed the door behind him and leaned against the cool wood waiting for the pounding in her chest to subside.

Constantine had seemed manageable in Sydney—barely. A mere hour ago she had been happily operating under the assumption that on a business footing, at least, she could handle him.

But this was not the Constantine she had known two years ago. The way he had seduced her so easily the other night was a case in point. He had ruthlessly used his fall and the power outage to maneuver her into having sex with him. The fact that she had wanted the sex wasn't at issue as much as the fact that Constantine was harder, sharper, more manipulative and dominant than she had bargained on.

And she was almost certain he knew exactly what she was up to on Medinos.

Eight

Constantine tracked Sienna's leisurely progress across the crowded reception room. Even if he hadn't been informed that she had entered the ballroom of Medinos's newest and most spectacular hotel, it would have been easy to spot her by the turning of heads as she strolled past.

Terminating a conversation, he placed his drink on a sideboard, his temper flashing to a slow burn when he saw what she was wearing.

Her hair was caught up in a knot, emphasizing the dress, which was designed to induce a stroke. A pale champagne halter, the gown was deceptively plain, the silky fabric an almost perfect match for the color of Sienna's skin so that at first glance he had thought she was naked. Added to that, the halter neck meant she wasn't wearing a bra.

His jaw tightened against a throb of mingled desire and irritation. Ankle length and discreetly cut, the gown paid lip service to the dress code he had demanded she follow, while subtly undermining it at every turn.

Beside him Lucas let out a low whistle.

"Look too long," Constantine said calmly, "and I'll put your eyes out."

When he had been dating Sienna, to avoid the press they hadn't gone out together at night. Normally, when he had been in Sydney, he had picked her up from work and taken her back to his apartment, or he'd followed her home to her place. The clothes she'd worn had been elegant, sleek, businesslike and sexy; he had barely noticed them.

The only other clothes he had seen had been her casual at-home gear, a bikini that had driven him crazy and her underwear, which for the most part had been tantalizing, but practical. What Sienna did or didn't have in her wardrobe hadn't interested him. Until now.

Zane, who had flown in from the States that morning for the resort opening, watched Sienna with his usual cool assessment. If Lucas was a shade on the wild side, Zane was worse, but he had the good sense to stay quiet about it. A couple of years on the streets of L.A. after he had run away from his mother's fourth marriage, and before they had managed to track him down, had left their mark. On the surface Zane was cool and calm with a killer charm. He never lacked for feminine company, but it was a fact that he didn't trust any of the women he had dated.

Zane sipped the beer he'd been nursing for the past twenty minutes. "It could be worth it. I notice she didn't bring her accountant with her."

Or anyone else, Constantine thought with grim satisfaction.

Lucas lifted a brow. "No briefcase, either."

No briefcase. No bra.

Zane took another swallow of his beer. "She doesn't look happy to be here."

Rub salt into the wound, Constantine thought bleakly. But at least she wasn't carrying that damned sample case.

"You don't need this," Lucas said bluntly.

Constantine's expression remained impassive. He hadn't discussed what had happened in Sydney, nor would he, but he was aware that Lucas knew exactly how focused he was on the CEO of Ambrosi Pearls.

He could have left the talking to their legal team. The options were clear-cut and his people were very, very good. Unless Sienna produced a large check, The Atraeus Group owned Ambrosi. But since those intense moments across the gravesite, this had ceased to be about the money.

At least for him.

He watched as Sienna paused to talk to an exquisitely dressed Japanese couple, her cool poise at odds with the off-the-register passion and fire that had seared him in Sydney.

The reason Sienna was in Medinos was simple. Aside from the fact that he wanted to make love to her again, he needed to know just how far she would go to clear the debt. The thought that she would agree to sleep with him in order to influence the negotiations wasn't something he wanted to dwell on, but after the debacle two years ago, and the fact that she had let him make love to her so easily the other night, he couldn't afford to ignore the possibility.

"The situation with the water rights has...complicated things," he explained to his brother.

Lucas shook his head. "The only real complication I can see is ten meters away and closing."

Zane finished his beer and set the glass down, his expression wry. "Ciao. Watch your back."

Constantine's gaze narrowed as a male guest moved

in on Sienna. His jaw tightened when he recognized Alex Panopoulos.

His phone vibrated. He registered the Sydney number of the security firm he had used to investigate the Ambrosi family. As he lifted the phone to his ear, Sienna turned to speak to Panopoulos. If he'd thought the front view of the dress was daring, the back of the gown was nonexistent. "It's not my back that's the problem."

Sienna managed to extricate herself from Alex Panopoulos on the pretext that she had to check her wrap. Pausing in a quiet alcove decorated with marble statuary and lush, potted palms, she folded the transparent length of champagne gauze into almost nothing and stuffed it into her evening bag. What she really wanted was a few moments to study the room and see if she could spot Northcliffe, the de Vries rep she was scheduled to meet with in the morning.

She caught a glimpse of Constantine, darkly handsome in evening dress as he talked into a cell phone, and her heart pounded hard.

Nerves still humming, she merged with the flow of guests while she examined that moment of raw panic.

Every time she remembered that she had encouraged Constantine to make love to her, her stomach clenched. Like it or not, where Constantine was concerned she was vulnerable, and the emotional risk of getting too close was high.

A waiter cruised past. She refused an array of canapés, too on edge to either eat or drink until she had identified Northcliffe. Pausing beside a glass display, she studied a series of gorgeously detailed pieces of jewelry, advance samples of tomorrow's product launch. For a timeless moment the room and the nervy anticipation dissolved and she was drawn into the fascinating juxtaposition of lucent tourmaline and smoothly worked gold.

She wasn't a designer. When it came to creating art or beautiful jewelry, she was utterly clueless. Her passion had always been the business side of things. Her father used to jokingly proclaim that she had the heart of a shopkeeper. It was a fact that she was never happier than when she was making a sale.

A faint tingling at her nape made her stiffen.

A glimpse of broad shoulders increased her tension.

If that was Constantine, then he had crossed the room, which meant he had seen her.

"Sienna. Glad you could make it."

She saw taut cheekbones and a tough jaw, but it wasn't Constantine. It was his younger brother, Lucas.

With his slightly battered features, courtesy of two seasons of professional rugby in Australia, and his smoldering bad-boy looks, he was undoubtedly hot.

Lucas had once tried to date Carla. Fatally, he had made his move after Constantine had walked out on Sienna and before Lucas had realized the wedding was off. Carla, who was loyal to a fault, had taken no prisoners and the public spat at a fabulous new nightclub had become the stuff of legend.

Magazines had lined up for the short time both Ambrosi girls had hit the publicity limelight, although Carla had handled the attention a lot better than Sienna. With her PR mind-set she had decided to view the fight with Lucas as a gold-plated opportunity to boost Ambrosi Pearls' profile, and thanks to her, orders had flooded in.

"You know me, Lucas." She checked out the last place she had seen Constantine. "Gold, jewels, objets d'art. I couldn't resist."

"You look like one of Constantine's objets d'art your-self."

Sienna countered his comment with a direct look. The dress she wore was sexier and more revealing than anything she would normally have worn to a business occasion, but in this case it was warranted. The gown had been used in their latest advertising campaign. Harold Northcliffe, who should have received the glossy press kit she had expressed to his Sydney office, would instantly recognize it. The jewelry itself was a set of prototypes they had designed with de Vries and the sophisticated European market in mind. "If you want to score points off me, Lucas, you're going to have to try harder than that. The dress belongs to Carla."

The amusement flashed out of his dark gaze. "It was the jewelry that really caught my eye."

"I didn't know you were interested in jewelry design." Lucas was known as The Atraeus Group's "hatchet man." His reputation was based more on corporate raiding than the creative arts.

"Not normally," he murmured, an odd note in his voice, "but I'm certain Constantine will be. When I first saw you I thought you were wearing a traditional set of Medinian bridal jewels. Quite a publicity stunt considering that you used to be engaged to Constantine."

Dismayed, Sienna touched the pearls at her throat. The pieces she was wearing were based on her grandfather Sebastien's original drawings. The delicate choker consisted of seed pearls woven into classical Medinian motifs, with a deep blue teardrop sapphire suspended from the center. Matching earrings with tiny drop sapphires dangled from her ears, and an intricate pearl bracelet studded with sapphires encircled her wrist.

"Speaking of the devil," Lucas murmured, looking directly over her shoulder.

A hot tingle ran down Sienna's spine. The knowledge that Constantine was directly behind her and closing in was so intense that for a moment she couldn't breathe.

Even though she was prepared, the confrontation was a shock. Dressed in a formal black evening suit, Constantine seemed taller, physically broader and, in that first moment, coldly remote. Although the impression of remoteness disappeared the instant she met his glittering gaze.

"We need to talk."

The curt demand sent another hot tingle through her. She resisted the urge to cross her arms over her chest. Suddenly the dress seemed too thin, too revealing, definitely not her best idea. "That is why I'm here."

A muscle pulsed along the side of his jaw. If she hadn't known he was angry before, she knew it then.

"Outside. Now."

Her jaw tightened at the low register of his voice, the unmistakable whiplash of command. "I don't think so." The last time she had taken orders she had been five and she had *wanted* that Barbie doll.

His hand closed around her arm; his palm burned into her naked skin. A pang of pure feminine fear shot through her, making all the fine hairs at her nape stand on end, but she dug her heels in. To anyone watching they would no doubt appear to be engaged in an intimately close conversation, but Constantine's grip was firm.

When her resistance registered, he bent close. His lips almost brushed her ear and his warm breath fanned her neck, sending another fiery pang through her, this time straight to her loins. She froze, pinned in place by the potent lash of sensation. For a split second she couldn't move. Worse, she didn't want to.

"We're leaving now. If you make a fuss, I'll carry you out and no one will stop me."

"You can't do this."

"Try me."

Wildly she checked for Lucas, but he had conveniently disappeared. "This is assault."

He laughed, and the weird primitive female thing that had frozen her in place and which was probably designed as a survival mechanism for the race so that women would have sex with men even if they were hideous and had no manners at all, dissolved. Suddenly, she was back. "I'll call the police."

"Before or after our business meeting tomorrow?"

Her teeth snapped together at his blatant use of the power he had over both her and Ambrosi. "That's black-mail."

He applied pressure, unceremoniously shunting her out of the room. "Babe, that's business."

Nine

Sienna dug in her high-heels as they entered a deserted gallery with tall, arched windows along one wall, softly lit works of art on the other. "This is as far as I go. We're out of the ballroom, which strangely enough you wanted to leave despite the fact that it's your party. But if we go any farther, I'm afraid no one will hear my screams."

"Calm down, I'm not interested in hurting you."

Ignoring her protest, Constantine swung her up into his arms.

Sienna pushed at his shoulders and attempted to wriggle free. "You could have fooled me."

Constantine strode a short distance then set her down directly in front of a large oil painting, grunting softly when her elbow accidentally caught him in the stomach.

Just when she was congratulating herself on finally ruffling his steely control, one long tanned finger flicked the sapphire teardrop just above the swell of her cleavage. "Part of the new promotion?"

Her cheeks burned with a combination of irked fury and a dizzying heat. "How would you know about that?"

"I'm still on your client mailing list. I get all of your pamphlets."

"I'll have to speak to my assistant."

Better still, she would edit the list herself. Those glossy pamphlets were too expensive to mail out to people who were never going to buy their products.

Constantine's expression was grim. "When you walked into the ballroom wearing Medinian bridal jewels you caused quite a stir. Was that planned, or a coincidence?"

She followed the direction of his gaze. The jewel-bright colors of the large oil painting that loomed overhead came into sharp focus. She studied what was, without doubt, a wedding portrait. "I had no idea these were wedding jewels."

"Or that the press could put two and two together and make ten." Constantine's expression was frustratingly remote. "This isn't a game, Sienna."

She flushed. The only thing she was guilty of was trying to save her family business and she would not apologize for that. "I'm not playing a game or pulling a publicity stunt."

Constantine folded his arms over his chest. "Prove it."

She was tempted to explain nothing, pack her bag and leave on the earliest flight out, but until the loan situation was resolved, she was stuck. "Very well. Come to my room and I'll show you."

Unlocking the door to her suite, she stepped inside and flicked a switch. Lights glowed softly over the marble floors and luxurious white-on-white furnishings.

She set her evening bag on a coffee table flanked by cream leather couches and walked to the wall safe. Punching in her PIN, she dragged out the sample case, which was sitting on top, removed her laptop then quickly shoved the sample case back in the safe, out of sight.

She placed the laptop, a girly pink model with all the latest bells and whistles, on the coffee table. Booting it up, she accessed the jewelry design files, which contained a photographed portfolio of designs that had belonged to her grandfather. She found the scanned page she wanted then removed the jewelry she was wearing and arranged it alongside the laptop. "These jewels are prototypes. They're not in production—"

"Until you locate a buyer."

Sienna drew a calming breath. "—until we have received expressions of interest."

"Otherwise known as a sales order."

Her jaw tightened. "The Ambrosi versions aren't an exact match of the jewels my grandfather sketched. The designs have merely been based on his drawings. We had no idea they were bridal jewelry."

Constantine was oddly still, the pooling lamplight softening the taut line of his jaw, the chiseled cheekbones and the faint hollows beneath. In the lamplight, with his coal-dark hair flowing to his shoulders, he looked fierce and utterly male, much as she had imagined ancient Medinian warriors must have looked. "It seems I owe you an apology."

"Not at all." Grimly, she powered the laptop down and then had to go through the whole risky rigmarole of taking the sample case back out of the safe in order to slot in the laptop.

"Allow me," Constantine said, smoothly taking the sample case from her grasp.

Heart pounding, Sienna reclaimed the case and jammed it back in the safe. If Constantine discovered she was here trying to make a deal with de Vries, that would not be good. With any luck, he hadn't seen the discreet branding on the case because the printed side had been facing away from him when he had taken it from her.

A tiny clinking sound drew her attention. Constantine had picked the necklace up off the coffee table. The delicate combination of pearls and sapphires looked even more fragile against his hands. He gently touched a pearl. Sienna shivered, as if his finger had stroked across her skin.

His gaze connected with hers. "So, who did you wear those pearls for, if it wasn't me?"

"I don't know what you mean." Desperate for a distraction, Sienna walked through to the small adjacent kitchenette and bar, opened a cupboard and found glasses.

After filling the glasses with chilled water from the fridge, she handed one to Constantine, taking care to avoid brushing his fingers.

Constantine finished his drink in two long swallows.

Intensely aware of his gaze on her, she placed her drink on the coffee table and gathered up the sample jewels. The sooner they were out of sight the happier she would feel. If she had understood the potential for disaster inherent in the Medinian designs, she would have stuck to the more modern flower-patterned pearls.

Walking through to her bedroom, she wrapped the jewels in a silk scarf and placed them in the top dresser drawer. She would put them back in the sample case and lock them in the safe once Constantine had left.

When she returned to the sitting room Constantine was pacing. He picked up a small bronze statuette then set it down almost immediately. If she didn't know better, she would think he was nervous.

He glanced at his watch. "Have you eaten?"

The complete change in tack startled her enough that she answered without thinking. "Not since the flight."

"Then I'll order dinner in." He picked up the sleekly modern phone, which was situated on an escritoire.

His suggestion was subtly shocking. Her heart sped up at the thought of spending any more time secluded and alone with Constantine. "No. I'm not hungry."

"You need to eat, and I've made you miss dinner. If you don't want to eat here, we can go somewhere more public."

Sienna considered her options. Constantine had made no bones about the fact that he wanted her. The realization that she was actually contemplating sleeping with him again stopped her in her tracks.

Just days ago she hadn't been ready for a sexual relationship with anyone. Yet, despite being burned twice by Constantine, a stubborn part of her was still dizzily, irresistibly attracted.

Sex had to be out of the question.

She was here on business. For her family and Ambrosi Pearls' sake she had to stay focused.

To shield her blush, she busied herself with the unnecessary job of checking the lock on the safe. "I do need to eat, but not here."

If they ate out it would be easier to avoid talking business and it was a fact that she needed to stall Constantine until late morning at least. By then she would know whether or not de Vries was going to place an order.

"Suits me."

Constantine's unexpectedly mild tone was surprising. For a moment, she thought she saw relief in his gaze, which didn't make sense.

Confused, she walked to her bedroom and grabbed a silk shrug that would cover her bare shoulders and décolletage better than the wrap she'd worn earlier. When she returned to the sitting room, Constantine was replacing the telephone receiver.

"I've booked a table at a small café on the waterfront."

"Sounds great." She sent him her brightest, most professional smile. At this time of year, the height of the tourist season, a waterfront café would be crowded. They would be lucky to hear themselves think, let alone talk. A business discussion would be out of the question.

She picked up her evening bag and her key, and preceded Constantine through the door. She glimpsed their reflection in the ornate hall mirror as they strolled out of the suite. Constantine was tall, broad-shouldered and remote in his formal evening dress. She looked unexpectedly provocative, the soft silk clinging to her curves as she walked.

A powerful sense of déjà vu gripped her as she closed the door behind her, laced with a cocktail of emotions she thought she had dealt with, and dismissed, two years ago.

The image could have been a film clip from the past. They had looked like a couple. They had looked like lovers.

Renewed panic gripped her when she considered that technically they were lovers. That all she had to do was give in to the pressure Constantine was exerting and she would be back in his bed. Again.

The restaurant was tiny and packed with customers but Sienna's relief faded when the two dark-suited bodyguards who had shadowed them since they'd exited the hotel suddenly disappeared and the proprietor led them to a private courtyard. A lone table, which had obviously just been vacated by early diners, was in the process of being set.

Within seconds they were alone.

Girding herself for an unpleasant discussion that would spell the end of Ambrosi, Sienna took the seat Constantine held for her, but instead of launching into business, Constantine seemed content to relax and enjoy the meal. Listening to his casual banter with the proprietor who served them personally and observing his teasing charm when a small child ventured out of the kitchens to chatter shyly at them, she found herself gradually relaxing as well.

An hour later, after dining on creamy goat cheese and figs, followed by an array of fresh seafood including spicy fried squid, the local specialty, Sienna declined dessert.

Her tension snapped back as soon as they reached the enclosed gardens of the resort. The security team melted away once again and she found herself alone with Constantine. Warily, she studied a walled garden with its limpid ornamental pool. Nothing about this part of the resort was familiar. "Where are we?"

"My private quarters. I was about to offer you a nightcap."

Something kicked hard in her chest. Disappointment. "If this is a proposition, believe me, right now sex is the last thing—"

"What if I cleared the debt?"

His words were like a slap in the face, spinning her back two years to the scene in her apartment when Constantine had point-blank accused her of agreeing to marry him in order to guarantee the financial health of Ambrosi Pearls.

It had taken months but she had finally decided that if he didn't know who she was, or what was important to her, that was his problem not hers.

It was difficult to believe that she had ever been naive enough to imagine that he had fallen in love with her, that they had spent six weeks together making love.

Not making love, she corrected. Get it right. Having

sex. Doing exactly what they had done on his couch three nights ago in Sydney.

Constantine hadn't moved. He was simply watching her, his arms folded over his chest, utterly cool and in control. She was suddenly sharply aware that she was being manipulated.

He wanted a refusal.

He had deliberately goaded her in order to get one. Interesting.

Why ask if she would sleep with him for money now, and in such an insulting manner, unless he had finally realized that he had been wrong about her two years ago?

"Last I heard," she said quietly, "you weren't finding it that hard to get a date."

"I take it that's a 'no.'"

"Take that as a definite 'no.'"

"Would the answer have been different if, instead of a temporary arrangement, I'd proposed marriage?"

Bleakly, Sienna decided, that question hurt even more than the last. She scanned the garden in order to get her bearings and find the quickest route back to her room. "There's no point to this conversation since you didn't propose. But since you're so interested..." Hating the huskiness in her voice, she started toward an indentation in the wall that looked like a door. "If I ever do marry, the relationship and my husband will have to fit around my needs."

"I take it that means Ambrosi Pearls?"

A sharp thrill coursed down her spine when she became aware that Constantine had padded up close behind her. As she stepped deeper into the inky shadows that swamped the courtyard, the notion that she was not only being maneuvered but actively hunted, intensified. "Not anymore, since you're intent on relieving me of that particular burden."

Halting at the wall, she studied the door, searching for a way to open it. Like the problems in her life, there did not appear to be a simple answer.

"Interesting," he muttered, "that you should use the word burden. I would never have guessed that you craved freedom."

"Freedom. Now there's a concept." The thought of being free of the debt burden was suddenly, unexpectedly heady, even if it did mean the demise of the company.

Guilt for the disloyal thought fueled her irritation as she pushed at the door. It gave only slightly. Frustration gripped her. She was over being a victim, especially of garden designers. "Please tell me this opens."

Constantine reached down and released a small latch she hadn't noticed in the dark. His arm brushed hers, sending a small shock of awareness through her. Her frustration mounted, both at her knee-jerk response and the fact that the door swung open with well-oiled ease. She was certain that at some level, Constantine was enjoying this and, abruptly, she lost her temper.

Two more steps and the conversation would be over, for tonight. "Back to the hypothetical marriage." As she stepped past Constantine, she deliberately trailed one finger down the lapel of his jacket.

The gesture was intimate, provocative, a dangerous form of payback that registered in the silvery heat of his gaze. "If you are considering a proposal, like I said in Sydney, if the prospective husband just happens to have a healthy bank balance and a flair for financial matters, as far as I'm concerned the situation would be win-win."

Constantine controlled the fierce heat flowing through him as Sienna strode down the path that led back to the resort's main reception area. She mounted a set of stone steps, the champagne silk gown swirling around outrageously sexy high heels. For a split second, the garden lights glowed through the dress, outlining her long, shapely legs, giving the momentary illusion that she was naked.

As distracting as the thought of Sienna naked was, it was the image of her naked and wearing Medinian bridal jewels that was consuming him at that moment.

Constantine briefly acknowledged the security guard he had tasked with protecting Sienna as the man stepped past him and followed her at a discreet distance. There were no serious threats on Medinos but, after the stir she had caused by attending his hotel opening wearing bridal jewels, the paparazzi were bound to hear about it.

Added to that, Alex Panopoulos was here and on the hunt. Constantine didn't regard the Greek as a serious threat, but if he tried to approach Sienna, Constantine wanted to know about it.

When both Sienna and the bodyguard had disappeared from sight, he closed the courtyard door with quiet deliberation and locked it.

It had gone against all of his instincts to let her go, when what he'd really wanted was to cement his claim. But there would be time enough for that, and he knew if he touched her now he wouldn't be content with playing the part of a restrained lover.

He hadn't liked hurting her, but she had pushed him with the jewels and the dress. He had needed to see her reaction to his proposition and he had gotten the result he had wanted. Despite ruthlessly using his company's promotional event to target new sales avenues for Ambrosi Pearls, she had refused to sleep with him to save her company.

What he hadn't bargained on, ever since he had seen her at the funeral, was his own response.

Just days ago he had been certain of Sienna's involvement in her father's scam. But the second she had lifted her head and looked at him at her father's funeral, as if they were still lovers, he had been the one who had been unmasked. He had wanted her whether she was innocent or guilty.

He had studied all of the paperwork and Ambrosi Pearls' financials. There was no tangible link between Sienna and the money Roberto had siphoned out of his father.

Two years ago he had miscalculated. He was determined not to do so a second time.

He wanted Sienna, but as far as he was concerned there were now only two options. It was either strictly business, or bed.

Ten

Dawn streaked the horizon with shades of gold, purple and rose as Sienna walked to the largest of a network of tropically landscaped pools. Shivering slightly at the cool dampness of the morning—supplemented by the resort's sprinkler system, which jetted vaporized water into the air—she eased out of her sandals.

A faint movement caught her eye as she dropped her towel, key and sarong onto one of the resort's deck chairs. The bodyguard who had followed her to her suite the previous night was standing beneath one of the palms. Annoyed, but determined to ignore him so long as he kept his distance, she walked into the water.

She swam energetically for a few minutes then turned on her back to catch her breath. The snick-snick of the sprinklers had stopped, replaced by slow dripping as lush palms shed excess water onto smooth limestone paving.

The deep quiet of the early morning gradually sank in, mending the ravages of a mostly sleepless night.

Constantine had offered to clear Ambrosi Pearls' debt if she slept with him.

Taking a deep breath, she ducked and breaststroked the length of the pool underwater, using the discipline of the physical challenge to cool her escalating temper. When she surfaced at the opposite end her lungs were burning.

On a scale of insults, she guessed it wasn't any worse than the ones he'd leveled at her two years ago, but the fact that he still viewed her that way after all this time was infuriating. If she had wanted to marry money, she could easily have found herself a rich husband by now. She hadn't. Two years after their split, she had barely dated.

Unlike Constantine.

Which brought her back to the manipulation angle.

For reasons of his own, Constantine wanted her off balance. Given his stake in Ambrosi Pearls, the reason couldn't be a business one. He already held all of the cards in terms of money and power. Barring a miracle from de Vries, Ambrosi Pearls was at his mercy; whatever Constantine wanted to happen, would happen. All she could do was plea bargain for her family and the staff.

If it was anyone but Constantine she might assume he wanted revenge, except he could have had that two years ago. All he'd had to do was expose the scandal of her father's dealings and the press would have ripped her reputation to shreds. He had chosen not to do that, saving her that final humiliation.

She frowned, her thoughts going back to Constantine's proposition.

The fact that he had made an offer, couched in business terms, meant he would be prepared to pay, and that, she decided, made him insect material.

Feeling happier with her assessment of him, she swam another length, kicked toward the steps and walked out of the water, slicking wet hair out of her eyes.

Movement sent tension zinging through her. Not the security guy or Constantine. Alex Panopoulos was ensconced on the deck chair next to hers.

He pushed to his feet, her towel in his hands as she approached. "Do you usually swim alone?"

Sienna smiled coolly, her gaze missing his by a calculated few millimeters. "I swim for exercise, not company."

Predictably, he didn't let go of the towel when he handed it over, so that she had to engage in a miniature tug-of-war to pull it free.

Annoyed by the game, and feeling exposed in her bikini when he was fully dressed, she forced another cool smile. "Mr. Panopoulos, if you don't give me the towel, I'll walk back to my suite without it."

"Alex, please." With a shrug he let the towel go. "I was hoping you would agree to be my date at lunch."

"Sorry, I already have a date." She quickly dried off as Panopoulos persevered with a predictable stream of conversation then wrapped the sarong around her breasts.

A flash of movement caught her eye. Constantine, dressed in low-riding gray sweatpants and a soft, faded muscle shirt, as if he'd been jogging, was strolling toward her from the direction of her room. Realization dawned. Constantine's bodyguard had informed him that she had company at the pool.

Constantine nodded at Panopoulos, his greeting curt. His gaze locked on hers. "Are you ready to go?"

Suddenly any male threat that Panopoulos posed seemed ridiculously tame. Panopoulos's face actually paled as Constantine collected her things.

Sienna scooped up the damp towel. "What took you so long?"

His hand cupped her elbow, and they were moving. She managed to pull free without making it look like a fight. Reflexively, she rubbed her elbow, which tingled with warmth. "Thanks for the rescue, but you don't have to take it this far. I can cope."

Sunlight glanced off the grim line of his jaw. "What did Panopoulos want?"

"That's none of your business."

"If he's bothering you I'll take care of it."

"The same way you deal with newspaper reporters?"

A glint of amusement entered his eyes. "No." Sienna was transfixed by an emotion she absolutely did not want to feel: a primitive surge of satisfaction because her man had stepped in and claimed her.

Her man. Her heart pounded once, hard. She must be out of her mind. She should resent Constantine's actions; she should be fighting with him. Instead her body was in the process of a slow, steady meltdown.

She stopped walking, forcing him to halt. "Why are you having me watched?"

"Not watched, looked after. A couple of the major tabloids have published speculative stories linking us romantically. And Panopoulos hasn't exactly kept his mouth closed about what he wants."

"I can deal with Panopoulos."

His gaze narrowed. "Like you did just then?"

A door slammed. Voices and laughter pierced the air, unnaturally loud in the morning stillness. Sienna was suddenly acutely aware that the sarong had soaked up the dripping moisture from her hair and her bikini and had become transparent where it clung.

Two young children barreled along the path, followed

by their parents. Sienna stepped aside to allow them passage. It was time to take some control back.

She held out her hand, palm up. "Sandals and room key, please."

Annoyingly, Constantine handed them over as if there wasn't an issue. She slipped her feet into the sandals, and wished she had thought to bring dark glasses. They did a great job of shouting "distance," which right now she desperately needed.

The rising sun shone directly in her eyes as she rounded a curve in the path, determined to put some distance between herself and Constantine. Because her feet were wet, her sandals kept slipping, making walking awkward.

Constantine easily kept pace beside her. "Be careful, those pavers are slippery."

"I'm fine."

In an effort to put more space between them, she edged sideways, and then she did slip.

Constantine's hand briefly closed on her arm, steadying her. "Why don't you ever listen?"

She jerked free and stalked the rest of the way to her door. "When you say something I'm interested in hearing, I'll listen."

"That'll be when hell freezes over, then."

The words were bitten out, but laced with an amused exasperation that, frustratingly, charmed her and made her want to bite back and bait him a little more.

Grimly, she fitted the key card in its slot. "You know what, Constantine? Maybe you should stop worrying about what I'm doing and get yourself a life."

"What makes you think I don't get exactly what I want?"

The low, sexy register of his voice froze her in place. Now was the time to back off, to step inside and politely close the door, but his gaze held her locked in some kind of stasis. She knew what it was; she had spent enough time analyzing why she had fallen so hard for Constantine in the first place. It was the alpha male thing; he took control and for reasons unknown, she responded. In this case he had dealt with Panopoulos as easily if he had been shooing a fruit fly away and she couldn't help but be impressed.

"I came over this morning to apologize. I'm sorry about the position I put you in last night, but I had to know. I also owe you an apology for what happened two years ago."

She blinked, struggling with the abrupt mental shift. Of all the scenarios she had gone over in her mind, she had never imagined that Constantine would apologize for their breakup. "What made you change your mind?"

"I did some research—"

"You mean you had me investigated."

"Call it what you like," he said flatly. "All of your financial dealings and business practices are straight down the middle. Roberto was the taker; you were the giver. Nothing in your pattern indicated that you would resort to fraud. And after what happened two years ago, and the fact that you had never tried to contact me again for money or anything else, I decided it didn't make sense that you were involved in this deal."

Sienna briefly saw red over the way he had arrived at his verdict. "Let me get this clear. Because I didn't ask you for money after we split up, I'm okay?"

A pulse jumped along the side of his jaw. "It's standard practice to run security checks on business associates."

"Tell me, did you have me profiled two years ago before you decided to date me?"

"Calm down," he said curtly, as if she was actually going to follow that order.

Fingers shaking with outrage, she started to tap in the

PIN that unlocked her door but before she could complete the sequence, he snagged the key card out of the slot and slipped it into his pocket.

"Oh, this is good. A repeat of the he-man tactics."

His brows jerked together. "What he-man tactics?"

She began to tick them off on her fingers. "The threat over my father's grave, holding me against my will in your car, forcing me to meet you the night after the funeral—"

"I didn't hold you against your will. We were in a supermarket parking lot. If you hadn't avoided me for four days, the meetings would have been conducted in a conventional business setting."

"I had no reason to want to see you. If you'll remember, the last conversation we had wasn't exactly pleasant."

"Which is why I'm apologizing now."

"Two years too late, and it's the worst apology I've ever heard."

His gaze glittered in the dim coolness of the portico that shaded her door. "Nevertheless, you're going to hear the rest of it. I tracked the loan payments. They were all deposited into one of your father's personal accounts, not Ambrosi Pearls' working account."

"That's right, one of Dad's gambling accounts, which was why I couldn't be sure the money wasn't winnings. If you knew that, why ask if I'd sleep with you for money, when you already knew I wouldn't?"

"You weren't involved in your father's loan scam, but that didn't mean you didn't know about it."

"So you tested me." Okay, she had expected that. She understood that a lot of women would be attracted to Constantine simply because he was so rich and powerful. But that didn't excuse him for thinking she could be one of them, or the fact that he still didn't get her.

She met his gaze squarely, which was a mistake, because Constantine's eyes were one of the most potent things about him. They pierced and held with a steady power that had always made her go weak at the knees. "Apology accepted, as far as it went, but I'd prefer that we just stuck to business. Like, for example, what time can we meet today?"

She knew about the official luncheon, because she had an invitation. There was also some kind of photo shoot for Medinos's most famous export, gold, scheduled for later in the day. "I've got meetings most of this morning, so I've slotted you in after lunch."

"Good, because I'm booked to fly out this evening." An early afternoon meeting would also give her the time she needed to meet with Northcliffe and hopefully wrap up the de Vries deal.

"I don't believe you personally wanted the money two years ago," he said abruptly. "What I could never accept was the fact that you gave your loyalty to your father and your company instead of to me."

"I was afraid you'd break the engagement if you found out, which you did, so I guess the lack of trust goes both ways."

His fingers tangled in her wet hair. "Two years ago," he muttered huskily, "I wasn't thinking straight."

Her stomach tensed against the tingling warmth of his touch. "Are you saying you were wrong?"

"I'm saying I shouldn't have let you go."

His answer neatly slid away from the admission she had wanted, but when his palm cupped her nape, a pang of old longing mingled with a raw jolt of desire shafted through her.

Eleven

Constantine's head dipped. Sienna had plenty of time to avoid the kiss, a long drawn out moment to understand that this was exactly the result she had wanted, and then his mouth settled on hers.

Her palms landed on his chest, curled into soft interlock. The hot scents of male and sweat filled her nostrils, triggering memories. Flash after hot flash of his long, muscled body against hers, the damp drag of skin, his hands on her hips, the intense pleasure she'd derived from every touch. The shattering intimacy of making love…

She went up on her toes, leaned into the kiss. A small sound shivered up from deep in her belly. He stepped closer, moving her back a half step until her spine settled against the cool barrier of the door. His hold was loose enough that she could easily pull free. One hand still cupped her nape, the other was spread across the small of her back, but, contrarily, having the choice granted her the freedom to stay.

Somewhere in the back of her mind she was aware that she shouldn't be responding to a man she had spent two years avoiding for a whole list of excellent reasons. Surrendering to him physically went against common sense and plain old-fashioned pride. But a reckless, starved part of her wasn't interested in reason and logic.

Her arms curled around his neck. The unmistakable firmness of his arousal pressed against her belly, sending a shaft of heat through her, and a fierce, crazy elation. Two years, and nothing had changed.

She still wanted him and she had no earthly clue why. For example, why didn't she feel this way about the occasional nice man she had dated since Constantine? Why hadn't she fallen into adoring lust with any one of the hundreds of bronzed, attractive stockbrokers and nine-to-five guys who littered Sydney's Central Business District?

She could have a pleasant, comfortable life with someone who actually loved her. A home, babies…

His mouth slid to her throat. The rough scrape of his jaw sent another raw shudder through her. Gulping air, she dragged his mouth back to hers.

The problem was she responded to Constantine in a way she didn't respond to any other man. It was depressing to think that she might actually be drawn to him because he was so difficult to handle, that after years of suppressing her own desires in order to save Ambrosi Pearls, she needed the battle to feel alive.

Lust was lust, it didn't impress her overly and it had never gotten the best of her before now. She was healthy, with a normal sex drive, but she was also ultrapicky. She didn't just like things so-so; they had to be perfect. Flowers had to be perfectly arranged, her accessories had to complement what she was wearing, otherwise she couldn't concentrate on anything but the fact that something was wrong, even if it was only one minor detail.

A natural extension of that pickiness was that the men in her life had to be right. They had to look right, smell right, feel right, otherwise she just wasn't interested.

Though he was too big, too experienced, too dangerous—nearly more than she could handle—Constantine did smell and taste and feel right, when no one else had ever come close.

His hand slid up over her waist and rib cage. The heat of his palm burned through the sarong as he cupped her breast and gently squeezed. The pad of his thumb rasped over her nipple. A sharp, edgy tension gripped her and for an endless moment her mind went utterly blank. His thumb moved in a lazy circle. The tension coiled tighter, and her mind snapped back into gear.

Oh, no. No way.

She pulled free, banging the back of her head against the door in the process. "I can't do this, not again. I need my key."

When he calmly handed it to her, she lodged it in the lock, tapped in the PIN and shoved the door wide.

She swiped up her towel, which she must have dropped at some point. "That kiss was a mistake. I'm here on business. I can't allow anything to mess that up."

"Don't worry, Ambrosi Pearls will be taken care of."

The breeze plastered the soft tank against the muscled contours of his chest. A resurgence of the hot, edgy tension that had gripped her when he had cupped her breast made her stomach tighten and her nerves hum. "What does that mean, exactly?"

He dipped his head and kissed her again, and like a quivering, weak-kneed fool she let him.

"Simple. I want you back."

Heart pounding, Sienna locked the door. After showering, she blow-dried her hair, applied makeup with fingers that were annoyingly unsteady, then checked her reflection: cream pants, cream camisole, Ambrosi pearl accessories. Cool, calm and classy, the exact opposite of the way she felt.

Constantine wanted her back.

He had said Ambrosi Pearls would be taken care of, although that didn't make sense because the one fact Constantine had always made clear was that he had no interest in committing the cardinal sin of mixing business and pleasure.

After collecting her sample case, she walked to Northcliffe's suite. Just minutes into the meeting, when Northcliffe discreetly checked the time on his watch, Sienna realized her sales pitch wasn't going well.

A short time later, Sienna replaced the sample case in the safe in her room and booted up her laptop. Stunningly, despite keeping her dangling for weeks and showing a good deal of interest, Northcliffe had declined to place an order.

Without a major deal in the pipeline, Ambrosi Pearls was officially in financial jeopardy. With no further sources of revenue, there was nothing to stop Constantine taking the company.

Still in shock at her utter lack of success, Sienna opened up her sheets of financials then put a call through to the company accountant. Sydney was eight hours ahead of Medinos, which meant that her early morning call came in midafternoon for Brian Chin.

After a terse conversation regarding their options—basically none—she asked to be put through to Carla.

Carla was predictably to the point. "Have you talked to Constantine?"

"Not yet, but he has indicated that he will look after the company."

"I'll bet."

They both knew that Constantine was entitled to take the company and break it up if he wanted; after all he had paid for it. If he allowed Ambrosi Pearls to keep trading, that was the best-case scenario.

What worried Sienna most now was that the heavily mortgaged Pier Point house and her mother's small apartment in town, which were both tied in with the company, would go. They had already sold the town house to meet debts. After everything her mother had been through, and in her present fragile state, the thought that she would literally lose everything made Sienna sick to her stomach.

"Did he give you any details about just how he's going to look after Ambrosi Pearls?"

Sienna's cheeks heated. "He didn't go into fine detail." Unless she could count the slow stroke of his fingers at her nape, the glide of his mouth over her throat…

"I'm getting subtext."

"We were…arguing."

There was a taut silence. "He is after you again. I saw the way he was watching you at the funeral. And he went with you to the house afterward. I mean, why was he there at all? Why didn't he just send his legal counsel?"

Sienna finished the call, but Carla's words had sent a small unwelcome shock wave through her. Since she had closed the door on Constantine she had kept herself busy, specifically so she couldn't think, because every time she considered his statement that he wanted her back, her brain froze and her hormones kicked in.

The thought that he had wanted her back before he had landed in Sydney added a layer of calculation to his motives.

He had apologized. Not in a way that made her feel good, but in a factual, male way that told her he was telling the truth. He believed she hadn't been involved in the current scam, but not that she couldn't be an opportunist when it came to money.

He wanted her back, but she couldn't go back into a relationship when she knew Constantine still didn't trust her. Something was going to have to change. He was going to have to change, and she didn't know if that was possible.

The bedside phone rang while Sienna was changing for lunch. Her stomach performing somersaults, because it was most likely Constantine, she picked up the receiver.

It was Tomas.

"Good morning," he murmured in his precise English. "Constantine is busy with meetings until twelve and has asked me to brief you."

"Let me get some paper." Sienna tossed the floaty floral dress she planned to wear over the bed and found a pad and pen in the top drawer of the bedside table. She picked up the phone, expecting to jot down numbers and legal details.

There was a brief pause. "I'm afraid you misunderstand. The briefing concerns lunch."

"Lunch?"

"That's correct."

Tomas followed up with a clipped list of do's and don'ts that sounded like something out of a Victorian diary. Modest dress was essential, with a discreet décolletage and a length preferably below the knee. Low-key makeup and jewelry were advised.

There was a small pause. "There will be a large press contingent at the product launch. Mr. Atraeus has requested that you adhere to his requirements."

The receiver clicked gently in her ear. Sienna listened to the dial tone for several seconds before putting the phone back on its rest.

She stepped out onto her private patio and took a deep breath. Unfortunately, her patio garden, aside from a gorgeous view of Ambrus, also framed the Atraeus fortress where it commanded the headland and a good deal of the island.

Not good.

Her temper still on slow burn, she stepped back inside, repacked the floral dress and shook out a sleek white Audrey Hepburn–inspired sheath that came to midthigh and extracted the flower pearl set from the sample case.

After the disappointment of the meeting with Northcliffe, she had no desire to drink champagne and smile and pretend that everything in Ambrosi Pearls' world was fabulous. Now that the company's fate was sealed, she would have preferred to stay out of the public eye and away from the press.

She had even less desire to follow Constantine's orders.

Minutes later, she checked her hair, which she'd pinned into a smoothly elegant chignon. The style was sophisticated and timeless, a good match for the opulent pearls at her lobes and throat.

The hair and the jewelry were perfect; the dress, however, failed to meet the criteria Tomas had outlined. The scoop neckline displayed a tantalizing hint of golden cleavage, the dress was short enough to reveal the fact that she had great legs, and in no way was the dress inconspicuous.

She sprayed herself with perfume then, on impulse, tucked a delicate white orchid from the tabletop arrangement behind one ear.

The flower transformed the look from sexy sophistication to something approximating bridal.

Satisfied with the result, she slipped into strappy white heels that made her legs look even longer, picked up a matching white clutch and left the room.

Constantine wouldn't miss the message, and that was fine with her. The sooner he realized she would not allow him to control her, the better.

Twelve

Lunch was an elegant affair, with a marquee on the lawn, a classical quartet playing and a well-known opera diva singing.

As Sienna strolled through the garden she spotted Constantine, who was wearing a gauzy white shirt over dark close-fitting pants. He glanced at her. She smiled coolly at a spot somewhere over his left shoulder and pretended she hadn't seen him.

A number of willowy models, dressed as brightly as birds of paradise, swayed through the crowd, weighted down with Atraeus gold. Sienna stiffened as she recognized two prominent gossip columnists sipping champagne, one of whom had relentlessly defamed her following the breakup.

She paused by a heavily guarded display cabinet showcasing exquisite gold and diamond jewelry. The reason for the two armed security guards was clear. Aside from the small fortune in jewelry displayed, the centerpiece was a pale pink baguette diamond ring that glittered with a soft fire. Very rare and hugely expensive.

"Sienna?" The editor of a prominent women's magazine paused beside her, smiling brightly.

Sienna braced herself to make polite, guarded conversation, ignoring a hot pulse of adrenaline when she realized Constantine was walking directly toward her.

The editor briefly studied Sienna's pearl necklace. "I love the pieces you're wearing." She made brief notes about the pearls and Ambrosi Pearls' upcoming collection.

When she moved on, Sienna's attention was drawn back to Constantine who had been waylaid by a pretty woman dressed in an elegant pants suit. She recognized Maria Stefano, the daughter of a prominent European racing magnate, because she had recently been photographed with Constantine at a high-profile charity function.

Maria wound her arms around Constantine's neck and leaned into him for a cooing hug. Constantine's expression as he gazed into her upturned face was amused, bordering on indulgent, and the sudden tension in Sienna's stomach intensified.

Realization hit her like a kick in the chest. She needed to walk someplace quiet and bang her head against a brick wall, because she was jealous of Maria Stefano.

The reason she was jealous was just as straightforward: she was still in love with Constantine.

Her chest squeezed tight. For a long moment she couldn't breathe, then oxygen whooshed back into her lungs, making her head spin. Constantine was single, fatally attractive and hugely wealthy. It was a fact that if he wanted a woman, he usually got her. Over the past two years he had dated a number of women, but until now they had mostly been blank faces and bodies. It had been easy to ignore the gossip because he had never had a steady girlfriend.

A photographer aimed a camera their way. Maria slid her arm around Constantine's waist and posed. By then several other cameras were clicking. Seconds later, Constantine excused himself, cutting the photo session short.

When he reached her side any trace of indulgence was gone. "You don't have to be jealous."

Sienna concentrated on the jewelry in the case and tried to ignore her body's automatic reaction to Constantine's piercing gaze, the clean masculine scent of his skin. "I am not jealous."

"Then stop worrying about other women."

Heat and a totally male focus burned in his eyes. If she'd had any doubt about his intentions or the lovemaking in Sydney, they were gone. He really did want her back.

Although, she was certain that a long-term relationship or marriage were not on Constantine's agenda. All he wanted was a wild, short-term fling.

That he expected her to jump back into bed with him after the sneaky way he had used her financial situation to maneuver her made Sienna so furious she had to unclench her jaw before she could speak. "Why don't we just go to your office now and talk about the loan agreement your father and mine cooked up and see where that takes us?"

Wariness flickered in his gaze. "Not yet," he said mildly. "Unless you came all this way to hand me a check."

"If there was a check, I would have mailed it."

"That's what I thought, in which case we'll stick to the schedule and discuss finances after lunch."

A camera flashed almost directly in her eyes. The photographers who had been so interested in Constantine and Maria were now concentrating on her.

A waiter offered her a glass of champagne. She refused

the drink, although for a split second tipping the chilled contents down Constantine's shirtfront was an irresistibly satisfying image. She had a better idea.

She half turned, brushing close to Constantine as she continued her perusal of the jewelry in the display case.

His gaze dropped to her mouth, and a small hot thrill shot through her. She had been so busy concentrating on Constantine's power and dominance, she had forgotten that she wielded her own power, that two years ago, for a short time at least, he hadn't been able to resist her.

His gaze rested briefly on the white orchid in her hair. "Damn, what are you up to?"

She kept her expression bland. "If you don't want to talk about business now, that's fine by me, but I'm in the jewelry trade and I am here on business. I'd like to take a closer look at the contents of this cabinet."

One hand was casually propped on the display cabinet behind her. To a casual observer they must have looked cozily intimate. For long moments, she thought Constantine was going to refuse, that she had overplayed her hand with the bridal theme—that he could see the sudden crazy plan she had formulated.

Just when she thought he would refuse, he nodded at one of the security guards, who stepped forward and unlocked the case.

Feeling wary but exhilarated, because what she was about to do was risky, she examined the array of beautifully crafted jewelry. Before she could change her mind she selected the largest ring, the pink diamond baguette. As engagement rings went, it would one day make some woman blissfully happy. "Four carats?"

Constantine's gaze was coolly impatient. "Maybe five."

"But then diamond rings aren't your thing, are they?"

He had never given her one, because their engagement had ended before the ring he had commissioned was ready.

After two years the lack of a ring shouldn't matter but in Sienna's opinion, and her mother's, not presenting a ring when he had proposed had been a telling factor.

According to Margaret Ambrosi and Aunt Via if a man didn't humbly offer a ring when he proposed—the best possible ring he could afford—that was a *sign*. The ring wasn't about money; it was about sacrifice. If a man truly loved a woman then he would be more than happy to demonstrate his love to the world by putting his ring on her finger.

To make matters worse, the lack of a ring had somehow made their weeklong engagement seem even more insubstantial. To Constantine the exquisite jewel was just a pretty, expensive trinket, without meaning beyond the calculated profit margin. No sentiment and definitely no emotion involved.

They were almost completely encircled by media now and the security guards weren't happy. Jaw taut, she held the ring out to Constantine. When his hand automatically opened, she dropped it into his palm. She registered the stir of shocked interest, his flash of surprise the moment he logged her not-so-subtle message that this time she wouldn't accept anything less than marriage.

The cool metal of the ring burned Constantine's palm. As his fingers closed around the band, his annoyance— at Sienna for wearing a dress that had every red-blooded man drooling, for wearing the same set of pearls she'd had on when they had made love on his sofa—dissolved.

The reporters and the buzz of conversation faded. He felt as if an electrical charge had just been run through his system, lifting all the fine hairs at his nape.

The bridal white, the pearls and the ring were a statement.

He had gotten the message—loud and clear.

Grimly, he decided he should have expected that she would hit back. In a moment of clarity, he realized that if he had wanted a woman who would allow herself to be dictated to, he would never have chosen Sienna. The CEO of a company that would have been highly successful if Roberto Ambrosi hadn't drained its profits. Sienna was formidable and a handful, and in that moment he was clear on one fact: she was his.

Instead of replacing the ring in the case he clasped her left wrist and slipped the ring neatly on to her third finger. "I would have chosen the white diamond," he murmured.

Shock registered in Sienna's gaze as he slid his arm around her waist, curving her into his side. "Looks like the wedding's on."

His expression controlled, Constantine made brief eye contact with the head of his security team as cameras flashed and the questions started.

Keeping Sienna clamped firmly to his side, he forged a path through the reporters. Moments later, with the help of security, they were clear.

Sienna sent him a stunned look. "Why did you do that?"

"The gesture was self-evident."

She made a strangled sound.

Constantine's jaw tightened. "After what you pulled, both last night and today, no one will believe you didn't angle for marriage."

"You didn't have to compound the issue by putting the ring on my finger."

"It was a spur-of-the-moment thing."

Unlike the past two years which had been ordered and precise, and without any discernible excitement. Seven days ago, he had been okay with that. As the Americans would say, all his ducks had been in a row. Now he wasn't sure if he could live without the chaos. "What I'd like to know is why you decided on the bridal theme?"

For a moment, he was caught between amusement and frustration and a definitely un-PC impulse that would ensure they were front-page news.

The glass doors of the hotel slid open.

Sienna threw him a suspicious glance. "Where are you taking me?"

Constantine felt like saying "To bed," but managed to pull back from that precipice. "The manager's office."

"Oh, goody," she muttered. "I've been wanting to check out all day."

Ignoring startled looks from hotel staff and guests, Constantine hustled Sienna down a corridor and into the large executive suite he had been using as his office, and kicked the door closed behind him.

Sienna spun to face him. "That was a press announcement out there."

He leaned against the door and folded his arms across his chest. "You wanted to play, those are my rules. Last night you turned up at my hotel opening wearing what looked like Medinian bridal jewels. On Medinos that amounts to an engagement announcement."

Her cheeks heated. "I've already told you, I had no idea the jewels we designed on the basis of Sebastien's drawing were wedding jewels! How do you think my family will feel when they open up tomorrow's newspapers and discover we're now supposed to be engaged?"

Her dark gaze held his and another one of those sharp, heady thrills burned through him. The past two years had definitely been flat. "You want me to issue a denial about the engagement?"

"It wouldn't be the first time." She yanked the ring off

her finger and dumped it in his palm. "And in the process it's entirely possible that this time you could look bad."

Given the string of stories dating back to the first broken engagement and the fact that she was presently grieving for her father, make that very bad. Worse, he decided, he would look like a man who couldn't make up his mind or control his woman.

Turning on her heel, Sienna paced to the French doors, which opened out onto a patio. A shadowy movement, visible through the sheer curtains that filtered the overbright sun, stopped her in her tracks.

Constantine dropped the ring in his pocket and strolled behind the large mahogany desk that dominated the room. "If you're thinking of making a break for it, I wouldn't advise it. That could have been a security guard, but more likely it's a reporter trying to get an exclusive through the windows."

Her gaze snapped back to his. "Any publicity generated will be brief. Without a wedding, the story will die a natural death. Just like it did last time."

For a long, drawn out moment silence vibrated between them. Time for a change of tactic.

"All right," he said calmly. "Let's talk. As it happens, now is the perfect time."

He gestured toward one of the chairs grouped to one side of the desk.

A tension he hadn't been aware of eased when Sienna finally moved away from the French doors and took one of the seats he'd indicated. Picking up the briefcase he had deposited in the office earlier in the day, he extracted a set of documents and slid them across the glossy desktop.

Sienna frowned as she skimmed the first sheet. "I don't understand. I thought this would be a straightforward transfer of shares to cover the debt."

She returned her attention to the contract. Overhead a fan slowly circled, with a soft, rhythmic swishing.

Too tense to sit, Constantine took up a position in front of the French doors, standing in almost the same spot that Sienna had, unconsciously blocking at least one exit. He frowned when he realized what he was doing. He guessed, in its crudest form, the paperwork was another form of exit-blocking.

Sienna skimmed the final page of the document. He logged the moment she found the marriage clause.

Shooting to her feet, she dropped the contract on the desk, her eyes dark with shock. "This is a marriage deal?"

"That's correct." Grimly, Constantine outlined the terms, even though he knew that Sienna, with her background in law, would have no problem deciphering the legalese.

Part of the deal was that she signed the transfer of the lease on the old pearl facility on Ambrus and the water rights to The Atraeus Group. In return, her family would retain a minority holding in Ambrosi Pearls. All debts and mortgages would be cleared, including those on the family house in Pier Point and Margaret Ambrosi's city apartment. Constantine had undertaken to reinvest in the company and retain all jobs. With the income from their shares, all three Ambrosi women would be able to live comfortable, debt-free lives.

Sienna shook her head. "I don't understand. If you need a wife, you could have any number of women. You could marry someone who has money—"

Relief loosened the tension that gripped him as he had braced for a refusal. He had known she wanted him, but until that moment he hadn't known whether or not she would agree to marriage. "I want *you*."

"Two years ago you threw everything away because of a loan."

"Two years ago I made a mistake."

He had a sudden flash of the night they'd first made love, the roses and the champagne, the sweetness and laughter when he'd let her seduce him. The chemistry between them had been riveting. He had spent two years without Sienna. Despite his crammed schedule and the fact that he had been absorbed with the challenge of running The Atraeus Group, it suddenly felt like he'd spent two years in a waiting room. "There is nothing complicated about what I want."

Shaking her head, she picked up her clutch, which she'd placed on the desktop. "You and I and marriage... It doesn't make sense."

He covered the distance between them and drew her into a loose hold. She had plenty of time to pull back, and he was careful not to push the physical intimacy, but it was a plain fact that, right now, touching her was paramount. He needed to cement his claim.

Taking the clutch from her, he placed it back on the desk and linked his fingers with hers. This close he could smell the flowery sweetness of her perfume, the faint scent of the orchid in her hair. "We share a common heritage. Marriage made sense two years ago."

"Two years ago we had an ordinary, normal courtship."

"Which is precisely why this should work now."

He lowered his mouth to hers, keeping a tight rein on his desire. One second passed, two. Her lips softened beneath his. She lifted up on her toes, and in agonizingly slow increments wound her arms around his neck and fitted her body to his. His arms tightened around her, exultation coursing through him at her surrender.

His cell phone buzzed, breaking the moment. Curbing

his frustration, Constantine released Sienna to answer the call.

Tomas. He strolled to the window and listened, his attention split as Sienna picked up the contract and studied the pages, her profile as marble-smooth and remote as a sculpture.

She wanted him. He was almost certain that she loved him, but he was aware that neither fact would guarantee her acceptance, and he wasn't prepared to compromise. When serious money had entered his parents' relationship equation, his mother had used the wealth to finance her exit from their lives. His father had remarried, but his wealth had also opened the door to a number of stormy extramarital relationships. With the debacle of his previous engagement to Sienna, Constantine had decided that the one thing he required in his marriage was control.

The contract was cold-blooded, directly counter to the way he felt, but if they were going to do this, he needed clear-cut terms. He would not live the way his father had done, at the mercy of his desires, or allow Sienna to run roughshod over him. This time there would be no gray areas and no hidden agendas.

Sienna's head jerked up as he disconnected the call. The orchid, he noticed, had dropped from her hair and lay crushed on the floor.

Her gaze met his, outwardly calm and cool but dark with emotion. "How much time do I have to think this over?"

Constantine slid the phone into his pocket. "I need a decision now."

Thirteen

Sienna lowered herself into the chair she had previously vacated, the leather cool enough against the backs of her thighs to send a faint shiver down her spine. "What happens if I say no?"

Constantine's gaze was unreadable. "I can have another, more straightforward document drawn up if you don't sign this deal."

The alternative document would be the one she had expected, taking everything—the business, her mother's house and apartment. It would, no doubt, make a large number of Ambrosi employees redundant, and could spell the end of Ambrosi Pearls altogether.

Constantine had made his position clear. There was chemistry enough to smooth the way, but this wasn't a courtship, or even a proposal. It was a contract, a marriage of convenience.

For a moment, after the softness of that kiss, she had

hoped he would say something crazy and wonderful like, "I love you."

Although the time for those words and that moment had been two years ago and they hadn't ensured happiness.

The flowery romantic love that had originally swept her off her feet was long gone, and she wasn't sure she wanted it back. The illusion of love had hurt.

Despite the pragmatism, hope flared. Maybe Constantine didn't love her, but this time, despite the enormity of what her father had done to the Atraeus family, he had fought for her.

Instead of abandoning her to his legal team, he had stepped in and protected her and her family from bankruptcy proceedings and the press. He had also gone to great lengths to protect and care for her mother and make sure she retained an income and her dignity. That counted for a lot.

Sienna aligned the pages until they were neatly stacked. Two years ago she had frozen like a deer in the headlights. She had let her father's actions dissolve her chance at happiness.

Her chin firmed. She didn't like the businesslike approach to something as personal and intimate as a marriage, but she acknowledged that business was Constantine's medium. The explanation for a contract like this, which practically corralled her with obligations to her family, to Ambrosi Pearls and to him, was so that Constantine could feel secure that she was tied in to the marriage. If he needed the extra assurance, that meant she really did matter to him. She didn't know if this would work, but she would never find out if she didn't try.

She took a deep breath. "All right."

Constantine didn't try to kiss her, for which she was grateful, he simply handed her a pen.

When they had both signed the documents, he called in a witness, one of the hotel receptionists. It was all over within minutes.

Constantine's phone buzzed as he locked the documents back in his briefcase. He answered his cell then checked his watch. "I need to be on-site with the contractors on Ambrus in an hour."

She picked up her clutch purse feeling faintly giddy at the leap she had taken. She needed food, and she needed time alone to come to terms with a future that just minutes ago had seemed wildly improbable. "I'll wait here."

"Oh, no, you won't." His jaw was grim. "You're coming with me. Now that we are officially engaged, I'm going to make sure you don't get another opportunity with the press."

Heat blasted off the enormous skeletal structure that was the construction site on Ambrus, shimmering like vapor in the air as the helicopter touched down on a huge slab of concrete.

Hot gusts from the rotors, peppered with stinging dust, whipped at her face and hair, as Constantine helped her out of the chopper. Sienna, who'd had just enough time to change into casual clothes and sneakers, grabbed her briefcase, which she had refused to leave behind.

Constantine would be busy with the contractor who was managing the construction of the hotel complex for a couple of hours, which suited her. There was an office, a modern concrete bunker she had spotted from the air, where she planned to crunch some numbers and catch up on some paperwork. If she found herself with time on her hands, she could always take a walk along the exquisite jewel-like bay.

Clearly, this wasn't a part of Ambrus that had ever been

used for anything more than grazing goats, nevertheless, it was beautiful and from a family history point of view any part of Ambrus interested her.

Anchoring dark glasses on the bridge of her nose, Sienna ducked to avoid the rotors. Constantine's arm clamped around her waist, tucking her into his side as he hustled her beneath the rotating blades. Disorientation hit her along with a wave of heat as she adjusted to his hold.

Ever since she had agreed to the marriage she had been off balance and a little shaky, although Constantine hadn't given her time to think. Ever since they had left the hotel's office, he'd kept her moving. She'd only had bare minutes alone, and that time had been pressurized, because she'd had to change clothes and pack her briefcase in time to make the flight.

She stepped off the concrete pad. Her pristine white sneakers sank into coarse sandy grit and were instantly coated. Automatically, she lengthened her stride, stepping out of Constantine's loose hold, but he kept pace with her easily, underlining the fact that they were now a couple.

Her cheeks burned at the knowledge, although no one in their right mind would attribute her flush to anything but the intense heat. Already her clothes were clinging to her skin and she could feel trickles of perspiration running down her spine and between her breasts.

Behind them the engine note of the chopper changed, the pitch higher, as if the pilot was preparing for takeoff. Sienna brushed whipping tendrils of hair out of her face as the helicopter did lift off then veered back toward the coast. "If that was our ride, how do we get out of here?"

By her reckoning, at this end of Ambrus, they were forty miles at least from Medinos. Not a great distance as the crow flies, but complicated by the barrier of the sea.

Constantine, who had walked on a few steps, calmly

waited for her to catch up. In faded jeans and leather boots, his eyes remote behind dark glasses, he no longer looked like a high-powered business executive but as much a part of the wild landscape as his warrior ancestors must have been. "Don't worry about the transport. I've taken care of it."

Sienna watched the helicopter turn into a small black dot on the horizon and the disorientation hit her again. "I could be crazy to trust you."

Out here there were no taxis and, according to Constantine, no cell phone service until they installed a repeater on one of the tall peaks in the interior. Telephone and internet communication was limited to the satellite connection in the office.

He held out his hand. "You've trusted me this far."

Sienna laced her fingers with his, the sense of risk subtly heightened by the casual intimacy. No matter how right it felt to try again with Constantine, she couldn't forget that just hours ago she had been uneasy about his agenda and certain that no matter how intense the attraction, there was no way a relationship could work.

The office was modern, well-appointed and wonderfully cool.

While Constantine was immersed in a discussion with the site manager, Jim Kady, Sienna appropriated an empty desk. She hadn't yet called either her mother or Carla, because Constantine had asked her to wait until they could inform both of their families. Although with the media stir following Constantine's announcement, she needed to call either that evening or first thing in the morning.

Setting her briefcase down on the desk, she eased out of her sneakers and shook the excess grit into a wastepaper basket. Padding through to the bathroom in her socks, she grabbed paper towels, dampened them then grabbed an extra handful of dry towels. When she returned to the office, Kady had left and Constantine was propped on the edge of the site manager's desk, taking a call.

She sat down, cleaned her shoes and brushed off her socks, which had a brownish tinge. She became aware of Constantine watching her, obviously amused by her perfectionist streak.

"You'll pay for this," she said lightly, trying to defuse the mounting awareness that she was alone with Constantine for the first time since they had signed the agreement.

His expression was oddly intent and ironic. "That I do know."

Her breath caught in her throat and her heart began to pound. It was a weird moment to understand that he liked her quirkiness, that he didn't just want sex and a controllable wife; he wanted her.

The sound of rotor blades filled the air as a helicopter skimmed low overhead.

Constantine checked his watch. "That'll be the engineer."

Relief flooded her. Rescue and reprieve. And the transport was back.

Just over two hours later, when Constantine's meeting was wrapped up, he walked back into the office.

Sienna kept her head down, ostensibly working on Ambrosi Pearls' figures, although it was little more than doodling with numbers. She would no longer be in charge of the major investment decisions, but after years of financial stress and buoyed by the heady opportunities ahead, it had been a pleasurable way to pass the time.

The heat hit her like a blow as she stepped outside with Constantine. In the distance the helicopter, which had been sitting on the pad, lifted into the air taking the group of suits attached to the contracting firm back to Medinos. Sienna checked to see if there was a second helicopter, just in case she had missed hearing it come in.

The pad was bare.

Constantine halted beside a four-wheel drive pickup truck that looked like a carbon copy of the truck Kady had parked outside the office, except this one had a bright blue tarp fastened over the bed.

When Constantine opened the passenger-side door, indicating they were driving somewhere, she dug her heels in. "I thought we were going back to Medinos."

"We are, but not just yet. While we're here, I wanted to show you the old pearl facility."

Which meant he had planned this. "If I don't get back soon, I'll miss my flight out."

"The company jet is on the runway at Medinos. You can catch a flight out on that when we get back."

His hands settled at her waist, and suddenly there was no air. He muttered something in Medinian. "I wasn't going to do this yet." Bending, he captured her mouth with his, the kiss hot and hungry and slow.

She froze, for long seconds caught off balance by the ruthless way he was conducting their so-called engagement and her knee-jerk response.

His mouth drifted along her jaw, she felt the edge of his teeth on her lobe. A small smothered sound escaped from her throat. His lips brushed hers again and her arms closed around his neck as she lifted up against him, returning the kiss.

He lifted his head. His forehead rested against hers. "Are you coming with me?"

Sienna let out a breath. This time he was asking, not demanding, but she was also suddenly aware that in spending time alone with Constantine she was agreeing to much more than a sightseeing tour.

The panic she'd felt in the office hit her again. She felt as jittery as a new bride, but she had agreed to marry him and it wasn't as if they hadn't made love before. "Okay."

Feeling distinctly wobbly, she climbed into the truck. Setting her briefcase down on the floor, she fastened her seat belt.

Constantine swung behind the wheel and put the truck in gear. Despite the fact that she had agreed to go with Constantine, the feeling of being herded was strong enough that she was about to demand he drive her back to the mine office when the VHF radio hissed static. Constantine answered the call and the moment passed.

Several minutes later the construction site was no longer visible. There was a rooster tail of dust behind them and the heat shimmer of the rugged island wilderness in front.

Time passed. At some point, lulled by the heat and the monotonous sound of the truck motor, she must have fallen asleep. Straightening, she brushed hair out of her eyes and checked her watch. A good thirty minutes had passed.

She frowned as she studied the road, which was now little more than a stock road running beside a wide, deep green river.

At periodic intervals along the narrow ribbon of road, marker poles had been placed indicating floodwater levels, in places a good meter above the road. There was further evidence of a previous flood and occasional washouts, where portions of the road had been eaten away by the destructive power of the river.

"How far are we from the pearl facility?" The road they were following appeared to be getting narrower.

"Five miles."

Five miles there, then a good thirty miles back to the construction site.

Minutes later, after driving through a deep gorge, Constantine picked up the radio handset again, tried the frequency then set the handpiece down. "That's it. We're out of radio range for the next few minutes. Now we can talk."

His voice was curt as he outlined the business plan for Ambrosi Pearls. He had taken a look at the structure and none of the staff would go, although that would be open for review. Given that the business had been tightly run and had only stumbled because of the debt load imposed by her father, redundancies weren't an option at this point. "Ambrosi Pearls stays in business." There was a brief, electric pause. "But you have to go. Lucas is taking a block of shares. He'll be stepping in as CEO."

Blankly, Sienna wrenched her gaze from Constantine's profile, her mind fixed on his statement that she would have to go.

"Let me get this straight, you want me out of the company completely?"

"That's right, and I'm not asking."

She stared at the stark line of the horizon, rugged hills and more rugged hills threaded by the road they were presently following. She had been braced for demotion. She had not expected to be fired.

She peeled her dark glasses off and rubbed at the sudden sharp ache in her temples. She could feel Constantine studying her, the ratcheting tension.

Although she should have expected this.

Constantine lived on Medinos, therefore it would be difficult for her to remain based in Sydney.

Constantine slowed to a crawl as he drove across a stretch of road that looked like it served a double purpose as a streambed during the wet season. "We signed a contract. You agreed to be my wife."

Her jaw set. "At no point did I agree to give up my job."

Ambrosi Pearls was her baby. She had nursed it through bad times and worse, working crazy hours, losing sleep and reveling in even the smallest victory. She knew every aspect of the business, every employee personally, and their families; they were a tight-knit team. Despite the stress and the worry the company was hers. She was the captain of the team. Ambrosi Pearls couldn't run without her. She felt the cool touch of his gaze.

"I want your loyalties to lie with me, not Ambrosi Pearls. We'll be based in Medinos. Running an Australian business won't be an option."

She stared at the road unfurling ahead, the blinding blue intensity of the sky, the vastness of the sea in the distance. "You run any number of hotels and companies from Medinos."

"Each one has a resident manager. In this case it will be Lucas."

He was right—she knew it—but that didn't make relinquishing Ambrosi Pearls any easier. From childhood she had grown up with the knowledge that, love it or hate it, she would run the family business. "I'm good at what I do. I've studied, trained—"

He braked, allowing a small herd of goats to drift desultorily off the road. "I know how focused you've been on Ambrosi Pearls. No one better."

"Plenty of women juggle a career and marriage."

"Ambrosi Pearls will not be part of this equation."

"Why not?"

His gaze sliced back to hers. "Because I refuse to take second place to a briefcase filled with sales orders."

Sienna jammed her dark glasses back on the bridge of

her nose, abruptly furious at Constantine's hardheaded ruthlessness. "You still don't trust me."

Less than an hour ago she had let him kiss her. He had manipulated her into agreeing to a lot more, despite knowing he was going to sack her while they were driving. "Looking after Ambrosi Pearls has never been just about business. It's part of my family. It's in my blood."

Gaze narrowed, she stared directly ahead, searching for a place where Constantine could comfortably turn the truck around. "I've changed my mind. I want to go back."

"No. You agreed to this."

"That was before you fired me."

"We're spending the night at a beach house up ahead. I'm taking you back in the morning."

Her head snapped around. "I did not agree to that. I do not, repeat, do not, want to spend the night with you. Take me back to the construction site. There must be some kind of regular transport service for the workers. If I'm too late to catch whatever boat or helicopter they use, I'll use the satellite phone in the office to call in my own ride."

"No." His voice was calmly neutral. "The beach house is clean, comfortable and stocked with food."

She could feel the blood pounding through her veins, her temper increasing with every fiery pulse. "Let me guess, no landline, no cell phone network, no internet connection…just you and me."

"And no press, for approximately twelve hours."

With movements that were unnaturally calm, given that she was literally shaking with fury, she unlatched her briefcase and retrieved her cell. She stared at the "no service" message on the screen. Any hope died.

The pearl facility was sited on the western side of the island, tucked into a sheltered bay directly behind the range of hills that was presently looming over them, blocking transmission. "Turn the truck around. Now."

She repeated her request that he turn around immediately.

When he ignored her for the second time, she studied the tough line of his jaw, the dark glasses that hid his eyes, and gauged her chances of yanking the key out of the ignition.

"I don't want to spend the night in some beach house," she said, spacing the words. "I don't want to drive one more mile with you. I'd rather crawl across the island and die of thirst, or swim to Medinos. And if you think I'm going to have sex with you, you can think again. Think dying or rabid thirst, because either of those two things will happen first."

The stare he gave her was vaguely disconcerted, as if he was weighing up which parts of her statements she would actually carry out. It was then she realized that he really did think he was still going to be having sex with her.

He turned back to the road, his jaw set. "We're almost there."

The landscape had changed, flattening out as they neared the coast. Blunt outcroppings smudged with grayish-green scrub and the occasional gnarled olive tree dotted the roadside.

He negotiated another bend and suddenly they were driving alongside the deep, green river again.

Her frustration escalated. Apart from throwing a tantrum, she was almost out of options—and she didn't do tantrums. She liked coolness and precision—pages of neat figures, relationships that progressed logically. She liked forward planning because she liked to win.

Briefly, she outlined plan B. Drive to a place where she could get cell phone service—there had to be a viable high point on this island somewhere—and call in a helicopter. Out here, with the primitive lack of any telephone or power lines, it could land virtually anywhere. If Constantine did what she asked, she wouldn't take this to the police or the newspapers. But if he kept driving all bets were off, and she would sue his ass.

Constantine had the gall to laugh.

A red mist actually swam before her eyes. Her hand shot out and grasped the wheel. He was momentarily distracted while she lunged at the key.

Any idea that she could get out of the truck and make it to a high point on her own was just that, a wild idea. All she wanted was to jolt Constantine out of his stubborn mind-set, stop the vehicle and make him listen.

Constantine jerked her hand off the wheel. Not that that was any big deal, because the maneuver was only a distraction while she grabbed at the elusive prize of the key. Unfortunately, when she had lunged forward, the seat belt had locked her in place, so she'd had to regroup and try again, which had cost her valuable time. Even then her fingertips could only brush the key.

Constantine said something hard and flat. Her head jerked up, not so much at the word, but at the way he'd uttered it.

She saw the washout ahead, which had gouged a crescent-shaped bite out of the road, a split second before the front wheel dropped into the hole. If Constantine had had his full attention on driving, he would have negotiated the hole. A floodplain fanned out on the driver's side. He could have detoured for fifty meters without a problem.

Constantine swung the wheel and gunned the motor, but with the ground crumbling under the rear left wheel there was no way he could pull them back on an even keel.

With a lurch, the truck tilted further.

There was a beat of silence, because Constantine had achieved what she had been trying to do and had turned the engine off. For an endless moment they teetered on two wheels then, with a slow, lumbering grace, the truck toppled sideways.

Fourteen

The distance from the road to the river below wasn't horrendous. From the vehicle it had looked tame, just another eroded riverbank, softened by time and not even particularly steep. But, like the moment when a roller coaster paused on the edge of a drop, no matter how small, the distance suddenly seemed enormous.

Sienna's seat belt held her plastered against the seat as the truck made a clumsy half revolution. Her glasses slid off her nose and a dark shape tumbled past her jaw—her briefcase. The vehicle rocked to a halt. They had stopped rolling, but they had ended upside down, hanging suspended by the seat belts. And they were in the river.

For a heartening moment they bobbed, the murky waterline changing as the truck settled lower. The light began to go as they were almost completely submerged by tea-colored water, tinted, she realized, by the mud that had been stirred up when the truck had disturbed the riverbed.

"Are you all right?"

She turned her head and stared at Constantine. He had a welt on his cheekbone, but otherwise he was in one piece. Apart from the fact that the truck had turned into a submarine and there was something trickling across her scalp—at a guess, blood, which meant she must have banged her head—she was good to go. "Just show me the exit sign."

"Good girl."

The truck was stationary, which meant the roof was sitting on the bottom of the river. That indicated that the depth was shallow, probably not even deep enough to cover the truck fully, but since water was hosing in at various points, getting out was a priority.

A sharp metallic click drew her attention away from the swirling mud and she realized that Constantine had been talking in a low voice. She forced herself to pay attention.

Constantine had already unclipped his seat belt. Using the steering wheel as a handhold, he lowered himself to the roof, which was now their floor, and reversed his position so that he was upright, his back and shoulders wedged against the dash. To do so he had to slide right next to her, because the steering wheel and the gear shift made maneuvering his big frame in the limited space of the cab even more difficult. There was no way he could stand upright.

Constantine leaned across her. She realized he was checking out her door. "The roof crumpled slightly when we went over. Not much, but enough that the doors won't open, so we're going to have to go out through the windows."

He unsnapped her seat belt and caught her as she fell, torpedoing into the deepening puddle of water. With her nose squashed against one rock-hard thigh, she hooked her fingers into the waistband of his jeans and awkwardly jackknifed in the confined space while he kept a firm grip on her waist, holding her steady. She ended up plastered against him from nose to thighs, his arms clamped around her like a vice and with the back of her neck jammed against the edge of the seat. But at least she was finally up the right way, which was a relief, although with her head in the darker floor cavity, the feeling of claustrophobia had increased.

"We're going to have to swim for it, but that shouldn't be a problem since we both know how good you are in the water."

Was that sarcasm? But with water creeping up her ankles she couldn't drum up an ounce of righteous indignation.

Constantine reached across her. She realized he was groping for the window which, luckily, was a manual wind-up type and not electric.

She tried to shuffle sideways, allowing him more room. In the process the top of her foot nudged against a hard object—her briefcase.

She had an instant replay of the sleek, black leather case flying around the cab—the probable cause of the stinging on her scalp. But the injury wasn't what obsessed her in that moment. The accident, stressful as it was, had had a strange effect. Her fury had zapped out of existence and the tension that normally hummed between them was gone. For the first time in two years, stuck upside down in a cab with Constantine as he took control in that calm, alpha way of his, she felt content and almost frighteningly happy.

It was a strange time to realize that despite the constant battles, at a bedrock level she trusted Constantine, and that two years ago when everything had gone wrong this was what she had needed from him.

"You're going out first," he said quietly. "I'll follow."

"No problem." Now that the mud had settled she could see that they were only a couple of feet from the surface. The biggest issue would be the few seconds wait while the cab filled with water. The moment most people would panic would be when the water gushed in. The important thing was to stay calm and hold her breath while the cab filled, because the last she wanted was to swallow a mouthful of river water.

"I'm going to unwind the window. Once the cab is full, you'll have to squeeze out the window. Are you good to go?"

Her head was throbbing a little, but she still felt pumped. Constantine's gaze was inches from hers. With water creeping up her legs and the muscular heat from his body blazing into her, if she hadn't been so at odds with him, she might have given into a *Poseidon Adventure* moment. "Just a second."

She bent her knees and slid down the front of his body. "Don't get any ideas."

She felt around in the water. Her fingers closed around the briefcase handle.

"Leave that."

Leave her laptop underwater? "No. I can use it as a flotation device."

"You can swim like a fish. You don't need a flotation device."

Sienna's head jerked up at his tone, connecting sharply with the back of the seat. A stab of pain shot through her. She had somehow managed to reinjure the same spot, which was now aching. She met his glare with her own version of a steely look. "I don't see why I should lose something I love just because you think it's a good idea." And with any luck the briefcase would be waterproof enough that the laptop would survive.

"I wonder whose idea it was to 'lose' the truck?"

The dryness of his tone flicked her on the raw.

Maybe the briefcase shouldn't be a sticking point, but suddenly it very palpably was. She had lost her company and her career, there was nothing she could do about that, but the briefcase was *hers*. "I'm happy to take the blame for the truck. Just don't blame me for the fact that you haven't gotten around to repairing your road."

"Why did I ever think this was viable?" Constantine jerked her close and pressed a brief, hard kiss on her mouth.

Adrenaline and desire shot through her. Constantine's gaze locked with hers and she had another moment, one that made her heart simultaneously soar and plummet. Her head was stinging and she was angry at the way he had all but kidnapped her, but those considerations were overridden by one salient fact.

No matter what he did, how badly he behaved, she still wanted Constantine. And not just in a sexual way. Her problem was that she wanted all of him—the overbearing dominance and the manipulative way he had pressured her into going into the wilderness with him so he could fire her then keep her prisoner until she forgave him. She wanted the aggravating challenge of his cold, ruthless streak and take-no-prisoners attitude, the flashes of humor. And last, and by no means least, she really, really wanted the heart-pounding sex.

"What now?" he growled, although that didn't fool her. He wanted her, too, and no amount of bad temper could hide that fact.

"Nothing," she snapped back. "As you can see I'm ready to go. I've been ready for ages."

A bare second later water flooded into the cab. The swamping flow would have shoved her sideways but Constantine held her firmly anchored against him. Closing her eyes and holding her breath, she counted and waited until the cold pressurized flow stopped. She opened her eyes on eight. The cab, now filled with water, was dimmer than before, although sunlight shafted through the windows.

Keeping a firm grip on the case, she levered herself out of the window, and kicked to the surface, into blue sky and hot sunlight.

She gulped air and treaded water while she got her bearings. The truck was completely submerged, the only sign of its presence in the river a muddy streak where silt and dirt stained the water. A raw gash on the bank marked the spot where they had gone off the road, but that, she realized was receding.

The current was carrying her downstream at a steady pace. Crumbling banks, eroded by time and scoured by flash floods, rose on either side of her. Despite the sunlight, the water was icy, but that wasn't her biggest problem. Constantine still hadn't surfaced.

Sucking in a breath and, yes, using the case as a flotation device, she kicked toward shore. She could swim against the current, but she would get back to the truck faster by getting onto dry land and jogging back.

Seconds later, her feet found the bottom of the river. Slipping and sliding on rocks, she slogged toward the shore, scanning the smooth green surface as she went. It was entirely possible that Constantine had surfaced for air then gone back down to the truck to retrieve something—maybe the radio set—and she had missed that moment. When she had surfaced she had been too busy hanging on to the briefcase to notice.

Setting the case down she jogged toward the gash in the bank that was now the only marker for the place the truck had gone in, since the muddy streak in the water had cleared. Simultaneously, Constantine surfaced from the now dimly visible shape of the truck, a pack in one hand.

Sienna used the strap of the pack to help pull him to shore. When they stumbled onto the riverbank she dragged the pack out of his hands, dropped it to the ground and checked him out for injuries, relieved when she couldn't see any blood. "Why didn't you surface straightaway?"

He slicked dripping hair back from his face and jerked his chin at the pack. "First aid. Food and clean water. And a portable radio, if it stayed dry."

Explosive anger burned at the back of her throat. Despite his practical reason for staying under and the fact that he had obviously felt confident he could hold his breath for all that time, it didn't change the fact that he could have been in trouble. "That pack wasn't in the cab."

Which meant it had been secured on the truck bed, underneath the flatbed canopy. Instead of following her to the surface he had stayed underwater, holding his breath while he unlaced the tarp, swam beneath it and retrieved the pack. With the swift-flowing current anything could have happened. "I thought you were trapped."

His hands closed around her upper arms, rubbed against her chilled flesh. "It's okay, babe, I had a knife. I cut the canopy open. There was no way I could have gotten trapped."

Babe? Something snapped inside her. "Don't you dare do anything like that again."

Maybe she was overreacting, but the thought that something could have happened to Constantine made her go cold inside. For several seconds she had been forced to consider what life would be like if she did lose him. She hadn't known how much that would matter to her.

She was in love with Constantine. She had to face the fact that if she still loved him after the past two years then it was an easy bet that she would continue to love him, regardless.

She didn't know how long she would feel this way. Maybe sometime in the dim, distant future, whatever it was that sparked her to respond to him would fade and she would love someone else. She was certain love was possible, but she didn't know if she would ever be desperately, hopelessly in love again.

An emotion that made her heart stumble flashed in his gaze. He muttered something in Medinian and hauled her against him. Her arms clamped around his neck as his mouth came down on hers.

Heat radiated from him, swamping her, and the kiss pulled her under. For long seconds she drifted, still locked into the expression she had glimpsed in his eyes. The truth he had hidden from her for two years—that he wasn't either remote or emotionally closed down, that as much as she needed him, he needed her.

He lifted his mouth and she could breathe again, but it wasn't oxygen she wanted. This time there was no thunder and lightning, no thick darkness pressing down, hiding motives and intentions. Her fingers slid into his wet hair and pulled his mouth back to hers. The passion was white-hot and instant.

She found the buttons of his shirt and tore them open. Seconds later, she felt the rush of cool air as he slid her wet, clinging shirt off her shoulders. A sharp tug and her bra was gone. He pulled her close, the skin-on-skin contact searing. The uncomplicated relief of being held by the man she loved spiraled through her as she lifted up on her toes and deepened the kiss.

His fingers pulled gently at the pins in her hair, destroying the remnants of her chignon so that wet strands tumbled around her shoulders. She found the fastening of his jeans and tugged, then they were on the ground. For long minutes, between heart-stopping kisses, she was consumed with buttons and zippers and the breathless humor of constructing a makeshift bed with discarded clothing.

Another drugging kiss and her arms coiled around Constantine's neck, pulling until he ended up on top of her, and suddenly the humor was gone. Despite being in the water for longer than she had been, heat radiated from him, swamping her. The rumpled, wet clothing beneath was rough against her bare skin, but the discomfort slid away as her hands found the satiny muscles of Constantine's back and she stretched out against the smooth, sleek length of him.

His gaze locked with hers as with infinite gentleness their bodies melded, the fit perfect. For long moments they simply stayed that way, soaking in what they hadn't had time for in Sydney, the slow intimacy, the hitched breaths and knowing glances.

Warm, melting pleasure shimmered through her as they finally began to move together, their breath intermingled, their bodies entwined. Past and present dissolved as the burning intensity finally peaked and the afternoon spun away.

Long minutes later, Constantine rolled onto his back, pulling her with him so she lay sprawled over his chest.

Sienna cuddled close, ran her palm absently over one bicep, stroking the pliant swell of muscle. He moved slightly, shifting his weight. She adjusted her position, making herself more comfortable.

In that moment she faced a small detail that, caught in the maelstrom of emotion and urgency, they had both chosen to ignore. This time they hadn't used a condom.

The moment had been primal and extreme, but the fact that Constantine could have made her pregnant didn't terrify her. She had wanted him inside her, touching that innermost part of her.

His eyes flickered, his gaze found hers. She bent down and kissed him, her hair a damp tangled curtain enclosing them. His hands slid up her back, tightened on her waist and she was lost again.

The rising breeze roused Constantine. He hadn't gone to sleep, and neither had Sienna. Like him, she had been content to lie quietly, her breathing settling into an even rhythm.

"We're going to have to move." His skin was darkly tanned and used to the hot sun, but Sienna with her creamy skin and honey-gold tan would burn.

Regret pulled at him as she eased out of the curve of his arm and snatched up an armload of wet clothing. The skittish alacrity with which she draped their clothing over warm boulders then walked into the river informed him that her thoughts were running parallel to his. They had made love without a condom, twice.

It wasn't something he had planned, nor would he ever force this situation on any woman, but now that it had happened he had to reassess and act.

A child. He went still inside at the image of Sienna round and pregnant. Sienna with his baby at her breast.

Raw emotion grabbed at his stomach, his chest. Until that moment he hadn't realized how powerful lovemaking could be, or how imperative it was to him that Sienna was the mother of his children.

Sienna had always been attractive to him, almost to the point of obsession.

Almost, but not quite.

Two years ago he had been able to control his involvement. To a degree, he admitted grimly. When he had discovered that Sienna had known her father was using their engagement to leverage a loan, he had been able to step back. But at some point between their lovemaking in Sydney and now he had crossed a line.

That shift had happened when Sienna had walked into his hotel ballroom wearing what he had thought were Medinian bridal jewels. In that moment he had wanted every promise inherent in the intricate weave of the bridal jewels: purity, passion and commitment.

Rising to his feet, he followed Sienna into the water. Despite the possessive urge to keep her close, he was careful to allow her space and not push any further than he already had.

Ducking down, he rinsed his hair. Water streamed down his shoulders as he surfaced just in time to see Sienna wading to shore.

By the time he walked out of the water, she was wearing her shirt, which had already dried in patches. With swift movements, he dried off with his shirt and pulled on his underwear and jeans, then replaced his shirt on its rock to dry some more, along with his socks and boots. The jeans were still damp, but the weather was so hot they would dry almost as quickly while he was wearing them.

Sienna, who had already finger-combed her hair and tied it in a neat knot, unlaced her sneakers. "That can't happen again. Making love without a condom is crazy."

"I didn't exactly plan to have unprotected sex."

His gaze narrowed when she calmly ignored him in favor of turning her jeans and socks over and aligning everything with military precision. She selected a rock, sat down and started brushing grit off her sneakers. He could feel his temper slipping then he finally got it. Sienna was a perfectionist; it had always been one of the things he had liked about her. He had even thought it was cute on occasion, although it periodically drove him crazy. Like now.

But suddenly the reason she fussed and tidied was clear. It was her way of coping when she was stressed or worried. She had done it in the office this afternoon and she was doing it now, which meant the cool distance wasn't a brush-off; it was simply a means of protecting herself.

Relief dissipated some of his tension as he walked over to Sienna. Crouching down, he cupped her face and gently kissed her. "I'm sorry I didn't use a condom, but given the way things were and the fact that I didn't have one, there was no avoiding it this time. Next time we make love I'll take care of the protection. There are condoms at the house. They were delivered along with the food."

Her gaze flashed. "You really did plan this."

"You knew as well as I did the minute you climbed in that truck what was going to happen. I asked, you agreed. I didn't make you do anything you didn't want to."

This time she avoided his gaze altogether, but he didn't need the eye contact to know exactly what was going through her mind.

Frowning, he straightened. Any woman would worry about an unplanned pregnancy. But if Sienna was pregnant, as far as Constantine was concerned, the situation was cut-and-dried. They would be married within a month.

Fifteen

Sienna studiously avoided Constantine's gaze as she finished cleaning her shoes. Heat and silence shimmered around them, broken by the cooling sound of river water sliding over rocks.

She was lacing one sneaker, when Constantine crouched down in front of her and picked up the other one.

His hand encircled her ankle and something snapped. Images flickered in her memory: the way she'd melted the first night they'd met when Constantine had crouched down and fitted her missing shoe to her foot. Not a glass slipper exactly, just a black pump with black beads, but the moment had been incredibly, mind-bendingly romantic.

She swiped the shoe out of his hand. "Don't."

She sucked in air, tried to breathe. Maybe she was being stubborn and picky, but she didn't want those kinds of gestures unless he really did love her. Pulling at the laces, she loosened them off enough to put the sneaker back on her foot.

Constantine frowned as his gaze skimmed critically over her. "You're bleeding. You should have told me."

She touched her scalp. There must be a cut because there was dried blood, but it was so small she had difficulty finding it. "It's nothing, a scratch."

He unfastened the pack and tipped the contents out on the ground, one of which happened to be a pack of emergency supplies. Standard issue, she guessed, for anyone who worked out at the construction site. The other was a first aid kit.

While he was sorting through the supplies Sienna went down to the river to rinse the blood out of her hair.

When she returned, Constantine appeared to be busy, tinkering with the portable radio. Dragging her gaze from the powerful line of his back, Sienna finished dressing except for the still-damp bra, which she folded and slipped into her jeans pocket. She strolled a few steps down the rocky beach, staring at the wild beauty of the landscape. With every moment that passed the commitment she had made in making love to Constantine without protection seemed more and more foolhardy in light of his glaring lack of any kind of emotional declaration.

A flicker of movement caught her eye. Constantine was by her briefcase.

Her brows jerked together as he picked it up and sneakily carried it up the bank. Out of sight.

Her temper shredding, she stormed up the bank and retrieved the briefcase. She didn't know what it was with Constantine and her things. He wasn't just satisfied with taking her company and her job; now he didn't want her to have her briefcase.

He frowned. "You don't need that. You'll only have to carry it."

"I do need it, and it's no problem carrying it." And if he

wanted to take it off her now, he would have to pry it out of her cold, dead hands.

His gaze narrowed, glittering with an edgy frustration that sent a zingy sensation down her spine. "Jewelry samples and order forms are the last thing you need out here."

She felt herself blushing at the confirmation that he had recognized her sample case back in her hotel suite. She stared at his muscled chest and a small, red mark on his shoulder she could remember making. She felt herself grow warmer. "It's not a sample case. For your information it's a portable office."

"The same thing in my book."

For a taut moment she thought he was going to say something further then he turned back to the assortment of tools he had assembled on the ground.

Still tingling with the heady knowledge that Constantine wasn't as distant and controlled as he seemed, she took the briefcase back to her rock, sat down and unlatched it. Water had seeped in, wetting the order forms but, because her laptop was zipped into a soft case inside the briefcase, it was still bone-dry.

She set the damp forms down on the ground to dry, extracted the laptop, powered it up then closed it down. She packed it away, and tidied her appointments diary and the jumbled mess of pens and pamphlets then placed the damp order forms on top. They were no longer any use, but since there wasn't a trash can out here, she would have to keep them until she could find one.

When she had finished restoring order to the briefcase, she slipped her cell phone out of her pocket and tried that, without much hope. As she'd thought, it was as dead as a doornail.

Constantine strolled over with a first aid kit. He sat down on a rock in front of her and leaned close, sandwiching her between his thighs. She was suddenly overwhelmingly aware of the broad expanse of his chest and just how physically large he was.

He tilted her head and she found herself looking directly into his eyes. His face was close enough that she could study to her heart's content the intriguing dark flecks in his irises, the red welt on his cheekbone that was rapidly discoloring into a bruise.

He cupped her face, his hold seducingly gentle. "If you get pregnant, we'll talk about it. Until then, we'll go back to using protection."

Sienna edged the briefcase away from his booted foot, ignoring his irritated frown. "Assuming there is going to be more sex."

"How likely are you to get pregnant?"

She drew in an impeded breath, suddenly floored by the thought that she could be pregnant, right this second. It was documented history that Ambrosi women got pregnant at the drop of a hat. They were psychotic power freaks when it happened, but certifiably fertile.

She did a quick count. "There's a possibility."

More than a possibility.

His thumb brushed across her mouth sending a hot little dart of sensation through her. "I'll leave you alone for now, if that's what you want. Now stay still while I take a look at that scratch on the side of your head."

Obediently, she tilted her head so he could examine the area. He took his time smoothing her hair out of the way then used some antiseptic wipes from the first aid kit.

"Ouch."

His mouth quirked at one corner. "Don't be a sissy."

"That's easy for you to say. You're not the one who's bleeding."

"The cut is small. It's hardly life-threatening."

"Then I don't know why you're bothering with the first aid routine."

He didn't reply, just angled her head again, pinched the wound together with his thumb and forefinger, which made it throb and sting, and smoothed on a small butterfly strip.

She stared at the welt on his cheekbone as he packed the first aid kit away. The bruise, which had started to turn a purplish color, made him look faintly piratical. "How did you get that?"

His gaze was slitted against the sun making him look even more dangerous. "The same way you got that cut on your head—from that damn briefcase."

She purred inside and inched the briefcase closer to her leg. She almost felt like patting it. Good briefcase, it had never meant to hurt her; it had been after Constantine.

He pushed to his feet. "The house isn't far, but we need to get moving. I checked the radio, and it still works, but we're out of the transmission area so we'll have to wait for the helicopter, which will be out to pick us up first thing in the morning."

Sienna watched as Constantine repacked the supplies and finished dressing.

He passed her a water bottle. Wordlessly, she drank. With the risk of giardia and other contaminants she hadn't drunk any of the river water, as tempting as the notion had been.

Constantine stored the bottle in the pack and held out his hand. "I'll take the briefcase."

"No. I'll carry it."

There was an explosive silence, but when she stole a sideways glance at Constantine she was certain his mouth was twitching.

The beach house, which had been less than two miles

away from where the truck had overturned, was not a cottage so much as a multilevel statement in design.

Decks merged into the side of a striated cliff and overlooked a windswept beach. Inside, the floors were glossy, the ceilings high. Huge plate-glass windows provided an unimpeded view of the sea.

Constantine pointed out the large adjacent bay, which held the old pearl facility, but by then the light was fading. Sienna could make out the tumbled remains of a building and little else.

Constantine touched a switch and air-conditioning hummed to life, instantly cool against her overheated skin.

Feeling dusty and tired, Sienna did a quick tour of the kitchen. Stainless-steel appliances were hidden behind lacquered cabinets, and a state-of-the-art oven, large enough to cater for a crowd, took pride of place. She opened a cabinet door and found a gleaming microwave and, on a shelf beneath it, an array of small appliances. "This place is fabulous. It doesn't look like it's ever used."

"It's a family retreat, but since we have to spend so much time overseas, it isn't used often. There are bedrooms upstairs and on this floor."

Constantine crossed the broad expanse of the living area, which was tastefully decorated with comfortable leather couches, and pushed open a door.

She followed him into the broad hall, which had several rooms opening off it. After a quick walk through, she chose a room with floaty white silk draperies.

Constantine showed her the bathroom, which was fully stocked with an array of products, including toothbrushes and toothpaste. "There's fresh underwear and clothing in the dresser if you want it. Freshen up, I'll go and organize some food."

After showering and changing into fresh underwear

and a thin cotton robe she'd found hooked on the back of the bathroom door, Sienna gathered up her soiled clothes and carried them through to the living area.

The aroma of a spicy casserole, which evidently had been prepared and left in the fridge, drew her to the kitchen. Constantine must also have showered, because his hair was damp and slicked back. He had also changed, pulling on a pair of clean cotton pants and a thin, gauzy white shirt.

He showed her where the laundry room was. She put her clothes and his in to wash, then walked back to the kitchen.

They sat out on the deck, a casual option that appealed more than the formality of the dining room, and ate the traditional Medinian dish followed by slices of juicy mango. The sun sank slowly, throwing shadows and investing the ocean with a soft, mystical quality that caught and held her gaze for long minutes.

When the sun finally slid below the horizon, the air temperature dropped like a stone. After the burning heat of the day, cold seemed to seep out of the rocks, raising gooseflesh on her skin. The night sky was unbelievably clear, the stars huge and bright and almost close enough to touch.

Sienna offered to clean up and make coffee, abruptly glad to escape the romantic setting and the growing tension. She stiffened when Constantine put on soft music and sat beside her on the couch but, when he didn't do anything more than drape his arm along the back of the couch, she finally relaxed.

After what had happened that afternoon, she had been prepared for a passionate interlude she wasn't sure she could resist. Instead he seemed to be doing exactly what she had asked: backing off and giving her some time.

Exhaustion pulled at her as she listened to a Beethoven adagio. But she could not forget what had happened that afternoon. She had to wonder if she was pregnant.

Her hand moved, cupping her belly. Constantine's gaze followed the movement as if he was entertaining the exact same thought.

She was suddenly acutely aware of her body.

The first shock of the idea had passed. Having a child would definitely narrow her options, but the notion of having a baby had taken firm root.

As if he had read her mind his hand smoothed down one arm, his thumb absently stroking her. The touch was pleasant rather than sexual, as if he was aware of her turmoil and wanted to soothe her.

Gradually, she relaxed against him. She was dropping into a delicious dark well of contentment when his voice rumbled softly in her ear.

"If there's a likelihood that you're pregnant, then we should get married soon."

Her eyes popped open. Suddenly she was wide-awake. He hadn't proposed, either back at the resort or here.

Maybe there was no need for an actual proposal. Strictly speaking, that formality had been taken care of by the contract, but that didn't change the fact that she would have liked one. Although demanding that would let him know exactly how vulnerable she was about their relationship. "When did you have in mind?"

"A week. Two at the most."

"I'll talk to Mom and give you some dates." It was a surrender. The only thing left to extract from her was an admission that she loved him, but she would hold back on that for as long as she could.

Maybe denying Constantine that final victory was childish, but she was afraid that if she surrendered emotionally he would no longer feel he had to fight for her. If Constantine deemed his battle won, she could lose any chance that he would eventually love her.

He wouldn't walk away this time, so the outcome would be much worse—they could end up locked together in a loveless marriage. She may have given up on the romantic fantasy of having him fall in love with her, but gaining a measure of love, however small, was vitally important.

"That's settled then," he said quietly. "I'll take care of the arrangements as soon as we get back."

Shortly after daybreak the *chop-chop* of a helicopter split the air as it set down on a concrete pad a short distance away.

Fifteen minutes after boarding the helicopter, they set down at Medinos's airport. Less than an hour later a car, driven by Tomas, deposited them at the *castello*.

Constantine had arranged to have her things delivered to the *castello* from the resort, so as soon as they arrived she was able to change into fresh clothes.

When she was dressed in a cool, ice-blue summer shift that ended midthigh, she slipped on sandals and strolled through broad, echoing hallways and vaulted rooms, looking for Constantine. When she didn't find him, she checked the ultramodern kitchen.

Classical music had been playing, but in the lull between CDs she heard voices. She walked down a hallway, which led to the front entryway and a series of reception rooms.

As she padded closer, she noticed a door that had been left slightly ajar. The conversation, originating from that room and naturally channeled by the acoustics of the hall, became clearer. She recognized the distinctive American accent of Constantine's legal advisor, Ben Vitalis.

"…good work getting the water rights transferred so quickly…"

Her fingers, which had closed around the brass doorknob, froze as Vitalis's voice registered more clearly. "…if Sienna had contested the estuarine lease, the marina project would have stalled indefinitely. We would have lost millions in contractor's kill fees."

There was a pause, the creak of a chair as if Vitalis had just sat down. "…Clever move, inserting the marriage clause. Even if she tries to contest the transfer of the lease, under Medinian law the rights will revert to you. Where are we with the loan?"

"The loan agreement is cut-and-dried."

The deep, incisive tones of Constantine's voice hit Sienna like a kick in the chest.

She went hot then cold. The reason Constantine had proposed a marriage of convenience in the same contract that settled her father's fraudulent debt was suddenly glaringly obvious. Somehow her father had messed up Constantine's development plans. Constantine had wanted to ensure that his marina went ahead unchecked and she had succumbed to his tactics with ridiculous ease.

A painful flood of memories swamped her—the clipped conversation that had ended their first engagement two years ago, Constantine's detachment after their lovemaking in Sydney.

She could forgive the way he had gone about seducing her. Even knowing she was being maneuvered, she had been helpless to resist because she had known with every cell of her body that the desire was heart-poundingly real. But this level of calculation was not acceptable. She would have to be willfully blind, deaf and dumb not to understand that a third, even more profound rejection, was in the works.

"Okay, then…" There was a click as if a briefcase had been opened, the slap of a document landing on either a table or a desktop. "Cast your eye over the child custody clause."

Feeling like an automaton, Sienna pushed the door wide and stepped into the room just as Vitalis flicked his briefcase closed and rose to his feet. Constantine's gaze connected with hers and her heart squeezed tight. She had wanted to be proved wrong, to discover that she'd gotten the conversation wildly out of context, but in that moment she knew she hadn't.

Nerves humming, she stepped around Vitalis, picked up the document lying on the desk and skimmed it.

Seconds later she literally felt the blood drain from her face. She didn't care about land or money. She cared that Constantine had manipulated her over the water rights. It was a betrayal of a very private kind that cut to the bone because it emphasized that he didn't simply want her; she was part of a business agenda. Even knowing that, she would have gone through with the marriage. But the children she might have were a different matter.

She didn't know what it was like to bear a child, but even without the physical reality of a child in her arms, she knew how fiercely she would care about her babies.

Vitalis had prepared an amendment to the marriage deal, granting Constantine custody and rights for any children. If she walked out on the marriage, she would be granted limited access to her children, but she could never take them with her.

Before he even knew she was pregnant, should she decide to leave the marriage, Constantine had arranged to take her babies from her as coolly and methodically as he had taken Ambrosi Pearls and her career.

She transferred her gaze to Constantine. "Did you actually think that I would sign this?"

Constantine pushed to his feet. Vitalis had already retreated, melting out of a side door she hadn't noticed.

"It's a draft Ben put together. You weren't supposed to see it yet. I intended to discuss options with you next week."

Options.

She could feel herself closing up, the warmth seeping from her skin. She had known she would have a struggle breaking through the protective armor of Constantine's business process. He thought she was tied to Ambrosi Pearls, but her focus on the family business was nothing compared to his. It was possible that she was even partly responsible for the way he was handling their relationship—as if it was a business merger—because of what had happened two years ago. "But this is the deal you want?"

His expression was guarded. "Not...exactly."

Not the answer she needed.

Blankly she struggled to readjust her internal lens. "I've spent two years beating myself up because I agreed to marry you knowing that my father had organized a finance deal with yours. That was such a crime."

She replaced the pages on his desk. She was toweringly angry and utterly miserable. Marriage was personal, intimate. When she had said she would marry Constantine, she had done so imagining that he could feel something real and special for her, that if it wasn't love right now it would grow to be one day. She had been operating on hope.

The exact opposite of this cold agreement.

Constantine pushed to his feet. "I want a wife who is committed to marriage and family."

She registered that he was still dressed casually in the

jeans and loose shirt he had been wearing when they had left Ambrus. The reminder of the hours they had spent together on the island was the last thing she needed. "So you drew up a contract."

"It wasn't as cold-blooded as that. We're sexually compatible. We share a lot in common."

With the bright glare of the sun behind him throwing his face into shadow, she was unable to discern emotion either way, and in that moment she desperately needed to see something. "From where I'm standing, the only true bond we share is a seven figure debt."

In a blinding flash, being part of Ambrosi Pearls ceased to be important. For years she had been consumed with saving the company. The struggle had taken every waking moment, but with the safety of the company employees and her family assured, she didn't have to continue fighting. None of them did. Constantine would fight the battle for them. She could let go, step back, because Constantine was more able to manage her family's company than she would ever be.

But the last thing she wanted was to step into a relationship that was defined by a maze of legal traps. "And to think, I let myself fall for you all over again."

Secure in the glimpses of the old Constantine, with whom she had fallen in love. Secure in the illusion that she had some womanly power and a measure of control.

Something shifted in his gaze. "Sienna...I didn't mean to hurt—"

"No. Just control, because that's what works for you. Control me, control any children, control your emotions." There would be no messy divorce or outrageous property settlements, because the bottom line was clear-cut. "You told me that you usually get exactly what you want. I guess that really is a marriage of convenience and two—"

Blindly, she flipped pages and checked the fine print, but couldn't distinguish individual words because her eyes were filmed with tears. "Or is that three children?"

Constantine speed-dialed Tomas as Sienna walked out of his office and bit out orders, sheer, blind panic making him break out in a cold sweat. Sienna was leaving the *castello* and the island. As much as he needed to keep her with him, he knew that if he tried to physically detain her, he would lose her forever.

The fact that he had considered holding her in the *castello*—in effect, perpetrating the kidnapping she had accused him of when he had taken her to the beach house on Ambrus—demonstrated his desperation.

When Sienna had registered the contents of the child custody clause he had understood the mistake he had made, that no amount of financial or legal pressure would make him first in Sienna's life, or bind her to him the way he needed her to be if she didn't want to be there.

In that moment he had recognized her; he had seen the steady fire and strength that had always unconsciously drawn him. He had seen flashes before—in Sydney after they had made love, in the walled garden of the hotel when she had thrown his blundering attempt to make her choose between Ambrosi Pearls and him back in his face.

She had said she had fallen for him and in that instant he had known that was the reason she had agreed to marriage, not the financial breaks.

That moment had stunned him. He realized he had been first in her life all along. It was his approach that had been flawed. He had been the one who was focused on business.

His only break was that she hadn't mentioned the marriage clause. They were still engaged, on paper at least.

Tossing the agreement in his briefcase, he strode upstairs to his suite and threw clothes into an overnight bag. Tomas would make sure Sienna couldn't get on a regular flight out of Medinos even if that meant he had to buy every empty seat on the outgoing flights.

Bleakly, he recognized that when it came to Sienna, the bottom line had never mattered. The first time he had laid eyes on her he had tumbled. He had known who she was, had recognized her instantly, and he had been entranced. The problem was he hadn't believed she would simply want him. In his own mind he could still remember what it was like to have nothing, and how lacking in popularity he had been then.

Money had changed their lives. Maybe he was overly sensitive, but he knew that when women looked at him now they saw his wealth. Like it had for his father, money had been the dominant factor in almost every relationship. He had made the mistake of assuming that because Sienna needed money, that she would need him.

He had been wrong.

Now, somehow, he had to make up for his mistake, to convince her that they still had a chance.

He didn't care what it took. He just wanted her back.

Tomas rang back. The private jet was fueled; there were no longer any available flights out of Medinos. If Sienna wanted to leave today, it would have to be on the Atraeus jet.

Constantine hung up and returned downstairs to collect the keys to the Maserati. She wouldn't like it. That was an understatement. Sienna would hate the forced proximity, but he knew with gut-wrenching clarity that he couldn't afford to let her go completely. Every second she was away from him would widen the gulf he had created between them.

Thirty minutes later, Constantine parked the Maserati at

the airport, completed the exit details and walked through to his private hangar. Tomas had informed him that Sienna was already on board.

During the flight Sienna barely acknowledged him, choosing to either sleep, or feign sleep, most of the way.

Constantine forced himself to remain calm. This was damage control. If he didn't fix the mistakes he had made they were finished, and he had made a number of serious errors.

Given the choice, he wouldn't have used a marriage deal. The document had filled him with distaste, but when it had come to dealing with Sienna and her attachment to Ambrosi Pearls, shock tactics had made sense.

She had cared about Ambrosi Pearls like most women cared about their child. From a teenager, she had literally had responsibility shoved at her. She had been so focused on sacrificing herself to make up for the damage her father had done, it was a wonder he had managed to get close to her at all.

He hadn't known every one of those facts when he had walked away from their first engagement, or understood the emotional battering she had taken. He had been so used to seeing her as in charge and ultraorganized that he had overlooked the fact that Sienna, herself, was a victim of her father's gambling problem.

Two years ago he had been coldly angry that Sienna hadn't told him about her father's losses or the loan Roberto had leveraged with his father. He hadn't wanted to address the reason he had reacted so strongly, but he did now.

What he felt for Sienna was different from anything else he had ever experienced.

The thought that she was pregnant, that there would be

a baby, had expanded that feeling out to a second person he could possibly lose.

The constricted emotion in his chest tightened into actual pain. He had always known what that feeling was and the reason why he had been so furious at what he had perceived as Sienna's betrayal.

She was right. He had tried to control her and any children they might have and, in the process, his own emotions. But the legal clauses he had used to bind any children, and thus ensure that Sienna stayed with him, had achieved the exact opposite.

He had ensured that what he needed most, he would lose.

Sixteen

When The Atraeus Group's private jet landed in Sydney it was after eight in the evening and it was raining. After the heat of Medinos, the chill was close to wintry.

Numbly, Sienna refused a ride with Constantine. "I can take a taxi. All I need to do is pick up my car from my mother's house, then I'm driving back to my apartment."

Constantine's expression was grim as he skimmed the airport lounge. "I'll drop you at Pier Point. She'll be expecting it. But if you're not coming home with me—"

"I am not staying with you."

He cupped her elbow and steered her around a baggage cart. "Then stay out at Pier Point." He released her before she could shake free.

Sienna's stomach tightened at the brief, tingling heat of his hold. "If that's an order—"

He massaged the muscles at his nape, the first sign of frustration he'd shown since he had boarded the jet. Up until that moment, he had been frustratingly cool and remote.

"It's not an order, it's a…suggestion." He nodded his head in the direction of the press waiting in the arrival's lounge. Almost immediately the cameras started whirring and the questions started. "And that's why."

Thirty minutes of tense silence later, Constantine parked his Audi in her mother's driveway. He carried her luggage and the briefcase in, then stayed to talk with her mother and Carla for a few minutes. His gaze captured hers while he listened to her mother's stilted congratulations and for a moment she saw past the remote mask he'd maintained to a raw throb of emotion that made her heart pound.

Just before he left, he handed her an envelope. She checked the contents and saw the child custody agreement Vitalis had drawn up torn in two. When she glanced up, Constantine was already gone.

When the sound of the Audi receded, her mother fixed her with a steely glare. "Don't you dare sacrifice yourself for the business, or for us."

Her fingers shaking, she shoved the agreement and the envelope into her purse. "Don't worry, I'm not. If you don't mind, I need a cup of tea." Despite the comfortable flight, the fact that she had faked sleeping meant she had barely eaten or had anything to drink.

Carla frowned and motioned her onto one of the kitchen stools at the counter. "Sit. Talk. I'll make the tea."

Sienna sat and, in between sips of hot tea, concentrated on giving a factual account without the emotional highs and lows. When she'd finished, her mother set a sandwich down in front of her and insisted that she eat.

"To think, I used to like that boy."

Boy? Sienna almost choked on the sandwich. Constantine was six feet four inches of testosterone-laden muscle who could quite possibly have made her pregnant. *Boy* was the last descriptive she would have used.

Margaret Ambrosi lifted an elegant brow. "So did you agree to marry Constantine to save the business?"

"No." She took a bite of the sandwich, forcing it past the tightness in her throat. It was a fact that she wouldn't have agreed to marriage if she didn't love Constantine. "It's complicated."

"You're in love with him. Have been for years."

Sienna's cheeks burned. "Just whose side are you on?"

"Yours. Marry him or don't marry him, but stop worrying about us. If Ambrosi Pearls and this house have to go, so be it, it's your decision. You know Ambrosi Pearls was never my passion."

Sienna stared at the rest of her sandwich, her appetite gone. Constantine had hurt her, deeply enough that she had done nothing but consider refusing to go through with the marriage. After the long, silent flight, and the glimpse of raw loss she had seen in Constantine's gaze, she was almost certain that he would let her go. An ache rose up in her at the thought.

Her mother, with her usual clarity, had cut to the chase. They could survive without Atraeus money. When it came to the crunch, the only question was could she survive without Constantine?

She had told him point-blank on the ride out to Pier Point that she needed time to think things through. He hadn't liked it, but he had accepted her need for space.

That, and the fact that he had surrendered unconditionally on the child custody agreement, constituted progress. She didn't know how long it would take her to heal, but those two things at least signaled a painful step forward.

Her decision settled into place as she slowly sipped her

tea. She could go ahead with the marriage for one simple reason: as hurt as she was she couldn't contemplate not having Constantine in her life.

Two weeks later, the morning of the wedding in Medinos was balmy and relentlessly clear. Although, judging by the pandemonium that had broken out in the last half hour, with cousins, aunts and the hairdresser and makeup team descending en masse, it sounded more like a street riot than a wedding in progress.

Margaret Ambrosi had insisted that if she was getting married in Medinos they needed a house for her to be married from, so Constantine had arranged for a private villa to be made available. It was an old-fashioned idea, but Sienna hadn't minded. The extra fuss and bother had at least taken her mind off the risk she was taking.

Her mother, in combination with Tomas, had pulled all the elements of the wedding together with formidable efficiency, ruthlessly calling in favors to get everything done on time and using Constantine's name to smooth the way. They had organized the dress, the flowers, live music and a church choir, plus a full-scale reception at the *castello*.

Carla poked her head around the door and handed her an envelope. "This arrived for you. Thirty minutes to go. How are you feeling?"

Sienna's heart thumped in her chest as she took the envelope and checked her wristwatch. "Great."

Skittish and unhappy, because she had barely seen him after their stilted conversation the day after arriving in Sydney, when she had agreed to go through with the wedding. When she had, they had never been alone. She was beginning to believe that the loss she had glimpsed in his eyes had been another mirage.

The limousine was booked for eleven; it was ten-thirty.

So far everything had gone without a hitch. Her hair and makeup were done, her jewelry was on and her nails had finally dried.

Her dress was an elegant, sleeveless gown with a scoop neck, simply cut but made of layers of floaty white chiffon that swirled around her ankles as she walked. The petal-soft fabric was a perfect match for the pearl and diamond necklace and earrings her great-aunt had given her as a wedding gift. They were rare, original Ambrosi Pearls pieces.

When Carla shut the door behind her Sienna studied the envelope, her heart thumping hard in her chest when she recognized Constantine's handwriting. When she ripped the envelope open, she found all three copies of the marriage deal she'd signed along with a scribbled note. Constantine hadn't activated the deal or filed any of the paperwork. No shares had changed hands. Ambrosi Pearls was still registered as belonging to her family. The water rights were also enclosed.

In short, he had frozen the entire deal. With the paperwork in her hands she was free to destroy it all if she pleased. To all intents and purposes, it was as if there had never been a deal.

Her legs feeling distinctly wobbly, she sat on the edge of the bed. Constantine had chosen to walk away from exacting any kind of reparations for her father's scam. He now risked financial disaster with his new resort development. She should feel relieved, but all she could think about was, did this mean the wedding was off?

There was a second knock at the door. Carla again, this time with a telephone in one hand. "It's de Vries."

Not Northcliffe as she had expected but Hammond de Vries himself, the CEO of the large European retail conglomerate. The conversation was crisp and to the point.

They had reconsidered, and now wanted to place the order. The sum he offered was staggering. After a short conversation, Sienna hung up and set the phone down just as her mother stepped into the room.

In a lavender suit her mother looked elegant but frazzled. "Sienna—"

The door was pushed wide. Constantine, darkly handsome in a morning suit, stepped past Margaret Ambrosi. "If you'll excuse me, Mrs. Ambrosi, I need to speak to Sienna. Alone."

There was a startled exclamation when Constantine ushered her mother out of the door. "Five minutes," he said smoothly.

Sienna rose to her feet, her heart pounding, because Constantine was dressed for the wedding and because she suddenly knew, beyond doubt, the only fact she needed to know. "I turned de Vries down," she said calmly. "I know you're behind the offer, and I know why you made it."

His gaze was wary. "How did you know it was me?"

"Hammond de Vries doesn't normally call us. One of his buyers does. Besides, they've had my number for months. It was too much of a coincidence that he called today with an offer that would cover the loan. Plus…" She let out a breath. "I happen to know that The Atraeus Group recently bought a percentage of de Vries."

Constantine leaned against the door, his gaze narrowed. "Who told you?"

"An industry contact."

"That would be your mother."

"Who just happened to have a conversation with Tomas—"

His mouth twitched. "—who is putty in her hands."

"Most people are. So…the game's up. You gave me an

out. Or…" She was suddenly afraid to be so ridiculously, luminously happy. "Did you want the out?"

He pushed away from the door, his hands settled at her waist. "By now you have to know what I want. Marriage. But this time it has to be your choice, not just mine."

Sienna wound her arms around Constantine's neck and met his kiss halfway. Long seconds later, he loosened his hold and reached into his pocket. "Just one more thing."

Emotion shimmered through her as he went down on one knee and opened a small, black velvet box. He extracted the ring, a princess-cut white diamond that glowed with an intense, pure fire. "Sienna Ambrosi, will you marry me and be my love?"

Her throat closed on a raw throb, her eyes misted. "Yes."

Constantine slid the ring onto the third finger of her left hand.

"You do love me." Giddy delight spread through her as he rose to his feet and pulled her close. She wound her arms around his neck and held on tight.

He rested his forehead against hers. "I've loved you since the first time I saw you. I can still remember the moment."

"Before the shoe incident?"

"About five seconds before my clumsy attempt at Prince Charming." His mouth curved in a slow smile. "I just had some growing up to do. Make that a lot of growing up."

He bent his head and touched his mouth to hers, and for long seconds she seemed to float. Although the moments of dizziness she had begun to experience in the mornings had an entirely different source.

When he lifted his head and she could breathe again, he ran his hands down her back, molding her against him. The touch was reassuring. She was vulnerable, but so was he; it had just taken him longer to know it.

There was a sharp rap. Margaret Ambrosi's head popped around the side of the door. She wanted to know what was going on, and she wanted to know now.

"It's all right, Mom. The wedding's on."

"Oh, good. I'll inform the limousine driver. I'm sure he'll be delighted, since he's waiting out front."

The door snapped closed, Constantine kissed her again.

Another sharp rap on the door had Sienna pinning on her veil and reaching for her bouquet. She glanced at Constantine, who was showing no signs of moving.

He twined his fingers with hers and gave her another sweet kiss, this time through the veil.

She pushed at his chest. "You need to leave. We'll be late."

"I'm not leaving," he said simply. He tugged her toward the door, a smile in his eyes.

"This time we go together."

* * * * *

MILLS & BOON

THE HEART OF ROMANCE

A ROMANCE FOR EVERY KIND OF READER

MODERN

Prepare to be swept off your feet by sophisticated, sexy and seductive heroes, in some of the world's most glamourous and romantic locations, where power and passion collide.
8 stories per month.

HISTORICAL

Escape with historical heroes from time gone by. Whether your passion is for wicked Regency Rakes, muscled Vikings or rugged Highlanders, awaken the romance of the past.
6 stories per month.

MEDICAL

Set your pulse racing with dedicated, delectable doctors in the high-pressure world of medicine, where emotions run high and passion, comfort and love are the best medicine.
6 stories per month.

True Love

Celebrate true love with tender stories of heartfelt romance, from the rush of falling in love to the joy a new baby can bring, and a focus on the emotional heart of a relationship.
8 stories per month.

Desire

Indulge in secrets and scandal, intense drama and plenty of sizzling hot action with powerful and passionate heroes who have it all: wealth, status, good looks...everything but the right woman.
6 stories per month.

HEROES

Experience all the excitement of a gripping thriller, with an intense romance at its heart. Resourceful, true-to-life women and strong, fearless men face danger and desire - a killer combination!
8 stories per month.

DARE

Sensual love stories featuring smart, sassy heroines you'd want as a best friend, and compelling intense heroes who are worthy of them.
4 stories per month.

To see which titles are coming soon, please visit

millsandboon.co.uk/nextmonth

JOIN US ON SOCIAL MEDIA!

Stay up to date with our latest releases, author news and gossip, special offers and discounts, and all the behind-the-scenes action from Mills & Boon...

 millsandboon

 millsandboonuk

 millsandboon

It might just be true love...

MILLS & BOON
True Love
Romance from the Heart

Celebrate true love with tender stories of heartfelt romance, from the rush of falling in love to the joy a new baby can bring, and a focus on the emotional heart of a relationship.